A
PATIENT
DEATH

A
PATIENT
DEATH

AN ÉMILE CINQ-MARS NOVEL

JOHN FARROW

EXILE
editions

singular fiction, poetry, nonfiction, translation, drama, and graphic books

Library and Archives Canada Cataloguing in Publication

Title: A patient death : an Émile Cinq-Mars novel / John Farrow.
Names: Farrow, John, 1947- author.
Identifiers: Canadiana (print) 20230469663 | Canadiana (ebook) 2023046968X |
    ISBN 9781550969856 (softcover) | ISBN 9781550969887 (PDF) |
    ISBN 9781550969863 (EPUB) | ISBN 9781550969870 (Kindle)
Classification: LCC PS8561.A785 P38 2023 | DDC C813/.54—dc23

Published by Exile Editions ~ www.ExileEditions.com
144483 Southgate Road 14, Holstein, Ontario, N0G 2A0

We gratefully acknowledge the Government of Canada and Ontario Creates
for their financial support toward our publishing activities.

Canada   ONTARIO CREATES

Canadian sales representation: The Canadian Manda Group, 664 Annette Street,
Toronto ON M6S 2C8 www.mandagroup.com 416 516 0911

North American and international distribution, and U.S. sales:
Independent Publishers Group, 814 North Franklin Street,
Chicago IL 60610 www.ipgbook.com toll free: 1 800 888 4741

FSC
www.fsc.org
MIX
Paper
FSC® C100212

for Lynne

A PATIENT DEATH

Joris Pul knows it to be true, that human kindness flows through his bloodstream like honey. The proof is demonstrated in the time he takes to do a job. Being methodical guarantees the outcome, yet gives his target a few more precious minutes to live. People don't think of that. If he's knocking on a side door into heaven one day and nobody opens up, he'll mention his generosity.

"I'm the wildflower honey-man," he'll announce to the guardian at the gate, heaven's bouncer, some angel-face. Bleary-eyed, maybe, with a pug nose to give him character. Hungover after a night out sipping sarsaparilla, or whatever side-door angels drink. "Take it into consideration. I let my victims live longer than necessary."

Whether he's admitted through the pearly gates or spun off into the flames, his target here on earth appears to be enjoying his few extra moments alive.

Pul lines him up in the rifle's scope.

What does it feel like, he has contemplated in the past and ponders now, when you don't know that your next breath means death? Do you sense it anyway? Does a shadow cross your eyes? Do you feel the dread in your bones yet don't recognize the sensation? A stranger to you, this hunch that a threat is near, so you do nothing? That it? You carry on as if life will carry on. Is that what happens when you don't know enough to run?

As a kid in his town, Joris Pul shot crows early on Saturday mornings. He noticed that all he had to do was aim his rifle with an intent to kill and the bird flew off. If he aimed with no intention of pulling the trigger, or with no bullet in the chamber, the crow stayed put. As if mocking him. Cawing. *Ha! Faker!* Do people get warnings like crows do when their lives are in peril? Not knowing how to respond, they do nothing?

People aren't crows.

They're not that smart.

They don't fly off their branch.

The same way you can turn a man around by staring at his back, you'd think you could line up a man's face in your crosshairs and get him to look up. Do you that courtesy.

Even – *come on, now, buddy, look up* – stare death in the eye.

His victim today remains intent on his rod and reel.

Hidden amid the foliage on his side of the river, Pul makes certain that no branch, no leaf, no insect, will interfere with the bullet's trajectory. He's shot people at close range with a handgun. Something removed, almost unreal, doing it this way. In his estimation it's regrettable. He's kept his hands clean in the neighbourhood – *well, everything's relative, right?* – and since when has killing a cop been anybody's idea of a smart move? This is different. He knows that. The old fart's retired, a guy with a big rep but no street cred in this part of the world, no badge anymore, who can protect him? Doesn't even pack a Glock. He's a foreigner who has no business on this side of the border and he should never have interfered. His time to be dismissed has arrived. Pul's job: carry out the man's immediate permanent dismissal.

What he finds intriguing is that he'll fire his weapon in one state and his target will fall down dead in another, for shooter and victim stand on opposite sides of the Connecticut River. He's hidden in bushes in Vermont, while the old tall nag of a retired cop is fishing off the opposite riverbank in New Hampshire. Pul will be interested to learn how state troopers divvy up their jurisdictions on this one.

He finds the thought amusing.

The cop casts a line.

A good way to go, when you think about it, fishing rod in hand in the early morning light. So peaceful-like. Then *bam!* Death. You never see it coming. He himself could go that way. Wouldn't squawk if it happened.

The guy doesn't seem like much of a fisherman. Crummy cast. Maybe he should let him have one last try.

Birds chitter. Flit about. Morning mists lift off the water.

I'm the honey-man, giving you more time. Pure wildflower honey. Flows through my veins.

The ex-cop's name is a strange one. Cinq-Mars, which doesn't sound like any name at all. French, he was told. How that crazy name was explained to him: French from Canada. First name, Émile.

He should never have come here, this French guy, this Émile with the reputation. Never have meddled. Now he won't live to regret it.

The guy doesn't have the sense to reel in his line and try again.

Hopeless.

All righty, then. Your funeral.

"So long, Mr. Frenchman from Canada," Joris Pul whispers as he lines up the centre of the man's chest in his sights. "Next time, don't tell nobody you planned to go fishing in the a.m." The safety releases with a click. He settles his aim through the crosshairs. Looking down the scope, through the mists rising off the Connecticut River, he fires.

The shot echoes off both wooded riverbanks. Instantaneously, birds take flight. The old man lies face down in the water. Motionless. The river turning red there. A good clean hit. If by some fluke or miracle the man's not dead yet, he will be. He'll bleed out in the water. Or drown.

The birds in flight respond. Crying out. A racket.

Joris Pul's work is done. He could take another crack at him, but a man needs to show pride in his profession. Demonstrate efficiency. With the rifle's strap slung over his shoulder he heads back up the steep embankment on the Vermont side of the river to make good his escape. A bit of a scramble on a patch of loose earth, but there's no chance he's been seen. No chance that he'll be caught. The only man who might have been able to put him away, so he was told, is now either dead or dying.

A doubt sets in as he nears the summit of the steep riverbank amid the trees. Voices. Of women. Caterwauling. Oh, God. Those two junkie friends. The young one, the smart one, crippled up on crutches with braces on both knees, and the older one, the ninny, the heavy one getting started in the life. Pul didn't forget that the women would be nearby but never thought they'd be up this early and already dressed. Losers. Probably never went to bed. The numbskulls, you'd think they'd run *away* from gunfire, not *toward* it. They're crying out and arguing and dragging the old man out of the stream. A big body for them with their infirmities although they seem to be managing. Probably they'll call a goddamn ambulance next. Which'll arrive too late. *No skin out of my nostrils*. A clean hit. Their caterwauling means he has less time to get away, and Joris Pul grabs hold of a low-slung tree limb, then pulls himself higher. Hurrying now. Huffing. He crabs on, up through the maze of boulders and trees to freedom.

His recent troubles are at an end. This Émile Cinq-Mars guy? This ex-cop from Canada who had no business showing up here, meddling in? Whacked. He's dead. He's gone.

I

ONE

Five days earlier.

Floppy ears, like wings.

Decorated in the ceremonial style of India, the elephant figurine pilfered from the mantelpiece is draped in coloured beads. The trunk curls skyward. The thief hates that a tusk suffered a chip. People can be so damned careless when one teensy insignificant nick can cost you.

He has no clue what the figurine might fetch as he carries it to the foyer. Delicate, it could be worth a mint. From the entry closet amid the coats and jackets – hats on the top shelf, boots on the floor – he extracts a wool scarf folded away for the summer in a suspended storage unit. He wraps the elephant keepsake in the scarf, then gently stows his treasure in a canvas bag he's been stocking by the door. The bottom of the bag is already lined with silver tableware, a pewter vase, candlesticks, napkin holders, and assorted jewellery culled from cupboards and drawers on the main floor, and from the old lady's fingers and wrists. Fragile items go on top. A pair of bead and bone necklaces that he figures are Native American have been packed in an egg carton confiscated from the fridge. At first, he removed the two eggs left in the carton and watched as they swivelled on the countertop before nesting together. That provoked an awareness of being famished. He stowed the necklaces, then fried the eggs in a pan, over easy in butter, enjoying them with ketchup and a slice of cold ham also plundered from the fridge. Wolfing down a meal while committing a burglary gave him a kick.

Now a stillness pervades the house, as though the air congeals. An afternoon hush into which his own heartbeat evaporates. Outside, no leaf stirs beneath the cooling arbour of the trees. The chirp of birds. Summer flies buzz. He hears bees. He likes the sound of busy bees.

Lined up by the door, he has his grocery bag of odds and ends, as well as the flat-screen TV, a Dell Inspiron, a run-of-the-mill stereo and four dining chairs which he's convinced are handmade so together they must be worth a grand. You don't come across that quality every day. On each chair rests a painting he's pinched from a wall. None impress him, but they do look really old; three farm scenes and one of mountains in winter, a sleigh in the foreground. He's seen people on TV told that their granddad's depiction of a swing hanging from a mighty chestnut in the backyard could fetch, at auction, 30 grand, more if they had it cleaned. Whether or not those folks got their money, he doesn't know. They often claimed they planned to keep the painting anyway, happy to learn that they now had to insure it for an arm and a leg. He could never get his head around that. Nope, he'd take the dough, then dash out the door, taunting, "*Suckahs!*"

But who knows if you can trust what they show you on TV?

Not that it matters. The paintings are spoken for.

A sound disrupts his peace. His joints seize up. How will he explain his collection of stuff? How to talk away the old lady when he's got a bag full of her personal belongings and a pile of her furniture lined up by the door? Is she even dead yet? What if she can still talk? Should he run? Hide?

He quells his panic. Listens.

No second crack of a branch or floorboard snap or whatever that sound had been ensues. Either someone is lurking, listening for him to make the next move, waiting to hear an intruder's breath, his footfall, or no one's there.

Silently, he makes the next move. Creeps toward the rear of the house.

Looks out the kitchen door.

No one's around. Nothing of consequence to be seen.

He's alone. Except for the old lady. He's safe.

The incident serves as fair warning. The time has come to get a move on. Load the van. Then skedaddle.

He moves back through the main floor of the house to confirm that nothing's been overlooked, an item that at auction might break the bank. He's supposed to make this look right. Professional. Initially, he thinks he's done, before his eyes catch a glint of light.

"Sweetheart?" he asks in a whisper. "Are you holding out on me?"

He had removed the old lady's rings and bracelets without noticing a necklace. At this angle, a fold in her blouse reveals a glint, and when he lifts the collar, he spies his prize.

Her eyes are open; her mouth agape.

He checks her pulse.

He closes an eyelid. It opens on its own again.

A sure sign.

"Excuse me, sweetie pie, you won't be needing this now, will you? Who knows what it might fetch in New York or Boston, hmm? Could be … nothing … if glass." His breathing is laboured, as though the necessary concentration obliges him to hold his breath, then gulp air. He goes on murmuring. "I won't hold it against you if that's the case. But hey, if the bauble's worth something, then shame on me. I'd hold it against myself, wouldn't I, that missed opportunity? Let's do this without a hacksaw."

The clasp proves ornery. Too tiny for his chubby fingers. He's wearing latex gloves, they don't help, but he dares not remove them. He only took them off to cook, not wanting to melt one on the handle of the frypan. He still means to wash that pan. Since the necklace is long and rests under her blouse, the simplest solution is to lift it over her head, which he tries, but it catches in her grey hair done up in a bun. He has to extricate several links and that's difficult, too. He permits her head to fall back against a cushion at the top of the sofa when he's done, adjusts her hands that tumbled from her lap – she's still pliable – and makes her comfortable again. He puts the new treasure in a jeans pocket and reminds himself not to forget it there.

She's settled once more.

Her skin hangs limply. Less a sign of death than of old age. Liver spots dignify her right temple. Another along her jawline. A beauty in her day, he's thinking.

He casts his eyes around.

Satisfied, he says, "Rest in peace, old girl." He packs up, which doesn't take long. Inside the van, his loot seems a rather pathetic haul. Before starting up, he listens for vehicles careening down the highway. The house and driveway are sheltered by trees. He can't see the road. Which means no one on the road can see him. He heads out without bothering to stop at the end of the drive, just gives the brake pedal a precautionary tap. No more cars. A moment later, he's accelerating. He will mind the limit.

All is well. He has done his good deed for the day.

As for her things, she won't be needing them anymore.

He's put the poor old soul to rest.

TWO

A year into retirement, Detective Sergeant Émile Cinq-Mars is discovering that four oil paintings hanging in the reception area for the law offices of Hodges M. Marsh, Esq., are having an effect. He feels welcome. Not to the offices *per se*, but to the state of New Hampshire.

On his right, a torrid rushing stream in springtime animates a forest.

To his left, the shoreline of a placid lake bespeckled by an afternoon fall of yellow and red leaves provokes a restive mood.

At his back, the aptly named White Mountains gleam in their full winter radiance, although he gives that season a cursory glance only.

Through no fault of the artist, summer is tinged by sadness. A portrait of the Old Man of the Mountain commands Émile's attention on the wall opposite his chair. For millennia, the iconic figure, carved by nature in rock, assumed the likeness of a massive human head protruding from a precipice high above Franconia Notch. For as long as people traversed below – for ages the Abenaki, then new arrivals – and for eons before any human step, the Old Man observed the passage of time. He succumbed in 2003, giving way in a mighty collapse.

Death tracks us all down, Cinq-Mars reflects. Ain't that the truth.

The end is patient for some, but as the Old Man of the Mountain found out, death can rear up in a twinkling. He speculates on whether the jut of red granite ever had a premonition that a hairline fracture might rupture across its throat. Or did it come on like an arterial clot, or an aneurism, or an assassin's bullet, without warning, drastically altering one moment from the next? He'd like to believe that the gigantic rock had an inkling, choosing a time when no one was around. The world slept soundly as the Old Man tumbled down the mountainside, taking out only a swath of trees.

Cinq-Mars long nurtured an affinity for the chiselled visage. They were connected, as both he and the natural formation have been identified by their august and rather gargantuan noses. Teasing him, his wife once remarked that the Old Man might have been the template from which Émile's own face was fashioned. In a pique on another occasion she recanted, insinuating that *he* had probably stood as the model for nature's carving, meaning to imply that he was an ancient fossil, or as thick as a brick.

A blessing: The Old Man of the Mountain died a natural death. Émile was never called upon to investigate his murder.

An apprehension: Did the dramatic fall of his likeness presage his own?

He's uncertain why he's been summoned to talk to the lawyer, although he's armed with a reasonable guess. The man may wish to offer on the property his wife and her sister inherited following their mother's passing. That's been the inference, but why would the lawyer decline to view the house or discuss the matter out on the farm? Why was Sandra asked to present herself at the man's offices instead, without any assurance of his interest? Why is the lawyer not talking through *his* real estate agent to *their* real estate agent? Émile chose to come on his own when Sandra suddenly had a conflict, an emergency with a farm animal. No deal can be struck as he lacks authority to represent the sisters, yet he has all the power in the world to be dismissive if that feels warranted.

He suspects it will.

Lawyers. He doesn't believe in killing them all, as a Shakespeare character suggested. That would keep his pals in homicide far too busy. He does believe in caution. He's wary around any lawyer he hasn't had a chance to size up.

When a plump, middle-aged receptionist marches out to summon him, Émile remains skeptical. She's perfect in her role. Her smile too friendly. She's dark-haired, rosy-cheeked, polite and inviting.

What is she up to as she leads him down a corridor? He expects her to admit him to an august chamber, about to have his wallet fleeced, his car keys confiscated, asked to pay a king's ransom for a minute of the man's time. Instead, she's a necessary guide along a serpentine hallway that winds and turns, curls back on itself and detours again, until Cinq-Mars regrets that he hasn't been dropping bits of Kleenex. She's talking to him about the weather and this year's overabundance of mosquitoes. Is she deliberately trying to distract him? He'll never find his way out again and supposes that that's the purpose of the maze.

Smiling still, she finally opens a door. In he pops.

Modest digs. Not a corner office, although a broad, second-storey window overlooks the town of Hanover's Main Street. Law books line shelves but do not constitute an extensive library. A white fireplace mantel is a visual attraction.

A marble dolphin breaking the surface of a glass sea inhabits the hearth.

The man's desk is defined by tidiness, the antithesis of the sprawl on any of Émile's workspaces. He's distrustful of a tidy man. No speck of dust can survive here. Two smallish chairs for visitors are counterpoint to the high-backed, black leather executive seat behind the desk. A machine to the right of the chair defies identification, although it has a screen.

The single distinguishing feature of this lawyer's office: No lawyer is present.

Émile is willing to speculate that he's been left on his own to snoop.

Three glass cases are affixed to the mantelpiece. The largest in the centre displays a trio of men's watches. The flanking cases exhibit two apiece. The instruments glitter. Together they constitute a collection, as no man needs seven wristwatches. Cinq-Mars fingers his own, a gift from his department upon retirement. How does it stack up to an expert's eye against these deemed worthy of display?

"Apologies," a voice behind him submits. Cinq-Mars didn't hear a door open – different from the one he entered. "Sorry to leave you at loose ends, sir. I no sooner asked my secretary to admit you than realized a trip to the men's room was necessary. I trust my modest collection has amused you."

Cinq-Mars faces a man of average height, which makes him four to five inches shorter than himself, and of slim build with the grey-white hair of a 60-year-old. Tufts are out of place. A cowlick sticks up from the back of his head. Curious that a man, a professional to boot, never bothered to check his grooming while in a washroom. Otherwise, the man's done up as expected. Subtle pinstripes to his suit. Navy blue. In summer yet. Lawyers.

"They tell the time, that's all I know about watches," Cinq-Mars remarks, a simple truth. "These look good. If they're antiques, they're well preserved."

The man laughs lightly, and Cinq-Mars is curious about what's odd here. Something's amiss as the lawyer stands without moving much, and without looking directly at him.

"I would love to collect old timepieces, Mr. Cinq-Mars, but how do I validate their authenticity? Mine are not antique. You're alone?"

As if with a click of his fingers, Cinq-Mars zeros in on what's odd. For a split second he assumed that the man was inquiring if anyone else is on the way – is his wife in the washroom, for instance? Immediately, he gets what is distinctive about the man's presence, for his question is meant to be taken literally. The lawyer is asking if anyone else is in the room, concealed in a corner perhaps. In the same flash of insight, Émile deduces the purpose of the machine to the side of the man's desk. The contraption is a reading magnifier for the visually impaired. So the man is not wholly, but he is legally – and can so attest, being a lawyer – blind.

THREE

A peculiarity. Across the highway, something's not right.

Penelope Gagnon is a gallant old bird. Through long hours each day, she wears a bathrobe blighted by soup and sauce stains. As she has regaled her friends: "No one takes a woman in her bathrobe seriously. Hugh Hefner got away with it. How come? Because he's a millionaire man. Make him a pauper, he'd put his clothes on real fast. I'm better off than Hef because I'm as poor as a mouse in my house, and I can still wear a bathrobe."

She is waiting for her friend across the highway to come over.

Penelope believes her physical appearance does her in. "The word for it: *nemesis*. Look it up. My appearance is my nemesis. What a person looks like should not count for nothing nohow."

Her friends agree that she has a point, although they don't get the bathrobe, except for the desire to emulate Hef. No one knows what constitutes her beef with him unless she's riled by his addiction to youth and beauty. Pen feels she's lost out on both.

She wears her pink hair in curlers to give it body.

Someone once asked, she thinks it was Bitz, "Is it the curls that give your hair body or the curlers?"

She was not amused back then. Still isn't.

Whoever asked, she's pretty sure it was Bitz, was amused.

She's been known to say, "I'm not bald yet but I'm trying!" Quite often she picks a few flowers from her garden and places each stem inside a curler. She's fond of the effect, yet when her friends call her a flower child, she doesn't understand the reference. She can't imagine why anyone would use that word, *child*, with respect to her. "I'm saggy. You can't see?"

She should go over, she's thinking. Cross the highway, find out what's up.

Known to be a jabber-mouth and an avid gossip, her tongue is never wicked, only mildly mean if someone has it coming. "That's not so bad," she contends. Penelope's style is to talk as though someone asked her a direct question when no one did. In part, it's why she joined a support group without needing the kind of support being offered.

Penelope tweets. Not like the birds in the trees with whom she has a fine rapport and feeds daily but on "my mobile device," as she calls it. She tweets out the news of the day. "Blue jays in the cedars @#whataracket!" Or, "The garbage truck spills more than it hauls off @#lettertothecounty!"

She keeps an eye on things to give herself good tweets.

Through trees, Penelope noticed a white van depart from her good friend Muriel's house across the road. Muriel is also in her support group, although in her case she needs the support. She and Muriel have a pact. They look out for each other. If a plumber replaces a washer or if the furnace man drops in to do an annual cleaning, Muriel will saunter across afterwards to convey the gist of the experience. Penelope has given her enough time. She puts on clothes: a pair of oversized dungarees and a man's plaid shirt that drapes over her belly. Off she toddles.

Traffic. She utters her first two cuss words of the month. *Potty mouth is me! I'll tweet that!* Before she does, there's a lull: traffic parts like the Red Sea for Moses. Even after she makes it to the other side and trudges up Muriel's drive, flip-flops slapping, no deluge of pickups or Toyotas cascades behind her. She is alone in the stir of the light breeze and the assurance of bird chatter. She breathes freely, without a stitch in her side, hardly panting despite the incline. Most days she huffs and puffs, often with a little putt-putt-putting percolating out of her bottom, but for that she blames beans.

Penelope knocks on Muriel's screen door, then walks straight in, as is her habit. She and Muriel only lock up at night to thwart raccoons.

In the living room, she murmurs, "Oh my," and sits beside her pal.

She can tell right away.

She's seen the dead before.

A dead body is not what a living person looks like.

This is what a dead body looks like.

Except that Muriel is sitting up. Sitting up dead.

She wants to hold the woman's hand, then thinks better of it. The palm might be cold. That could cause a shiver to run through them both. She doesn't want to startle her friend. Then she feels something. A presence, she thinks. She looks around the room, half-expecting a presence – not a ghost, but a sense of Muriel lingering on, having last words to say – then realizes what spooked her. The television is missing. As if it walked out the door! The dining room chairs are gone. The paintings, too. Mouth open, she looks at the deceased for an explanation and sees that Muriel's not wearing her necklace, or her rings, or her bracelet. Penelope knows what it means.

She slams the depravity of a man – had to be a man – to rob the dead.

If Muriel was only dead, Penelope might not know who to call. But as Muriel has been robbed, Penelope's duty is to inform the police.

Yet she hesitates. The situation is complicated. Perhaps she should make a different call first. Such as to their mutual support group, although Muriel doesn't need the support anymore and Penelope never has.

Penelope stands up to take all this in, to weigh her options.

She looks past her friend as if hunting for something else that might have been snatched. She knows what she's looking for, but it's gone, too, or perhaps was never there.

"I'm sorry you're dead," she says out loud. "I'll call Bitz, okay? She'll know what to do."

Yes. Bitz will know.

Penelope tiptoes out of the house. She hurries – a gyrating waddle, really – down the drive and is pleased that a rampage of vehicles hasn't returned. She hurries on as if she needs to take a whiz. Her screen door slams behind her and that's when she reacts to her friend's sudden demise. Nerves break across her chest, and she gasps. She needs to take hold of herself, grabs a chair and sits, crossing her legs as she goes down. Her breath has gone short. Tears blur her vision. She stretches for the phone, but it's beyond her grasp. *Oh, my God, Muriel, what happened to you?* Then she remembers her mobile device in a pocket of her clown-sized dungarees. She didn't think to use it in Muriel's house but goes to it now instead of her landline. *Why do I need both? It's confusing!* She won't tweet this. You don't tweet something like this. This is something you keep to yourself until after you have talked to Bitz.

Penelope is about 20 years younger than Muriel was, and 20 years older than Bitz. That's the benefit of a support group. Different kinds of people mingle, different ages. When Bitz answers, her kids are screaming in the background. Anybody would think Penelope was phoning a Middle East war zone.

"Are you in Iraq?" Penelope asks.

"Pen? No. Hi. They're out of control. The kids. What's up? Did you say Iraq?"

"Muriel's dead."

"What?"

"She bought the farm."

"What!"

"Oh my GOD! Bitz! My best friend is dead!"

Bitz wants the details, and Penelope is careful to tell them properly, about how Muriel was sitting up and looking quite pretty, really, overall. "She looked good for a dead person."

"You looked all around her?" Bitz asks for the third time.

"All around. Not there. Nothing."

"Yeah. Okay. Well. We know where she keeps her gear, don't we?"

"I'm not sure."

"I do anyway. So you looked?" For the fourth time, she asks.

"I looked."

"Good," Bitz says, and Penelope is happy to hear that. She's done something right. Bitz would know. "You're sure she's dead?"

"I could ask her but that won't do much good."

"Okay. Okay. Let me think."

"What should we do?" Penelope inquires earnestly.

"I'm coming over," Bitz tells her, and Penelope is happy to hear that, too. Then she remembers the most important detail. Or the second most important detail, after Muriel being dead.

"She's been robbed."

"What? Pen? What do you mean, robbed?"

"That's what I mean. Her TV, gone. Chairs. Gone. Her jewellery. Gone. Paintings off the walls. Who would rob a dead woman?"

"My God. Pen, are you home right now? Or at Muriel's?"

"My house."

"Pen, what if someone, you know, killed her?"

"What? Who?"

"The thief."

"Who? Oh. The van. The man in the van!"

"What man? What van?"

"I saw it drive off, the van. I didn't see a man though, that's true."

"Pen," Bitz announced, "I'm coming over. Hell, I'll bring the kids. Don't call the police. Not yet. We need to look around. You need to lock your doors. I'm calling Libby right away. She can get there on her bike before me in my car. If she's around. Keep an eye out for her. Maybe I can get a neighbour of mine for the kids. We'll see. Pen, don't call the police yet. Call after. Libby and me, we need to look around first. Do a thorough search. Yeah, get down to the riverbank and all that."

"The riverbank."

"Never mind. I need to get off now and call Libby."

What occurs to Penelope at that moment is a strange thought, what people call *non sequiturs*. She knows the phrase well and tries to use it in a proper context once or twice a month. Non sequiturs. She likes to say that one out loud, she likes the sound of it, just as she likes to say *nemesis* or *brouhaha*, which is her favourite. The air is filled with wailing, the soft light through the trees is flashing reds and blues, and she's walking back out of her house onto her porch with the mobile device stuck to her ear. She's thinking that she's about 20 years younger than Muriel, and about 20 years older than Bitz, and that Bitz is about 20 years older than Libby. Maybe a little more. Which is a non sequitur. She is also thinking that Libby won't be able to get here on time but that has nothing to do with how young she is. Instead, it has to do with the pending brouhaha.

"You can call Libby, Bitz, but it won't do any good."

"Why not? What's going on?"

Penelope doesn't know for sure, but she suspects that Bitz hears them too, the sirens.

"The police. They're here. More are coming down the highway. They're turning into Muriel's driveway."

"You called them?"

"I didn't call them."

"Pen—"

"I didn't!"

"Well if you didn't call, who did?"

"It wasn't me!" Penelope maintains. "I don't think it was Muriel. Are you still coming over? Are you calling Libby?"

"No, Pen, don't be silly. I'm not going over there now. I'm still calling Libby."

"What do I do?"

"Pen, sit tight, okay? Can you do that? Sit tight."

"All right," Penelope sighs. "I can do that, I think. Can I tweet this?"

"Pen, absolutely do not tweet this! As a favour to me. No tweets."

Penelope agrees not to do that.

"And Pen?"

"Yeah, Bitz?"

"As a favour to me?"

"All right."

"Don't say a thing to anybody. Also, stay away from the river completely. Don't talk to the police unless they talk to you and then don't tell them you saw the body. That will only cause you trouble. Don't tell them you were over there. They'll think things."

"What things?"

"Like, where's her TV? Stuff like that. Like, did you rob her yourself?"

"I didn't take her stuff!"

" 'Course not. But you see the problem? Better to say you never saw a thing."

Penelope is silent a moment or two, taking all this in.

Bitz says, "Pen?"

And Penelope says, "Sure, Bitz. No problem. You can count on me."

Because she can. She doesn't have Muriel anymore, which is starting to hit home. She only has Bitz. And Libby, too, in a way. She's been in the support group even though she doesn't need the support they offer because Muriel was her friend and believed she could use the company of people who wouldn't judge her if she wore a bathrobe half the time or sometimes from dawn to dusk. Muriel thought she could use the company of people who had problems of their own. If Penelope is to stay in the group, she'll need Bitz for that, now that Muriel's passed. Not that she needs the kind of support they go on and on about, but she doesn't mind the company and the chat. She doesn't mind hearing about people's down and lonesome woes. She'll do what Bitz says. She doesn't want to start a brouhaha with the police. She'll stay quiet instead.

FOUR

The attorney is partially, or largely, blind. No view across the fields will enchant him, which explains the choice of venue: His office, not the farm. "My wife is indisposed. I came in her stead."

"Thank you for not cancelling, Mr. Cinq-Mars."

The man knows the path to go behind his desk. A mouselike scurry moves him effortlessly.

"I understand now why you don't collect antique watches, given that you can't see them properly."

"I'd be taken to the cleaners. An easy mark for any bait-and-switch."

Cinq-Mars is accustomed to giving someone a hard look, which often compels the other person to reveal more. His high forward, hawkish nose, and penetrating gaze generate results. That won't happen here. Any searing scrutiny is rendered ineffective when the other person can't properly notice. "If I may say so, it still begs the question."

"Why collect *new* watches when I can't see them, either?" As the man extends his hand, Émile adjusts his position to shake it. "Hodges Marsh. Pleased to meet you."

"Good to meet you, sir."

They sit. The lawyer swivels in his chair. Émile's large form struggles to find comfort in an ultra-modern, low-backed seat. These days he counts himself as six-two, down from an inch taller. He hopes this is due to stooping more, rather than shrinking, although another possibility has occurred: perhaps he was never as tall as he once believed. Six-three could have been the result of a short nurse measuring his height at a police medical exam and getting it wrong.

"Why collect what you can never really see?" Cinq-Mars inquires.

"If I limit myself to cherish only what others also can't see, how does that help me with anything?"

Cinq-Mars is stymied. He has no response. He likes the attorney's reply, the more for being posed as a tricky question. He finds himself warming to the man.

"For starters, I'd be without a wife and two children. Complete strangers see them better than I do. Should I then deprive myself of my own family? Does that make sense? Carry it out from there."

"Interesting point," Cinq-Mars concedes.

"We're a strange breed, Mr. Cinq-Mars," Hodges explains. "Us collectors I mean, not the blind. With respect to the enjoyment of a fine watch, I believe I'm the equal of sighted men. No one needs an expensive timepiece to tell the time. A cheap quartz from China can be more accurate. Yet a timepiece that almost perfectly measures the earth's orbit using a mechanical spring and an array of forks, gears, and delicate turnings too numerous to list – *that* inspires my awe."

People have their things. He's enjoying the man's company, getting past a prejudice against his profession. "I appreciate hearing about someone's passion."

"I wear them on special occasions," Marsh adds, a calculated shift in direction. "The other night, I chose the Vacheron Constantin for a dinner party where your name, Detective Cinq-Mars, came up as a subject of conversation."

The day is offering a few curios.

"How's that?" he asks.

"I was dining with the Governor. Posh, but a political fundraiser, so ultimately tacky. You're a hero in this state, sir. The serial murder of students on our beloved campus stunned us all. Your help in solving those crimes is deeply appreciated. You're a famous local hero now. Prepare yourself."

Cinq-Mars is not comfortable with the turn. Reputation's wardrobe, he has found, never fits properly.

"In New Hampshire, our criminals now tremble," the lawyer tacks on.

"You are definitely making fun of me."

"I am. Apologies. Shall we discuss the farm?"

Émile Cinq-Mars is more willing to do so than when first he arrived. He's sensing that he may have found what can be elusive when arriving in a new community, namely the discovery of a potential friend.

"My wife will be interested in a buyer's plans," Cinq-Mars makes known. "The transaction is not solely based on price."

"Ah, Émile," Hodges Marsh observes, "you sound like a man who wants to sell me a fine watch."

A laugh closes their gentle gabbing, and they begin their financial dickering.

FIVE

Libby St. Croix learns about the death of her good friend Muriel Cuthbert while zipping down a hill on her bicycle. Despite her infirmities, she's as free as a bird until her phone vibrates in the cargo pocket of her left thigh. She takes her hands off the handlebars, digs it out, and answers while gliding with similar ease to the red-tailed hawk above her head. It hovers over the Connecticut River Valley. Gracefully swooping, its shadow intersects with the girl's ride.

Libby shouts into the phone at Bitz. The woman's kids are braying in the background. "Bitz! Speak up!"

Bitz screams back at her that Muriel is dead.

Tacking on that she was robbed.

The last part fails to register. Libby can only repeat, "Dead? Bitz, what do you – ? What're you saying?"

"Can you go there?"

"Where?"

"You'll need to be discreet."

Libby isn't sure what she's hearing with all the background pandemonium.

"What are you talking about? Muriel's dead? Is that what you told me?"

She nearly crashes. Not noticing a rough patch in the pavement, the girl makes a frantic grab for the handlebars, losing her grip on the phone. It bounces off the asphalt. Libby brakes hard, turns around, goes back. The phone is her lifeline. She hears Bitz shouting through the phone to her, "Libby? Libby!" She also hears the raucous kids. Prevented from picking the phone up by her damaged hip and by her knees which are confined by braces, she works her crutches out from a plastic sheath attached to the seat of her bike and rear fender. By a serendipity they serve as an upper backrest when she's in full glide. No sooner is she successful at working them free than the bike rattles to the pavement under her and Libby catapults to the ground. Engaged with the crutches, she fails to stop her fall and lands hard on a shoulder, twisting her face away to save it from ruin.

She hears Bitz, only now the mom is yelling at her kids to be quiet "for the love of Mike or I'll murder you both."

On the ground, Libby is crying. Whether from the sudden jolt her body received or the horrid memories a fall invokes – or the sudden news of a friend's passing – she doesn't know. She's upset and in pain. Blinded by tears.

Bitz is calling to her across the asphalt.

"I'm coming!" Seventeen years of age and crippled by a calamitous slip a year ago while scaling a cliff, Libby inches her way over the roadside dirt toward the voice of her older friend. At last, she retrieves her phone.

"Can you go, Libby? Be *extremely* discreet. Stay away from the river-bank. We'll save that for later when no one's around. Libs, keep an eye on Penelope. Tell me if she gets unglued."

Libby promises to do all that; no easy vow to keep. She sees that she's skinned a kneecap and an elbow. Willing herself upright, she's onto her bike again. Tricky business. Stabbing pains – familiar ones, unre-lated to the fresh cuts – make her gasp. Also the new one: Her heart is burning. She's never lost anyone before. Never had to deal with death. Muriel was 60-plus years her senior yet to her she's been the most important person in the world. Hard to fathom that she's gone. That can't be right. Bitz must have it wrong. Or Penelope mixed up the facts, told the story wrong. Which is easier to believe. And yet, when Libby makes the next hill, then descends, tears fly off her face in the wind her momentum creates as though she's her own storm.

She pedals in a fury, even downhill.

SIX

Émile Cinq-Mars has accompanied his wife to New Hampshire, taking up residence in a charming century-old farmhouse that belonged to Sandra's deceased mother. The estate has been settled, with the disposition of the farm being shared between the two surviving daughters. Should Émile and Sandra follow through on a move to the state, they will have a horse farm in Quebec to sell. Proceeds from the two properties, added to the estate's liquid assets, less the couple's existing mortgage and the cost of a new home, will augment their income during Émile's retirement years. That's the plan.

Everything depends on the marriage remaining intact, which has been up for discussion. After initially announcing that she was considering calling it quits, Sandra has elected to stay on. They're together, yet the strength of her commitment remains uncertain. Too young, too energetic to think about retiring herself, she covets a change from raising horses but has not chosen a new career. When Émile asks, she murmurs only that she's still not sure.

Everything in their lives these days appears governed by uncertainty.

In lieu of decisive decision-making, they've been drifting along to see how things pan out. Uprooting to New Hampshire has taken hold without great discussion. They both allude to the possibility that it could be permanent, but no one has declared it so. Émile frets that they've suffered a general breakdown in communication. The potential move has instigated a subversive stress, one that's crept up on them undetected, yet it does not account for Sandra's mood when, upon Émile's return from the lawyer's office, she seems miffed for no apparent reason. She shows no interest in the content or the progress of his meeting, and

Émile is immediately annoyed when she mutters something about a message.

"What message? San? Who from?"

"Who do you think, who from?"

"How should I know?"

"Émile, you travel. What happens? Every time like bloody clockwork."

He's baffled. "Tell me."

"Somebody dies a gruesome death."

What used to be a joke between them is less humorous as time goes by.

"There's been a murder," Sandra confirms. She's just returned from a meeting as well, hers with a veterinarian about her mother's aged goat. She's also carting in a week's supply of groceries. Leaning over the fridge's veggie bins, she stuffs items away.

"What murder?"

She must be yanking his chain; to what end is another puzzle.

"State Trooper Hammond, remember him? What's his rank again? I forget. Anyway, he called. He wants to talk to you."

In goes a bag of Brussels sprouts.

"That doesn't mean there's been a murder. Maybe he wants to nail me for speeding." Two can play at baiting the other.

"We have an appointment at 3:15, Émile. To see a house."

"I didn't forget." He's not convincing. "We'll be there."

"Not if you've been arrested." She beats him at his own game. At last, she flashes a smile.

"Sandra— "

The fridge door closes, and she pops up again, nosily folding brown paper bags. "Honestly, Émile," she incites over the racket, "you don't know how long it'll take if you start – *investigating*. You don't know where the murder is or how long it'll take to get there. New Hampshire's not that small."

"Hang on, San, who says I'm going anywhere? What will I investigate? What murder? I have no clue why he's calling me. What don't people get about the word retirement?" Suddenly his voice seems too loud as the last of the bags is tucked away in a niche.

"Look who's asking."

"Sandra."

"Émile. Go. Find out who killed Cock Robin for all I care. Apparently, the crime scene's close enough. Maybe you can do both. Arrest a killer *and* buy a house the same afternoon."

"You're in a mood."

"I'm not. Really. Call him. I don't care."

"San, I never agreed to work for Hammond again. I never suggested that he should call me."

"He's of the opinion that he can tempt you. Like waving a red flag before a bull maybe?"

"It's not— .—. Anyway, we're not ready to buy a house yet, are we? We're only looking."

"You know, some men are tempted by pretty young things. You, by cadavers with bullet holes. They're not as sexy, but in the long run, safer. I'm not complaining. And, yes. For sure. We're only looking."

"Anyway," he mutters, "how do you know the death was gruesome?" He's guessing that Hammond did not impart that detail. Unprofessional, to provide a description to a civilian. He hunts for the number on his new mobile phone, the first of its kind that he's enjoyed. "I don't recall his rank," he grumbles in answer to an earlier question, as though that should count in his favour, and presses the screen to his ear. He weighs if he should correct her on one aspect: that he, too, vastly prefers "pretty young things" to any bullet-riddled corpse.

Sandra is sifting through a closet for something, then emerges with an old tennis racket. Maybe she's not so miffed. A portion of her umbrage may have been an act.

Retirement, Émile has discovered, requires imagination. He hasn't yet imagined his own. Initially, he expected to work on his wife's horse farm, until she revealed that she wanted to quit taking care of animals. The labour is exhausting and unrelenting; over time, physically debilitating. Freezing-to-the-bone barns in winter are never fun. Hot, humid, dusty summers no improvement. And yet, with police work behind him, and with no horses to groom, feed, train, and – his specialty – to buy and sell, what then? He's not unhappy to be making this call, and while he's keeping that to himself as Hammond's phone returns a *burrup-burrup* to his ear, he reaffirms that Sandra knows him too well. If there's been a murder, if a case has surfaced interesting enough that the New Hampshire State Police think to call him in, he wants to know about it. To be involved, at his age, in his position – which is no position at all – could be an opportunity difficult to pass up.

He won't admit it to Sandra openly and tries to keep the thought secret, even from himself.

Answering, Hammond asks that he hang on before Émile can say hello.

Sandra says, indicating the tennis racket, "This is for Hank." The goat. She blows a whiff of hair off her face. In summer, her cut comes halfway down her neck. Still no trace of grey, he notices. She pulls it back over her scalp with her free hand, revealing the face he adores. Those large and soft brown eyes, the lines of perpetual concentration etched across her forehead. "The vet's suggestion. Whack his flanks when he's stubborn. To help his circulation."

"Really? You're going to whack a goat?"

"Either that or drive him to the glue factory. I'll give it a try."

"Hope you don't have anything similar in mind for me," he adds. That he's 19 years her senior often provokes gybing between them.

Sandra is up for it. "First, let's see how it goes with the goat."

SEVEN

Someday, Reece Walter Zamarlo might die here. A suitable setting for a kill. Men exist who'd look upon him as a suitable victim. If ever he's not needed, or people grow suspicious of him, or the secrets he's accumulated become too onerous, this could be the spot. On a day like today, without omen or warning, a bullet might rupture his brain.

In his mind, a paradox: A death unforeseen, yet anticipated.

The canopy of branches overhead protects the site from observation from above. In winter, an eye-in-the-sky could spot him there. This time of year, no chance. All around the woods are thick, the escarpment dotted with rock outcroppings, giving the area a gloomy, unwelcoming cast. If someone he works for decides to off him, he could be shot here repeatedly. Empty the chamber. No one likely to hear. Any wandering hunter up on the mountain could never pinpoint the location as the shots echo into infinity.

Not only could he be killed here, Zamarlo figures he could be buried here, too. The killer could take his own sweet time with the dig. Once the weeds and grasses grow back and the seasons turn through a full cycle, there'd be no trace of his bones throughout eternity.

Every trip to the site seems special that way. Fraught with risk. He drives up the ancient logging road in his white van onto a separate trail. Men who scouted the path generations ago have passed. Few men today are aware of its existence. He crosses a creek bed that's dry in summer, and the van picks its way along a hunter's trail. No great distance. The forest closes in. He has solid rock to drive on for a brief stretch.

He'd hidden here as a child, when his old man was on the run.

That was then. This is now.

He's shared knowledge of the location, when he trusted some people. He regrets it. He'll really regret it if they off him here. Their good relations have corroded, although he still uses the site when an exchange requires privacy.

His white van settles into a spot next to the other guy's blue.

His counterpart sits on his rear bumper smoking. He looks weird. The man's changed his hairstyle and maybe it suits him but in Zamarlo's judgement he looks ridiculous. He hates the guy's hair and hates that anybody smokes up here. What if an ember starts a forest fire? The man on the bumper leaves his butts behind in the wilderness and that offends him, too. He won't smoke up here himself or leave anything behind. He clambers out of the van, miffed.

The man acknowledges his arrival; the cigarette still stuck between his lips. "Zamarlo," he says. His idea of a hospitable greeting.

"Pul." Last names only. Nothing too friendly in case one guy has to shoot the other guy someday. Easier done if there's no friendliness between them.

He opens the tailgate on the white van, and Pul looks inside. They begin a quick negotiation.

Pul will take the chairs off him. They go at a half-decent price.

"For obvious reasons," Zamarlo reminds him, "I keep the TV."

"Knock yourself out," Pul says. "You know what to do with the pictures?"

"Spoken for, yeah. They're next, soon as I bug out of here."

Whether or not they're worth something he's happy to have had that deal arranged in advance. He wouldn't have a clue how to get rid of them himself. For the jewellery he asks a few bucks, nothing much. Less haggling than expected. Both sides understand the circumstances. These are dangerous goods. They constitute much more than mere contraband.

He's told to keep the elephant figurine. The trinket's worth squat.

"Better yet," is Pul's advice, "dump it. Toss it on your way back down, off the logging road. Shatter it to smithereens."

He feels bitter about that. He still believes it has value. The old lady liked it. He doesn't want to disrespect her by being critical of her stuff. What does this guy know anyhow? Smithereens. Big word. When Zamarlo returns to his van and sits, he feels the old lady's necklace in his jeans pocket. He should show it to Pul. Sell it right here, right now, except that he's feeling put out. He decides to keep it, along with the elephant.

Pul raps on the passenger window. Zamarlo rolls it down.

"Don't need to know the details," Pul says. "Curious is all."

"About what?"

"About why. Why you do what you do. It's unusual."

Zamarlo looks at him more directly than he has done to that moment. He has questions of his own about this guy. For instance, Pul's new hairstyle. He doesn't understand why a guy does that. Change his hair. The man's shaved his head on one side, then combed the hair from the top of his crown over it. A conspicuous look. He doesn't know why a man would give himself a look like that when the last thing he'd want in life was to be noticed. Zamarlo is noticing him. He isn't comfortable with the man's query.

"I don't talk about it," he says.

He sees that Pul gets that, and even concurs. "Me neither. Difference is, nobody asks me why. People figure they know. With you, I find it peculiar." He slaps the side of the van. "See you around, good buddy."

He won't be shot today.

Zamarlo backs up, then waits. He lets Pul depart in the blue van first. They choose to stay separated, and never travel in tandem. That's their rule. He hangs on for a bit, then gets out again when he decides to clean up the cigarette butts. Scratching in the ground that way, he can't escape musing about what it might be like to die on this hill, to be buried in this dirt, to spend eternity right here in an unknown, unmarked grave.

Gut instinct tells him that he might find out.

He might become part of the mountain, like rock.

Really, when he goes over everything, not so unwelcome a fate.

For now, he'll take the butts with him. Keep the place tidy, in case the patch ever becomes a gravesite. His.

EIGHT

"I'm back," the trooper answers. "Who's this?"

Émile returns his attention to the phone. "Trooper Hammond, it's Émile."

"Hey, thanks for the callback. Heard you were in town." Being a minor celebrity may have perks, but it has its own irritations, too. "I got something up your alley."

"Sandra mentioned a murder."

"I wish it was that obvious."

He's already interested. "Murder's not obvious?"

"This one's in dispute."

"Which way do you lean?"

"Homicide, beyond a shadow. My colleagues contend natural causes."

"Majority rules, no?"

"Nonsense. I rule. But even my suspect wants to call it God's will."

Cinq-Mars smiles, cradling the phone. He appreciates surprise. To have a suspect lined up for a homicide that no one agrees is a homicide is a nifty turn.

"Your colleagues, the smart ones in the room, say natural causes. Why?"

"Because they're not necessarily the smart ones. Up yours, too, Émile. They make a few good points, though. No sign of violence. The deceased is a little old lady. Looks as sweet as can be, sitting up on her sofa. Hard to imagine anyone doing her harm. My colleagues are sentimental that way."

"You're not sentimental, just bored?" A trace of disappointment has entered his voice. He might side with the majority in this instance.

Hammond is smart enough to call him, but he's not the brightest lamp post on the block, either.

"She's a robbery victim. Nobody disputes that. A felon was in her house. That's how we found the body."

"I don't follow."

"The thief, bless his heart, came across the woman already dead. Robbed her anyway. Then departed the premises with her valuables."

"How do you know the chronology?"

"He told me so."

Cinq-Mars is interested again. "You caught him? Red-handed?"

"He phoned it in, see."

Cinq-Mars doesn't see at all.

"He robs her, he takes off," Hammond continues, "then drops a dime. Says he came across the dead lady in the middle of his job, finished up, then beat it. Called to let us know. His conscience demanded it. The Christian thing to do."

"Considerate thief. Religious, too."

"Looking out for his own skin more likely. He doesn't want her death to land on him, whether he did it or not."

"Doesn't point to murder."

"Nothing does, Émile."

Sandra has been listening to one side of the talk. The lack of information from Émile's end has intrigued her. She leans against the door jamb, arms crossed.

"I take it he never identified himself."

"Life should be so kind."

"Why be keen to call it homicide?" Émile asks.

"She's not the first elderly person to die like this."

A series? He'll keep the interest out of his voice. He doesn't want Sandra to know that rather than a single investigation, there could be a bunch.

"You said elderly." He wants to ask how many others but bites his tongue. "The old pass away by natural causes sometimes. Even during, after, or before a robbery."

"The others weren't robbed. No similarity that way."

"What then?" He remembers this about Hammond: Talking to him can be like riding a yoyo. The trooper will wind him up, then drop him into disappointment again before swinging him through loops.

"Émile, they were sitting up. As if enjoying a cup of tea. The elderly don't usually die sitting up in their armchairs. Sometimes, yes. Consistently? Also, if they died like that, one or two would've toppled over."

Then he whirls him about, yoyo style.

"You're a real detective. That's observant of you." Cinq-Mars smiles at Sandra, to reassure her that he's not involved in anything sinister.

"The first ones, Émile, I signed off on natural causes. I wasn't on-site and now we can't exhume. They were cremated. This much later, I can't say for sure they were homicides, but they've been accumulating. The reports say they were sitting up. Could be a signature a killer didn't realize he left behind."

Cinq-Mars is thoughtful. "Curious." Yet in no way conclusive.

"If you show up, I'll let you in on something else. It'll knock your socks off, Émile. Even yours."

He doesn't need the carrot to totter off to the crime scene, although the inducement is effective.

"I'll pop over. My wife and I have a chore later, so my time is tight."

"I'll stall the removal. You're 15 minutes away with a heavy foot."

"Hammond?"

"Yeah?"

"What's your rank again?" He also wants to ask him for his first name, as he's forgotten.

A captain. Cinq-Mars keeps the more personal query to himself, to give his memory banks a workout. He has a devil of a time with non-French names.

That the drive will be relatively brief and also straightforward is good news. The deceased has been living by the Connecticut River, off the main highway that parallels the waterway south.

"Keep the lady company until I arrive, Captain."

"She's not rushing out. By the way, we call ourselves 'trooper.' No matter the rank. It's our way."

NINE

The Connecticut River draws breath as a ripple on a beaver pond 300 yards south of the Canadian border, then wends for 400 miles to empty into Long Island Sound. Half the length demarcates the border between Vermont and New Hampshire. As Émile Cinq-Mars traces a brief section of the waterway where Highway 12A mimics the curvature of the shore, he's beguiled by the stream. In buying a new home, he considers a predilection for riverfront.

A river running through his days. Like time.

Opposing traffic heats up. A slower truck causes the vehicles behind to accordion. Transports and contractor pickups jumble together with SUVs, sedans, and motorhomes seeking cooler mountain air. Some intend to remain in New Hampshire, others will take the I-87 East into Vermont. A few trucks will merge onto the major thoroughfares, ply their way north to his homeland, *la belle province*. Yes, a beautiful province. He mulls that over when he spots a Quebec plate with that very inscription pass by. His beautiful native province marred by the ugliest tax rates in North America. The thought irritates him in the moment. It's one reason he contemplates leaving, now that he's on a pension – a tick on the side of the ledger that favours departure. In the corresponding column, he's noted a number of practical reasons to stay. Health care is huge at his time of life, along with cheap, clean electricity, the French language, the *joie de vivre* of the people, his long-standing familiarity with the place. Quebec has been home for so long that that counts for something.

It counts for a lot.

He has no kids and that's connected to the move. He married late. Although younger than him, Sandra also married relatively late. Their age difference is an element in the move. He's seeking his retirement home, but if all things go according to normal expectations, Sandra will live there for a significantly longer time. Where she wants to be counts for more than any check mark in a column.

The death of her mother spurred her to contemplate a return to her original home in New Hampshire. He understands. Now, if he can interest her in riverfront property, this whole moving thing might come together.

He can see himself casting a line in the early morning light.

After crossing Bloods Creek, he catches sight of a civic address on a post at the end of a driveway. His destination is near. He keeps an eye peeled. Along this stretch, the road has veered away from the stream. Hammond said to look for a house set back amid the trees on the side of the highway opposite the river. He slows. When stationary cop cars rise into view, he expects to wait before making his left. A driver, perhaps in deference to the police presence, spots his turn signal and stops. He's permitted to turn onto the scene of the crime.

If, he reminds himself, it is the scene of a crime.

Official vehicles cram together. Cinq-Mars steers his Escalade partially down the driveway's ditch. The vehicle is on a significant tilt; clamouring out is a struggle. He braces himself on the running board, then hops down. With a flick, the door slams shut.

He's challenged by a trooper. Even in rural New Hampshire he has only to identify himself and obstacles vanish. His recent local fame has been earned by solving a few interconnected murders on a college campus. Biggest news of the year locally. A good reputation is not only difficult to build and easy to lose, but it will also come under continuous attack if left out in the open. Folks will find a fatal flaw soon enough, he expects, and condemn him. Not that he could care less.

"Émile!" Hammond calls from the porch door. Cinq-Mars is unaccustomed to detectives who wear uniforms. Each force to its own culture. A white man of solid build, the trooper's features in his mind are too typical. The brush cut, broad shoulders, square jaw, and a posture that looks chiselled into form by the Marine Corps strike him as conspicuous, as if the man had been cast by Hollywood.

"How goes the battle, Trooper Hammond?" He's still failing to pull up the officer's first name.

"It's been joined. Good to see you again, Émile."

The cottage is characteristic of a dwelling inhabited by an older woman. Small, sheltered, tidy. The dark screen porch offers protection from rain and bugs. A favourite sitting area in summer.

He's introduced to the Medical Examiner at the bottom of the steps. "Marcus Easton," Hammond states. "Not only was he born with the initials ME, but he's also our best excuse for one in the state. Don't let him bitch that he's underfunded. He can bore a librarian to death with that talk. Marcus is a smart cookie, only on this case he's dead wrong."

Cinq-Mars extends his hand, and the tall, balding, rather handsome black man takes it, grinning. "How can I be wrong," he wants to know, "if I don't have an opinion?"

"Good point," Cinq-Mars agrees. "Glad to meet you."

"He's wrong because he doesn't have an opinion, that's why, and he doesn't have an opinion because he refuses to see the light."

"Keeping my options open," Easton says.

"See what I mean?" chirps Hammond. "He stands by his ignorance."

Émile enjoys the easy banter. He revels in being at a crime scene, having thought it would never happen again.

"What's here that'll knock my socks off, as promised?" he asks the trooper.

"Inside, Cinq-Mars. Prepare to lose your innocence."

Marcus Easton tags along and returns indoors with them. Hammond guides them into the living room where the deceased is sitting up. Émile gazes at the old lady on her sofa, half expecting her to say hello. No cup of tea is set beside her, so Hammond's earlier analogy doesn't quite pan out, but she does look as though she's set to watch television. If she still had a TV. A cable wire indicates where it used to be installed. The thief apparently forgot the remote control, which lies on an end table next to an empty plate.

"She does look peaceful," Cinq-Mars admits.

"Pull up her sleeve. Either one. Check the crook of her elbow," Hammond instructs him. "We'll talk about peaceful then."

Cinq-Mars can hear the ME inhale deeply, frustrated by Hammond's insistence on this point. He gives him a look, and Easton nods to go ahead.

He undid a button. Hammond must have done this himself, then meticulously buttoned the old gal up again. The soft forearm, especially by the elbow, shows telltale track marks, really a long, pocked dark bruise.

Ugly.

"She doesn't seem so sweet now, hey?" Hammond points out.

Cinq-Mars looks back at Easton. "Diabetic? Bruise easily? Not to mention badly."

"I think what he thinks," Easton says. "Unlikely to be insulin. Most probably heroin."

"Come on," Cinq-Mars says, and straightens up. Bent for a close look, his lower back objected. He feels a familiar twinge. "A junkie? This sweet old thing?"

"Breaks your heart, don't it?" Hammond remarks, although he doesn't appear to be broken-hearted himself.

Easton explains. "We have an issue in New Hampshire, also in Vermont. Maybe the whole country by now, but it started here. A lot of heroin comes in that doesn't serve your traditional addict."

"An epidemic, Émile," Hammond attests.

"A few years back, the formula for OxyContin was changed," Easton continues. "Food and Drug wanted to stop abuse, make the pills difficult

to crush, less easy to alter. Folks were bypassing the time release, injecting full-on. Those with chronic pain who'd been abusing the old Oxy
started looking for an alternative when the new Oxy showed up. They
needed, or they wanted, stronger relief. Some folks no longer had pain,
now they're addicted to the rush, the high. With the new Oxy available,
pushers don't sell illegal Oxy as much. Either one is expensive. Meanwhile, heroin's gone cheap. A pack of cigarettes costs more than junk.
These aren't the old days. *H* is now the go-to drug of choice for people
in pain willing to self-medicate. That's true for Oxy addicts who switch
over. In that demographic, you can include a few sweet old ladies."

Cinq-Mars blows out a gust of air in mulling this over. What the
world is coming to. Grandmas are junkies now? He shares a nod with
Hammond. "Still, doesn't point to murder."

"Where's her gear?" the trooper challenges him.

The Montreal detective looks around. No needle in sight. No
stretch band to magnify the veins. No lighter, no spoon. And the sleeve,
he presumes, had been buttoned up. If she OD'd, what happened to
her rig?

Cinq-Mars concludes, "Points to natural causes. She wasn't doing
up at the time, so she didn't OD. Even if she did OD, it's still not
murder."

"She's an addict," Hammond argues back.

"Alleged to be," Easton points out. "We haven't tested her yet."

"Where's her kit?" Hammond asks again, with a touch of anger. "I
don't mean that we haven't found it right beside her. We haven't found
it, period. Not in her bedroom, bathroom, kitchen."

"She has a hiding spot," Easton suggests. "It *is* her dirty little secret."

"You said that already."

"I'm saying it again."

"What's your thought?" Cinq-Mars puts to the ME

"Somebody took her kit away," Easton postulates. "She injected. She
had a coronary. Her time was up. She died. A friend came over, found

her, took away her kit to protect her reputation. Or our thief did. Don't ask me why. Or, third option – this is what I really think – she never injects herself. Maybe she doesn't know what drug she's taking. Somebody comes over, injects her, then takes off while she's still alive. A kind of personal service for the elderly. So, no gear. No heroin on the premises. No murder, either. She quietly popped off, natural causes, or worst case, a simple overdose. It happens."

"Or somebody knowingly gave her lethal juice," Hammond interjects. "Self-medicating or administrated by a person unknown, either way, that's murder."

Cinq-Mars folds his arms over his chest for a moment, then lets them fall again. "It's curious, I'll grant you that much. But Hammond, come on, why be convinced she was done in?"

"Because little old ladies and little old men have died sitting up in the countryside and how many of them are also addicts, and how many of them left their gear lying around?"

"How many?" Cinq-Mars asks.

"None that we know of," Easton says, which infuriates the officer.

"Because we didn't do autopsies!" Hammond bursts out. He has to fight for control of himself. "Because nobody checked their arms."

"Needle tracks aren't invisible," Cinq-Mars points out.

"What do families do with their dead junkie aunts and their dead junkie grandfathers? Demand an autopsy? That's the last thing they want. Do they write in their obituaries that the deceased died while high on smack? Do they write, 'Grandma loved her grandkids, playing the piano, and shooting H?' Or do they forget about that last part? This is the fourth elderly person in three months to be sitting up in the afternoon as dead as the Old Man of the Mountain."

Him again.

Hammond has a point although Cinq-Mars remains unimpressed. This doesn't seem like a case that merits his intrusion. If there's bad dope going around, police need to find the source. He's more suspicious than Easton, who clearly expects a logical explanation somewhere down the line, but even if Hammond is proven to be on to something, this is a legwork job, your basic meticulous investigation, nothing that requires his input or talents. He's certainly not going to slog around New Hampshire, which is foreign turf to him, trying to find out who sells killer heroin to senior citizens.

And yet, Hammond did say one thing that has snagged his attention. In the trooper's estimation, previous deaths may have been mishandled due to negligence. The elderly died, and an assumption was made that nothing was amiss. Cinq-Mars checks himself, recognizes that if he had been a beat cop back in the day and was called to a scene where an old person was merely dead, looking peaceful and untouched, he'd probably accept natural causes as the likelihood and call the morgue, all within the same half hour. Most families prefer that their senior loved ones be spared an autopsy and usually deny permission unless they're pressured. They may still deny it. In any case, few families permitting an autopsy learn the results. If it merely showed an addiction to heroin the medical community wouldn't bother alerting the police, or the police the family. Too common. If Hammond's hypothesis is anything close to being correct, care should be applied not to perpetuate previous mistakes.

He's impressed by Hammond today.

"Do you mind?" he asks. "Can I have the room?"

The trooper and the ME wait for an explanation that doesn't arrive.

"How much of the room?" the trooper wants to know.

"The whole kit and caboodle. The works. The house."

"For how long?" Easton inquires. "I want my examination concluded by the afternoon."

"Fifteen minutes. Unless something comes up. I have a house to look at with my wife, one we might buy. Get carried away here, Sandra will have my hide."

The latter statement satisfies them. Protocol is out the window, but the man has a reputation and Hammond has benefitted from his expertise. He owes him. He also asked him to come over, so can't reasonably deny the request. Easton passes the guest investigator a pair of nitrile gloves, then the two men usher their colleagues out the front door ahead of them.

Émile Cinq-Mars is left alone with the corpse.

He puts on the gloves.

TEN

She goes by the name Bitz.

Mousey blonde hair and a washed-out complexion. She blames the drugs for how she looks and how she looks in her own judgement is not great. The drugs make her look bad, she says, then the drugs undermine her interest in looking good. At her support group meetings, the other women nod. They understand. The men at the meetings don't care, but sometimes they nod, too.

Being an addict is a bitch.

Especially today. Not because the kids are misbehaving and she's too high to bring them into line, but because she probably looks like an addict and a hopeless mother.

She's crossed the state line to do this.

Being an addict is a bitch when you look like one, but she hopes the kids will remedy the situation when she gazes at the shopkeeper and he checks her out and instantly knows that she's higher than the White Mountains, higher than a kite above the White Mountains, that he's staring into a junkie's eyes.

He'll ask, "Can I help you, ma'am?"

She'll say, "Sure. I'd like to buy maybe a gun?" A subtle touch. A statement, but also make it sound like a question.

He might ask her why she wants one. She's rehearsed her response. "For protection mostly. Mostly, yeah." Her two kids will be at the front of the store raising cane. He'll agree with her. A woman on her own with two kids needs protection. He'll forget about the fleeting thought that went through his head minutes ago when she walked in. Addicts mean trouble. He's already let that one fly out the window.

Bitz yells at her kids to pipe down once more, then opens the door to the gun shop and shoos them in ahead of her. She goes near the back where the cheaper weapons are displayed on the right-hand side. She's done her research. All she's needed is further incentive. She has that now.

The shopkeeper wants to know what she wants the weapon for.

"To keep beside my bed at night," she says, and doesn't know where the thought comes from. She never rehearsed the line and can't remember what she planned to say. "Or under my pillow. Or in my handbag. Something small. Handy. For protection." She plays this card: "You know, for me and my kids."

I might be an addict, she's thinking, but I'm a mom, too. You gotta sell a gun to a mom, right? You can't say no to a mom even if she's high.

ELEVEN

Throughout his career, Émile Cinq-Mars has enjoyed this part of his profession. Not time spent with a corpse, which has usually left him feeling dingy, but loitering in the aftermath of a crime scene. His senses grow prickly. He hates how cops often conduct themselves, the ones who are chatty and prone to theories. Running down their checklists. As if routine or racket or accusations ever solved anything. No lowly suspicion has a chance to float free from the mire while they mindlessly natter on.

He seeks, instead, to absorb the atmosphere of a crime scene *before* the event took place. Not unlike a scientist with an ear and an eye to the cosmos, he attunes himself to the infinitesimal, to an odd blip, a deflection of light. He's after what went on prior to the Big Bang going bang, or what occurred in the moments preceding this woman's death. Forensics will address how it happened. To illuminate an earlier moment, before an embolism erupted or a killer struck, requires a malleable mindset.

His meditation seeks to extract the atmosphere of a time that's passed. Cinq-Mars is intrigued by the theory of quantum information stored on event horizons. As matter is being compressed into an unfathomable black hole, information escapes. He's gunning for that, the mechanics of what *preceded* a homicide, of what happened *before* someone tragically was sent packing into oblivion.

He wants to know what knowledge escaped the silence of death.

Other cops call it motive.

He stares at the space where a television stood proud from the wall. A coaxial wire hangs limp. He's betting that the woman enjoyed TV. She lived on her own. There's no sign of a dog or cat. Perhaps she was allergic, or she never replaced a pet she lost, worried she'd not live long enough to provide care. Instead, she watched nature shows on television.

A modest home, yet the woman lacked little of importance. Wine and a variety of spirits in a cabinet – the thief is not a drunk for he left an ample supply behind. She had a choice of fancy dinner settings or those for every day. A closet exhibits quality outerwear, including hiking boots and a pair of fishing rods. Their forward positioning in the closet suggests the rods were used. You fish? He needs Hammond to tell him her name. Of a sudden he can't wait, goes out the front door and across the porch and shouts through the screen.

"Cuthbert," the trooper fires back. "Muriel. Middle initial J."

He goes back inside.

Muriel, he muses, what happened?

Calm in repose, as though the moment of her death arrived without alarm. If this was a death by injection, she cooperated.

He contemplates what's stolen. TV and dining room chairs. That's an oddity. He likes oddities, they offer telling clues. Who steals chairs? He leans over to examine the tabletop. A light trace of dust, almost imperceptible, is present. Twin circles set along the longitudinal centreline indicate that candlesticks stood side-by-side. A thief who steals electronics, chairs, and … candlesticks.

A thought returns him to the corpse. Muriel sits bereft of jewellery. Her lightly tanned fingers and wrists indicate that she normally wears rings, a watch, a bracelet. All gone. This is one enterprising thief. He drove a truck, a van or open box pickup. Not necessary for anyone heisting rings, but for furniture, yes. Either he steals furniture on a regular basis, necessitating the van, or he has other reasons to own one.

A family man, with kids. Or he needs the vehicle for work. Or he's a hunter. Or a man who needs the size and power of a truck to bolster his self-image.

Below a sideboard Cinq-Mars spots a modem. Muriel had Wi-Fi.

A drawer reveals a Dell User Guide. A laptop, then, now gone.

Visually skimming the sheen of the mantle, which is dustier than the table – probably a two-week spell without attention – indicates that a knick-knack has been pilfered. A small item on an oblong base. A photo of Muriel with the mantelpiece in the background tells him exactly what's absent. He raises the snapshot in a frame and gives it close scrutiny in the light. Now he's looking for a burglar who's into chairs, electronics, paintings – given the brighter spaces on the walls – and elephant figurines.

The thief called to report her death, how nice of him, but neither her death nor the goodness in his heart stopped him from sliding rings off her fingers. What was his primary interest, the valuables or the chairs? The electronics or the figurines? Or did he come here to take it all and end Muriel's life, too?

In the snapshot, he sees her smiling face and a necklace, which he suspects she wore regularly. It suits her.

What happened here, Muriel? Speak up now or forever…

He wanders through to the kitchen. A wooden cutting board in the shape of a lamb lies on the countertop, a skillet on the stove. The lamb is lightly littered with cracker crumbs, telltale bits of cheese and apple. Two cheeses in the refrigerator match tiny bits left behind after she sliced a portion for lunch. Lifting up the waste bin he finds the apple core and an empty soup can. Chicken noodle. A clean pot sits upside down on the drying rack by the sink, next to a bowl. The skillet shows the remains of an egg or two fried up in butter. Why clean the lunch dishes but leave the breakfast debris untouched? Not even left to soak in the sink.

He checks the refrigerator's lower freezer compartment.

Three frozen trout lie sealed in tinfoil.

Muriel! This your catch? Good for you!

Émile stands away from the counter and the stove, one hand supporting himself on a half-wall that divides the kitchen from the dining room, where he falls into deep concentration.

Muriel? he ponders.

Breaking from his spell he goes upstairs and enters her bedroom. Always an intimate room, where someone who lives alone is bound to let a guard down, reveal a secret. This woman put in a daily effort. The bed's made. In a corner, the laundry hamper is empty. Nothing is left lying around and when he checks her dresser, he notices that nothing has been stuffed away. All is folded and neatly arranged. No bra mingles with the socks. No sweater hangs out with a blouse. Cinq-Mars is quietly proud of someone as old as Muriel taking such meticulous care of herself into her near 80s.

And fishing, too. Successfully.

The far reaches under her bed are dust-bunny free.

You're fussy. What's with you and heroin? Is that true?

Nothing in the bathroom indicates that it is. She's tidy and capable. Clearly determined to live on her own and not in an old-age home. If she wanted to protect a secret, this woman possessed the wherewithal to do so. Still, he has difficulty believing it. Downstairs, in death, she looks so sweet. Heroin? Really?

Hard to imagine her injecting into a muscle, or intravenously, or under the skin, then turning on *Jeopardy!* Did friends come for lunch and chase the dragon – octogenarians sniffing heroin – while gossiping about socialites? Do they get together for a gabfest, then try criss-crossing heroin with cocaine, or enjoy an afternoon tea while working on a quilt for the church bazaar whereupon, done for the day, they try she-banging both drugs together?

In this house, with that woman, he could only imagine routines involving illicit drugs as comical.

He knows he's wrong to think that way. That this is sad.

Interesting what the ME reported about people seeking out a better painkiller. Heroin is misunderstood in America. A powerful drug, lethally addictive, no doubt. Yet, when scores of thousands of soldiers came back from Vietnam hooked on smack, observers believed the country was in for an epic human disaster. That tragedy never materialized. More than a few soldier-junkies were lost, of course, yet the overwhelming majority unhooked themselves once they slipped free from the war zone and the noose of the military. Cinq-Mars knows of experiments run on rats. Free a junkie-rat from a lab prison, provide him or her with companions, fun games to play and a life to look forward to, and junkie-rats voluntarily unhooked. Offer the junkie-rat a choice between filtered water or heroin-laced and the rat was more likely to choose clean-living as long as he had pals and a happy life. The junkie-rat just said no. Environment counts. Pleasure in one's situation is a stronger remedy than the drug is a vice. Society has struggled to comprehend that reality.

Drug addiction, Cinq-Mars has contended, should not automatically be blamed on the drug, but on a society where people feel isolated and abandoned, where friendships and social connections and institutions are shorn. Lives lost to drug addiction are often lost before they slide into a drug-induced abyss.

He considers the environment as it pertains to Muriel.

Lonely. That's self-evident. Frail in death, perhaps true in life as well, thereby restricting her interests and enjoyments. Although she fished. Add to that the pain from one joint or several or from an old injury that necessitated OxyContin, then take away the OxyContin after she's addicted, or merely jack up the price, and he can imagine her as vulnerable to accepting heroin as a substitute once it's accessible and cheap.

Alone all day – the rooms secrete that sense – bored from dawn to midnight, in pain, desperate, exploited by a gentle pusher, not by some thug who cinches the belt on his torn jeans below his bum-crack, but by a casually dressed, smooth-talking, good-looking gentleman, or a friendly woman, and even Muriel J. Cuthbert becomes a junkie soon enough.

He gets it now. How it works. The quantum mechanics of addiction.

His conclusion is disconcerting. Standing in the hall outside her bedroom, he feels the deceased somehow has influenced his thinking. Cinq-Mars is adversely spooked. He returns downstairs.

A dingy feeling on his skin or not, he takes time to view the corpse.

Then goes out and beckons Captain-Detective Hammond – *Trooper* Hammond; he wants to get that straight – back in. The ME traipses along also and signals men from his lab to fetch the body. The room transforms from museum quiet into supermarket frenzy. Cinq-Mars takes the two through to the relative calm of the kitchen.

"So?" Hammond presses.

"You're right," Cinq-Mars assures him. "Murder."

"Whoa," Easton interjects. "How do you make that leap? Our Trooper, I understand. He has a vested interest in calling this a homicide. You? Do you get paid, too, if you freelance on this?"

Cinq-Mars ignores the insult. He leans back against the edge of the counter, the sink behind him. "On the table next to Muriel," he begins, then stops himself. "Was she a widow or single?" Posing the question to Hammond.

"Twice married, a neighbour said, twice divorced. No kids."

"Did the neighbour help out with your pain theory?"

"Broke a hip, four, five years ago. Never healed to her satisfaction."

"I want to hear about *your* theory," Easton reminds him.

He faces the ME. "Next to her," Cinq-Mars explains, "by the sofa, you'll find the remote and a lunch plate. Breadcrumbs. Cheesy bits."

"You followed breadcrumbs. Great. Where'd they take you?"

Easton is less enamoured than others with the retired detective's reputation.

"Muriel cleans up after herself. Wise enough in her old age to not let anything get ahead of her. She had a bowl of soup for lunch. The can's in the waste bin. She finished the soup, then washed the pot, bowl, and spoon. Left them to drip-dry."

"How does that give us murder?" asks the ME, persistent and sceptical.

Hammond expects something good. He's seen Cinq-Mars in action before. As the retired detective has already indicated that he'll back him on the murder scenario, he's happy to grant him full rein. Having drifted over to the half-wall, he braces himself against it and shoots a glance at Easton, who remains upright, hands on hips in a challenger's stance.

"After the soup and clean-up, she prepared a cheese plate with apple slices," Cinq-Mars goes on. "The cutting board shows that, and the plate by the sofa. She died before she got a chance to clean up that part of her meal. When you do your autopsy, you'll find cheddar and brie in her upper stomach."

Cinq-Mars waits, as though he expects the other men to get it now. They don't.

"Who cleans up their lunch dishes as they go," he asks them, "but leaves their breakfast dishes dirty?"

That's when their eyes move to the stovetop. Nothing The drying rack doesn't show the breakfast kit, either. They must assume that it's found in the sink if Cinq-Mars is asking the question.

"Not even with water on it to soak," he emphasizes. "She has breakfast, leaves a mess, then has lunch and cleans up only that part? I say no. She had lunch, and after she had lunch, somebody else came in and had breakfast. Your thief, who alerted you to her death, are you telling me that he comes in here, finds a lady dead, and decides to carry on with robbing her anyway?"

"It takes all kinds," Marcus Easton maintains.

"Okay. Let's buy that. We won't pay much for it, but we'll cough up the going rate. Tell me, does he come in here, rob her, then say to himself, Hey, look, since the lady's dead anyway, I might as well have breakfast?"

The men's gestures acknowledge that it sounds peculiar.

"But he *did* have breakfast, you're saying," Hammond points out. "So that *is* what happened, in your opinion."

"No, sir. If that so-called thief walked through the door and found a dead lady, and if he was cold-hearted enough to take the rings off her fingers and steal her furniture, he wasn't stupid enough to hang around and have a meal. Even you said he called back to report the body because he didn't want this pinned on him. What happened here is this. He killed her. He may have found her on the verge of dying, so waited for her to die and passed the time by cooking up some ham and eggs, or he killed her himself, which is more likely, then took his sweet time robbing the place afterwards, given that he'd accomplished what he came here to do. To commit murder."

Probably neither man is convinced, but Easton is more willing to let his skepticism show. "I wouldn't want to take that to a jury. He was hungry, ladies and gentlemen, that proves he did it."

"He robbed her afterwards, to make it look like he didn't kill her, that's what proves he did. An innocent man with a guilty conscience would've agonized over being implicated. But a guilty man? His primary focus is to get away with it. He's not trying to protect his innocence, only to maintain his cover. There's a difference. He calls back because he's guilty and wants to look innocent. But if he was innocent, he would never have stayed to have breakfast. He would either have dropped that dime immediately, or cleared out, pronto."

The ME concedes an inch or two. Little more.

Cinq-Mars placates him. "Don't sweat it, Marcus. That won't be all that goes to the jury. Remember, he called back. He admitted to the theft. Why?"

Hammond bites. "You just said, so he won't be implicated in her death."

"Why is he worried about being implicated in her death if it was from natural causes? Why does that even cross his mind? If he didn't kill her, why would he think it was *not* natural causes? Even your ME is inclined to go along with old age as the cause."

"That's true," Hammond concedes.

"Why did he call?" Cinq-Mars asks.

"I presume you know," Easton says.

Cinq-Mars accepts that the comment is not meant to be antagonistic.

"He's no thief," Cinq-Mars tells him. "This whole burglary thing, steal the TV but forget the remote, take the chairs and an elephant figurine—"

"How do you know that?"

"A photograph. You didn't see it? Upstairs there's a small jewellery box with a few nice items. Other knick-knacks lie around up there, too. Why not take them? Answer, he never bothered to look. Because he wasn't here to steal. He was here to kill and only stole so that Trooper Hammond, or any other officer who might conclude that this was a murder, would busy himself hunting down a thief as being the killer. At the very least, go after him as a material witness. But he's no thief. You won't find him in any mug book among thieves. He was only pretending to be one."

"Why?" Hammond asks. He has a tendency to be slow.

"To throw you off his scent. You'll look in all the wrong places."

"That's interesting as far as it goes," Easton declares, his tone respectful now. "Your theory doesn't allow for the fact that none of it is necessary. As you said, why would the killer assume we'd call this a murder, when we never would have if Geoff didn't take the call?"

"Who?" Cinq-Mars asks, a slip.

"That's me," Trooper Hammond says.

"Of course. Sorry. What? No. You see, the killer knows that the deaths are adding up. He may have gotten wind that you've been looking at the cold cases again. Have you talked about them out loud, Captain?

I mean, *Trooper* Hammond? To other ears? Any way you slice it, he takes steps to protect his identity. You know what that means."

Hammond knows, but the logic skips past Easton this one time.

"He's not responsible for only one homicide," Cinq-Mars tells him. "He's committed a few."

The kitchen goes quiet. Even Marcus Easton seeks out the top of the refrigerator with a hand and leans against it now. This is not a town or a state familiar with multiple murders, at least not until Cinq-Mars showed up and resolved the campus case. The use of the word *serial* in their investigations has been exceedingly rare.

They still don't want to use it now.

"Actually," Hammond admits, "I half-expected this to be easy. Run down a burglar, hope he did it. If not, pump him for more intel. Now you're telling me there's no burglar to run down."

"A false lead. A deliberate smokescreen. So inept at stealing that he didn't know what to take. A little of this, a little of that. Ridiculous. You're looking for a guy with a van who's a lousy thief, but he has a head on his shoulders. He thinks before he speaks, then thinks again before he acts. Even here, he only messed up by giving in to his appetite. At least, he makes mistakes."

They dwell on that a while, then Easton takes his hand off the fridge. He's the first to look as though he has somewhere to go.

"I'll follow the body out. Check her stomach for cheddar and brie. Do a tox screen. Run down whatever's in her veins."

"I have to look at a house," Cinq-Mars says.

"I'll hunt for a van loaded with furniture in a land of vans hauling furniture," Hammond remarks. "Be nice to get lucky."

"You said he dropped a dime?" Cinq-Mars puts in.

"Metaphorical. Not from a booth. We already checked the call with the FBI. A throwaway. No trace."

"There you go."

"Where do I go?" Hammond wants to know.

"He came prepared. You see? He planned to make that call all along. Which means he knew coming in the door that someone would be dead by the time he left. He knew he had to have a throwaway to make a call, then threw it away."

They leave together and separate outside. Cinq-Mars sees that Muriel had satellite. He strolls down to the highway. The house is nicely sequestered. Highway 12A is within earshot but invisible behind a barrier of trees, the bend in the drive enhancing the home's privacy. A few sightseers have dropped by, gabbing on the other side of the road. A girl on a bicycle circles around. Murder, a spectator sport. He looks back at the cottage. What fortified Muriel during her time was the home's privacy. In the end, it made her the easiest of targets. A killer could take his time, even enjoy a late breakfast. But *why*? That's the bugaboo. Murder is too big a risk for nothing more than a TV and a few chairs. He doubts that the paintings are valuable. Ones left behind upstairs are strictly amateur hour. No, a bigger picture has to come into focus here. He's convinced of that but he's not seeing it, nor can he imagine what it might possibly reveal.

TWELVE

Émile Cinq-Mars arrives at the listing, turning up a short drive. His wife appears cross. Sandra waits with Patricia Shaftesbury, their agent, an ebullient strawberry blonde – if left to nature's palette she'd be revealed as grey. Her do is wavy and creates an overall impression of perkiness. While her demeanor is too professional to be considered bubbly, she sashays through life in a way that comes across, at times, as delirium.

"Cavalry's arrived!" she trumpets as Émile steps from the Escalade. Not fond of effervescence, he makes allowances in her case. Putting a bright spin on everything is part of her job, although he'd prefer if she put a plug in the relentless colour commentary.

Sandra is not exhibiting similar enthusiasm. He's quite sure that he's not *that* late, 12 or 15 minutes, but resists the temptation to check his watch. She's propped against the front fender of the agent's Acura SUV, drawing late afternoon sunlight upon her face. Partly the light: he's struck by how he adores this woman as he leans in to kiss her cheek.

"Short and sweet," she whispers.

"We have time," he whispers back.

"Not my point."

He manages the kiss.

She adds, "Not love at first sight. You?"

"Have you been inside?"

Patricia Shaftesbury grins on, unaware that the couple's private exchange shoots down her potential sale.

"Why bother? Too dreary."

The bungalow is long and dim, the cladding an unfortunate hue of brown. Probably the exterior was meant to blend in with the bark of surrounding trees but succeeds at disappearing below the foliage.

Cinq-Mars is not averse to saying, "We'll pass on this one," and yet, he's curious. In terms of knowing what constitutes good value for the area and what's overpriced, he must do his homework. Here's a chance to learn what four-and-a-quarter buys in this neck of the woods. He returns a facsimile of the agent's smile and asks to go inside.

"Fair warning," she reveals. "The owner – her name is Cara Drost – is on the premises."

"Unusual, no?"

"She suffered a calamity. Ski accident. The reason she's selling. The upkeep is too much in her condition. It's difficult for her to leave when prospective buyers drop by."

He wishes he'd taken a pass. No gracious way out now.

The interior is brighter than expected as the rear of the house is predominately glass. The view is onto a brief lawn that slopes to a wood-lot. Pretty enough, but Émile is accustomed to a longer vista, and anyway there's no river and he has that in his head today. The fixtures are dated. The kitchen cupboards will have to go no matter who buys this place. Wallpaper needs to be stripped, the Gyprock repainted and, in places, replastered. In the dining room, a middle-aged woman who does not distribute her modest weight well and looks nothing like an active skier, is splayed out next to her crutches. Cinq-Mars notices her eyes. A wobble to the cornea. The pupils dilated.

"Please," Cara Drost requests, "pretend I'm not here."

Not easily done. In her state, she summons attention.

"Sorry about your accident. That had to be nasty."

"Break a leg skiing, the risk you take, right? But *two* busted ankles? Seriously? Two? I snapped the first one on my third cartwheel, the second on about my sixth. Then hit a tree."

Émile and Sandra fear they might be held up by this story for a chunk of the afternoon. The agent comes to their rescue. Patricia Shafts-bury bobs into the fray, thrills to the view, is charmed by the open arrangement of living and dining rooms, gushes about the stonework on the fireplace mantel, and is solicitous to the owner while at the same time shooing the reluctant couple along. They cut the tour short even under the barrage of her enthusiasm, having zero interest. Sandra and the agent, then, are astonished when Cinq-Mars tracks back to the proprietor for a quick chat.

"What do you do for the pain?"

Cara Drost balks. "Why ask?"

"I'm curious."

"You're that policeman, aren't you? I heard you were. That police-man."

"Retired. I police nothing and no one anymore."

"Newspapers say different. The TV. Oh my God, the radio."

"You watch a lot of television. Due to your injuries."

"I'm stuck to my chair. I haven't taught since Christmas."

"High school?"

"Elementary. Long-term disability, thank God."

"That's good."

She laughs. "I don't want you to think I'm desperate. My price for the house is quite firm. Stuck in this chair or not."

He's deliberately slow to respond, then says, "Speaking of desperate. May I use your facilities?"

"Sure. Ah…I guess you know where the little boys' room is by now."

He does. He does not choose the closest option, selecting instead the master bedroom's en suite. Cinq-Mars had agreed with Sandra that the mauve tiles are hideous, the tub both too short and too shallow. He goes in and flushes the toilet, then opens the medicine cabinet and rif-fles through it. His wife would never have allowed this while she was in the room, the agent hovering. This way, alone, he turns on a tap and makes quick work of the cabinet under the sink, where he finds the woman's gear. A supply of needles in sterile packs. A spoon. Elastic wrap. The most damning evidence: twin sachets of brown nubs. He'd bet his life on it: heroin.

Émile is doubting if he still wants to live in New Hampshire, where little old ladies and elementary school teachers are addicted to brown sugar. His test sample is too insignificant to call it an epidemic, and yet, as a new arrival, these discoveries are disconcerting.

Her eyes and voice gave her away: Cara Drost shot up within the last hour. She's as high as any hawk that swoops over these hills and valleys. He wants to warn the schoolteacher that her life might be in danger and not from New Hampshire ski trails. With no crafty way to do so, and aware that his musings may be inaccurate, he turns off the tap.

Sandra has gone outside, taking the sun again. Standing in the light, she seems distant to him, as if deliberately keeping something to herself. The agent remains raring to go. She's added another house to their itinerary.

"New on the market. It'll go fast. We better hop to it!"

Cinq-Mars looks back upon the bungalow. The schoolteacher's habit may have prompted this sale. The teacher's inability to care for the grounds herself may have motivated her, and yet, into the mix, she's indulging the needle. He wonders if her long-term disability payments go south if the authorities learn the money is for heroin. They will if she's incarcerated, and who looks after her home then? He's gazing upon a tragic scene.

THIRTEEN

Known to her friends as Bitz, Betsy Kincaid commands her kids to "Stop shouting! Someone's at the door." Mules slap her heels as she goes down the hall to answer. The children, a girl and a boy, seven and nine, suspend their mayhem a moment. By the time she opens the screen door they're boisterous again. In the early evening light, she gazes outside, and asks, "Who's there?"

Pushes the door farther out.

Peering to her right, Bitz declares, "You."

The man is 10 feet away on her porch, leaning his back against the house, one knee bent, a foot up against the siding. His posture feels like a threat.

She can't take her eyes off him. Not yet.

He's not a large man. His size does not mark him as intimidating. His shoulders are remarkably broad for someone of average stature, but she's been around muscular men in her day, slept with a few. She turned a few into candy floss. This one though, his stance, his bearing, carries not only a subliminal threat but arrives with the fear of instability. The unknown. She half-expects him to go off his rocker for the most inconsequential slight. She suspects the man is aware of the effect he puts out. He's intelligent, yet she intuits that one day he'll be unreasonable, a sodden soul off his meds, prone to violence because she happens to blink at the wrong instant.

"My kids are inside." She means by that: *Keep your head screwed on.*

"Behave yourself," he tells her. He still hasn't looked at her.

Bitz clutches both her elbows to stem a sudden shiver. She steps out onto the porch.

She has no intention other than to behave. She'd never risk a scene with this man. She finally takes her eyes off him and scans the neighbours' yards, both hoping that no one's around to see him while praying for the proximity of others for her protection. She doubts that if he goes off on her he'd care about who's around. Interference is not something he fears. He exhibits an attitude that he's free to commit harm with impunity. He doesn't view anything the way normal people do. He exists in his own world as if he commands everyone in it.

"What's this about?" she asks. "Is something wrong? My kids are inside."

"Who's gonna bother your kids? Won't be me."

That's saying something anyway. A reassurance. "Is something wrong?"

"I'm standing here, aren't I? If I'm standing here, something's wrong." He finally looks at her, and she sees for the first time that he's smoking. He takes a last drag on his cigarette then flicks the butt into the hydrangeas that border the porch. He looks at her for longer than she'd like. His eyes, at least, don't look crazy tonight. "I don't do kids," he says, and suddenly she's more fearful than ever. The threat hangs in the air that such a thing can be arranged if he decides to bring her children into this.

His way to underscore that their talk is serious.

"You don't usually show up this time of day. Not your usual day, either."

"Bitz, don't talk to me about what's usual, okay?"

"Okay. I won't."

"Special situation, Bitzy."

"Did I do something wrong? Joris, tell me what it is. I'll fix it."

"For sure you'll fix it. I know what you intend. It won't happen. I know what you're planning, Bitzy."

"What do you mean? I don't understand. I'm not planning anything."

"Christ, don't lie. You been caught out."

"I don't understand. What did I do wrong?"

"Do you care about your kids or not?"

The fear clenching her gullet spawns panic. This can't be happening. She starts breathing more deliberately, more deeply. "Don't hurt my kids."

"I said that already. Do I have to fucking repeat myself around here? Calm the fuck down. I don't need nobody hyper-the-fuck-ventilating on me."

Since the last time she saw Joris Pul he's shorn one side of his blonde scalp, the hair on top draped over the clearing. An attempt to be contemporary, hip. The severe overhang of his brow won't permit him to be either. She takes deeper breaths and tries to be calm. Or calm enough to suit him.

"I'm sorry," she says.

"Better be," he tells her.

Her exhale is loud.

"For the kids' sake," he says. "That's why I'm here. You want to see them grow up – nobody's going to touch them, nobody's going to harm them, Bitz, you got my word on that. You'd think I'd harm a kid? You don't know squat. But – if you want to see them grow up, then you have to be here, right? You have to be around. If they don't have a momma how sad is that? Me, I know how sad it is. You'll miss out on everything. Tell me you agree with me."

She's hugging herself and trying to breathe normally. She nods.

"I need you to say that you agree. I want to hear it out loud."

"I agree. Yes. Right. Of course."

"How does it help your kids if their momma ain't in the picture?"

"Right. Yes. I agree."

"Good. So, forget about what you're doing."

"I—. I don't understand. What am I doing?"

"You tell me."

"I don't know."

"The wrong answer. Think about it for five seconds" – for the first time he raises his voice – "then tell me what you won't do no more."

She does think. Her chest cracks open then. She gasps.

"I was thinking about—"

He waits for her to recover, then turns to face her again. "You'll feel better once you get it out."

"I was—. You know. I was thinking, an idle thought, nothing more than that, I was thinking maybe about maybe trying rehab."

He waits in the evening light as if searching far across the street, perhaps into a neighbour's window where a light's come on. "See?" he points out to her. "Think about your kids. Not about yourself. About seeing them grow up. About being around to see them grow up. Rehab? In rehab, they ask you to talk about your problems, shit like that. You don't need those dumbass conversations. Who knows what you'll say in there? We can't have that. I cannot tolerate it myself. Tell me you agree with what I'm saying. It's a major inconvenience for me to come here. Am I wasting my time? Tell me the truth straight up."

Bitz nods again, not sure what she's confirming.

"I need your agreement here."

"Sure. Joris. Yeah."

"I'm only thinking about what's best for you. Off you go to rehab, what's the next step? Social Services. They get an idea about you, they hear things, take your kids away."

"No, Joris—"

"People phone in, with stories, to make sure you never get them back."

"You wouldn't do that!"

"Me? Why do you think it would be me? Shame on you, Bitz. I'm only trying to get you to understand the situation, the consequences of your actions. So, tell me straight out. Think about your kids and tell me if you're going to rehab."

She understands him now. "I won't. No rehab."

"That's right. You're a single mom. You're getting by. All is good in the world. You're a junkie. Keep it that way. Otherwise." He gives her that long stare again. He doesn't have to say anything more, but he does. "Otherwise you don't want to know, Bitz."

The man steps down from her porch and turns to look up at her from the bottom step.

He says, "You honestly think I got no friends in rehab? I mean, like, who work there?" He shakes his head as if he can't believe that anyone could be that naïve. He heads back to the street and by the time he climbs into his black Mustang with the top down Bitz has returned inside. She can't bring herself to tell her children to be quiet. They're shrill and loud and being mean to each other. She goes into her laundry room where they are unlikely to invade. Shuts the door and the whole of her body quakes. Shivers engulf her on this warm night, and she hugs herself tightly as her back slides down a wall until she's sitting on the floor in a lump where she weeps a while, and weeps some more before she pulls herself together. She knows what she must do next. She pitches herself upright. Suddenly determined. Usually, she waits for the kids to be in bed. Tonight she'll do it early. Bitz goes upstairs to her bedroom for a fix. She needs to get high. That's the only answer for everything right now. Forget about rehab. That's it. That's all. Find a vein. Drill the next hit into her skin, and blood, and soul. That's all there can ever be. The kids'll look after themselves for now. Put themselves to bed. They do that anyway.

FOURTEEN

Evening falls as glorious viewed from the farmhouse porch.

Sunset lacks drama in the mountains. Cooler breezes slide from the hills, relaxing the senses. As the sun subsides below a peak, a summer concert is in full throat. The farm's cattail pond substitutes as a bandshell. From the arc of maple, oak and ash along the far shore, reggae tree frogs regale them with a cacophonous hullabaloo, a rendition of uptempo insect bedlam, then release themselves to total silence as though expecting to spark applause. A beat that returns, roaring.

One momentous caterwaul, not unlike that of an infant in desperate bray, knifes through.

"What *is* that?" Émile wants to know.

Sandra sits curled on the wicker sofa's cushions. "What's what?"

"*That*. That wailing."

Through the chattering frenzy, one scream separates from the rest.

Sandra flashes a smile. "That, dear sir—" She's interrupted by a companion wail, at about a 30-degree angle from the first. "*Those* are Fowler's toads."

"Are they being murdered?"

The reference makes her laugh. The famous detective has aimed his spyglass mind upon amphibians in search of incriminating clues. "Don't muck through the pond to investigate, Émile. They only want to be noticed."

"They've got my attention. So the pleasant songs, in the middle of the register, what are those? They sound more like birds."

She concurs. "Marsh wrens. They're nocturnal."

He observes her a moment, aware of her intimacy with this environment.

When they turn themselves over to the music, the night is spell-binding. "Tree frogs and crickets also, just like back home," Émile mentions.

"I'm hearing chick-will's-widows, too. They're nightjars." Sandra stretches in the ease of the evening, then unwinds with her feet returning to the floor. "Did you know, crickets make four distinct sounds?"

"All of them grating."

"Not true. Some go soft."

"Don't they tire of all that leg-rubbing?"

"Émile, that's a myth. They don't rub their legs. They have a row of teeth on their wings, which they rub with a membrane on the opposite wing."

"Hold on. Teeth? On their wings?"

"It's what they rub against. The wings also form a funnel to act as a speaker to project the sound."

"I'm surprised they're not plugged into an electrical outlet."

"Internal batteries, I'd say."

This works, Émile is thinking on another level. Meaning, the marriage. An easy-going talk at the end of the day with no grinding issues in sight. Forget about packing up, buying a house, moving. Forget about everything. Set it all adrift on the evening air. Thinking this way delivers an inkling, perhaps an insight, into how Sandra feels. This move they've been contemplating: She wants out from caring for horses, but does she want to give up her life in the countryside for the joys and challenges of populated neighbourhoods? Surrender all this? He only realized today that he'd like to wake up by a riverside, but Sandra? Suburbs or in-town? Countryside or village? Mountaintop or valley? Rustic or modern? They haven't discussed any of it, and perhaps such a talk should come before being towed around by a real estate agent.

"Four distinct calls for crickets," Sandra continues, wanting this essay out. "The loud one you noticed. A declaration. *I'm here! Come visit!* A quiet one is the courting call. *Female in the house!* The male sounds sweeter then, the phoney. Of course, boys will be boys: there's the fight call, which means another male is too close for comfort. The fourth call, believe it or not, is post-coital. Kind of like having a smoke afterwards."

"My God. What goes on out there. The shenanigans."

"We won't discuss fireflies. They're so obscene. Not to mention murderous. Your bailiwick. The snowy tree cricket, did you know, calculates temperature."

"I did not know that." He thinks she's pulling his leg.

"Count the number of chirps over 14 seconds, add 40, that's the temperature in Fahrenheit. I don't know about Celsius. You Canadians are stuck using a thermometer, I suppose."

They laugh together, at peace, a mood broken by headlights turning off the highway onto their property. The lights jounce in the ruts. Trooper Hammond phoned ahead; they've been expecting him.

"What level of hospitality is required?" Sandra asks.

"He doesn't require feeding. That bottle of Talisker Storm should do. I've got it covered."

"Good. I'll pop into the tub, read in bed for a bit. If he entices you to view an axe murderer's bloody handiwork, honk twice so I know you're gone. Don't forget to shower afterwards."

"Ha-ha."

An undercurrent critical of what he's up to may reside in her quip, yet she's signalled that his activity is fine with her. Sooner or later, they'll get into it, figure out what's up with each other and with what they're doing. Where they're moving. In the meantime, he has a cop to chat with and a case to ruminate on. He forgoes snifters for a couple of shot glasses in one hand, the bottle in the other, and steps off the porch to greet his guest.

The man who departed Bitz's house in a black Mustang keeps a hectic schedule. Joris Pul visits old Mrs. Birman with whom he enjoys a rapport. They have a beer and shoot the breeze. He reminds her to keep her mouth shut.

"Who am I supposed to talk to? Never mind I know nothing about what?"

"Doing my job, Mrs. B. Some folks might snoop around. Probably won't find you. If they do, don't talk. Got that?"

"You mean cops."

"The *who* don't matter."

"My lips are sealed, sonny boy. But what if I squeal? What then, Joris? Do you shoot me between the eyeballs, or break my legs?"

"With you, Mrs. B., I'll tickle you until you holler. You'll be sorry then." They have that kind of relationship, trusting and friendly. Mrs. Birman does a pantomime of the shivers, as though she's terrified by his threat. He swigs down the last of the beer and he's off again.

Overall, Joris Pul appreciates the variety of his daily chores.

A waft of dust kicks up from the car's wheels. Cinq-Mars shelters the shot glasses. The motor is switched off. He places the glasses on the hood and uncaps his bottle which is only a quarter full. They won't be doing grave damage to their livers if the talk goes deep into the night. Hammond clamours out. Cinq-Mars would invite him up to the front porch except that he's been on his keister long enough. Houselights cast sufficient illumination for him to pour and for the trooper to pick up a glass, although the two men remain dimly lit, as if standing in their own shadows.

"Did you know," Cinq-Mars inquires of the New Hampshire State Police trooper, "that the snowy tree cricket can tell you the temperature?"

Hammond draws his first sip with appreciation. He might have downed it as a shot but sets the tone for the evening differently. They'll go slowly.

"I prefer to hear the weather on the radio," he says. "Or stick my head out the door. Better than a stopwatch on a chirping bug."

"You knew that?" Cinq-Mars double-checks.

"Count the chirps over fourteen seconds, add forty."

"I'm impressed. I just found out."

"My mom taught me that kind of stuff. I guess a few lessons stuck. I'd ask her how do we know there's only one cricket? What if there's two or three? Does that skewer the count or raise the temperature? I'd get her goat that way."

They sip their drinks. The pair have not enjoyed an easy acquaintance. Early on, Hammond was belligerent toward the outsider and floundered on his rampant insecurities. Eventually, things settled, respect ensued, and now the trooper has sought his counsel. Cinq-Mars accepts that the man is no longer suspicious of him but knows it's bizarre to be let in on a case. Odd that a retired old fart's two cents matter. He was never the most collegial of officers himself, merely tolerating the proximity of a partner until the man – in his day, usually a man – either proved himself or shoved off. Frequently, he shoved off because Cinq-Mars pushed. Only by the tail end of his career did he partner well.

"What's the good word?" Cinq-Mars asks, the Scotch on his tongue.

"Our gal pal. The late Muriel J. Cuthbert. For over thirty years she ran a beauty salon. Pillar of the community. Kept to herself lately. Retirement will do that. She likes to fish. That's a new one on me. Old geezers, sure, they fish. But women? Well, what do I know? Hard to keep up."

"I saw her rods. Lures and stuff. Trout in her freezer."

"I never saw that. My guys asked her neighbours. I read the reports."

"What's eating you, Trooper?"

"Injection of pure heroin," he states. "That's what killed her, the ME confirms."

Hammond drinks again, then lets his breath expire in a long, low gush. "Pure. She did not take too much; she took it too *pure*. She didn't know what hit her. In a coma in minutes, then the bodily functions are confused and off she goes into the great beyond. On a high or as mental sludge. Who knows? Who lives to tell the tale?"

Cinq-Mars is wistful a moment, although he's not sure whether the pause is for the dearly departed or for the pleasure of the whiskey. "She's doing H, at seventy per cent, or sixty or forty, then injects at one hundred and she's dead."

"If the increase is substantial, given how frail she's been, it's all she wrote. She stays sitting upright and dies a bit slowly without fuss."

Cinq-Mars takes that in. "I hate to say this. It doesn't categorically indicate murder. Manslaughter, maybe. I hate to cast dispersions on a victim, but suicide remains a possibility. She could have requested the ways and means, someone to stow her gear afterwards. Keep her reputation intact."

As host, he uncorks the bottle again, and Hammond isn't shy to offer his glass for a refill. He leans his rear against the car's front door and Cinq-Mars does the same over the wheel well, the bottle on the hood between them. Stars begin to sprinkle the sky as darkness deepens, a quarter moon expected eventually.

"It's a puzzle," Hammond agrees.

"Also, if somebody did her in, who wanted a little old lady dead? It should be a safe gig, being old, little, and a lady."

"Plus," Hammond puts in, "if she requested pure heroin, who would give it to her? Who had it to give? No down-the-chain pusher is supplied with pure mint. As I see it, no other indicator points to suicide. No note. No evidence of depression or remorse or bad news out of the blue."

"Insurance?"

"As far as we've discerned, she had no one to leave it to."

Cinq-Mars acknowledges the validity of all that. He doesn't want to be persuaded that she committed suicide, he hates when that happens, so holds the thought in abeyance. "Assuming we're talking about murder," he ponders, "the biggest question is why? Motive and opportunity are issues. It doesn't look like anything of value was stolen, and that's another question. Why would a thief steal so many items that aren't worth much? I've answered that already, I know – to make it look like he's there for a reason other than murder – but why so much stuff? He could have made it easier on himself. Stuck to the jewellery. Opportunity suggests that she knew the thief. Whether he injected or she did, he was aware of her habit. Heroin could be the connection between them. She was a junkie. Maybe the thief, too?"

"Or her pusher," Hammond puts in.

"Or her pusher, obviously. But what pusher wants to kill a client? Unless she'd run out of money and wasn't paying. But junk is cheap, and, like you said, what pusher in this neck of the woods can get his hands on pure *H*?"

"The thing is, if a supply is out there, if somebody is putting pure *H* on the market, we'd see more deaths. I've checked. The hospitals have not discerned any uptick in heroin overdoses lately."

Hammond slaps a mosquito on his neck.

"Want to go inside?"

"That's okay. I'm wearing repellent. That little bastard got desperate."

Cinq-Mars makes a gesture with his chin that the trooper questions. He explains, "Maybe that's who we're looking at. Someone who got desperate and took a chance. Why I don't know. When something that's going on didn't work out, our Muriel got swatted."

Hammond grunts and drinks. "Any ideas?"

"Somebody buttoned up her sleeve, after she injected. Wanted to cover up the injection. Hide the murder. Clever, that. Look, I met a woman today who's selling her house. Schoolteacher. Cara Drost."

"I know her."

"You do? In what capacity? Don't tell me she has a record, that will really damage my view of the world."

"No, she's fine. We both grew up near here. Down the highway about seventy miles. Same village. We were in school together."

"Do you know about her?"

"What's to know? She teaches school."

"She's a junkie."

He might as well have told him that she'd been running a whore-house, with herself as the standard-bearer. Hammond is floored by the news.

"Found the evidence under a sink."

As the other man appears stricken, he proffers an excuse on her behalf. "She broke both her ankles skiing. She's in pain. That's the cause right there."

"Skiing? Cara? I can't imagine that."

"Can you imagine her as a junkie more?"

"No. No way. You're sure?"

"Well, I didn't ask for X-rays of her ankles—"

"That she's a junkie?"

He rocks his chin from side to side. "Strong first impression, put it that way. Borderline irrefutable."

"My God. Cara Drost. I can remember yanking her pigtails."

"That's probably why she's a junkie today."

"Not funny."

"Yeah. I don't know if you have the manpower, Trooper Hammond, but I suggest keeping an eye on her. See who walks up to her door."

His nod is slow, deliberate, wheels are churning. "Sure," he says. "Thing is, Émile, we've got at least one murder on the books, plus a drug connection that's scary. We don't want hundred per cent proof on the street, so I'm pretty sure I'll find the manpower."

The two men gaze up at the stars, and Cinq-Mars intuits that their time together will soon be up for the night. He lobbies for what he needs next. "We have this death and the previous deaths. Speaking of man-power, I'd like to go door-to-door on the old cases. See what that reveals."

Hammond smiles, then finishes his drink. What he says next causes Cinq-Mars to jerk his head around. "Why I called you in the first place."

"Excuse me? What do you mean?"

Hammond puts his empty glass down on the hood. "I can make you look semi-official, Émile. Deputize you if I want. What I can't do is stick a line item on the books to investigate a series of natural deaths. No way do I have the budget for that, no way can I push for it. I've already tried. We have budgets. We have oversight. Pulling out manpower to do a rundown of natural deaths veers toward the impossible. Plus, if it's not done right, it'll infuriate citizens who lost a loved one. Delicacy, insight, care for how people feel, that's all necessary. Folks who think they lost a loved one from old age or an act of God might become touchy if cops promote a conspiracy. The state won't be keen, I've validated that."

"Your troopers won't be thrilled with the assignment," Cinq-Mars interrupts, understanding his dilemma.

"Why I called you in. Look at the older deaths. Real delicate like."

Cinq-Mars is dismayed by how he's underestimated this man and bowled over by how well his own scheme is panning out. He doesn't have to twist the guy's arm. The contrary, it's his wrist being burned. "More to you than I suspected, Trooper Hammond."

"It's Geoff. You hold a negative view, Émile. No secret."

"I'll cop to not being fully cognizant."

"Not my best foot forward when we met. Now, at the risk of taking a step backwards, getting you to help out hasn't been only my idea."

Cinq-Mars is puzzled.

"I'll own it," Hammond explains, "but I had to plant a certain seed, you know? I had to get another man to think this was really *his* idea. Thanks to that, if you help to convict, I can free up reward cash."

Extra money sounds nice, but who had he been talking to? Who else is a party to conscripting him? Cinq-Mars doesn't have to ask, he just keeps staring down the lengthy beak of his nose until the other man yields.

"The Governor," Hammond admits.

"The Governor wants me on the job?"

"Tickled pink. Will he pay extra funds to investigate deaths marked down as natural causes? He will not. Will he free up funds to have *you* do it? Off on the side? You can do no wrong in the Governor's mind. Even so, we'll require convictions before paying out."

"I barely met the man. Shook his hand briefly." He won't say that he was not terribly impressed and is not now, either. He'll be paid if he convicts, which is not how the brakes of the law are best applied when careening downhill.

"You'll do it?" Hammond wants confirmed.

An opportunity, knocking. Cinq-Mars takes a breath. "Try and stop me," he confirms.

"I have files. Back seat. They're not exactly thick. Skimpy as can be. That's half our problem right there."

Émile Cinq-Mars is on the job again. Heading into retirement, he never imagined that.

On her bike, Libby St. Croix is cut off by Joris Pul in his car. The skinny teenager was captain of her high school track team before falling off a cliff on her summer holidays. Pul didn't know her in those days but knows her now. She depends on crutches, the kind that snap onto her forearms, and she depends on him. Although she can ride a bike, she can only put weight on the balls of her feet, not on her heels, and she has a hard time braking between his car and the curb. He gets out and shoves her off the bike, which he stuffs into his trunk. She's lies in a lump on the pavement. He pulls her up and waits while she struggles into the front seat. Pul drives her far away from her familiar neighbourhood. He doesn't want her recognized in his company, and she likes that. They approach a building in an industrial park off the highway where he draws up a big garage-type door, then gets back in the car and drives right in. Now she's afraid. Scared outright. She hobbles out of the Mustang on her crutches. Pul doesn't hold the door open or help in any way. She doesn't know where they are or what this is about. This is something new and she's frantic and wary.

He closes the garage door.

"Something wrong, Joris?"

"People keep asking me that today. Must be the fucking moon. Yeah, something's wrong. You could say that."

The warehouse is almost empty, save for a desk and a phone and a few boxes and a table with a coffeemaker on it, and a chair in the middle of the room where he tells her to sit. More or less in the dark. Scant light is available from a pair of exit signs, so she can see an object on the table that, when she looks more closely, she identifies as a mousetrap. Old-fashioned with a wood base and a large rusty spring. There's cheese in the mousetrap. She thinks the trap should be on the floor, but it sits on the table. Maybe that's where the mice go. The windows are high up in the warehouse and small. Through one a quarter moon transits a bank of cloud. The man switches the light on that hangs from the ceiling and for a few moments she squints.

She's seated. She's scared.

The room is dead quiet.

At her back, Joris Pul yanks a section of duct tape free from a roll.

The man binds her arms to the chair.

She watches him do it. She doesn't move. She doesn't resist.

Her heart is pounding now.

Her own kerchief is taken from her hair and tied tightly across her mouth.

The terror dances in her eyes now. This is all new to her.

"Problem is, the way I see it," the man quietly explains, "you don't understand what *need* is. *Real* need. I have a need and you don't seem to understand that. The reason you can't grasp it, little girl, is because you're so damn selfish. You're pathetic. I need more young people to depend on me the way you depend on me. I like that, but I also *need* that. You have friends. Classmates. You meet kids when you go to mass, you run into them at the Dairy Queen. Why is it you never brought me one yet? Fortunately for you, I'm smart, see. I know why you let me down. You're so damn selfish, you don't appreciate my need."

She squirms and battles her restraints and bounces her chair off the floor a couple of times but that hurts. Both her knees are in braces.

The man says, "I know what you want to say. Word for word, I bet. Oh, poor you, you don't have any friends. Oh, poor you, you're shy. But when are you going to learn what's important? No friends? Other kids have no friends. Make friends with those kids. If you can't bring me a few kids your age, bring me old people. I need to expand my base. You hang out with old folks, right? You're twisted that way. I take care of old people, too. See? I'm not so fussy why should you be? Bring me someone. Anyone. Is that a lot to ask? Too much? That's what they call a rhetorical question by the way – rhetorical – and the answer is no. You see, I'm not going to hurt you, Libby. You think I am, but we'll wait here until you need a fix real bad, then you can get a better grip on what it means to have a real need, one that must be filled, and only then, when we have that mutual understanding, when you're not feeling so goddamn selfish, we'll have our talk. Everything will come out in the open then."

He walks away from her.

He calls out, "I'll be nearby." His voice in the warehouse echoes. "Waiting on your every need. That's me. I understand the importance of need, of want, of desire. You will, too, Libby."

She's 17 years old.

Not the time for her fix yet, but already she wants it.

The terror dances in her eyes as she looks up into the glare of the overhead lamp and begs for a salvation that she's quite certain will never come.

FIFTEEN

He's in a drunken state.

As a boy, Reece Zamarlo grew accustomed to the dead. He grew up in a small New Hampshire town across the street from a funeral parlour operated by his aunt and uncle, and with his dad often in prison or on the lam and his mother working, he spent most of his time there. His aunt raised him. In her company one time, he saw cops across the street aim rifles at his front door, demanding that his father come out.

Little Reece could have told them back then that his dad was not home.

Only his mother emerged, half-dressed and shaking so much she could barely keep her arms raised.

At his aunt's, the front rooms were reserved for viewing the dead and for services commemorating their passing. When the dead arrived from the morgue they were ministered to in the basement. He and his sister saw naked corpses often. Once, his sister dressed up the toes of a deceased with bows and homemade rings. She was disciplined for that, a trespass soon forgotten.

Growing up that way, Zamarlo doesn't mind the dead or death; it's illness that upsets him. He might have taken over his uncle's practice had he not chosen his father's path. He landed in trouble as a young whelp and did time. In prison, he saw both death and sickness, and between the two death did not trouble him. In a way, sickness became his mortal enemy, and in the war between sickness and health, he decided that death can be a friend.

Life taught him that.

Prison reinforced the opinion.

He saw firsthand the ravages of disease. His aunt, a woman he adored and whose kindness reshaped his life, suffered horribly from jaw cancer. The hideous ugliness ate away at her face. Periodically, a vision of her awakens him in a slick sweat. He trembles then, until dawn permits him to sleep again.

Reece Walter Zamarlo, with a beer clasped by the neck between two fingers, steps outside his home under the starry heavens and a fleet scud of cloud. Above a low-slung hill, a quarter moon pokes out, a mischievous grin on its mug. Zamarlo mentions it to his three-year-old son, who's not there. The boy no longer lives with him but sometimes Zamarlo keeps him around for imaginary conversations. "That moon's like you."

"Like me?" the kid's voice in his head says back.

"Up to something."

He concedes that he's two sheets to the wind. He tips an elbow up and tilts his head. Polishes that bottle off. Puts it down on a front step.

Zamarlo digs keys from a pocket as he crosses the gravel parking lot where the whiteness of his van shines like a satellite. He slips a key into the padlock that secures his workshop. Inside, he lowers venetian blinds on either side of the door and bolts the door shut before he switches on the overheads.

Fluorescents blink, then light the room.

On his worktable lie the gutted remains of televisions and computers. Folks once upgraded their computers by installing new hard drives and more memory. Twice, three times; same machine. Now? They buy new machines. Same with TVs. Used to be lots of work for a good repairman. These days, a man with a problem TV carries it down to the dump, or to a damn ecological centre, then drives to a box store and buys new. The best that Reece Zamarlo can do is occasionally take a set off someone's hands, or a computer, effect a repair if it isn't too onerous and put it up for resale. Scratch a few bucks that way. Beer money, at most. Anyway, it gives him cover. Which is important in life. Meanwhile, he can fix anything else in need of repair. Fridges, dishwashers, washing machines. He can usually squeeze in a repair on one before it quits for good. In the northland, not every small store has a sufficient client base to afford the luxury of a repair department, so he picks up occasional warranty work. Small stores call him in, which usually means replacing a part that's inadequate, or making an adjustment to a gizmo gone out of whack in the shipping stage; or filling out a form that states why the machine ought to be replaced or taken back to the factory for a do-over. Nothing that requires being a bona fide genius.

For many appliances, he is *officially authorized*.

Which keeps the wolf from gnawing at his door.

Although, as he likes to say, he still can hear the beast howl.

Reece Zamarlo wants to do better than merely get by. He wants better, but for that he needs a cover. Fixing stuff is a good cover.

He opens the doors of a tall steel cabinet, revealing multiple shelves. His wife, who left him, used to say that some people use shelves to organize their stuff, and other people use shelves to hide their mess. He's the latter, she said, and he assumes she's right. But he has something now that he doesn't want to hide. Why did the old lady who died today have this figurine out on display? Probably it provoked a memory for her, some trip. One she'd taken, or one she dreamed about. For him, he likes the elephant's happy, colourful look.

It's worthless. He checked *online*. Joris Pul was right about that.

He lifts it off a shelf.

He places the figurine on a stand against a wall, clearing space by removing a three-hole punch and a stapler, which he dispatches to a drawer. The elephant looks good there. Brightens the space somehow and he feels proud in a way. Maybe if someone comes in, that client will think, as he did when he stole it, that the thing is worth a mint.

Back to other work.

The jar of pure heroin is an eighth full, yet he unwinds the cap with care. This is the real stuff, nothing that belongs on the street, and the last thing in the world he wants to have happen is to drop a rock that rolls under the table and down a drain. He treats each rock as a gold nugget. And why not? Each is worth more than the elephant, although that's not saying much.

Though to some, a rock like this means life. To others, death.

He uses a dinner plate as a working surface. From a table drawer he extracts an empty plastic satchel, a small baggie, enough for one dose. A single lethal dose. Using tongs he extracts a marble-sized amount and places it on the scale, checks the weight, then centres it on the plate for cutting. About a third needs to come off. He makes the cut, reweighs the nugget. A teensy bit over but he can let that go. Important to provide the right amount, or always a little in excess.

Even to someone about to die.

A matter of integrity, really.

Not to mention the dead person's dignity.

Not to mention the person's last comfort.

Not to mention getting away with murder.

He places the dose in the baggie.

Again being careful, he removes the cap from the jar a second time and places the remainder inside. He puts the baggie inside for safe keeping, relatively free from humidity. Screws the cap back on, returns the bottle to the shelf and shuts the cabinet doors.

Sometimes, you have to fight sickness with death, when there's no other way. Charge him with murder if he gets caught? Ridiculous.

Many who are dead are glad he's alive.

A growing number will become grateful.

As will be the person next on his list to die.

Reece Zamarlo knows who that will be.

SIXTEEN

The man with his blond hair shorn along one side sits still while Libby St. Croix moans in her discomfort. Her limbs ache. The gyroscope of her inner ear is out of whack as though she's a seasick duck. Her alimentary canal wants to be expelled from her body without preference for an orifice. Libby screams, her voice muffled by the kerchief across her mouth. The man doesn't care how loud she is and that scares her. She moans, and the sound prompts her to moan more. Her blood curdles, wants to erupt, to vacate her skin. Her heart blisters. Her blood can't stand her mind entrapped in these bones and she wails and feels deformed, as though her flesh shrivels and turns scaly. The man with the shorn hair observes her, then says, "Libby, don't take it so hard."

The gag is across her mouth. She can't answer or plead. Only a moan.

"Do you feel my need, Libby? How great it is?"

She tries to say yes. She murmurs something similar.

"Then it's your lucky motherfucking day. Know why, Libs? Because I believe you. We could go on all night, no skin off my nose. Instead, let's jump to the next step."

She's not lucid, but thinks he means sex. Her body so wracked she doesn't care. She doubts she'll notice. She tries to burst her restraints but cannot and topples over in her chair, then lies cockeyed on the floor. In one angry motion he plunks her back upright.

"Don't do that! Sit in your chair for fuck's sake like a fucking lady."

He leaves her, then returns. On the table he places a beaker and the whole of her body convulses, a rhythm of pain and gladness. A beaker!

He returns with a knock-off Bunsen burner and her body twists in ecstasy. Her bones tear apart from her tendons. This can't be ecstasy. This must be misery. She can't tell the difference anymore.

He leaves again and comes back with heroin, and a needle pack.

She's so happy. Her misery intensifies.

"Prove yourself," he says.

She nods furiously in agreement.

"If I'm the cat, Libby, you are the mouse. I have great plans for you. But tonight, you are the mouse."

He places the mousetrap on the floor where it should have been all along. Adjusts it near her right foot. Then he stoops over and slips off both her shoes. No socks, she's barefoot now. He stands above her, touches her scalp gently.

"Be the mouse," he whispers. "Take the cheese out of the trap. Go on. You can do this. What, you're confused? Use your toes."

She recoils from the notion and fights against her restraints and the whole of her body screams *no* at him. He dangles the lump of heroin in a packet in mid-air, and she concedes. She wiggles her toes, slowly, slowly, toward the trap.

"Good girl. Almost done. Get the cheese out, Libby."

She wiggles her toes closer.

The trap snaps shut on her advancing toes and she screams as her torso distends and contorts in an agony she has never known.

She wants out from her body.

He says, "Excellent. You're a good little mouse, Libby."

He opens the trap, frees her, and sets the trap again.

She keeps yanking her foot back as if to snap it off. She shimmies as pain traipses through her right leg like the slow constant slicing of a knife.

He smiles. "Now the other foot."

She makes the chair bounce.

He soothes her scalp with his hands.

"I know," he says. She wants to trust in his sympathy. She has no other hope to clutch on to. "This gets harder. It'll be more difficult before I make you better. But I'll make you better, Libby. Just never fail me. Learn your lesson. Don't hesitate. Let your toes wiggle-waggle, see if you can reach the cheese."

The toes of her left foot creep forward even as she cranes her face and neck away. She can't look. The trap snaps and she screams to the rooftop.

"Oh Christ!" Joris Pul shouts out, in an ecstasy of his own. "You nearly sliced a toe right off! Good girl, Libby! You're doing great."

Toes are bloody.

He resets the trap and this time puts it back on the tabletop. Libby, her eyesight blurred by tears, gazes at it.

"Now," he says, "I'm bringing the table closer, okay? Okay."

He draws it closer then adjusts her chair. Her belly moans.

"This time," he encourages her, "the cheese. Fetch it. Use your fingers."

Her upper arms are bound, but she can move her forearms slightly. A moment occurs when she is somehow outside herself if not actually outside her body, where she can observe her own fingers as they move on their own volition, as though she has disowned them and does not respond to them anymore, nor do they to her. She can regret this trespass on her life and the incidents and choices that conspired to bring her to this juncture, a moment when she can believe that she can endure whatever he asks of her. She can survive, if not intact, then as separate from the pain, as though the pain that transfixes her body will evaporate and she will, in her own way, triumph. Then the trap snaps viciously on three fingers and Libby screams to awaken beasts from their snares and her hand flaps frantically with the trap attached to her and she knows a terror apart from the snake of pain up and down her arm, and the man, this beast from his lair, pins her hand down upon the table so that he can remove the trap in his capricious manner as he cackles and still the pain is so slithering and wretched even as her fingers are freed.

"Christ that hurts!" he exclaims.

She moans.

Libby recovers in her chair, but is delivered to another oppression, the disobedience of her body, and her ineffable servitude to the drug.

He turns the chair around and her other hand must creep forward now, stretch, await then undergo a similar slaughter. Believing, praying, this to be the last act of her passion, she is the more willing supplicant this time, to get it over with. She keeps her eyes open this time and tries to trick the mousetrap. She succeeds. When it snaps it clips only an edge of her little finger.

But that hurts. She screams again, and the man is well pleased.

He reworks the trap yet again.

Why has he reloaded the trap?

Her nerves are snapping in her brain against her.

He bends her head low to the table. He removes the gag.

He knots it into her hair again.

He whispers. "I don't want you to be the cheese, Libby. I don't want you to be the mouse. I don't even want you to be the cat. No. You, Libby, will be the one who springs the trap. When the time comes, spring the trap." He pokes it with a pencil and the trap clamps shut, splintering the wood. She flinches in fright. "Say you will do that. That you will become the one who springs the trap." He applies it again and pokes it with the remnant of his pencil again and the trap snaps into another paroxysm, which makes Libby jump once more.

"Yes," she agrees. She will spring the trap? *Where's my H?* "I'll spring the trap."

"You will," he says. "Easy, see?" He shows her once more, although she has no need for the demonstration.

"Yes," she says. She doesn't know why.

He resets the trap yet again.

He says, "Now, try to get the cheese out, Libby. Just once more."

But turned this way?

"You don't know how? Think. Let me see. Ah, how about this? Use your tongue. That's the way. This is the last time, see? Use your tongue, Libby."

The whole of her being rebels but he was expecting that, holds her head to the table, forces her chin down on the table and pushes her head forward slightly then nudges the mousetrap, on its side, closer and closer.

Quietly, he instructs her. "Stick out your tongue now. Do it now, Libby."

She doesn't know why she has to do this, but she does this, she pokes her tongue out and seeks the cheese and the trap springs on her and no agony can know this, no ache comprehend this remorse, no humiliation cross this border as violently she slams her head around under his hands and still the trap sticks to her tongue and she must cooperate now with the man, beseech his assistance, hold still with her mouth open wide while he pulls the lever back. And she collapses and, in her chair, topples to the floor.

The man places the trap back on the table and does not bother to reset it. He crouches over her. He places a hand on her shoulder.

"That was rough. I know. Life is shit sometimes. But now we both know, don't we? You will spring the trap when the trap must be sprung. You will not let me down. Relax now, Libby. You're only bleeding. The bad stuff's over. Now we open our presents. Like it's Christmas."

He pulls the chair and Libby upright again.

He lights the burner.

He tears open the little package and removes the plug of *H*.

Her pupils dilate, her mouth gaping. Her tongue lolls in pain and in anticipation. The *H* is heated. She waits. She exhorts the plug to liquefy. The drug never disappoints her. It liquefies. The man pulls up a vein by compressing a band on her arm. As the needle touches her, she believes him. The misery is behind her now, and she will spring whatever trap needs to be sprung. She will not be the cheese. She will not be the cat. Never again will she be the mouse.

Never again will she be the girl who inserts her tongue into a mouse-trap.

He releases the band and the drug swims up into her veins and she falls, falls, she's falling, under a blessed cloud, a clouded blessing.

II

SEVENTEEN

Émile Cinq-Mars acquired his Escalade as honourably as the next man's used Corolla. Helping an innocent woman slip a murder rap earned him the keys, and she even ponied up for the fees and taxes. On the morning after Muriel J. Cuthbert's murder, a Thursday, Émile assumes he'll be behind the wheel of his big red palace-on-wheels. Sandra puts the kibosh on his expectations.

"I've got four people to see," she reminds him. "Then our agent wants to give me an overview."

"What overview? You were born and raised here."

"Of what's for sale, Émile. Prices. Value on the dollar. New communities have popped up I know nothing about."

"I won't live in some pop-up new *community*." His emphasis on the word makes a slum sound inviting.

Sandra's shoulders fall with exasperation. "Then she should know that. Not to mention me. She can educate me on what's available and for how much, and I can educate her on what we're looking for."

"San, why doesn't *she* drive *you* around? Which leaves me the Escalade, no?"

She tends to say Cadillac. He says Escalade. *Cadillac* rattles his teeth, as if he really can't get his head around being in possession of the marque. Had he been buying with that kind of money up his sleeve, he'd probably have chosen his old favourite, a basic Jeep, then pocketed the change. Not only does the upscale chic of the Caddy confound him – its opulence, prestige, the size of the thing, the gas bill – nothing about the car conforms to his personal style. For years he drove a VW Bug. Yet he's admitted that, environmental matters aside, the gas bill is immaterial weighed against the cost of purchase. Free pays for a whole lot of premium.

He's lectured himself: Graft takes hold that way. One moment you're content with your lot in life, the next you're noticing the high price of octane.

In his mind, the morning argument's been won. Sandra will requisition her mom's old jalopy for her errands, then embark in the real estate agent's Acura SUV for their scouting trip. Makes sense.

But he's wrong.

"Émile – think – if I go in Patricia's car, she'll own me for the afternoon. I'll never break free. In my car, I can ask: Where do I drop you off? Drive her there and we're done."

Good point. "Yes, but in her car, just say you're ready to go home."

"Like she'd listen. There's always one more neighbourhood, or street, or house, or *development* for me to see. Anyway, be fair. I've been driving the clunker for days. The right and left hemispheres of my brain have realigned. Your turn, bud. Get used to the idea."

Which cinches the deal.

Losing an argument early in the morning puts him off his feed. This does not augur well for being back on the job. Émile steers the clunker in behind the Escalade and follows Sandra out, only to promptly slow down on the potholed drive so as not to chip a tooth. By the time he gains the highway, she's gone, out of sight, vanished.

The old rattletrap Ford lurches along. Sandra's mom had used it to go up the driveway to retrieve the mail, then drive back to the house, probably not exceeding five miles an hour, maybe 10 in the straightest section. It's not left the property in a decade. She'd have a farmhand change the oil in the barn but otherwise accept any broken part as a providence not worth combating. She kept it licensed, but as the car was never spotted in the open, the vehicle's street legality has not been challenged. Driving it, a high whine mystifies Cinq-Mars, as if he's in the cockpit of a relic airplane. A low scrapping rumble is onerous. He's tempted to check that he's not dragging a bumper, or the transmission.

Miraculously, out on the asphalt, the manual window rolled down – no air-conditioning – an elbow resting on the sill, tugging at the wheel to bully the beast through curves, Émile feels young again. Never mind that the Ford was an old lady's car and seems imbued with her scent, a mix of perfumes and ointments. Never mind that going from zero to 60 is too slow for a stopwatch to calculate, that he's better off with a sundial. Never mind catching the seat with his left hand to prevent himself catapulting into the steering wheel while braking, and never mind that the horn sounds more like a suppressed burp. He feels like a teenager in his first roadster, back when the word still existed. "Woohoo!" he calls into the wind and tries sticking his head out the window. One happy mutt.

Should he try his luck at picking up chicks?

Not that he managed to do so when he was the appropriate age.

The thought of it, the embarrassment of it all, the fun he might have trying to induce, say, a grandmother into the shotgun seat, gives him a laugh.

Dutifully, Émile heads for Muriel Cuthbert's abode to see what he might glean a day after her demise.

No chicks to pick up, he's thinking, no grandmas, either, not that he ever would. *This* is what old detectives do. Both youthful beauties and the well-preserved ignore him. Only the dead welcome his arrival now.

He won't be entering Muriel's house. Ploughing the same ground is often useful, although it loses allure when he finds the doors locked. He elects to canvas the neighbourhood. If anyone saw anything the day before, odds are the police talked to them, yet he's after what the troopers were unlikely to ask. He wants to solicit impressions, catch a glimpse into how

Muriel Cuthbert spent her declining years. Forage through whatever her neighbours noticed recently that they might term *different*.

Having parked in Muriel's drive, he sets out on foot.

Penelope Gagnon – who's overly excited to share tales of her French-Canadian heritage after Cinq-Mars introduces himself – tells him more than he wants to hear. He tunes out her incessant barking. She tells him that Penelope's best friend Muriel was outgoing and friendly. She loved to fish, appreciated her solitude without being isolated, although the poor dear lived with pain.

"She loved to fish?" He knew that already, but seeks to slow her down a tad, see if he might sneak in a word of his own.

"Fish! Even in her pain."

"Tell me about her pain."

"Muriel won't tell you. She don't complain. To me, she mentioned it now and then. You just knew – I knew – in another person's mouth her words would sound like a … like a lamentation. How's that? A big word. I know some really big words. I practice them. Anyway, it's something in the Bible that's a lot like tooth decay. An old grocery list of complaints like the kind you get in the Good Book or down at the beauty parlour, all woe is me and my children are holy terrors. Future terrorists, maybe. With Muriel, no, everything was straight out, then she was done. You don't hear another peep. She'd go fish instead."

"How did she describe her pain?" Cinq-Mars wants to know.

"*My damn hip hurts*. That was it. But you knew, I knew anyway, that it was a bigger complaint than that. A lamentation." She lingered over the syllables, as if savouring the taste of candy.

"So she liked to fish?"

Penelope Gagnon's pink hair is up in curlers. A daisy pokes from one, which causes her not a smidge of embarrassment. A bright brown mole highlights each cheek, one a fraction higher and a touch closer to the nose than the other. The lenses on her glasses are tinted a light grey, which casts her eyes in an unnecessary gloominess.

"Every morning she walks past my house – *walks*! she *stumbles* past my house! I couldn't look outside, afraid to see her fall and bust her nose. She takes that path, that one, between the tall pines, hard to see. She goes down to the riverside. My property but, lordy me, I never begrudged her trespassing as long as she don't go break her neck then go sue me."

Cinq-Mars suspects that she did begrudge the trespass. Her inflection makes it sound akin to theft.

Penelope carries on. "Once I joined her down there. She's the friendly type and we were pals, but on that day I got a feeling Muriel was too polite for her own good. She's too gentle a soul to tell me go take a hike. I never disturbed her down there again. Some people need private time. I don't know why. That's all I get, private time. I don't need it myself."

"I want to thank you." What he really wanted was to leave.

"For what?" Penelope inquires. "What you asking me for anyway? Nobody asks me nothing. You're that famous detective. Your name was on TV and I said to myself it's French, like my name. I got descended from those French loggers from Canada, did I say? They worked in the mills later. After that if they didn't die in our great wars like so many of 'em did, they dispersed. Became English-speakers like everybody else. I don't know a word of French myself. Well, maybe two. *Oui* and *bonjour*. How's that?"

"Very good."

"Do you speak French yourself much?" Penelope Gagnon asks him.

"I do. Yes."

"Do you know a lot of words?"

"Quite a few. Why?"

He's been trying to extricate himself from the conversation for a few minutes but is now too dumbfounded to make a move.

"Why?" he repeats.

"Is there a reason for that?"

"A reason? Why I speak French?" Cinq-Mars can't hide his incredulity.

"Yeah. Why?"

"French is my mother tongue. My language."

"You're not dispersed?"

"Not yet. I guess I'm considering it." She's not using the right word, but he knows what she means, and there is that to bear. Can he live where he never speaks his own language? Where his own voice becomes a foreign tongue? "Thanks," he repeats, recovering. He suffers a desire to educate her. He would if the prospect didn't feel like climbing Everest. He lets it go.

Escape does not come easily. Penelope has more to say, and he listens, respectfully, as Penelope's talk becomes a wake for Muriel. His attention fades for a minute or two before his ears perk up. He's not positive, but he thinks she told him that Muriel looked peaceful.

"How do you know that?" he almost whispers, not wanting to frighten her.

Penelope may have detected the ramifications of her remark. Not all her gears meshed, but she is not without awareness. "The officer, yesterday, told me. She looked peaceful, right? Didn't you see her yourself?"

"Did you?"

"Did I what?"

"Did you see Muriel yourself, Ms. Gagnon?"

"Who? When? Where?"

"You know who. Muriel. You know when. Were you over there? After she died?"

"Why would I be, over there, after she died? I thought about it, to say a goodbye, but with all them policemen ransacking things, who'd go there?"

"They didn't ransack."

"No? No. I wasn't over there. Of course not."

He doesn't believe her, but sometimes he prefers a witness to think he does.

"Thanks. I'm sorry to trespass on your property, but I need to visit the spot where she fished."

"Why?"

"She spent time there."

"But why are *you* going to spend time there?"

Her question, he feels, derives from a budding defensiveness. He defeats her with honesty. "I'd like to get a sense of her life. To know who I'm dealing with."

"She was very old. She just died. Why is everybody, the police, walking around like chickens next to a deep fryer? Was she robbed?"

"Why do you say that?"

"The police were over there for hours. Just because somebody died? Death happens. One minute you're sitting up, the next, you bought the farm. On good terms, you hope. Was she robbed?"

"Do you think she was robbed?"

"Why would I think that? *I* didn't take anything!"

"Of course not," Cinq-Mars soothes her, although he's confirmed to himself that she knows more than she's willing to say. "Funny how she was sitting up, hey?"

"Yeah," Penelope agrees, and he knows he has her, that no policeman gave her that detail. If one did, he needs to be reprimanded. Cinq-Mars decides to come back for a second crack at her later on; first, he'll let her stew, and take the walk down to the riverbank.

He follows Muriel Cuthbert's morning path, a longer one than he expects, the way it winds, beneath the shade of trees and the ambience of birdsong, where he discovers her boots.

Having a secret path, he supposes, that no one else traversed, gave her license to leave her stuff behind rather than lug it back and forth each day. The boots reached the tops of her thighs for wading in cold water. They'd be difficult for the hobbled older woman to carry. Hidden, farther along, under a cluster of bushes, he finds a tackle box, containing a collection of lures and flies. Under a foldaway shelf inside the box, he locates her gear. Her real gear. Needles. A stretchy armband to tie off and bring her veins up. A spoon. Matches. A small camper's single element, alcohol for fuel. She came down here to fish. She also came down here to shoot up. No actual heroin, but then he remembers the boots, goes back to them and shakes them out. Two sachets tumble from the toe of one foot. She can now be arrested for drug possession and put away in prison for her final years.

Except that her final years are at an end.

While Émile was dozing through their talk, Penelope-the-neighbour revealed that Muriel not only fished but did so successfully, frequently bringing her a trout and sharing her catch with other neighbours. She kept fish for herself but also returned many to the river. So. She did more than shoot up here. Her private place. Where she could pursue her passion for a rod-and-reel and a hook on a line and a fish on the hook, and where she could be relieved of her pain, and in time relieved of her need for a fix by injecting herself under the cathedral-like sanctity of the forest. Émile is overwhelmed, briefly, by an honest sense of her, similar to what he experienced in her bedroom the day before, but today's reaction is nuanced. He gains an appreciation – that's what it feels like – of her gaunt loneliness. For the desperation of her affliction. For the hardship this caused her, this private blot on her public image, this warped secret imbedded in her being. She must have been saddened each day that she got high and known regret when she crossed a dealer's palm for her next hit. Nothing exciting or subversive about it, he believes. The thought takes a cue from the peacefulness of her speck of shoreline. She had a space to walk out into the water, a rocky bottom to negotiate to take herself away from the water's edge to cast her line without the impediment of overhead boughs. Here, fishing, the constant rush of water surging by, she was herself, delivered from pain for a time, while also imprisoned by the cure.

A short distance down, a small wedge of sand and pebbles amid the rocks and vegetation creates a clearing on the embankment. Cinq-Mars goes there, bending low to examine the patch more closely. The marks a few feet up from the water conform to the striations a canoe makes hauled onto a sandy landing.

Footprints surround these marks. Interesting.

He never knew her, yet everything he has sensed about her yesterday and what he's gleaned from a neighbour today, plus the assumptions that have cropped up while standing in her private sanctuary by the riverside, help him surmise that she was not a woman who desired death. He cannot declare this with certainty, yet intuition suggests to him that, being of an age, she was prepared for death, yet there's nothing to suggest that she was anxious to hasten the day.

He finds himself taking her side. He might even take up fishing when the job is done, perhaps to commemorate her. The hobby appeals, along the serenity of this shore. Whoever did her in – and she was murdered, that is no longer strong conjecture in his mind, he is now utterly convinced – that person is not going to get away with it, not on his watch.

He takes a moment to weigh this sudden notion – *his watch*. Retired? Collecting his pension, but for the time being no longer retired. Not with this fine lady in need of justice. Not in a pig's eye.

His affection for her, at least for his impression of her, takes root. He wants her killer caught. A desire that feels vaguely and curiously personal.

On the return walk, away from the riverbank and close enough to Penelope Gagnon's house that he can see her searching for him through a side window, Émile Cinq-Mars stops. He wonders if he's in his right mind. Time has passed since he last strolled through a woods. He's forgotten how shapes and shadows and the play of light can trick the mind into seeing what's not there. Still, he's an investigator by profession and habit. He takes two steps back. Looks again.

What he thought he saw appears different now; yet intriguing still. Initially, he spotted two parallel lines in the dirt, the kind that can be made by the heels of a person being dragged. Now they look like twin gullies carved out by heavy rain. Looking through the leaves he spots the colour white. An oddity in a forest. Could be rock. Could be wind-blown garbage. He tramps in off the trail. He doesn't go far, another eight to 10 feet. Stands there, mesmerized by the shock of it all, then slips his phone out of his pocket and buzzes Hammond. He has to cut off the man who answers in an ebullient mood.

"Trooper Hammond, sorry. Listen. Across the street from Muriel Cuthbert's place, on the property of a woman whose name is Penelope Gagnon—"

"Yeah, we talked to her. What did you find?"

"Another body. This one's not sitting up. A male, forties, with a knife sticking out of his chest. Lots of blood if you like that sort of thing."

The silence on the other end of the line is understandable. Cinq-Mars is feeling somewhat hollowed out himself. Hammond breaks in. "You've got to be fucking kidding me. But you don't kid, right?"

"When you're talking to the woman, there's something you should know."

"I've known her for decades. She's a ditz."

"I believe she was in the house across the street yesterday. She saw Muriel dead before you did. She's not admitting it. I take it she's kept that from you, despite your long-time acquaintance?"

"Christ, Émile," Hammond says, almost as though he's blaming him for this complication in his working life. "I'll be there soon. I'll bring the band. Hell, I'll probably bring the whole goddamned orchestra."

Leaving the dead man, heading toward the highway to await the state trooper, Émile spots the turn signal on a Honda Fit flashing. The man behind the wheel turns off and enters Penelope Gagnon's driveway at the same moment that a young bicyclist spins in behind the car as well. Cinq-Mars is 50 feet farther along when he reacts to the sound of another vehicle that's also slowing down. Obviously, a meeting of some sort was called, on which he's intruding. He has the nagging impression that his visit may have precipitated the sudden gathering, although he can't fathom why. More likely it was called previously. Either way, the woman with a dead neighbour and now a dead man on her property has friends who have chosen to congregate. As though they're swarming.

EIGHTEEN

As troopers lead her outside, Penelope Gagnon resides in a fog of bewilderment. The humiliation of being handcuffed thwarts her balance.

Neighbours and strangers rim the highway and a girl on a bicycle snags Émile's attention. She had shown up with others for a get-together that the police interrupted. Crutches that snap onto her forearms rest in a homemade apparatus behind her bike seat and whenever she stays too long in one spot, balancing on her toes, she brings the crutches forward to lean on. She's unable to walk properly, but he's impressed that she can ride.

He's cognizant that her attention repeatedly lands on him. She's intent on neither the troopers nor on Penelope. The person who summons the whole of her interest is Émile Cinq-Mars himself, standing on a rock, not doing much of anything.

A puzzle, that impression. What is she noticing? Is it his immobility that strikes her as odd? Or is it that he was across the street yesterday and on hand again today as she arrived, and that's made her curious? The girl is keen on the one man inside the police perimeter bothering to look outside. The sad spectacle of the woman she came to visit, either under arrest now or being taken in for questioning, intrigues her less than the man standing upon a knoll, doing nothing. Cinq-Mars feels the same way: He's primarily interested in her.

On her porch, Penelope suddenly twists away from her handlers and the troopers more forcibly seize hold. Cinq-Mars flinches, then crosses his arms in disapproval while holding himself back. These are not his cops.

Refusing to budge now and tilting to one side, the woman stands in a pair of floppy jeans and a faded green sweatshirt. Given her weight, she's difficult to move. One cop gently knees her thigh to get her moving again – people along the highway think to boo – and Cinq-Mars can no longer help himself.

He goes over at a clip and intercepts Penelope as she clears the bottom step.

"Penelope," he says, hoping familiarity will help.

"Oh my gracious." Tears plug her eyes.

Two officers, one male, one female, each clutch an arm. Cinq-Mars spots Trooper Hammond charging their way.

"A formality. The police need to talk to you. The security measures are difficult, but necessary. This is how they do things."

"I didn't do nothing myself!"

She has a way of disclaiming that opens her up to further questions. "Do you know who did?"

"I know nothing at all myself! I didn't see no dead man on my property! Only you did! Nobody told me. Why is a dead man on my property?"

"Don't worry if you don't know the answers to questions like that, Penelope. The police will ask, and you need to answer as best you can. If you know nothing, say so. If you can help them in any way, do that, too. All right?"

"Take these off me, please," she implores him, holding up her wrists.

"Tuck them under your sweatshirt. Then no one can see."

She complies, and he can tell that that helps, although her public shaming has already been comprehensive.

Hammond arrives at his elbow. "Problem?"

First, Émile comforts Penelope Gagnon as she's led away. "Take care now." Then asks the trooper. "Where do you take her?"

"Troop F. Twin Mountain."

Cinq-Mars has driven on that road. So far out of town she'll think she's being transported to the other side of the moon. "Mind if I observe?"

Hammond weighs the notion. "You can't exactly observe."

He thinks he knows why not.

"This isn't New York City," Hammond explains. "We're not on TV."

"No one-way glass."

"In Concord. Not here."

"Then, can I be let into the room?"

Speaking privately like this, out of earshot of other troopers, Hammond is amenable. "Sure. I'll head out in a half hour or so, depending."

"Thanks. I'll be here."

"Yeah, you better stick around." Over his shoulder, as he slips away, he adds, "I have to talk to you, too."

"About what?"

Hammond turns and speaks while walking backwards. "You found the body, Émile. Makes you a witness. You might be a suspect. My one and only."

Good. At least now, in a roundabout way, he has official status.

Émile returns to the knoll he occupied previously, only this time he goes higher than before and discovers that he remains under the girl's scrutiny. He gives her a concentrated return gaze, and she reacts, tucking her crutches away and taking a tour on her bike. When she parks again, she's still in his line of sight. As is he in hers.

He observes the general commotion. Marcus Easton's forensics crew has returned to action today, although their efforts are small-town modest. He can't fault them for a lack of technical equipment. They're restricted to dusting the forest for fingerprints and footprints and collecting blood and tissue samples. Not much else. Left behind in the chest of the victim, the weapon may help identify the killer, although given that it was abandoned at the scene, Cinq-Mars doubts it will. The killer didn't think so, either, as he left it *in situ*. Blood might reveal the identity of the victim through DNA analysis, should it be on file, as this corpse has landed without ID. They'll wait on that.

When Penelope Gagnon was asked to have a look, she had a conniption fit. "I'm not looking at no dead man, all bloody! Not me! I'll faint!"

Marcus Easton breaks from his crew and comes over, peeling off his gloves.

"Not much to go on," he asserts. "Or did you solve this already?"

Still with the attitude.

Cinq-Mars suddenly blurts out at a member of Easton's crew passing behind their boss, "Hey! Watch how you carry those!"

The abrupt force of his edict spins Easton around, and stops the technician-in-training carrying Muriel's fishing boots up from the shore.

The shout also alerts Hammond.

"What about it?" the young tech answers, feebly.

"Did you empty the contents yet?"

Coming up behind the technician, Hammond asks, "What contents?"

"There's heroin," Cinq-Mars remarks, "in one of the boots. If he hasn't lost it by now."

The technician almost puts the boots on the ground to examine them, but Hammond smartly prevents that. Together they hold each boot up, and out of one, into Hammond's palms, twin sachets tumble forth containing the pair of heroin rocks.

Hammond gives him a look. "What else do you know?" he queries.

"I had a look around *before* I found the body. I haven't touched anything since."

"Three cheers. And you found the body how, Émile? It wasn't exactly exposed back there."

"Followed the trail made by the dead guy's heels when he was dragged into the woods. The same trail your troopers have stomped over and obliterated."

"Right," Hammond says, not at all perturbed. "That trail. Do you mind answering my question?"

Cinq-Mars admires a man who knows how to stay on topic, who even knows what it is. Hammond wants to know what he knows.

"I had a suspicion. Call it intuition. Could be that there was blood along with the heel marks and I was taking that in subconsciously, you know?"

"Whatever you say."

"If you haven't found it already, there's a tackle box down there, too."

"We found it. She fished, Muriel did. Is it hers? The boots, too?"

"I'd say so. Inside the box you'll find her gear."

Trooper Hammond's look drills through him.

"The needle packs are sealed. The one that did her in yesterday won't be there. On the other hand, I didn't do a thorough inventory."

"You left that to me. Thanks. I can earn my pay now. Anything else?"

"Penelope's innocent."

"Is she? Good to know. I'll take that under advisement."

"I don't know how much she knows. More than she's willing to say. But she's innocent of all this."

"You know that how?" Easton intrudes. Hammond gives the ME a look, as though he should not have posed the question, that he has no right interrupt in this company. Yet Hammond looks back at Cinq-Mars to provide the answer.

"I talked to her. She's not capable of killing either person."

"You're the one with the heavy background," Easton kicks in, refusing to be muzzled. "Nobody can say who is or isn't capable of murder."

"Anyone might be capable of murder," Cinq-Mars concurs. "At least on the surface. But Penelope is not capable of *meticulously* murdering Muriel, too perfect a crime. Nor is she capable of murdering a man by stabbing him in the chest then speaking to someone she takes to be an officer of the law – that would be me – a short time later without exhibiting a single note of tension, or panic, or fear." He glances at Easton as though to acknowledge that he is usurping his job, having decided on a time of death without the ME's input. "*That's* what she's not capable of, which you'll find out, Captain, when we interview. Speaking of my background, if it means anything to you, out of my experience I'm advising patience and to be gentle with her."

"My wife says that to me all the time. Sometimes I listen. But not usually." Hammond rocks his head from side to side, and determines, "You'll be in the room, Émile. *You* will be in the room." Then he looks at Marcus Easton, and although he doesn't need to say it, for what Medical Examiner would ever find his or her way into an interrogation room outside of some cockamamie TV show, he tells him anyway, "*You* won't be." He's clearly upset with him and perhaps for more reasons than Cinq-Mars is aware.

Left alone, waiting for Hammond to depart to follow him out, Cinq-Mars ambles up to the road, in part to see if any neighbour has something to report, but really he wants to meet the bike-girl. That turns out not to be possible: She retreats, riding away. He's sorry about that, although a girl who walks with crutches won't be difficult to locate later. When they first arrived, the troopers probably jotted down her particulars. He'll check her out as a person of interest.

NINETEEN

The schoolteacher Cara Drost is routinely transported to the Upper Valley Health Club in a specialized bus for the infirm, where she remains seated in her wheelchair with her two shattered ankles to be raised on a hydraulic ramp into the van then lowered again at the club's entrance. The first time she made the trip she felt miserable to be so dependent on others, a reaction that yielded to gratitude for her improved mobility.

She's made new friends onboard the van. The drive to the club in Lebanon, New Hampshire, becomes a boisterous affair as her pals catch up on recent news following their stints of isolation. "Heading to the courthouse!" someone once coined their trips, in deference to feeling extracted from prison cells – their homes – and carted off. The designation stuck. The Upper Valley Health Club is known among them as "the courthouse"; their homes as Cellblock One, or Two, and so on, as they're dropped off late in the afternoon.

Upon arrival, the women disperse to designated exercises, massages, routines and treatments. A few get down to brass tacks – learning to walk again or trying to budge a frozen shoulder. Others simply hang out, although these few don't gloat in front of the others. Cara Drost among them. In keeping with their prison-break mentality, they've given each other nicknames, such as Killer, Mugger, and Knuckles. Cara was originally Car Thief, gleaned from her first name. The tag never inspired her. She clearly brightened when someone dubbed her Crooked Cara, then just Crooked, and she loves it.

She spends time in the therapy pool, enjoying those minutes. Immersed in pulsing water and bubbles the women tell tales, or lament the state of the Union, or share Hollywood gossip. Never stated in so many words, a prohibition has been passed along from those with long-term infirmities to the newbies, that one's own misery never bears discussion. No matter the travesty of one's condition, someone nearby probably suffers more. Suck it up, friend. Whatever you do, don't bitch. Not in the courthouse.

Up to her neck in the therapy pool, feeling semi-comatose, listening to the latest gab, Crooked Cara can believe, briefly, that she is not suffering at all.

Then she's wheeled away to the change room. She takes her time to towel off and dress herself, something she can do on her own, *thank God*, sitting in her chair. Not everyone in her jailbreak crew is that fortunate.

After the pool she plays a few rounds of gin rummy until a darker spirit inhabits her veins, then Crooked mutters her apologies and decamps. Her excuse is always the same, that she's got her bloody infernal stretches to do. She acts as though she's headed for a torture session on a rack as she wheels off down the hall. An elevator lifts her up two flights where she disembarks and rolls her chariot left. Down a long empty corridor, then a right turn, and two doors farther along she's outside a broom closet.

She hears no one. This is not an enclosure frequented during daylight hours. No one will come by for a mop. Only the night cleaner's equipment is housed inside.

Or so people think. Her own gear is sequestered there as well.

A secret spot, a safe haven, to shoot up.

Always a relief and a joy to find a fresh supply of *H* waiting for her inside.

TWENTY

In the village of Twin Mountain, the principal interrogation room for Troop F is in use. Cinq-Mars sees why, catching a glance as a door closes. Plastic plates and cake crumbs litter a table's surface. Dregs of red wine visible in plastic glasses and a bottle lies on its side, as though for spinning. Someone's birthday, retirement or stag party, or a baby has been born.

The drive up was torturous in his mother-in-law's recalcitrant Ford. The car's shocks earned their nomenclature. The lip to every bridge caused his head to smack the ceiling. With each dip the car rebelled – set to fly off the road or careen into pieces – electing to shudder and shake through a series of kangaroo bounds. At intervals, the lazy progress of the Ammonoosuc River alongside the highway soothed his spirits, but inevitably he'd cross a pavement crack and feel the rattle chase up his spine to vibrate through his eardrums, while the steering wheel's jackhammer action commanded the whole of his focus and strength.

He's glad his wife isn't driving this thing.

He doesn't know how she's managed. He's made up his mind that the car is soon bound for the junkyard.

Émile arrived later than the others to find Penelope in a holding cell. Before he could object, he was informed that the door was open to keep her from going bonkers. That's when he noticed the party room. He was then called into the substitute interrogation space outside the cells. Empty of criminals but intimidating. Jumpy, beleaguered, cuffed, Penelope is guided in to join him, along with Trooper Hammond and a guard who positions himself at the door.

"I need a lawyer. I got a right. Where's my lawyer at?"

"You're not in custody, Ms. Gagnon." Hammond speaks softly. "We only want to talk. A woman was murdered across the street from your house yesterday. A man was found dead on your property this morning. When you think about it, you're here for your own protection."

A scam. Cinq-Mars might have deployed a similar ruse if he remained on active duty. Her request for a lawyer has not actually been denied, while her attention has been diverted.

A request for water is one they're willing to accommodate.

"Of course, Ms. Gagnon," Hammond states, and smiles, turning up the charm. "How rude of me not to offer. Would you prefer coffee, or a soft drink?"

"A Coke, sure, if you got. Not Diet."

"We got. No problem. You're helping us out here, so bang on, we'll set you up with a Coke. Thanks for coming in." He makes it sound as if this was her idea. The guard at the door trots off for the soda and Hammond pushes himself up from the table. "Let's get those darn cuffs off."

The woman vigorously nods. "I don't get it," she whispers. "Can you explain to me?"

"A mere formality. Just a few questions, ma'am," Hammond says gently as he hooks the cuffs onto his belt. "Let's begin with your name and address."

"What did you mean when you said that? Muriel, murdered? Was she?"

"Name and address, please." A slight testiness colours his tone. Cinq-Mars is hopeful but not certain Hammond has the patience for Penelope.

"You know where I live. You know who I am!"

"A formality, ma'am. For the record."

Penelope says instead, "She was sitting there. Quiet like. Nobody stabbed her or nothing stupid like that."

"Who?" Hammond presses.

"How do you know that, Pen?" Cinq-Mars puts in, although he's supposed to mind his peace.

Hammond slumps back in his chair, irritated now. "I need to ask your name and address, ma'am."

Penelope's eyes shift between the two of them. She's not so upset that she hasn't detected her gaffe, even though the remark passed Hammond by. Her glance trips over the trooper, then she stares down at his Smokey Bear hat on the table, then fearfully at Cinq-Mars.

"That copper yesterday said so."

"No, he didn't," Cinq-Mars objects. This is the second time he's caught her in that fib, and this time around won't let it fly by. He can't imagine that a trooper blabbed key details to her, and if one did, Hammond needs to hear it.

The captain is alert, finally. "Ma'am?" he asks.

"I didn't kill nobody. I don't know why that man's dead on my property. How could I report him if my own eyes never saw him lying dead like that?"

Hammond won't be distracted again. "Were you in Muriel's house yesterday? What did you see?" She hasn't really been a suspect in his mind, but now he's not so sure. "Ma'am?"

Silence is difficult for her. Runs against the grain.

"Penelope," Cinq-Mars probes, gently, "you'd report the man if you saw him on your property, lying down, not moving, wouldn't you?"

"All bloody, they said. I'd report that right away."

"Why didn't you report Muriel right away?"

She is about to answer before having another thought. "Report what?"

"That you saw her. Why didn't you report that you saw her?"

A quick spurt of tears overcomes her a moment. Although this is not an act, she quickly recovers, rubbing at her leaky nose.

Hammond, Cinq-Mars can tell, is up to speed. The trooper can take point; he no longer has to. They pause when the duty officer returns with the can of Coke and a file folder. A single sheet lies inside the folder; Hammond studies it, then closes the folder. He taps it twice with his ring finger, creating a knocking sound with his wedding band that draws Penelope upright.

"I was going to call," Penelope asserts.

"But you didn't," Hammond drives home.

"No need."

"A woman is dead in her home. You think to call the police, but you don't. Why was there no need?"

"You showed up."

"Pardon me?"

"Not you personally. Maybe you did right away, maybe you didn't, but the police starting showing up. So I stopped calling you. I had the phone in my hand. I put it down. There was no need."

Hammond opens the folder again, raising it up for a closer view. Perhaps by accident or by design, Cinq-Mars cannot view the page. The file goes down to the table again and Penelope follows it with her eyes.

The trooper taps his ring against it once more.

"Ms. Gagnon, you made a call around that time. You didn't call the police. Who did you call?"

"No one."

"That's not true. I have the information right here." He raps the folder again for effect. "I know who you called and when. We have your phone records. Best that you answer with the truth, otherwise we won't believe anything you say. Who did you call?"

Defeated, she sighs. "My friend Bitz. Bitzy. She's a friend of mine."

"Why did you call her?"

"I told you."

"No, you didn't."

"She's a friend of mine. That's why I called her. She's a friend of Muriel's, too. I called her, to tell her Muriel was dead. I didn't think she was murdered. Bitz thought she might've been, though."

"How come?"

Penelope is disinclined to answer. "I don't know," she says at last. "She just thought it out loud, I guess."

"You went to Muriel's house yesterday."

"Yeah. I guess so."

"Was she alive or dead?"

"Dead. I found her that way, yeah."

"Did you kill her?"

"Don't be so stupid," she states calmly, almost blithely, a sincerity to her tone that's impressive. "Wasn't she already dead anyway? I don't kill people. Not me. Even if I did kill people, and I *don't*, I certainly won't go kill my best friend for no reason."

"You went home after that?"

"To call the police, yeah."

"But instead you called Bitz."

"Yeah."

"Did you go down to the river?"

"What river?"

"What do you mean, what river? The river that flows by your house. The river on the edge of your property. Did you go down to the river?"

"Why?"

"Never mind why. Did you go down there or not? Just answer the question."

"Can I open my Coke now?"

Hammond almost laughs. He looks over at Émile. The older man smiles and leans forward. "Penelope, I'll open your Coke. Enjoy it."

The more she drinks, the more she gulps with each swallow. Half the contents are quickly gone. She puts the can down and wipes her mouth.

"Was that good?" Hammond asks her.

"Yeah."

"Did you go down to the river?"

"I don't know why you're asking me that. Why are you?"

"Don't evade the question. Just answer it."

She still wants to know why they're asking. Cinq-Mars repeats the question once more, an alternative inflection. "Did you go down to the river, Penelope?"

"Of course not. Muriel was dead. I was too upset to go on any stupid walk for no reason. Anyway, I almost never go to the river. I don't bother with it."

"Émile?" Hammond says.

"Yeah?"

"Any questions?"

The trooper is willing to let him take over for a bit. It's not that he's stymied, but the gentle strokes Émile can employ might be effective.

Cars zing by as she veers her bike onto the shoulder of the highway. A young guy in a blue pickup honks. Maybe he doesn't notice the crutches hanging off the back end of her bike, is what she thinks, or the contraptions on her knees. It's not a world she inhabits, boys in pickups, showing off how bold they are, honking their silly horns. Forget about it.

She's skinny. Sometimes she thinks that's all they care about.

She carries on past the driveway, swerving a little because her speed is slow, the shoulder rough. When the highway clears, she circles around. Sunlight spanks off the white van in the yard. She knows the driver isn't home. No signs of life. No barking dog. No wife, she's been long gone. No visitors. She swings down onto the property and parks her bike on the far side of the van where it won't be seen from the highway. She straps the crutches to her arms and hobbles toward the workshop.

The keys are in the lock. Right where she left them.

She enters.

Cinq-Mars engages Penelope with a tact that does not come naturally to him. He's determined to deflect her attention away from her early morning shockwaves – a murder on her woodlot, her swift incarceration. He coaxes her into talking about Muriel instead, and after a few false starts the disheveled woman finds her rhythm, forgetting that she's sitting outside the holding cells of Troop F. She returns to her customary chatty self. Cinq-Mars is hoping that one word or unconscious phrase, even a gesture, might tip him off on what she's not inclined to reveal.

That slip arrives in the midst of her babble.

Speaking of her friend, Penelope drops the word "group."

Cinq-Mars leaps. "What group?"

She's goes silent. Significant by itself.

"Penelope?" he encourages her quietly. Even Hammond, who was probably dozing off, is awake and listening now.

"What?" she asks him back, another clue.

"What group?" he asks again.

"What group?"

"What group?"

Rather than answer, she fiddles with her curlers.

She's lost the daisy that was there.

Cinq-Mars weaves his fingers together, an exhibition of patience. "You said, and I quote, 'Muriel and her group used to go to the farmers' market. You used to go along, too, didn't you, Penelope, to the farmers' market?'"

She's able to answer that question more easily than others. "Sometimes."

"In a group. Or you joined up with a group there, right?"

She nods, ever so slightly.

"So what group?"

The one query that snags her.

"Penelope?"

"A few friends, that's all. I didn't mean nothing by that."

"You didn't intend to tell us about it, you mean. Look, a few friends in a group is not a problem. I'd enjoy that. So tell us what group."

"A group of friends, that's all." She's building her firewall.

Cinq-Mars goes around it. "Tell us who else is in the group, Penelope." She's not seeing a way out and Cinq-Mars assists her. "Who were Muriel's friends? Who are yours? That's all we're asking, really. No big deal."

Put that way, she's more willing to speak. "Bitz. She's one. Libby, she's one. Me and Muriel. Kath. Walter. He's one."

"So there's men. Not only young ladies like yourself. Any others?"

"Buster. That's a dog's name, but he chose it himself. Who're you calling a young lady anyhow? Mmm, I think his real name is Dornhoffer or Dornhofferman, something like that, but his real first name is Heinz or Hans or one of those two, but we call him Buster, like he's some kind of yard mutt. He sort of is." She laughs.

"Apart from the yard dog, who else?"

"Libby, she's the youngest. Mrs. Birman's the oldest. That's what she calls herself, like she's too good for us to know her first name."

"Funny, though," Cinq-Mars ponders.

"What is?" She's checking her curlers again.

"You are part of a group of friends, but one friend doesn't use her first name in your company. Odd in a group of friends, don't you think?"

Penelope seems to agree. She doesn't add to the discussion.

"Maybe there's another reason these friends get together. Since they're an unlikely group," Cinq-Mars comments.

"Why do you mean unlikely? We're just friends."

"A motley crew. Old. Young. Men. Women. Going to the market on a regular basis. Strikes me as odd. Does it strike you as odd, Trooper Hammond?"

"Totally. Really unusual," the trooper concurs.

To which she shrugs, as though their point is beyond her ken.

"Are you an addict yourself, Penelope?"

"What?"

"Are you addicted?"

"Why say that to me? What a thing! You mean the drugs? I don't do the drugs. Why would I? Except the ones my doctor says."

"Muriel did."

Penelope looks down.

She takes a moment. She contemplates adjusting her curlers again but decides that that might be the wrong thing to do. Penelope forces herself to keep her hands down at her sides.

"I know," she says. "So?"

"In this group, does everyone take drugs? Did you use to take drugs maybe? Then stop? Would you call it a support group? Is that the reason these friends get together? They're addicts? You're in the group. Are you an addict the way Muriel was? She didn't get her drugs from the pharmacy. Maybe you took drugs like that in the past."

Penelope is adamant that she's not now nor has ever been an addict. Hammond asks to see her forearms and the woman is quite proud to roll up the sleeves of her sweatshirt and show them off. She knows to do that. Knows what he's looking for. "Clean as a whistle!" Penelope pronounces.

The two men concur. Regardless, she's aware of what they're talking about.

"So why are you in the group?" Cinq-Mars presses her.

A burst of pride ignites her response. "Because Muriel was my friend. She invited me. That's why."

"I see. Good. That was good of her. But the others. They were invited in for a different reason. You were special, you were Muriel's friend. The others, they were in the group in a different way, is that right?"

Her nod affirms his insight.

"A support group for addicts," Hammond seeks to confirm. "To help them quit drugs, or to stay clean?"

She shakes her head in the negative.

She doesn't want to say. When she looks up at Cinq-Mars, she's hoping that he will say it aloud himself, and not make her.

"For Muriel's sake," he says. "To help us find out why there's a dead man in your woods, you have to tell us, Penelope."

She seems willing but takes her time. "Like you said, more like a support group, but not to *stop* being addicts, that's not it. Not to quit or to stay quit."

"Then what?"

"More like," Penelope considers, and she does seem to be genuinely figuring this out for the first time herself, "more like a support group to *stay* as addicts. A way to *live* as drug addicts, I guess. A life like that is hard. That's what the mutual help is about. Nobody was trying to quit, see."

Cinq-Mars and Hammond, in sync, take deep breaths. They hazard a glance at each other, for this is a new one for both of them. A support group *to remain* a drug addict.

"What did you do in the group, if you weren't trying to get by as an addict yourself? Maybe they wanted you to join in with them?"

Penelope is adamant. "Wasn't like that, no. They used my house, that's all. They liked it as a place to meet. On the back deck you can't see the river, but you can hear it. They liked that. Inside when it rains, I have enough places to sit. They liked my place."

Hammond's voice emulates Émile's example, calm and low. "Ms. Gagnon, if you don't mind too much, we need you to help us write down the names of everyone in the group."

"I can't be a bad squealer."

"Oh, don't think that way. This isn't about drugs, about who takes them or who doesn't. We don't want anyone else to be harmed. We want to keep your friends alive. You mentioned quite a few already. Go ahead, repeat them so we know for sure. I'm putting Muriel's name at the top of the list. Who's next?"

Just then a trooper's aid, a civilian, passes a sheet of paper to the guard at the door. The guard brings it over and Hammond gives it a quick perusal before sliding it across to Cinq-Mars.

Émile gives it a longer read. The dead man has been identified. Hammond points to a relevant note. He drove a white van. Yesterday, Penelope reported a white van leaving Muriel's property.

Befuddled, Penelope resorts to the Coke. Three long swallows, then she wipes her mouth with a sigh. When she's ready, Émile has a notion.

"Start with the youngest. You called her Libby. Tell us about her."

She tells them that she walks on crutches.

She rides a bicycle.

She hurt herself real bad falling down a mountainside. "End over end. She's got the bad luck, that kid." That's why she does the drugs, Penelope explains. On account of her constant agony, her injuries.

Penelope doesn't have much to say about the others. Cinq-Mars leans forward and lowers his voice to draw her closer.

"Think now. Overnight, or early this morning, did you hear or see anything around your house that you might deem…" He searches for the right word. "…untoward?"

She doesn't have to think it over. "I didn't hear nothing. I don't go to bed early. I don't sleep so well. Oh! Wait. I did hear something. But that was only a dream."

"What did you think you heard?"

"Someone in the house. I got up. Nobody was there."

"Did you turn the lights on?"

"No. There was moonlight."

"Did you walk around the house in the moonlight?"

"I went to the bedroom door. I thought I heard something, but it was real quiet, so I went back to sleep. A dream is all. Must've been."

"Must've been. Thank you, Penelope. Thanks for talking to us."

"No problem. What's next? Do I got to go back in that jail again?"

"You're safe in there," Hammond points out to her. "It'll only be for a little while. Give us a chance to figure out what's going on here, okay?"

"Okay," Penelope agrees, as though being incarcerated as a material witness, or as a suspect, is a notion she's come up with on her own.

"While you're writing down the names of the people in your group you mentioned," Cinq-Mars suggests, "continue writing down any names from the group you forgot to mention. We need to hear about everyone. All right?"

Penelope agrees. "All right."

TWENTY-ONE

"Reece Zamarlo."

"Spell it for me." Émile Cinq-Mars makes the request of Trooper Hammond, then promptly changes his mind. "Never mind. Old habit. I don't need to keep track of those details anymore."

Hammond smiles. "You're flubbing this whole retirement thing, aren't you?"

"Haven't noticed a big change in my workday, no. The name again?"

"Last name, Zamarlo. First name, Reece. Fixes stuff. Electronics, mostly. Used to anyway, until somebody slammed a hunting knife into his chest."

Reece Zamarlo's white cottage is nondescript; it passes muster as a bachelor's pad. The TV room looks lived in, chips and pretzel bits line the edges of the La-Z-Boy and a few empties stand sentry duty on the floor. The kitchen imparts an impression that it's cleaned once a fortnight. For now, dishes litter the sink; a few are stacked in the dishwasher. The bread is four days old, the milk 10, and the recycling bin suggests that frozen dinners are generally favoured over honest cooking.

The single bedroom is not a bachelor's travesty although the drawers are untidy and the bed's rumpled. The sheets and pillowcases are clean enough though, and no clothes are strewn about. The only imposing clutter is reserved for the bathroom where discarded toothpaste tubes lie in an incomprehensible stack, as if Reece Zamarlo was building a toy fort. Also, three hairbrushes, old and new razor blades, an electric shaver, and an assortment of shampoos, deodorants, aftershaves, and various bandages. The bathroom is the least clean room in the house. Cinq-Mars concludes that no one other than Reece Zamarlo has showered there recently. Who would want to? If someone else did shower, he or she left no obvious trace.

A loner.

"What d'ya think?" Hammond asks in the kitchen.

Émile's absorbed in thought. "The dining chairs," he says.

"What about them?"

"They look like rescues. One found here, another there. No care taken. If he stole Muriel's, you'd think they'd be in place by now."

"He's not the only man in New Hampshire with a white van. Maybe he's not our thief. He's only a homicide victim."

"Or he stowed his loot somewhere else. On to the workshop?"

"Yeah. Check it out."

Outside, Cinq-Mars pauses by Reece Zamarlo's white van. He's struck by a finger-drawing in the dust on the lower portion of the rear side panel. Roughly, an elephant's head, with its trunk raised skyward. He digs out his cellphone and takes a picture of it, then makes a facial expression to Hammond to indicate that it could mean anything, or in all probability, nothing.

The shop does not appear to be revealing. Found unlocked. Some messiness pertains, although the tools are organized well. Reece Zamarlo won't be the first man to have permitted the counter in his kitchen to suffer the indignity of neglect but never his workbench. Despite the quiet hour, a sense of activity permeates the room. Troopers have already conducted a quick search, coming up empty. They'll continue after Hammond and Cinq-Mars conclude their browse.

"Nothing found?" Cinq-Mars inquires. The shop seems bona fide.

"A whole lot of nothing."

"Your men looked in everything?"

"Opened drawers, checked the boxes, the bags, the bottles, the tin cans. Almost everything is checked off. Nothing so far, but they're not done."

Cinq-Mars opens a rear door that reveals a closet larger than expected. Flicks the light switch on. The storage shelving is generally arranged neatly, mostly with spare parts and the gutted remains of old motors that might someday be brought back to life in a revived machine.

Cinq-Mars is struck by something. Hammond notices.

"What?"

"Zamarlo did it."

"Did what?" Hammond asks.

"Robbed Muriel. Which means he probably killed her, too."

"Why?"

"I don't know why."

"I mean, why do you think that way?"

He points with a gesture of his chin to where Hammond should look. They gaze upon an elephant figurine inside a glass jar.

"Muriel's elephant. You think? Could be, hey."

"Notice – the chip on the tusk. The photograph of Muriel with the elephant in the background? Had that chip. What a strange thing to do. Steal all that stuff, then put only one item away in here."

"In a glass jar."

"In a glass jar. Do you know what's strange about it?"

"You tell me."

"The elephant is on display. As though someone wants it to be the elephant in the room. Someone wants us to see this. I presume Zamarlo. The elephant is shining a light. Maybe."

"A light? Meaning what?"

"Pointing a finger. Don't you feel it? If this Reece Zamarlo just put it on a shelf, I would get that, but in a jar, right where this is the first thing we see in here – plus the elephant head on the van. It's like someone is taking a hammer to my head, saying, '*Boing*! Here's a clue! Now do something with it.' Then *boing* on my head again."

Hammond isn't feeling that way. He stares at the figurine as if hoping to derive a similar response. "What do we do?"

"Bring your people back in. Get them to go through the place once more. Especially this closet. Fine-tooth comb, Trooper Hammond. Super thorough. Fine-tooth comb."

The trooper gazes at Cinq-Mars. He can tell that he's not going to be handed further inducement or an explanation of what he should be looking for. He shrugs, then says, "Sure thing," and steps outside to call his team back in.

TWENTY-TWO

Émile Cinq-Mars wolfed down a less than satisfactory lunch at a road-side diner. A cold beer made the food palatable. A second improved his digestion. Seated on a stool, he attacks Trooper Hammond's files. Before finding a body in the woods, he had asked to peruse these cold cases.

The files outline the deaths of people where a dollop of suspicion persists. The oldest case lists a brother as next of kin. Cinq-Mars was expecting a spouse or a partner, or a child in the case of divorce. The brothers were twins. Together at birth, separated by death.

Grant Labryk is weeding in his garden when Cinq-Mars arrives. He stoops over an offending dandelion to stab it with an articulating claw. Cinnamon skinned. A frolic of white hair rises like wings from his scalp. Cinq-Mars walks halfway across the man's lawn before being noticed.

The fellow turns without straightening up. The curvature of his spine is fixed for the duration.

"Afternoon," Labryk declares. A strong voice, the gaze warm. The look of a man who hopes for viable company while anticipating disappointment. Perhaps his visitor will be a salesman, a proselytizer, or the more common intruder – a traveller requiring directions and limited to two choices, the way he's headed or the way he's come.

"Afternoon, sir." Émile offers a wry smile. "I'm looking for Grant Labryk at this address. Would that be you?"

"Last time I checked, yeah. Are you selling or confiscating?"

"Neither, I don't think." Cinq-Mars shows that he's amused. Each of many flowerbeds contains a stiff metal flag, Old Glory amid the roses and geraniums. "I'd like to talk about your brother."

"That scamp? What's he done?"

That scamp would be 76 years old were he not deceased.

"Ah, I mean your twin brother, sir." He speaks louder.

"Heard you the first time. Behaving himself, is he?"

"I'm not privy to that knowledge, sir, not being an emissary from the great beyond."

The gentleman with the crooked spine lets him off the hook. "Don't mind me. What's this about, since you know he's passed?"

"The circumstances of his death interest me. I'm here to check that everything went according to Hoyle, so to speak. We want to make sure folks receive appropriate care at that time of life."

The man's eyebrows contrast the stiff, rising white hair on his head. They flounder, dip low to impede his vision, and are a dirty grey.

"We?" the man asks.

"I'm representing, shall we say, the government."

"Shall we say that?" the man probes. Cinq-Mars doesn't blame him for his suspicions. "What government?"

"Sir. New Hampshire." By extrapolation, that's not entirely untrue.

Grant Labryk stares back another moment before he relents.

"All right. We'll talk about his appropriate care. Time of life, you said? More like time of death. Funny, I don't recall that he carried any insurance worth talking about, except for the burial fund. Is that what you want back? Couldn't we just dig him up instead? Ask him what he did with the cash?"

"I'm not in insurance, sir. I want nothing back."

The man grunts as though he doesn't believe him; yet invites him inside. "I'm ready for a cup of tea. Join me. You might as well."

"That's very kind."

"Is it? I'll do better next time. I'm a curmudgeon by nature. Not inclined to be cordial."

Émile follows him up the front steps into his home.

The house is one that suffers from being in the shade, feels on the dull side. Such details stand out now that he's looking to buy a home. Idly, he's thinking that Scotch in the afternoon, rather than tea, would make a fine new tradition. When he introduces himself, his name seems to hang in the air like a threat while the man holds the kettle under the kitchen tap at the rear of the house. He's looking back at him while the water overflows into the sink.

Cinq-Mars takes a guess. "You've heard of me."

"Should I've?" His reputation, for once, has not gone before him.

"No, I just thought— You look startled."

Labryk dries the outside of his kettle, then places it on a burner. His movements are ingrained, this tea ceremony intrinsic to his marrow.

"How do you pronounce your name again? Never heard one like it."

Émile must repeat his surname a few times before the man stops flexing his eyebrows at him.

"French," he explains.

"I believe you. What government do you work for? Not the French."

"New Hampshire." Not a total lie. He's been assigned by a state trooper. Then he recalls that the man's query has already been asked and answered. In this instance, he's not sure whether Grant Labryk loses track of things, or if he's deliberately doubling back to see if he'll answer the same way twice. "Your name is similar to your brother's. You're Grant. He was Garth. Were you close? I take it you lived together."

"He moved in after he got sick. That was about three years before he died, give or take. We lived apart until then."

"My condolences." The file hadn't mentioned an illness.

"Thanks. You think it was suicide?"

"Excuse me?"

"Why else be here if not to adjust the meagre insurance payout."

Émile is in no position to explain himself. "Do you think it was suicide?"

The man shrugs. "My brother was a good guy. Religious on Sundays, some other days, too. Mostly it depended on the weather. He didn't believe in suicide. Would I blame him if he went out that way? Given his illness, only an unjust God or an insurance company would hold it against him."

"His illness," Cinq-Mars starts up, then stops. He doesn't want to sound uninformed. He regrets that he's possibly wildly misinformed.

"The cancer," Labryk continues, "ate through his larynx. Horrific that way. Would I have done myself in under similar circumstances? Can't say. I'm religious, too, depending on the hour, the climate, and what's on TV. Alone in my bed at night, I'm a virtual saint. If cancer ate through my throat, I'm not sure I'd be saintly at any hour of the day or night."

"I know what you're saying."

The kettle whistles and the host fills a teapot, spills out the water, fills it again and deposits the bags.

"Listen," Labryk confronts him. "What's this about? If you're here to rob me, get the Christ on with it. If you want me to buy something, the start of the month is the best time, not now. If you're after the insurance money, say so. It was only for his burial. He left nothing else and that could be a big part of it."

"I don't follow. Part of?"

"His misery," Labryk clarifies. Then says, "The tea."

He covers the teapot with a cozy. Turning, he gazes at Cinq-Mars, his look harsh. "Is this about the heroin? Are you saying that? You must have a reason to be here, the government. I knew about it. Is that what you want to hear? I didn't give it to him. My brother had too much kindness in his veins, despite the heroin, to ask anything like that of me."

"You know about the heroin." Cinq-Mars sighs. "Do you think it killed him?"

There. Beating around the bush is officially over.

Labryk seems confused. "He took it for the pain. Why can't people understand that? Stick a fork in your eye, then see if you wouldn't be willing to put a needle in your arm to escape the anguish of it all. Not just the pain, you understand: the anguish of it all. My God, the man needed something. They dose you to the gills at the hospital, get you hooked on this and that, then put you back on the street with an empty syringe. What's a man, any man, supposed to do? But I'm not going to say another word, not one word—"

"Sir—"

"—until we've had our tea."

Cinq-Mars abides his silence and waits for the tea to steep. Similar to his opinion of Muriel, he's impressed by the good condition of the home. The walls could use a more cheerful colour, and he's betting the man has a housekeeper, but Grant Labryk is disciplined. Then he recalls the metal flags outside.

"Were you military, sir?"

"Navy. Never left dry dock. Logistics, they called it, what I did. I won't tell you what I called it."

He offers lemon and honey with the tea, and the visitor tries a little of both. Émile follows him through to the living room where they sit opposite each other, Émile on the sofa, Labryk in a wing chair.

"Your brother," Émile asks, "was he navy, too?"

Grant shakes his head. "I enlisted. Couldn't wait to see the world. I got as far as New Jersey. And a military base in Germany for a year, then four walls for about two years in Virginia. That was never as exciting as it sounds. Garth also wanted to see the world. He slung a backpack over his shoulders and off he went. He saw it, too, the world. Got laid a lot more than I did, too."

"Good for him."

"I used to resent it. After he got sick, it gave me some relief that he once lived like he wanted. Like I wanted, really. At least, when he was young."

He's warming to this man. If he's the curmudgeon he claims to be, the designation comes along with evident intelligence and humour.

"In life, with your careers, were you twins? Or did you do things differently?"

"Out of the navy, I worked for a company that made lawn sprinklers. Never left. Other than trying to withstand the excessive excitement of that career, I have no complaints. Garth bounced around but damned if he didn't make money. He invested, too. As the saying goes, he did well for himself. He made his momma proud."

"Family?" He sees no pictures.

"I married once. No kids. She died too young but not so long ago. He married twice, two kids. You'll never guess where those boys are today." Labryk doesn't leave him hanging. "Navy. Both of them. Neither Garth nor I could figure that one out. Maybe I was the bigger influence, or maybe it had something to do with me not being the dad, you know?"

Cinq-Mars nods.

"You? Kids?" Labryk asks him.

"Afraid not."

"Just your mysterious government job, which by the way, I don't buy for a second of your time or mine."

He's just been called out as a phoney.

"The government doesn't give two shits about you when you're alive," Grant Labryk reminds him, "unless your taxes are due. Once you're dead, all that care and attention goes out the window."

Cinq-Mars puts his tea down. "Sir, I'm working with the New Hampshire State Police. There's a reason they want to do this indirectly, without raising anybody's hackles. Folks might not be pleased to talk about their loved ones if the discussion doesn't show them in a squeaky-clean light."

"The heroin, you mean."

The man knows how to come to the point. "That's it."

Labryk sips. He ponders the news. When his cup goes down, Cinq-Mars knows that he's ready to talk seriously again.

"I would never say to a policeman, if that's what you are, that you got nothing on me. Policemen can have anything on anybody, and they don't have to try that hard. Do with me whatever you want, but I'll speak the truth. Garth bought his own horseshit. That dark side of his life he kept to himself. I don't know how the transactions took place. He would not involve me, and I turned a blind eye. Had to. He was in so much pain. What do you want to do with him now? Cause him more pain? Or are you coming after me? You can. I have no defences."

"Mr. Labryk—"

"Don't talk to me about the government! I don't want to hear about the government! That's all I ask. The military, I respect. But it ends there."

He'll remember that in the future. Down here, in the U.S.A., not everyone loves those in high places.

"One time," the man continued, "I told him I was staying home from my garden club meeting. I had the dizzies. He said no, I had to go to my meeting. We just looked at each other, nobody said nothing more. I went to the meeting, my head spinning like a top. So, he had his times, his arrangements, that coincided with my absences. That's the most I ever figured out."

Cinq-Mars got that. "Sir, I don't want to cause you, or your brother, more pain. I'm here to see that others don't go through anything similar. Did the heroin kill him? He was suffering, but did his death come out of the blue? Did he overdose on purpose?"

The older man shakes his head again, then speaks more quietly than before, as if someone else might be listening. "The fast way he went in the end made me question things. I refused an autopsy. The Medical Examiner—"

"Who was that, the individual, do you recall?"

"His name was Easton, I believe. Close to it anyway."

"I believe that's right."

"He asked me to agree to it three times. I said no each time. Garth had suffered enough. Leave his poor body in peace. The cancer killed him. Any fool knows that. But the cancer, the cancer brought on the pain, and that brought on the heroin, and that brought on, you know, the greyness, the sadness, the wandering in dark alleys. The good parts of your life are taken away by the cancer. The little that survives is taken away by heroin. Maybe that's what gave my brother a reason, if he needed an extra one. Why death came when it did and not sooner. I only found out after he died that he had nothing left. His savings, depleted."

"I've learned that heroin is no longer so expensive."

"I've heard that, too. On the TV. Used to be pricier. The drugs aren't that cheap when you're not only buying for yourself."

"Meaning what?"

"Cancer patients. They get to know each other."

"I see." The matter still does not compute for him. The patient was well-off. He could have afforded cheap heroin for the multitudes.

"That's what bothers me, sir," Labryk says. "He was too proud. He may have been ashamed to find himself depleted, and that's why it was that day and not earlier or later. Maybe he went only as far as his money could carry him." He remains contemplative a moment. "Or—"

"Or what, sir?"

"Or maybe he just got too tired to carry on. I can forgive that, too."

Cinq-Mars nods, retrieves his cup again, and drinks. "I'm sorry to invoke painful memories. I'm trying to find out if the heroin was bad, if that's what did your brother in. If it was, then perhaps we can save others. See that justice is done for those who passed. If you think it was because of money ..."

Émile's voice trails off, and the man is nodding as he gazes outside his window, his mind drifting back to the garden, perhaps. "Can't say. I think that – sometimes this vexes me – that the pain, never underestimate the pain, that the pain meant a continuation of heroin. That meant he might impoverish me as well as himself. When I found out that he died broke, it came to mind. Maybe he let himself go. To an overdose. What do you think?"

He has formed no opinion, and nothing today provokes a conclusion. "He never discussed dying? Never broached the subject?"

"My brother was a private man to the finish. Fact is, I don't really know what he did to make his money. That tells you something. When he moved in with me, he was embarrassed. It had an effect, suddenly being dependent again. He became even more private. He never took me for granted, despite being my twin. I also know that he was bitter, as much for what the cancer was demanding of me as for what it took away from him."

A thing that Cinq-Mars knows, departing, is that the surviving twin is in no way implicated in his brother's death. He accepts that perspective because he knows people and already trusts this man implicitly. When he was a cop he'd have to keep the pretense up, make sure the man wasn't putting anything over on him. Being retired, he answers only to his own instincts, which he prefers.

Why, he ponders as he drives off, is there ever a murder anywhere, when so many battle so hard to live? And why is there ever a crime, when men such as this one silently move through their days with such dignity? Shouldn't it be that people learn from their best examples? Some do, of course. Yet others, for all the wrong excuses, fail that simple test.

Cinq-Mars has more names on his list, yet the day has extracted a toll. He's drained. He feels depleted by death, by its slow creep, its patience, then suddenness in the lives of others. On no one's clock, he steers for home.

Émile Cinq-Mars now knows that his wife has put in yeoman duty driving around the countryside in her late mother's relic of an automobile. Behind the wheel for the better part of a day, he feels that someone has taken a jackhammer to his cerebellum while simultaneously locking his kidneys in a vise. He keeps looking for a place to piss only to decide that he doesn't need to go, that his bladder has merely bounced above his ribcage while his brain is on the spin cycle.

Home again, relishing a nap and a bottle of aspirin, he heads upstairs where he finds Sandra trying on dresses.

"What's this?" he asks.

"We're going out."

"Good to know. Any place special?" He lumbers onto the bed, stretches fully and holds the position a moment, then relaxes on his back. "More to the point, when? Later this month I hope." His hands fold over his tummy. He's not convinced he'll move again for a week.

"Come on, old man. I accepted an invitation."

"Oh. Social. The news keeps getting better."

"You weren't around so I made an executive decision. You still have time for a catnap."

"Good. They sleep for days, don't they? Your sister's?"

Sandra responds with a quick headshake.

"Your niece?"

"One last try. You snooze, you lose."

"I'll accept the loss if I win that prize – a good long snooze."

"Tiring day?"

"I hate that car now."

"Aha!"

"You're a saint. From now on, the Escalade is yours. I'll walk."

She laughs. "The Ford's not that bad."

"Come on. It's not safe. I'll have it towed tomorrow. But who invited us? Please, don't ask me to guess, San. My brain's jumbled."

"Your new best friend forever."

He's genuinely befuddled. Maybe the damage from the car is permanent. "Not Hammond."

"Your lawyer guy. Hodges Marsh. He and his wife invited us to Woodstock."

"Really?" He sits up an inch, his limit. Adjusts the pillow so he can prop his head higher. "Why?"

Sandra shakes herself out of a dress she's rejecting. "To make nice? To soften us up to buy the farm? Who knows? Whatever, I am not saying no to dinner at The Hill and Dale. Besides, I'm in the mood."

He thinks it over. He does feel that Marsh is being a tad presumptuous but supposes that this is what you do when you're anxious to make a deal. The man's blind: he has fewer options. "Sounds doable."

"Nap. I'll wake you when it's time to get ready."

He's neglected to kick his shoes off, and she slips them from his feet now, then wanders up to give him a kiss. He wiggles his toes as her lips touch his. Effortlessly, Émile succumbs to sleep.

When she wakes him, she's sitting on the edge of the bed, biting her lip. In his mind only a minute has passed – a glance at the beside clock states otherwise. He's had a good 40 minutes of shut-eye.

"What's up?" Something's on her mind.

"Ah … confession time? I messed up today. I committed a crime."

He tries to think of the worst possible thing. "You bought a house."

"No, silly."

"Then it can't be that bad."

"It involves our agent."

She hasn't given him much to go on. He's stumped. "Did you shoot her? I don't mind."

"Don't get mad. I mean, you're going to get mad, but don't go off half-cocked. This does not constitute the end of the world."

She needs time to gather her courage.

"So, I was riding around all day with Patricia, and we were talking, and the day is long. God, she can gab! I tried to drop her off, but she talked me out of it. Anyway … she asked me about you and what you're doing."

"Don't tell me." He has an inkling now. Sandra knows that he's a private person, that he'll find anything said about him to be annoying. In particular, though, one aspect needs to be suppressed. Namely, what he's doing now.

"I was talking and then, I was tired, Émile, it just slipped out. I told her, I swear, I told her not to tell anyone else. I said you were investigating natural deaths in case they weren't so natural."

"Sandra."

"I know! I asked her not to tell anyone. I impressed that on her."

He exhales. While he's not actually angry, he's not happy about this turn, either. "It'll be all over town by sunset. Stand on the green with a megaphone. Actually, this is worse."

"I only thought of that after I spoke, after she got excited."

"Oh! She's excited. Great. What did she say?"

"What didn't she say? Émile, I pleaded with her. She promised that she can keep a secret. But I couldn't, so she might not either."

"That's pretty much a guarantee."

"How mad are you?"

That she is confiding in him, whereas lately she's been secretive, proves a sufficient antidote to any slight umbrage.

"The theory goes that I'm better off coming upon people unawares. Maybe that's not true. This might work out. Volunteers might speak up. So, no issues."

"Thanks. I'll count myself as properly scolded anyway."

"Forget it. We're going out. I suppose you want me to wear something."

"Clothes would be nice." He's earned a few brownie points with his reaction: she's not demanding. "I woke you early. I thought you might like a nice long soak in the tub. Shave. Presto. You're done."

"Tie?"

"Jacket required. Tie optional."

"All right." He stretches. "Deal."

She kisses him then, a warmer, more prolonged intimacy than he's known lately. After his soak, he dons the optional tie. He senses her approval.

TWENTY-THREE

Entering Woodstock, Vermont, Émile Cinq-Mars wonders… *Live here?* Favoured in earlier times by the Rockefellers, the years have been kind to the community. For its ambience, the mountain village is hard to beat.

Another thought runs counter to that: hard to afford, too.

The restaurant for their evening is partially hidden, the front door accessed down a cobblestone side alley.

Sandra and Émile are led to a snug table, Sandra the first to spot their host arriving right behind them. She identifies Hodges Marsh by his dark glasses. As an equestrian, she can signal horses through their complicated maneuvers, her actions indiscernible to an untrained eye. Similarly, Mrs. Marsh provides imperceptible aids to her husband. That mutual trust between them has Sandra feeling fond of the couple before they're introduced.

First names are exchanged. Mrs. Marsh is Regina, and no sooner are they comfortable than a drink arrives for Hodges, a short daiquiri. The waiter then accepts orders from the others.

Émile's impressed. "How did you manage that?"

"Since I can't flag a waiter whom I can't easily distinguish from a patron, I place my drink order to arrive when I do when I make the reservation."

He's not knocking it back but savours a sip to make his point.

Hodges, Émile observes, establishes an exacting awareness of where his utensils lie, his water glass, his drink. Whenever he puts something down – a bun, a pad of butter – it goes back to where he'll find it again. The blind often are credited with auditory acuity; that may hold true with this man. Émile observes, though, that his hands also substitute for his impaired vision.

As if, once he's settled, his hands have eyes. Or antennae, perhaps.

Across the border in New Hampshire, Trooper Geoff Hammond takes a call. He considers notifying his new pal, then changes his mind. Grumblings have surfaced within his troop. The rank-and-file have their noses out of joint with an outsider granted access to crime scenes. Pissed off further when the rumour flew that the Governor himself wants the Frenchman's gargantuan nose in their business. Hammond believes the Governor seeks political advantage, given the detective's local fame, but he's not going to point that out to his troopers. Someone could work it against him.

He'll join his troopers to run down the call. Once he learns what there is to learn, he'll consider including the outsider. Hammond turns his overhead cherries on and departs at full wail. The siren alerts the countryside to his high-speed race to the Upper Valley Health Club in the Town of Lebanon. Apparently, a lady there is sitting up dead in her wheelchair.

At table, the couples dabble in a variety of topics, pausing once while Émile and Sandra have a mild spat about whether or not he enjoys gnocchi – she says never, he insists that it depends – and they pause again when Regina laments the epic incursion of heroin into the peaceable kingdoms of Vermont and New Hampshire. Hodges weighs in that the notion has been exaggerated. Taking Regina's side, Émile thinks otherwise. Hodges counters that the problem seems extreme to the detective because that's the pool he's dipped his toes into lately. "No offence, Émile, but if you were investigating burglaries, we'd all feel robbed."

"I should get out and walk the mountain trails? Clear the synapses?"

Hodges thinks it's a great idea and tries to convince his wife that the situation is not nearly as dire as the press attests. Unconvinced, she beats his arguments into the ground. The world as once they knew it, she contends, has come to an end. In the face of that full-on apocalypse, Marsh insists on keeping his own counsel and remains blasé.

"Rome's burning," Regina dissects. "You're fiddling."

Émile discovers that his name has been in the news again, which is how Hodges knows he's been around addicts and murder.

Regina chose the rabbit loin fricassee, with shell beans, gnocchi, and pancetta, doing so after canvassing her guests to ascertain that no one took exception. Sandra revealed that she hunted rabbits as a kid. She won't be standing up for the furry creatures. "There's always more rabbits, and more rabbits," she said, winning Regina's favour.

Sandra opted for the spring lamb, with yoghurt *spätzle*, fiddleheads, pistachio and mint. The dry-aged New York strip adorns the plate of Hodges Marsh, with dandelion chimichurri and red thumb potato. Émile might have gone that route himself, but something about following a lawyer's example created a prohibition in his head. He abruptly switched to the halibut with artichoke and fennel *à la barigoule* and sea beans.

Everyone's in thrall with their choices, and the handsome, university-aged waiter, who could serve as his school's poster boy or star quarterback, beams as though personally elevated by their praise.

Hodges Marsh has a question. "While you're out there, Émile, casting your investigative net, what do you ponder? Weighty wool-gathering, that's your reputation. What do you dwell on as you peer upon a corpse?"

"Hodges!" Regina all but clutches her rubies. "Macabre!"

The retired detective keeps his internal reaction to himself, which he might have phrased as, "What the hell are you talking about?"

"We've all heard it said, Émile, there's no free lunch. Extrapolate from that that there's no free dinner, either. Sorry, Sandra, we're not here to discuss the sale of the farm. Although we shall, in my office, in due course."

146

"Good to hear."

"And yet, I have invited you to dinner with a purpose. Indulge me. There's something I'd like to receive back, other than a decent price on the land deal. Something more difficult to come by."

Sandra and Émile are equally mystified.

"What would that be, Hodges?" he asks.

"I've heard, via the grapevine, of a certain esoteric mind at work. Émile, I listen at length to Democrats and Republicans, preachers and professors, businessmen and social activists. Perhaps a product of my liability, of my blindness – and please forgive me, I rarely play the blind man card – but the sound of a thoughtful voice enchants me. It truly does. I love good talk. I love debate. I love ideas, no matter how far-flung they may be. Now, please, don't pout. I'm not asking you to sing for your supper, at least not yet—" The ladies laugh, although Émile declines to be distracted. "I suppose that I *am* asking you to give me a glimpse into that renowned head of yours. Something off the cuff, Émile. A meditation you've entertained lately, or a deep discourse, whether taken to conclusion or not. Please. Indulge me. I beg of you."

The request does constitute singing for his supper despite the claim to the contrary. And yet, just as Marsh appreciates good talk and may be bereft of it in his daily environment, Émile is similarly limited in his opportunities to tear off into cosmological tangents. His inner speculations rarely find a receptive audience. An opportunity has arisen for both of them – the one eager to listen and the one willing to speak – to partake.

"Perhaps an effect to being on this case," Émile admits, "lately, my mind has been harping on black holes."

"Do you feel down one?" Hodges inquires. Émile has taken to observing the man's hands, the interplay of thumbs and fingers, to interpret what lurks behind his words.

"Murder, being on my mind, has dislodged a meditation on black holes, although not as anyone might assume."

Cinq-Mars gives his dinner companions the opportunity to cut him off. They mind their peace.

"I've brushed up against atrocities in my day. Some gruesome, all sad. Comments we hear from the general public – such as, who could do such a terrible thing? – are valid to a point. Psychotic killers – they dwell on their own lunar landscape. But those who have killed out of lust or fear or a craving for violence, who felt wronged or felt themselves superior – if we are honest we can probably say that we *do* understand them. To a degree. I'm not saying we'd do the same, I'd like to think not, but we can accept that it's possible to slide into a killer's mindset. At least at some frayed time in our lives.

"The deaths in this community," he continues after a final bite of the halibut, "are confounding. In a nutshell, old people have been sitting up dead and those deaths may not have been natural. Trouble is, for the life of me I can't see what's in it for a murderer. If he didn't make the mistake of having his people sit up, we might not be aware that a crime took place. That tells me he's looking to get away with it. But what does the killer glean from the act? We can imagine that in a certain warped state of mind there's a sick thrill to shooting or knifing someone. An emotional release, for example. But is there a satisfying jolt that comes from watching people permanently fall asleep? Similar to watching paint dry, no? Our killer is no thrill seeker."

The others dwell on this as they polish off their meals, before Hodges recalls the introduction to the talk. "We arrive at black holes, how?"

Cinq-Mars doesn't bite immediately. "Larceny. That's another excuse for murder. Somebody wants something and killing a fellow human being is the path forward. I'm not seeing that here. The killer does not get his kicks from killing and he does not gain anything worthwhile from the enterprise. What's up with that?"

Regina is impressed with his dilemma. "Where does it lead you?"

Cinq-Mars must wait to masticate and swallow a final sea bean. "Out into the universe, I suppose, onto an event horizon, slipping into a black hole." He's off on a spiel, then, enjoying the opportunity to give himself rein. "People who believe the earth is flat may be on to something. Can we really get our heads around walking on the surface of the planet without ever being upside down? I can't. I still expect to fall off. In any case, while the earth, I'll concede, is close to being round, like a partially deflated ball, the universe is flattish. The flat-earth people, who are idiots, missed out on being the flat-universe people, who are brilliant. Einstein entertained the notion of a universe that curved back onto itself, others speculated that it could be shaped like a saddle. But no. Our universe is flattish. Which is a good thing, for a host of reasons. So, as you recall, this meditation affects black holes."

He explains that the curvature of a black hole allows for time and space to be the inverse of the other. If he were to slide into one, with Sandra watching, she'd see his bones elongate like a giraffe's neck as he went over the edge. "Space warps the extreme curve at the opening to the hole." She'd also see him incinerate as he's struck by radiation waves. "From my perspective in the moment," he stresses, "being pulled forward by space rather than by time into the black hole's inverse spiral, I'd go on living as though not much is happening. Sandra sees me stretched out like a prairie then reduced to ash, like a prairie fire, while for me everything is old hat. She just seems a trifle distant."

The others smile. Sandra mildly chides him. "Émile."

"Just saying. Not the case now. Distortion is a matter of perspective on the space-time continuum."

Heady stuff. He knows they're not following him entirely, or at all. He can also tell that, like the image of himself being stretched as an elastic noodle sliding over an event horizon into a black hole, they can feel their own minds expand and incinerate. They sense an inkling of what it might look like.

"For me, thinking about such things actually creates black holes," Cinq-Mars goes on, leaving them even more befuddled. "As was said of God, if He didn't exist, we'd have to invent Him. Well, black holes do exist, and therefore we're obliged to recreate them in our heads if we want to figure them out. That's also what we are free to do with God, of course, although most people don't get that, neither the religious nuts nor those who are antagonistic about the whole idea. If God *does* exist, then we must recreate Him in our heads. Which we do. The question then follows, if we recreate Him in our heads, does He therefore not exist? Or exist? Slip your mind down a black hole to untangle that one."

The grin forming at the edges of Hodges Marsh's lips indicates his pleasure. His thumbs flick the tips of his ring fingers. The lawyer enjoys high-minded talk, although, as a practical man, he asks, "How does this help with your case, Émile? If at all?"

"Sandra sees me stretched out, in my example, but the person slipping into the black hole – that would be me – finds everything to be normal. For me, life carries on. For Sandra, I've been distorted and destroyed. That's what I'm looking for. The image that appears normal and typical to one observer, that may be distorted and destructive to another. The lesson here is to look at everything from different angles and with different mindsets. What seems normal is perhaps not. A schoolteacher seems normal, for instance. A schoolteacher on heroin, less so. But perhaps the latter is more normal than the former, if we change the time and space, if we alter the reality. We rely on time and space to be constants with respect to our frames of reference. The universe teaches that they are never constant. My job, in a sense, is to think differently. See differently. See what gets stretched. Or shrunken. See who's down a black hole but hasn't noticed yet that they've been incinerated. If I haven't noticed either, then maybe I haven't looked."

"Philosophy's loss," Hodges Marsh remarks, "—should I say theology's? – was crime fighting's gain."

"Hardly. Your remarkable wristwatches tell time, Hodges, yet you can barely read them. Which one do you have on tonight? I muse about this and that, yet flounder in the dark. Do you see the similarity?"

Marsh nods, takes it all in, like a fine meal. Then answers the question asked. "I'm wearing my one German timepiece. A. Lange & Söhne. This one was not at the office, Émile. A perpetual calendar. A time or date adjustment will not be required for one thousand and twenty-six years. Then wound back only a day. Or forward. I can't recall. By then it won't be my concern."

They are amazed by that.

The four make use of the washroom before departing. First out, Cinq-Mars waits in the corridor where he's approached by their waiter. Regina Marsh took care of the bill. Did she forget to tip? Was the check not added correctly?

"Sir?" The boy is shy to intrude on his privacy.

"Good service tonight. Discreet, warm, efficient."

"Thank you, sir. I just wanted to say – I know this is inappropriate – but I overheard a discussion at your table. About heroin. You're right. The other gentleman is wrong in my opinion. It's more widespread than people know."

Nothing is as important to Cinq-Mars with respect to an investigation as local knowledge. For that reason alone, he wants Hodges Marsh to gain trust in him, be willing to divulge what he might discern from time to time in the echelon of the society he inhabits. He's been working to gain that advantage through the evening. Similarly, he's willing to hear what the waiter has to say. "Go on," he encourages.

"My grandfather, sir. Nobody would think he'd take an illegal drug. In the end, drugs destroyed him. More than cancer, I think."

"I'm sorry to hear that. Sorry for your loss."

"A lot of heroin is going around among old people. My granddad had friends like that."

The women are coming out of the washroom, animated and talkative.

"I'd like to pursue this," Émile tells him. "Can I find you here another night, perhaps before your shift?"

"Sure. I'm in around 5. Wednesday through Sundays. Ask for Leo Ross."

"Thanks, Leo. My name is Émile Cinq-Mars."

"Yeah. I know."

"I see. I'll be in touch. Tell me, Leo, did your grandfather die sitting up?"

The question strikes the young man as peculiar. "No. He was lying in bed. He hadn't been able to sit up for quite a few days."

The boy departs as the women come by again, with Hodges Marsh finding his way behind them.

"What was that about?" Sandra asks.

"Another black hole to gaze into," Cinq-Mars replies.

They depart. "You were in fine form," Sandra quips in the Cadillac. Attitude behind her praise. The road out of town on up to the highway is slow speed, and the speed often changes, a trap for the unwary. "You've made a friend."

"Jury's out," Cinq-Mars qualifies.

"Why say that? Hodges was really keen on your whatever-that-was. Meditation."

"Not really. I don't think so."

"Émile? Why say that?"

"He wasn't interested in what I had to say. He was humouring me, actually. He was keen on getting me to talk. That's different. He's probably doing a victory lap."

"You," she says. She seems put out. "Always … *detecting*. Just be a friend. God knows you can use one."

In the moment, he fears she means as a replacement for her company.

His mobile buzzes, ending the talk. Sandra fishes it out of his inside jacket pocket for him while he drives. She takes the call. Hammond. He has a message. Another death. This time at the Upper Valley Health Club, and yes, the deceased is sitting up in a chair. Speaking through Sandra, Hammond assures him that they have every reason to mark the death as suspicious.

"I'm dropping you off. Let him know I'll be over," Émile responds.

"Remember, Émile," she says after conveying the message and clicking the phone off, "you're not thirty. You're not even sixty. You're supposed to be retired for heaven's sake, and you've had a long day. A few hours ago you looked half-past dead. At the very least, pace yourself."

He concedes that she has a point. The meal and company were fine, with dimensions under the skin that were intriguing, but he is tired. Still, up ahead, another death to brood upon. Another happily seated corpse.

TWENTY-FOUR

Sitting in her wheelchair, the dead woman has been stashed in a hall closet meant for mops and cleaning supplies. Cara Drost. Schoolteacher. Heroin addict. He had viewed her home and discovered her addiction. At the fitness club, he's privy to the mysterious circumstances of her death.

Mr. Markham Henry, the night custodian, found her.

"The shock of my life, sir. Right there."

According to Mr. Henry, the door was properly locked when he arrived. No keys are found on the woman to explain how she got inside.

"Dead or alive," Mr. Henry remarks, "she has no business in there."

What Cinq-Mars sees has him reeling. He keeps it to himself, with so many people around.

"What do you think?" Hammond asks, barely above a whisper.

"Later." In the closet, he's feeling mildly claustrophobic.

A colleague bumps into the trooper's arm, causing him to twist, then elbow a medical assistant in the head. Precious room to move and both he and Cinq-Mars squirm back out to the hall.

"You called it, Émile. You told me she did heroin."

"I didn't call her death. Did you put someone on her?"

"Daytime watch, yeah, on her house. No one arrived unaccounted for."

"Who arrived?"

"A couple of friends. A real estate agent. They checked out. Not that that means a whole hill of beans. We can take a closer look, but if first impressions count for anything, no one delivered narcotics to her door."

"Drugs don't have to come to her door, do they?"

"Meaning?"

"She can go to the drugs."

"Yeah. I see that. She comes here on a bus for people with special needs. She could've been supplied here."

"She and everybody else with special needs."

Hammond gives him a sharp glance to see how serious he is.

"Anything's possible," Cinq-Mars reminds him. "Even likely."

"My officer waited for her to get off the bus at her place today. Late afternoon, usual time. The bus never showed. Now we know why."

"She wasn't on it."

They both know what confronts them. The sports facility is a big operation, with a diverse clientele. Gyms and equipment rooms, pools and locker rooms, basketball and handball courts, martial arts and aerobics classes, dance classes, activities galore, and offices, hallways, quiet rooms, nooks and crannies. A phalanx of drug dealers could move through the premises with impunity and anonymity. A pusher could set up a tent, who'd notice? Security film is limited to the entrances and a scan of the parking lot.

"No footage in the shower rooms," Hammond states drily.

"Let's hope not. Mind if I talk to the custodian?"

"Be my guest."

Markham Henry has a pencil-thin physique that an observer might dismiss as frail until he shakes the man's hand. Cinq-Mars discerns a grip capable of bending steel. The man's eyes are spotted red, and he appears to be nervous, perhaps suspiciously so, but once he feels that he's under no special scrutiny he relaxes, and his smile expands.

"She must have given you a fright, Mr. Henry, when you walked in."

"Slammed the door right in her face, I did. Thought I was interrupting something, for a second there, like I accidentally forgot myself and walked into the ladies' toilet. A woman just sitting there. Then I thought, no. Don't think that way, Markham. No woman's john here is the size of my broom closet. I arrived back at my senses. Opened the door to my mops again like I do every working day. Except I did it slowly this time. Half-expected the woman inside to jaw me down for intruding on her private time. Or for slamming the door in her face. Either way I expected a berating. Turns out, she did not say a word in regard to my intrusion."

Émile catches the glint in the man's eye.

"Do you know this woman?" he asks him.

"Can't say I do. A lot of people pass through I don't know."

"What time's your shift?"

"I do nights."

"Graveyard?"

"Not that bad. No, sir. Is 7 in the evening to 2 in the morning. Sometimes, I go later when I'm moving slow."

"She usually comes in during the day, the trooper tells me. You weren't likely to cross paths. Do you use this closet every night? It's familiar to you?"

"Every working night," he qualifies.

"Who else uses it, on your shift or off?"

Markham Henry mulls that one over.

"I'd say is just me," he contends at last.

"Have you noticed anything odd?"

"Odd, sir?"

"Something missing. Something out-of-place. Something added that you know nothing about. Anything where you thought, 'Hmmpf, now how did that find a way in here?'"

He mulls that over, too.

"One time," Mr. Henry opines, then shakes his gnarly right forefinger, "now that you mention it. Two times, maybe. I never could figure it out."

"What's that?"

"Tire tracks."

"Excuse me?"

Markham Henry nods toward the corpse sitting up in her wheelchair. "A chair like that wheeled in out of the rain, or across a wet floor, leaves tracks. I thought maybe somebody in authority or whatnot stuck a wheelchair in the closet one day, maybe those two days I'm talking about, that's how I surmised it. Put it down to that, anyway. Yes, sir."

"That's interesting. Thank you."

"Then there was this other time."

The man is becoming a font of knowledge. "What happened then?"

"Swear I saw a footprint. A shoe print that been wet then tracked in here. There wasn't no match out in the corridor, but the corridor could've seen a cleaning machine by that time. Gone over with a waxing machine, too. Strange, a footprint in a closet."

Cinq-Mars surveys the corridor, and the custodian follows his glance with his own eyes, doing his own careful survey.

"After you found the lady this evening, Mr. Henry, did you look around in the closet? Have you checked if anything is different or missing, or if there's something new?"

The man looks apologetic. "No, sir. I saw that sight, the lady dead asleep, or maybe just dead, and I got downstairs to call. I locked up, went down, made the call, came back here. Waited outside the door until police showed up. I let them in. Yes, sir. I haven't touched nothing inside, not after what I seen."

"The right thing to do. Would you mind coming back inside with me?" They both look over to where Cara Drost is being wheeled out on her chair to be transferred to a body bag on a gurney. "It'll be free in a moment. I'd like you to go in there with me and see what's different, if anything."

"Sounds spooky. But I'll do it if you think there's merit."

"Thanks. Just hang on a second for now."

Émile crosses the corridor to ask Trooper Hammond for the room.

"What? The corridor? The floor? The whole damn building? You got to be reasonable this time, Émile."

"Take it easy. Just the closet. You can come in if you want. There's room for three."

"Three?"

"The custodian. Me and you can stay outside. I just want him to go in and look around. See if anything's new or changed, according to his perspective."

"What'll be new?"

"Let's find out."

They hang on as the body baggers take their leave, then Cinq-Mars signals Markham Henry to come over. The man enters on his own, with Hammond and Émile at the door. Nothing appears to disturb him until his attention is drawn upward, to a space on the wall above a shelf. Cinq-Mars is not looking in that direction but knows what the older man sees. He spotted it earlier. He already feels unnerved, even undermined, by what's there.

"Was it there before?" he whispers to the man.

"Never saw that. I would've. Never did. That's new to me."

"What is?" Hammond asks.

"Take a look," Émile instructs him, and follows him into the room so that the three men are huddled tightly together.

"What is that?" Hammond asks, seeing the crayon markings high on the wall for the first time, having missed it when inside the closet previously.

"Kind of a drawing," Mr. Henry remarks.

"Yeah," Hammond says, "of what?" His voice tapers off.

Cinq-Mars gazes at the crayon markings again. "The head of an elephant," he points out. "With tusks, mouth open, the trunk raised high. Now, where have we seen that before?"

Hammond doesn't bother to answer. He's stunned, too. He looks at Émile as though hoping for an explanation, but the former policeman is flummoxed and shakes his head.

"A message of some kind, a sort of signal, but don't ask me what."

"Look at the tusks," Cinq-Mars directs him.

He does so. "One's chipped."

"One's chipped," Cinq-Mars confirms.

"This means something," Hammond says. "We don't know what."

"I agree," Émile Cinq-Mars allows. "Geoff, I need to get home. I'm done in. Sandra says I need to pace myself. I think she's right. Check with your people in Twin Mountain. I need to know if Cara Drost ended up on the list Penelope was preparing of members in her group."

"I saw the list," Hammond responds. "Her name's on it." He adds, with a measure of kindness in his tone, "Safe drive home, Émile. Thanks for coming out."

III

TWENTY-FIVE·

Émile Cinq-Mars attempts to steal away from the farm before the sun pokes above the mountains. The effort is wrecked when he cranks up the relic of a station wagon. In the sweet quiet of dawn, the initial blast of the engine emulates a lion's mighty invective across the Serengeti.

He imagines that Sandra, asleep, shot up with a start.

One more day, he confirms to himself. Then it's the junkyard.

He chews a fried egg sandwich on the drive to the river by Muriel's house. A dollop of ketchup stains his shirt; he makes the matter worse trying to rub it off. Visually, not unlike a bullet wound to the heart. That gives him pause. He quit the police force in part to stay alive, yet he's now in pursuit of a killer, without a badge or weapon to protect himself. Funny how that goes.

Arriving at the riverbank Émile removes his shirt to soak the red spot in the water, then hangs the shirt on a tree branch. He uncaps his thermos and takes his ease amid the morning's birdsong.

He moves upstream to sit on a smooth boulder, drinks his hot coffee and feels the cool morning air on his bare chest. He visualizes Muriel Cuthbert casting a line here, her shadow at play upon these ripples. He devises a plan: He'll request access to Muriel's house, to probe her murder he'll say, but really to borrow a fishing rod. He'll find out if he enjoys the pastime well enough to equip himself with his own tackle. Who knows? How much he enjoys fishing might clinch or confound the decision to migrate to New Hampshire.

Mist rises as sunlight warms the air over the cold of the river.

Not quite dry, his shirt goes back on.

A curious analogy attaches to his mood. He's fantasizing about catching fish when catching criminals has encompassed his life's work.

Émile weighs the similarities. Not being expert in the sport, he presumes that to catch a fish means segregating one from its school, coaxing it along with a tasty-looking lure that artfully camouflages a hook. When he thinks about it, he's caught crooks that way, too.

His mental serendipity turns him back to the task at hand, and to why he's reflective by the riverside. He needs to cull a group of addicts for one or more members who may be of help. Typical policework, nothing new in that, but in appreciating the deft and patience required by those who fish, he feels encouraged by the process.

Being on the riverbank helps him out. He's been stymied by one curious unknown: *why*? Why the deaths? Why would anyone bother if there is no gain, not even a demented thrill? If murder is neither profitable nor exciting in some sick way, then why bother? That's the cerebral line he casts onto the surface of the stream, and when he reels it back in, he fabricates a response. He's caught nothing – a common frustration for fishermen and detectives alike. The nuance that lures his attention then has to do with the Connecticut River.

With respect to his case, he's only been noticing what flows past him. He's gotten nowhere with respect to where the effluence comes from, the dimensions of the watershed, where it all goes. Somehow he must cast a line, allow it to linger in the current, then reel the bait and the hook back in. Then try again. To fish successfully requires broad local knowledge, and to acquire that he must grasp both what's upstream and what's down.

A mathematical formula pops to mind, one that has long enchanted him. He's not sure where he learned it in the distant past. He could be talked into thinking that clever Muriel in a new guise as a river sprite tricked his brain into bringing it forward. He ponders how a mathematical formula – a myth, really – helps him now.

Trooper Geoff Hammond typically starts his day early. He called in and had a fit. His material witness had been held overnight.

"*What?*" he demands of his trooper over the phone.

"Penelope Gagnon was here overnight."

"Why?"

"What do you mean why? You never released her."

He'd pull his own hair out if it was long enough. He hadn't meant to keep her overnight. He simply forgot about her. He'd heard of these things happening, and thought little of the cops responsible, but this one's on him.

She had not fared well in confinement and the duty sergeant quickly wants her off his hands. A guard might jab her with a Taser, he's saying, she's been that infuriating. "Who knows how she reacts then." Hammond promises to be there on the double and, arriving, signs her release. He goes one step farther. To help settle her down and assuage his own guilt, he offers to drive the distraught woman home.

"He said I had to walk, that one!" Penelope complains.

"Figure of speech, ma'am. Saying you're going to walk means to set you free. To show you the door."

"That's not what I heard him say. I heard him say it, I had to walk myself home. I'd die on the way! I'd get lost, me."

Whether a misunderstanding, a deliberate attempt to bully her, ordinary meanness or an attempt at humour, he'll let it slide. "Shall we go?"

She all but kisses him on the way out.

"You said you'd let me go yesterday."

"That's what I'm doing today."

"That policeman back there, him, he wouldn't promise me nothing. Said, 'We'll see, we'll see.' What does that even mean? Am I going home or not?"

"Look out the window, tell me what you think."

A river flows on the right side of the car. Yesterday, driving north, it was on her left. Today, she's following their direction, going with the flow.

"Straight home, ma'am. No need for the pyrotechnics—"

"The what?"

"Relax, Penelope," Hammond says, taking a page out of Cinq-Mars' book by using her first name. "We're going right to your front door."

"That was a nice big word you said."

"Pyrotechnics?"

"I like it." She rattles off all the big words she knows. Fortunately for the captain, she doesn't know that many.

They ride on in silence for a time. Then Hammond chooses to review her statement, to find out if the dawn of a new day after a restless night has provoked any changes.

She sticks to her story.

"The list you helped us prepare, Penelope, you're positive you got all the names down?"

"I don't forget my friends."

"That's great. I thank you for that."

She appears to be mulling something. "Why was the dead man on my property? I can't keep his name in my head."

"Reece Zamarlo."

"That's a name?"

"Apparently. You didn't know him?"

"Not with a name like that. What was that word you said?"

"Pyrotechnics."

"I like brouhaha and non sequitur the best. I try to say words like that in a sentence once a week. Do you know brouhaha?"

"I know it, yeah. Can't say I've heard it used much."

"I was scared about a brouhaha in that jailhouse. I don't need guards around me when I sleep. Maybe I snore. Maybe I don't. Do I need them to tell me? They can go F off."

"Pyrotechnics means when something is like fireworks."

"I'm going to use that one. What did he do anyway?"

"Who?" In a way, even though he started it, he's lulled into this easy-going chit-chat. The morning sun rising, the highway lifting and falling under the wheels, the gentle purr of the squad car.

"The guy with the whopper name. The dead one."

"Zamarlo. Do? You mean like for a living? He used to fix things, ma'am. Washers, computers. TVs. Just about anything. Stuff like that."

"I'm going to tweet this. I'm glad I didn't need nothing fixed by him."

"If everything's working in your house, that's a good thing."

"What I mean is—"

"You didn't invite a killer into your home. I understand."

Penelope is quiet then and Hammond sees in the rear-view that she's concentrating, devising a notion. She says at last, "He got killed, that man. You called him a killer. Was he a killer, too? Not only a dead man? Who'd he kill? Not Muriel. She was sitting up. I didn't see no harm done to her."

At least she freely admits today what she failed to keep under wraps yesterday: She was in the dead woman's house. "We think he stole her stuff. That makes the whole deal suspicious."

"What would he want with Muriel's stuff? I guess he was a thief."

"That's a puzzle." Guilty for keeping her overnight, he's generous in speaking to her. "He seems more of a fix-it man than a thief, but we believe he robbed Muriel. A piece in a puzzle."

She's quiet again. He waits for her to resurface.

"I know a fix-it man. I don't mean I *know* him. Heard about one. An old friend of mine, her nephew. He fixed things, too. The aunt didn't have no such strange name. But she raised him. Reece – that might've been his name even, the nephew. She's gone now."

Hammond checks her in his rear-view. "Reece, huh?"

"Went like Muriel did."

He's alert. "What do you mean by that?"

"Sitting up," Penelope explains. "The aunt, she passed away sitting up and watching the boob tube. At least, nobody stole hers."

Hammond presses his foot down farther on the gas. He has something to check out now. He has something to relate to Cinq-Mars. One more name to add to their list, and this one arrives with a connection.

Caffeinated, his quiet time at an end, Émile Cinq-Mars starts up the path away from the riverbank that leads past Penelope's house. He stops where he discovered the body of Reece Zamarlo. The grounds have been thoroughly trampled. He's been party to police procedure superior to this. He's also been involved in much worse.

He walks into the woods the short distance to where the body once lay. Contemplates the scene again, the image of the dead man quite sharp. An itch is lodged in his synapses. He can't find a way to scratch it.

His immense beak warrants a rub, for he has walked through a spiderweb. He needs to get the sticky stuff off his hands and out of his nostrils. A thought skips into his head then, precipitated by the web. Spiders create two types of filament lines. Sticky and smooth. As they form their careful traps or visit their prey, spiders strut only along the smooth threads. Their victims, unable to discern the difference, get stuck on the sticky strands. The web, then, is analogous to general police practise. It's easy to get stuck on the sticky strands and miss the clean, sweet lines that lead to a central trap.

He wants to get to the core of the image in his head from a day ago. Sticky threads are obvious: blood on the carcass, a knife in the upper belly, the handle of the blade turned wrong way around – but what can that mean really? In the fray, the attacker might easily have gripped the knife upside down. As long as the blade pointed outward it did the trick, nothing else mattered. Émile kneels, as if over the body, revisiting the details more precisely. Momentarily, he understands something. And stands.

Voices.

Penelope's, he hears first, then Hammond's. They both would have seen his jalopy of a car in the driveway. A door closes, and a few moments later he detects footsteps on the path. Hammond is coming down the trail to see him. Émile stands still, then calls out when he's not been noticed amid the trees.

Hammond comes to a halt and Émile emerges as if he's a lesser Sasquatch, but related.

"Scared the life out of me. Not saying you took a year off but maybe a minute or two. Thought you were down by the river."

"I was."

"Going over the crime scene? Do you want me to leave? Park on the other side of the highway? Or leave the state entirely?"

"Aren't you the sarcastic prick this morning. Would you like a coffee?" Émile holds up his thermos.

Hammond seems touched. "That's okay, thanks. I'm good."

"What's new?"

"Hey," the trooper says, and he exhales with evident excitement, "I've got something." No word or silent gesture is shared, yet both men turn slightly and commence to mount the incline back toward the highway. "I drove Penelope home."

"Just now?"

"We held her overnight. Get off my case. It was a mistake. Let's not dwell."

"No problem," Cinq-Mars says; then murmurs, "Some mistake."

"Not the end of the world. She was babbling on the ride back. Reece Zamarlo had an aunt. Who died. Sitting up. The name she gave me doesn't match any on our list of suspicious deaths. Tells me, maybe we haven't gone back far enough. There may be others. Maybe this whole deal begins sooner than we thought."

"The headwaters," Cinq-Mars murmurs.

"Sorry?"

"Never mind. Was the aunt an addict?"

"She doesn't know. The death predates Penelope's involvement in the group."

"You're thinking what I'm thinking," Émile ruminates. "If Reece Zamarlo is our killer, did his campaign begin at home?"

"The aunt could've been the first. Or who knows? The list could be endless. If she was a victim, the trail goes farther back."

"It takes us upstream."

"Upstream?"

Émile ignores the question. "Yesterday, I stopped on the trail because I saw where feet had been dragged into the woods."

"Eagle-eyed of you. I'd've walked on by."

"Me, too, normally. Who can guess why I stopped?"

"You saw blood, you said."

"Or not. Maybe by then I saw Zamarlo's white shirt. I can't be sure."

They pause under a natural arbour. "What's new with that?"

"Some minuscule part of my brain wanted me to check out the drag marks. When I went back a step or two, on closer examination they looked less like drag marks than I initially thought. Good thing I spotted the white of his shirt, or he might be stinking up these woods by now."

"I still don't know what you're on about."

"Geoff, he was knifed in the chest. There was blood. But not that much blood. Enough to ruin his white shirt, like I kind of ruined mine this morning. This isn't a bloodstain, by the way, in case you were wondering."

"Ketchup."

"Good observation, Detective. With Zamarlo, he suffered a knife wound, to the upper gut, below the heart, so wouldn't you expect more blood? Blood on the trail, too, not just back in the woods. The actual wound, you know, was larger than the blade. Which means the knife was moved up or down a little."

"More blood that way," Hammond concurs.

"A fountain. Yet less blood on the body than you'd expect."

Hammond gets it. "If he got dragged into the woods after having his gut sliced open, why wasn't there blood on the trail?"

"Exactly. Go about this diplomatically, but can you suggest to Marcus Easton not to assume the cause of death?"

"You think he got dragged in dead."

"Then sliced. A knife wound to the upper gut, why is that even fatal? Or fatal so quickly? Or fatal without heavy blood loss. It also explains the knife being upside down. If Zamarlo's already dead, on the ground, then the killer can hold the knife rightside up, so the body's upside down."

"I can picture it. But how does this affect us? How Zamarlo was killed matters? Does it change anything?"

"For starters, a knife fight means I'm presuming a male killer. A person equal in size and strength to the victim. Some other form of death opens things up. Nothing conclusive but it also answers another question. A knife to the belly, the upper belly in this case, not only does that leave a blood trail and a mess as he bleeds out, but most likely the guy remains conscious for a while in unholy pain. I'm talking about screaming to wake the dead. At least, to wake a lone woman in a house nearby who's not known to sleep soundly."

"Penelope," Hammond mutters.

"Whereas if he was dead by the time he was stabbed, he stays silent. Explains that part of it anyway."

They've emerged from the cover of the woods into Penelope's yard. She's watching from a window. They don't mind. They expect nothing less from her.

"All right," Hammond agrees, and he promises further, "I'll get in touch with Easton," Hammond promises. "I also want to check out this previous death, Zamarlo's aunt. You?"

"I've got two lists to run down," Émile points out. "The quick and the dead: the ones in this drug cult or support group or whatever it is, and the ones who died in mysterious ways. The thing is, Geoff, that's a lot of driving around for one old guy in a prehistoric car. My wife tells me I need to pace myself."

Hammond smiles. "You mentioned that. I'm guessing you want something."

"I don't have the authority. How about your guys bring in the quick – the living – one by one, and I stay in a chair with my feet up, asking questions. Maybe in Twin Mountain? Out of the way. Won't cost the innocent any embarrassing exposure. Don't bother to tell me that a civilian interrogating private citizens in a police setting is not kosher. Ho-hum. I know that already. I'll be gentle. We'll say we're taking a survey, if that helps."

Hammond smiles more broadly. "It helps. One by one, you said. Any order?"

"I want to speak to Bitz, the person Penelope spoke to first after she found Muriel dead. Then I want to talk to the youngest in the bunch. Penelope said her name is Libby. She's on crutches and rides a bike."

"How do you know that?"

"Penelope said so."

"Yeah, I was there, Émile. But you asked her. You said, directly, 'Is she on crutches and does she ride a bike?' How did you know that in advance?"

Cinq-Mars shrugs. "I've seen her around."

"I'll arrange it," Hammond agrees.

When the mighty bellow of the engine on Émile Cinq-Mars' car erupts, Penelope Gagnon lets the curtain on her window fall back.

The voice behind her asks, "They gone?"

"Heading out," Penelope relates. "Good riddance, the buggers."

TWENTY-SIX

Sandra Lowndes breezily strolls through Hanover, New Hampshire. She knows her good mood won't last. Home lingers in the patina of a place, and she's sensing how *home*, for her, is imbued in this town and these people.

Lately, she's come to realize how foreign her life in Quebec has been. She enjoyed being immersed in a language she'd known only in school and loved latching onto a flamboyant culture. She's embarrassed to call the experience exotic, but initially her American perspective had her thinking along those lines. Trucks hijacked at gunpoint to steal maple syrup? Really? How is that not exotic? And her, married to the smartest cop in the land who'd come home with these wild stories.

Over time, what felt foreign to her – obliged to keep her maiden name a prime example – has grown familiar; the exotic evolved into the humdrum. Certain peculiarities, once comic or quaint, succumbed to being frustrating. By contrast, trips to her mom's house in New Hampshire provoked positive memories, even when at odds with past realities. Still, Sandra is not yet wholly convinced that a return to New Hampshire is her best alternative. A tad too cosy perhaps? More nostalgia than progress?

She likes it here. Yet doubts persist.

With her chores accomplished, her next rendezvous requires a 20-minute hiatus. She chooses to kill time in a coffee shop and shares a comment with the barista on the beautiful weather. Retrieving her cup, she scans the room for a table when a voice wavering on the edge of her consciousness penetrates.

"Sandra!"

She twists around and spies Hodges Marsh. At a loss to visually confirm her identity, he awaits a response.

"Hodges! So sorry! I was off in a daze."

He's standing. "I thought I recognized your voice. Will you join me?"

"Thanks, Hodges. Yes." She walks around a balustrade that separates the service bar from the lounge area. An old-school gentleman, he waits for her to be seated before sitting as well. Marsh wears a black pinstriped suit with a maroon tie and a blind man's wrap-around sunglasses. Apart from being grey, his hair resembles a cornfield in the wind.

"What a pleasure," he states, though not with any discernible enthusiasm. "Fortuitous, also. We have business to discuss."

"We do. Such as, would you like to buy my farm?"

He laughs. "No minor thing."

"Not in my eyes, no." She grimaces and regrets referring to eyes.

"I've had reason to be tardy. Matters are up in the air. Zoning laws for one. That's a huge hurdle."

"I take it you're not planning to keep it as a farm."

"Going forward with a multiple-unit project, water supply and sewage are issues that need to be resolved before I put my money down. Also, I never get into a big project alone. I'll need to cobble a partnership together."

"That takes time." In one sense, she's wanted to be in a hurry, to emphasize that a change in her life has gained momentum. Still, she has no pressing need for speed. Delay does not constitute a burden.

"My architect took the liberty of walking the property," he tells her. "His evaluation will include an assessment of its worth for my purposes. Until that report arrives, I will hold my interest in your farm in abeyance. After that, I might make the leap. Or not. I hope you understand."

"Take your time. Learning patience might be good for me. Hodges, were you leaving? Am I keeping you?" She's noticed that the lawyer has no coffee.

"I just arrived."

"Oh. Can I get you a cup?"

"Mine will appear shortly."

"Like magic."

"Presto!" he exclaims as, that quickly, his claim proves true. Table service is not generally available – an exception is made for him. A cappuccino is placed on their table. "People here know my order. I run a tab. Maybe someday I'll walk in and new staff won't know what to make of the blind man just sitting there. So far, it hasn't happened."

"Similar to the restaurant. You have everyone trained, Hodges."

"When young people ask my advice, which is rare, I suggest they acquire an affliction. If they already have one, milk it."

"You're terrible."

"I am! Which reminds me, how's that terrible man of yours? The one who strikes fear into the hearts of criminals? How's his case going?"

Having said too much to her real estate agent on the matter recently, she's not inclined to redouble her mistake. "If you read the papers, Hodges, you know what I know." Suddenly, she's unsure if he can read newspapers and is again infuriated with herself.

"Dreadful business," Marsh laments, undisturbed by her perceived faux pas. "How goes the house hunting?"

"We've not been decisive, Émile and me. We'd like to see the farm sold first."

"Well, you're in good hands. Patricia Shaftesbury is a dear friend. But tell me, that schoolteacher found dead at the Health Club, is Émile investigating that one, too? Surely, she was not on heroin. The paper didn't say."

She need not lie as Émile has not been gregarious regarding the case. "I can't say. Émile left at the crack. We haven't had a minute to talk about it." Looking to change the subject, she adds, "Hodges, are you wearing another of your famous watches?"

The instrument gleams. Even to her untrained eye, she can tell that the visible components are created with precision and artistry. He shows off his wrist. "The Audemars Piguet today. From the Jules Audemars collection."

"Lovely."

"Thank you. This one's my favourite."

"According to your wife, your favourite is always the one you're wearing."

He leans forward to continue whispering. "Here's a secret. This one really is my favourite."

She whispers back. "Do you not feel vulnerable? Wearing something so valuable?"

Straightening, he speaks in a normal voice again. "Sandra, I was born vulnerable. But the day I first put on a valuable watch and walked out in public, I felt like a young girl wearing her first training bra."

She neither understands, nor is inclined to appreciate, the analogy. "How so?"

"I realized that I was wearing a personal emblem. Something that was both a great and a private secret. As it is, I can't actually *see* people looking at me, but I can *feel* them. Who's the blind kid? Then, who's the blind student? Then, who's the blind guy in the courtroom? I now have something for others to take note of which has nothing to do with my dark glasses or, when I use it, my white cane. I don't show off the watch, but I'm aware of it on my wrist. A voice inside me – agreed, not a pleasant one – says to those who stare because I'm blind, 'Go ahead. But notice, I'm wearing an object of beauty you can't afford.' Me at my worst, of course. Bitter to be blind. But there you have it."

In a way, she's impressed, although she agrees his character is found lacking. "I get it. Some women bedeck themselves with jewellery. Similar, no?"

"Some men drape a hot young bimbo over a forearm. Maybe one on each arm. I believe a wristwatch has more charm."

She laughs. She wants him to hear her pleasure in his remark, aware that her smile goes undetected. "Some men have both, Hodges. A bimbo on their right sleeve, an exclusive watch on their left wrist."

"Oh, gross." Hodges Marsh makes a face. "I'm sure those men wear gaudy appliances, the size of a Frisbee, nothing elegant."

They're both laughing, and Sandra concurs.

After a spell devoted to their coffees, she says, "Émile may be looking for a friend in this neck of the woods, Hodges. If we move here."

"I did invite the two of you to dinner."

"Thanks. He admires you. He enjoys your company, I can tell."

"I heard – the grapevine – that your husband likes to explore esoteric tangents. That made me think he might be a friend I'd enjoy, conversation being my primary entertainment. By the way, I agree with him."

"His train of thought on black holes can be… serendipitous."

He cracks a smile. "I meant about heroin."

"That's not what you said at dinner."

"My wife gets into a panic about the situation. I try to downplay the reports."

"I see." She doesn't. "Hodges, lovely meeting you here, but I'm sorry, I must be off. An appointment."

She is cross with herself departing the coffee shop so abruptly. She's not in that big a rush. The talk has reminded her that Émile is chasing down another case that has galvanized a community's interest, and that makes her wonder if they haven't fallen into familiar patterns. He's off in a world of blood and savagery while she's preoccupied with transactions. Is this the path their relationship follows, no matter where they live, even when they abandon their jobs and attempt to conduct themselves differently?

The next meeting on her agenda is with Patricia Shaftesbury. Today she learned that Marsh and Patricia are friends. Which prompts the question: Has that friendship compromised Patricia's effort to sell the farm? Has the agent delayed getting on with it to accommodate the lawyer, even discouraged other buyers to give him extra time? Perhaps to get her to lower her price? She's apprehensive because when she and Patricia agreed to meet today, the agent insisted on hearing Sandra's schedule before setting a time. She then recommended the coffee shop as a place for Sandra to kill a half hour.

Now she wonders. Is Émile's suspicious nature rubbing off on her?

A few days ago Sandra met the schoolteacher who was found dead last night. Émile sheltered her from his suspicions at the time, given the way he went back to talk to her in the house, then visited the en suite when he could have used the vanity by the front door. He was up to something, she knew, which had dropped her into a pensive mood. Meeting Patricia Shaftesbury outside the agent's office, she tumbles into a similar blue funk. As though things are afoot that she'd rather avoid. Matters investigated by her husband are so often dire.

Another matter corrodes her mood. She is all but convinced that when she entered the coffee shop, a figure was standing on the periphery of her vision on the other side of a balustrade. That figure proved to be Hodges Marsh. Why was he already standing there, almost as if waiting for her, and why wait to call her name until she was served her coffee?

He could not have known she was coming. Except that Patricia suggested she kill time there. The coffee shop is a good hike from the lawyer's office, he passed other cafés – yet he goes regularly, which refutes her own argument. So why is she thinking this way when she precisely forbade her husband to run the man down, given his inclination to befriend him?

Her summation is not helpful. For some reason, his interest in luxurious timepieces provokes her distrust, a suspiciousness that now falls onto the brow of Patricia Shaftesbury. Does this come from years living with a detective who has made himself successful by peeling away the lies, the deceit, and the masks of humanity? Or, and this new thought suddenly seems both insidious and real – is she trolling for an excuse?

Is this her way to stop herself from moving back to her hometown, by dissing potential friends?

Suddenly, Sandra understands the source of her quick temper with Marsh, why she bolted so quickly. His wife, he said, was upset by the heroin epidemic in the state. At first, she was mad at him for making her sound feeble, or mildly neurotic, and that still holds. But beyond that, this is her home, too. Her *old* home. She, too, is upset that New Hampshire is mired in a drug crisis the likes of which was unimaginable in an earlier era. She has to consider the ramifications of the state's crisis and take stock of what her husband is involved in. This virulent epidemic on her doorstep is scaring her off. And she's not feeble. She's not neurotic. She's scared, and angry, and worried, with good reason.

TWENTY-SEVEN

The boy is nine, the girl seven.

They appear to be in awe of his height.

The pair keep craning their necks, their mouths agape.

Cinq-Mars takes the kids outside. They're both terrors but he won't stoop to bribery. He leads them to the rear of Troop F where the broad, grassy yard slopes to a woodlot. A picnic table is set up for troopers there to enjoy lunch and smoke while seated. Cinq-Mars stares down his eagle's beak without a stitch of compromise, and the kids look up. The little girl might be trembling.

For once, they are both still.

"Play here," he tells them. "A policeman will be out to watch over you. Don't skin your knees. If you skin your knees, you'll be arrested. If you fall over, don't cry. If you cry, you'll be arrested. Don't fight. What happens if you fight?"

The little girl says, "We'll get arrested."

"You can scream. You can yell. You can have fun. You can do whatever you want. What you can't do is come back inside. After I talk to your mother, she'll come back outside to get you. Understood?"

The little girl nods. The sullen boy won't argue with him, either.

"All right then. Have a good time. The policeman will bring you water when you need it. Unless you're good. If you're good, he'll bring you a pop. They have Dr Pepper here. Or Mountain Dew. Or both. I'll see you later."

He doesn't count the pop as bribery. More like a successful one-sided negotiation. Cinq-Mars shunts back inside and orders a trooper out, as if he has that authority. The officer complies, willingly enough.

He enters the cellblock where the woman known as Bitz is sitting at a small table with her hands folded and her head down. He takes her to be in her 40s. They're not using an interrogation room because this isn't a kosher interview and Hammond doesn't want his people grumbling about that too much. Waiting for him, the Bitz woman looks a trifle worn but also as though she brooks no nonsense. She won't look at him. They're alone, the cells alongside them vacant.

Cinq-Mars sits opposite her. He assures her that her kids are being looked after. "They won't be getting into mischief."

"That'll be a first."

"An officer of the law is keeping an eye out."

"Let's hope he doesn't make it a habit."

First impressions: she's quick, she's bright. She's afraid. "You're called Bitz. Is that short for something?"

"You don't know my name?"

"I'm checking to see if you do. Think of it as a test. Do you know why I ask?"

She shrugs.

"Gives you a chance to answer a question honestly. To confirm that you have the capability. Do you?"

He's guessing that she's a woman of some experience, yet she doesn't come across as particularly cynical or downtrodden.

"My name is Betsy Kincaid. I've gone by Bitz since birth. Should've been on my birth certificate, really. Don't know what my parents were thinking."

"How difficult do you intend to be?" Cinq-Mars asks.

"I don't know why I'm here," she tells him. "You're the police. I intend to be cooperative. I teach my children to honour the police."

"Not quite," Cinq-Mars says, and lets her confusion sit for a couple of beats. Then explains, "I'm not the police. Used to be. I only work with them now. I need to make that distinction."

She's puzzled by the discussion. Cinq-Mars likes that. Always a part of his kitbag, to keep the person being interviewed modestly bewildered. He likes to come at the individual from various angles simultaneously so that the suspect or the witness never knows when, where, or how to erect a barrier.

"Your kids are fine," he assures her.

"I wish people would stop talking about my kids," she says.

"Just letting you know."

"I'm being cooperative. I'm a cooperative person."

"Good. Don't worry about your kids, that's all I'm trying to get at. Who else talks about your kids?"

She won't answer that one. "What do you want to ask me?"

"I don't want to ask you anything. I want you to tell me about the group."

He sits back to examine her reaction. She looks to strike back but thinks better of it, then her gaze travels around the room, to the barred cells, the bare table, and finally into Cinq-Mars' eyes.

"Thank you," he says.

"For what?" She holds her stare. An inner resilience there.

"For not asking, *what group?* You were tempted to say that, but you didn't. So thanks. Like a poker hand. Sometimes you want to bluff by playing it slow, sometimes by being real quick. The only thing you can't do is change your mind. You're beaten if you do. So here's the thing, Bitz. Tell me about the group and I'll give you a free pass on whatever you say about yourself. Unless you killed somebody. Then I revoke that free pass. If you're going to tell me that you're a drug addict or something of that nature, just as an example, I'll forget about it as long as I have a reasonable assumption that I'm hearing the truth. Remember, I can do that, I can forget about the particulars because I'm not the police. That's why we're in here without a trooper present. I can forget about whatever you tell me the moment you say it. What I do with what you say is my business, but it doesn't include the incarceration of a single mother of two kids. One thing more. They're playing outside, your kids. You can join them. When, depends on you. One hundred per cent. Now, talk about the group."

The way her shoulders shift tells him she's willing to confide.

"Some of us, we help one another out. With our mutual problems. Give each other some comfort. To stay strong. We share a few laughs."

"What sort of problems?"

"Our injuries. Our pain. Stuff like that."

"Your addiction to heroin, you mean."

She takes a deeper breath.

To confirm that he has already heard the pertinent details, he says, "You help your friends out as drug addicts."

The designation may not sit well with her, but she concedes. "Yeah. If you want. As drug addicts."

"Nothing to do with what I want. What would you call it?"

"Look, we don't exactly fit the profile. We don't belong to some street gang. We're not down and out, we're not defeated. We try to get on with our lives. Do our jobs. Raise kids. The ones in the group who are old, they tend to their gardens or sit on a porch in a rocker. You say drug addict, we say…"

She stops in mid-explanation, seems to lose her concentration.

"What do you say?"

Her shrug does not reflect indifference, rather resignation, along with a dollop of denial. "We say … whatever. When we call ourselves junkies it sounds silly. A kind of joke among us. Reflects our situation."

Despite her expression of lassitude, Bitz Kincaid is willing to talk, perhaps motivated by a need to do so.

"Tell me how you guys came together. How the group got underway."

"Before my time," she contends, yet she's willing to open up. "Same way we expanded later on I imagine. The first few met in rehab. Not drug rehab. Outpatient rehabilitation. For our war wounds."

"War wounds?"

"Turn of phrase. Everything from car crashes to bad falls. Injuries to just plain old arthritis."

"What was yours?"

This one time, she's not inclined to answer.

"Bitz?" Cinq-Mars asks. "May I call you that? Tell me about yours."

A deep breath. Looking away. Then back at him. "Mine were actual war wounds."

"Meaning?"

"I was a soldier. Iraq. I was standing a long way from the bomb in the marketplace when it went off – by a long way I mean more than 30 yards – but it was loaded with nails and screws and pellets. I caught a shitload. Liver, one kidney, both lungs, my pelvis, my thighs. An internal mess. Don't let my sunny disposition fool you. The outside is only for show. Internally? That's why I'm a cockroach today."

"Cockroach."

She smiles. Caught. "It's what we call ourselves in our group."

"You're not in the army now?"

"Medical discharge. A few ribbons to go with that. Were you military?"

"I'm a natural-born civilian. But a cop almost from the get-go. Retired."

"Same difference."

"In terms of the line of fire, once in a blue moon. In terms of incendiary devices, not the same at all. I salute you."

"Yeah. Thanks. Salutes and ribbons. Add a couple of bucks to that and I can buy a cup of coffee."

"Where?"

"Excuse me?"

"Where can you buy a cup of coffee these days for two bucks?"

She permits a corner of her lips to bend.

"Would you like one, by the way? I can order a mug for each of us. The joe's not bad here. They have a fancy brewing machine. Won't cost a dime."

"Sure. Thanks."

"Just coffee or does it require a fancy name?"

"I'm good with mud. Load it up."

"Hang on a sec." At the door he puts in the request to an officer, then closes it again and returns to his chair. "Okay, so a few people got together – was it only women in the beginning? I only see women now. But there's been men."

The question doesn't interest her. "Don't know."

"You're not the group's historian."

"We don't take notes."

Cinq-Mars swipes a palm down his right cheek and concludes the gesture by circling his thumb and forefinger over his chin three times.

"How do you pay for your habit? Support your kids?"

"Not easy. Mostly a struggle."

"I believe you."

"Heroin's not that expensive."

"So I hear. Yet it takes a toll. Affects a person's working life. Their will. Heroin rearranges a person's priorities, no?"

She opens up her palms for some reason and places both face-up on the table. "The father of my first child, he was dying when we had sex. I didn't know he was dying, although he was hurt. He had to stay on his back, me on top, exciting at the time, but ... he died. Not in the act. Later. We were down the hall in the same hospital, gave each other some comfort. A real sweet boy. He'd already passed before Leon was four months in my womb. Daddy number two was a VA administrator, stateside, married, maybe he took advantage of my emotional and physical duress. A shrink said that, but I place no blame. I played my part. I get what we call child support from him but if you want to call it hush money, feel free. Either way, I take it. And then I'm a nurse."

"You're a nurse."

"You doubt that? I was a nurse in the military. I'm part-time now. Private practise. Mostly I run stress tests and take blood pressure. Minor triage. Jab folks during flu season. No hardship. All I'm cut out for, with the kids and everything."

"And everything."

"Being a cockroach and that."

"So you're good with needles. On the job and off."

Her palms come up in the air. "You want to say I helped out with that, lent my expertise, go ahead. Nothing wrong with helping your friends stay alive."

"Nothing," Cinq-Mars concurs, then goes back to the beginnings of the group. "The injured," he details, "get friendly at an outpatient clinic. Then one among them is feeling chipper. She reveals to desperate friends that she found a drug that gets rid of the pain and takes the edge right off. Am I close?"

"Pretty much bang on. I didn't know anybody knew about us."

"Word is making the rounds," Cinq-Mars tells her.

"Sorry to hear."

"So," Cinq-Mars leads her, "you help people out."

She perks up. As if, given that the secret is finally known, she's glad to talk about the group. A point of pride. "Like I said, we're not some street gang. We didn't know much. How to score, how to shoot up. What words to use. The basics. That leads us into what's not basic. How to pool our resources. Get a better deal. Good for everybody, us druggies and our connection, both. We help people keep their spirits up, that's way important."

Connection, the word she used. In the singular.

"You're like a union. Lobbying for member discounts."

"Something like that."

"Speaking of your connection."

"That's what it comes down to, right? This talk."

"Curious to know."

"One thing you learn in boot camp. You probably heard it at the police academy, too."

"What's that?"

"Whatever you do, don't shoot yourself in the foot."

"With us guys it was, don't shoot your balls off today or you'll probably regret it tonight. Maybe you heard it said differently."

A glimmer of a smile again. They'd get along in different circumstances. If he'd been a solider or she a cop, they'd have partnered well. Circumstances that are not to be.

"In other words," Cinq-Mars leads her along again.

"In other words, why would I give you the name of my connection if it means cutting myself off from my connection? Or. You know. Worse."

"Another dealer will take up the slack. Trust me on that one."

"Who wants to play that game? The devil you know. Trust me on that."

He takes her meaning. She has reason to be cautious. That's to be expected. He's sympathetic, although he's not going to let it show.

"Tell me about Reece Zamarlo, Bitz. He can't bite back. He's the dead man on Penelope Gagnon's property. I'm assuming you know that."

"I heard, yeah. I didn't approve of the man. I wouldn't call him a dealer, if that's what you're thinking. More like a delivery boy."

She suddenly goes quiet. "What else?" Cinq-Mars prods.

"He had a van."

"What else?"

"He fixed things."

"Keep going. What else?"

"Why? He was no one."

"What else?"

"His old aunt was one of us."

"She was in the group."

"Founding member. Maybe – like you said, I'm not the historian – but could be that she was the first to try heroin to cure what ails you."

"You don't think Zamarlo helped her along with that?"

She'd never thought about it, that's evident in her expression.

"Where were you early yesterday morning, Bitz?"

"Home. With my kids. Ask them."

"I will."

"Please don't. You'll scare the heck out of them. Leon acts like a bully. He is a bully. But really, he's a frightened little boy. I love my little boy Leon."

"Where were you before they woke up?"

"No kids of your own? I was in bed. Sleeping."

"She died like Muriel did, you know." Keep them off guard. Keep them guessing. Wary on different flanks. The time has come to alter both the tempo and the stakes.

"Who did?"

"Reece Zamarlo's aunt. She died sitting up. Was she your friend?"

"Zamarlo's aunt?"

"Muriel Cuthbert. She was in the group."

"Yeah, she was my friend."

"What do you know about her elephant?"

"I'm sorry?"

"That's not relevant to you?"

"Sorry?"

"Answer this question, please. What did Zamarlo do for the group?"

She throws up her hands a moment. "He was a delivery man. What elephant? What question?"

"He delivered drugs. You don't call that a connection?"

"He had a van. He fixed things. He could go places. Anybody looking would think he was inside fixing a sewing machine or some damned thing. He was useful that way. He delivered. That's it. That's all. Like FedEx."

"You want to make cracks? Really? This is what I want. Where were you yesterday morning when Reece Zamarlo was having his belly sliced open?"

"Oh fuck off. I told you that already."

"Don't get hostile."

"Don't *you* get hostile."

"Tell me the name of your connection then."

"Nope. Never. I have kids. Kids need their mother. You don't believe me, look outside."

"You can't be that great a mom."

"Oh, thanks for that. And yes, I know what you mean."

"You know who's boss. Not you. Not even your kids."

"You mean heroin. Cute. You don't know what I've been through."

"Bingo. We agree. On everything. Was Reece a junkie, too?"

"Don't think so."

"Is that what you called him – Reece?"

"Sometimes."

"Other times?"

"Zamarlo."

"Never Mister? Or Boss?"

She coughs up a sort of laugh. "Never."

"Tell me about Penelope."

"Why? What do you want to know?"

"She's in the group."

"So?"

"Tell me about her."

"She's not really in the group."

"You're contradicting yourself."

"She's not an addict like us. She's in the group because she's inquisitive. Better to have a person like that close to you, in this case close to

Muriel's house, too. Let her come in the front door instead of peering through the windows. She's no druggie."

"Do you hold that against her?"

"No. Of course not."

"Sounds like you do. Is she in the group, or isn't she?"

"I guess she's in. Look. She was Muriel's nosy neighbour. Muriel's place was where we met. Perfect except for the neighbour. So Pen got invited to come along, join in. And then, we started using her house, too."

"What did she do for the group?"

"Nothing. Except for meeting at her place."

"Nothing."

"Not that I'm aware."

"So there could have been something."

Bitz shrugs. He doesn't feel that she is holding back on that particular question. Yet she's deciphering as she goes along what knowledge she will impart and what she won't. He doesn't want her to be comfortable.

"Do you know why I'm asking?"

"About the group?"

"About whether or not you killed Reece Zamarlo."

"You weren't asking me that. I didn't! God!"

"I was, actually. You have no alibi."

"Neither does the rest of the sleeping world."

"Oldest lame excuse in the world. You were in bed. Asleep. Who's going to believe that? I don't believe it, just so you know. Don't take it personally. I never believe people are in bed asleep when something big happens. That's my nature. When do you shoot up?"

"Can I go now?"

"You want to go?"

"I never wanted to stay."

"That's not true. You actually want to talk about the group. You're proud of your group, maybe for good reason. Do you know who killed Muriel?"

"So it's true? It was murder?"

"You tell me."

"I can't. I know nothing about it."

"Do you know who killed Reece Zamarlo's aunt?"

"Cancer, I thought."

"Do you know who is systematically killing members of your group? Cara Drost. Wayne Samuels. Clara Lightwood. Do you think you're next, Bitz?"

"Are you trying to scare me? What do you mean killed? Murdered?"

"Murdered. You were a soldier."

"A nurse."

"A military nurse. I presume that means you don't scare so easily."

"It doesn't mean any such thing. Can I go now?"

"No."

"No?"

"No. Do you feel that your life is in peril?"

A knock on the door announces an officer with the coffee. Cinq-Mars keeps staring at Bitz as the trooper comes in and puts the coffees down with some sugar packets, a few creamers, and two crappy tin spoons. Then he leaves and shuts the door behind him.

Bitz drops a sugar and two creamers into her coffee and stirs with a spoon. Cinq-Mars ignores his. He'll take it black.

"When can I go?"

"Soon. Tell me about Libby."

"Libby St. Croix?"

"Tell me, did you ever go fishing with Muriel?"

"Fishing? What about Libby?"

"What was that like? Fishing with her?"

"It was all right. I had fun."

"Yeah? She had more than one rod and reel. She must've brought friends along from time to time. Other friends along or just you?"

"I don't know."

"Sure you do. Did you go early in the morning often?"

"Will you fuck off or what? I wasn't there yesterday."

"Was I asking that? Just generally, do you go early? I was down there this morning myself. Thinking about fishing that stream. Were you there yesterday? Don't answer by swearing at me."

She answers with silence.

"Tell me about Libby."

This time, Émile is the one to gesture with his hands, opening them wide above the table as he sits back, indicating that he is giving her time and space for this part of their discussion.

She asks a question first. She seems distressed. "Is there something you want to tell me about Libby? Do you know something?"

"No," Cinq-Mars answers. "Do you?"

"No. Well. Maybe."

"What can you tell me about her? She's in your group."

Bitz takes her time. Formulating. "Libby. Poor kid. She's special. Some cool young women, and I count her as a woman even though she's 17, a child, but some cool young women like to think they run with the wolves. Whatever that means. They say that. That's what they want to do and expect to do. Libby's not exactly like them. She runs with wolf-angels in my opinion. Muriel, since you want to know, took her fishing."

She waits to see what he'll make of all that. He responds: "Poetic. Romantic even. Wolf-angels. Why put it that way?"

"I doubt if I can explain it."

"Try. You said it."

"Find out for yourself. That might be the only way."

Perhaps for the first time they're neither jousting nor even communicating. Bitz has issued a challenge but Cinq-Mars feels no animosity behind her edict.

"I will," he assures her. Then he says, "I could tell you that we can protect you, keep you from harm, put a brick wall around your life, but

I don't suppose that that's actually true. I doubt you'd believe me anyway."

"You got that straight. I appreciate the honesty."

"What if we brought him in, your connection, what if we nab him without any assistance from you? Once we have him, will you help us out then?"

She only takes a beat to think about it. "Nope. He can be replaced. Then where would we be? Any of us. This isn't only about me. We're all in it together."

"He can be replaced," Cinq-Mars repeats. "So someone's upstream."

"Upstream?"

"Did you know this? The Connecticut River begins as a beaver dam. Your situation, same as the river. There's headwaters, then the river flows, then it empties downstream. I'm pointing out to you, there's someone upstream who will do the replacing if your connection needs to be replaced."

"Could be up," she says, "could be down. *H* moves upstream, I know that much. From the south, north. That's only natural."

"How so?"

"Out of the cities."

"Same in my country. The cities are south. Okay. I understand that."

"This isn't your country?"

"It might become my country. About your connection."

"Bread gets buttered. I'm not giving up my group. My connection neither."

"Do you feel that your life is in peril?"

"I'm trying to get through this talk, okay? Keep my head above water here. The short answer is no, I don't think I'm in peril. On the other hand, the world's a goddamn perilous place, isn't it?"

"Sometimes it is."

"A fucking war zone. I should know. Can I go now or what?"

"Sure. Why not? Thanks for coming in."

"I had a choice?"

"Let's say you did, Bitz. You've been cooperative. For your own security, we'll keep that to ourselves. My advice, tell no one about this talk."

"That suits you how?"

She's quick. She's bright. "It suits you, Bitz. That's what I'm saying."

As Émile rises from an uncomfortable chair his lower back complains. He secretly stretches trying not to make a show of it, then sees that Bitz Kincaid has remained seated.

"What?" he asks her.

She looks glued in place. "About Libby."

"Libby," Cinq-Mars encourages her. "Muriel took her fishing."

"The thing is."

"Go on."

"She's missing. I usually know where she is. Right now I don't."

"Since when?"

"Since yesterday. Doesn't answer her phone, her texts, and her folks – I rarely phone them – they say she didn't sleep in her room last night."

"Does that happen often?"

"Not too much."

"You think she's in danger."

Finally, Bitz stands. She looks up at the tall man.

"No guarantees. If you find Libby, who's with her might interest you."

Her connection.

"I'll keep an eye out. Shall we see if your kids have been arrested?"

"If they have, I can pretty much guarantee that you won't be letting them out anytime soon. Not for good behaviour, anyways."

They both smile. A reflex that quickly dissipates. They're in a war zone. Bitz knows that for a fact. Cinq-Mars is beginning to have an inkling.

TWENTY-EIGHT

Cherry Garcia from Vermont. Maple walnut from a Boston dairy. Both tubs are half-consumed. He keeps the cherry out, returns the other to the freezer drawer, and digs in.

Eating ice cream has a double effect. Victims worry while he relaxes.

One guy went berserk. Just because he ate ice cream.

Joris Pul had ambitions once. These days, if he keeps himself out of prison, he's satisfied. He was induced to come to New Hampshire from the wilds of New Jersey with a stay-out-of-jail card. Back home, same shit crowd, same lame screw-ups, the predictable betrayals, and lickety-split you're heading to your favourite Federal Correctional Institution, Ray Brook or Otisville in New York, or booked in-state so your family can visit – Fort Dix a couple of times, Fairton another. A deeper crime and you're off to Allenwood, Pennsylvania, where he did a stretch and hated it. In any lifetime of misery, nobody needs Allenwood.

Out of New Jersey into the peaceable kingdom of New Hampshire. Far less chance of incarceration. No dumbass friends to roll you over. A free get-out-of-jail card in your hip pocket thanks to people you know.

He gets bored. As a young punk he could not have hacked the dull part of his job now. Not enough action. Even now he misses the strip joints and the bar life. Older, he has a lady at home who knows not to ask, and a teen daughter who only wants a pony and when she gets one, a puppy instead. Two grown horses and three full-grown dogs later she's still asking, but he's learned his lesson. He has enough four-leggeds to support in his life.

No jail time since landing in the north, and he expects none. Which keeps things loose. His hands are clean, and his head stays low. Lately, though, stuff's been happening. Peculiar, people popping off that way.

He never had much contact with Reece Zamarlo but knew what he was doing. The big questions: Why do it? Then why get stabbed? Who did that?

These days, he can do his job as a thug without inflicting unnecessary carnage. Experience counts that way. Be creative, do the unexpected. Introduce a mark to his own natural fear that runs through his veins, reacquaint him with his own natural fright. Same with a woman. The rest is easy. A spoonful of Cherry Garcia. Usually no blood, at least not on him, usually no weaponry. All goes well.

Yeah. He likes the life.

He slows down on the ice cream. It gives him a thought. Joris Pul suddenly kicks himself in the nuts – the mental image he summons – for not thinking of this sooner. He opens the fridge door and does a quick survey of the contents. Then over to the pantry where he looks inside. This woman has one hell of a diet. Not the news of the day that she looks a wreck. Ice cream isn't cheap though and neither are cookies. Or chips. There's a steak in the fridge's meat drawer that costs 17 bucks and could feed a foursome, real food, but there's also six bags of pretzels in the pantry – six! – that altogether cost more. Two family-sized bags of chips. More than a dozen big bottles of various sodas. Penelope Gagnon is an untidy mess. She spends her loot on junk food and goes through it fast. She possesses all that anyone needs and owns her own home close to a riverbank. He assumes she owns the land down to the shore. How? She doesn't work. Who would hire her? She's too young to be retired. Too well-off to be on welfare. Everything about her tells him she's lazy and a layabout, so how does she stay afloat in this world?

Pul takes out the second bucket of ice cream, picks out another spoon, and carries both tubs into the living room. They're half-full. He drops the maple walnut onto the coffee table at Penelope's knees, and commands: "Knock yourself out."

"I don't want any right now." She's been ornery for an hour.

"You want to be force-fed? You want to be licking ice cream through a tube?"

"What does that even mean?" This one goes frantic fast.

"Joris, leave her alone," Libby interjects. She's at the opposite end of the sofa from Penelope, leaning back with her legs straight out and her feet resting on the coffee table. She's put her knee braces on over her jeans. She's not supposed to, but sometimes she can't stand them right on her skin. Her feet are bare, the heels and big toes smudged by dust.

Pul glares at her, and she turns away. Glum as shit. Poor Penelope picks up the bucket and the spoon and starts in on her ice cream.

"Eat it all," he says. "That's no hardship, see." He digs into his own tub. After a minute he says, "Maple walnut sucks."

"I like it," Penelope contends.

"You're an idiot."

Her sniffles start again.

"Stop that. Am I slapping your face right now? Believe me, I'm tempted. Ice cream is feel-good food. See, I'm eating mine, I'm feeling better. When you feel better, we'll talk. You will tell me everything you said to that cop, everything he said to you."

"I told you already!" she complains.

"Shut up and eat your ice cream first. I'll eat mine."

Nobody offers Libby any. She looks at the two of them, as though she can't believe where she is or what's going on. Once Penelope gets into the ice cream she keeps going and actually manages to finish her container first, although Joris Pul is not far behind.

"Good. Now, don't you feel better?"

"Pretty tasty," Penelope says.

"If you say so." Pul settles back into what he calls the piss-coloured armchair and says to the frightened woman, "Where'd you get the money, honey?"

"What money? I have no money."

"To buy the ice cream."

"What do you mean? It doesn't cost that much."

"Where'd you get the money to buy this house? How do you pay your bills? Who pays the electricity? How do you heat in winter? I don't see you out chopping firewood, know what I mean? Where'd you get that mobile phone you do your tweeting on? I'm asking, what scam do you got going?"

"Nothing to tell." Penelope's both timid and adamant, but Libby seems attentive, as though she's interested in the answer or already knows it. She seems to grasp what's behind the question, where he's going with this.

"I have a big fist," Joris Pul points out to Penelope. "Check out my rings. Not so fancy. But they're steel, see. I can crack a jawbone. Crush a cheek."

"Come on, Pul."

"Shut up, Libby." Only after he snarls at her does he look her way, then asks, "Do *you* know?"

Libby, in turn, shoots a glance across at Penelope. She says to Pul, "Long story."

"Get started. I don't got all day myself."

Penelope answers first. "I come from a big French-Canadian family." Pride in her voice.

"We all descend from the apes. Do I care?"

"She had a grandmother," Libby contributes.

"Who left her a stack of cash?"

"Not exactly," Libby replies. "This grandmother had a bunch of grandkids. She set up a trust fund for their education."

"This one?" Joris Pul juts his thumb to indicate Penelope. "Educated?"

"Not exactly." ·

"Everything is not exactly with you."

"Let me explain."

"I'm letting."

Libby takes a breath. Penelope is gazing at her now, waiting to hear her own story being told as though she's unaware of the outcome.

"Grandma leaves a trust fund to be divided up among sixteen grand-kids. They each receive a share, and here's the catch: they collect the money for as long as they're still in school. Penelope's the youngest, and surprise-surprise, maybe the smartest."

"This one?" Pul indicates her again.

"Yeah, even though the other ones have degrees. Her siblings and cousins graduate, and every time they do the ones who are still in school get a larger share of the pie. Someone gets a degree, takes a job, the money that used to be theirs now gets divided among the ones still in school. So, Penelope's turn comes up to enroll in university, and, well, nobody thought that was such a good idea. An exception was made. At the time, nobody thought twice about it because it didn't contradict grandma's will. A judge decided, Penelope can attend a training school instead. School after high school is still school, which was the basic idea. Good enough to receive her share. What was your first training school, Pen?"

"Baking class."

"You're a baker?" Pul asks. He sounds incredulous, although a glance at her waistline alters his viewpoint. He finds it hard to believe that she ever put in bakers' hours.

Libby shakes her head. "You're not getting this, Joris. She never grad-uated. But she found another school to attend later on, and then another, and another, until she was the only one of the grandchildren left in class. At that point, instead of getting one-sixteenth of the funds as the kids originally received, she's now collecting sixteen-sixteenths. She can't afford to ever leave school. Grandma's will didn't conceive of that contingency. Once everybody graduated, the trust fund money was supposed to go to charity. Instead, Penelope stays in school forever. The smart one. She's the charity."

He studies her. She's beaming. "What school you in now?"

"I'm in Muriel Cuthbert's hairdressing class."

Joris Pul stares back at her a while. He states the obvious. "The dead woman had a school?"

"One student," Libby explains. "Not that there were any classes. She only has to be enrolled to collect her trust fund cheques. From what I understand that fund has grown over time. It'll see her into the grave."

Pul keeps staring. Finally, he concludes, "You wouldn't know it to look at you. You're a smart cookie."

Penelope smiles back, delighted by the compliment.

"You need to find a new school. Your teach is dead."

"Funny you should mention it," Libby says. "I'm starting one. Rock-climbing."

Penelope's heard that one before and still finds it funny.

Pul is satisfied. He got to the bottom of her financial situation and he's happy with the result. She can afford what he has in mind. "You know what's next. The two of you. I'm going out on the porch. See, this has nothing to do with me, what you two get up to. I'm taking a bag of pretzels outside. Have a beer. Let me know, Libs, when she's done. Hang on a second."

The two women watch him as he goes over to his briefcase by the door. He looks like a man about to remove a contract to sign, to solidify a deal. Instead, he pulls out a mousetrap, inserts a square of cheese. He gently puts the mousetrap down on the coffee table between the women and sets it.

"What's that for?" Penelope asks.

"Incentive," Joris Pul explains. He heads out to the porch.

"What's that for?" Penelope asks Libby this time.

"Your tongue."

"What?"

"Or mine."

"Why?"

"To make sure we both understand. We have to do this, Pen."

"Do we?"

"Muriel can't keep you in the group."

"I know that but—"

"Time to join on your own."

"You explained it."

"I have to bring someone in. If I don't, I get the mousetrap on my tongue." She sticks out her tongue to show the damage that's been slow to heal.

Penelope is breathless. Frightened now.

"I don't want to bring him a kid like me. This way, he gets you. You're interested anyway, right?"

"Muriel wouldn't let me. She said no."

"I can't say no. If I say no I get the mousetrap. Or you do. Anyway, you're interested, right? All on your own, without me?"

A fatal shrug. "What's the brouhaha all about?"

"You'll find out. This way, you're in the group legitimately. You stay in the group for real. Everyone will accept you now. That's fair. Saves me from the mousetrap. Probably saves you, too."

"My God."

"We'll look after you, Pen. All of us will. In the group." She whispers, "This isn't forever. Real short term. Remember. I have a plan."

"I know."

"You're ready?"

"To be a junkie?" Penelope asks.

"Don't say it like that. It sounds silly when you do."

"I'll be a cockroach like you."

Libby turns her face away. She knows that Penelope has no idea. She's lied to her. She has no interest in addicting Penelope Gagnon to heroin, as Joris Pul is insisting she do. She's lied to her to make it seem that this is the next logical step in her life, when it's not, and she's coddled her enough to coax Penelope to agree. She hasn't told her that she has another plan, that she really won't let her become a junkie, except she will let her get high once. Libby has no choice if she wants to ease her friend's suffering, moderate the woman's initiation into a life of hell.

She has a plan. That's no lie.

Libby has not answered Penelope's last query, but the woman says, "All right, Libby. I don't want him to hurt you. I'll be in the group for real like everybody else."

That sweetness, that naïveté, could almost break her heart, Libby thinks, if she still had a heart worth breaking. She's not sure she does. Pul won't let her have her own hit of smack if she doesn't get Penelope high first. That's the priority at the moment.

When Joris Pul comes back into the house after time has passed he finds Penelope Gagnon flaked out on the sofa, her head lolling slowly from side to side. Her facial muscles relax in a way that contorts her appearance. She's grotesque. Nobody could fake that look. Pul picks up the mousetrap. Libby scowls at him.

"Don't give me your fucking attitude, kid. You want your hit or not?"

Her deportment shifts. She's holding herself with her arms clasped and the look she gives him expresses compliance. She'll need the hit soon. She gave herself a bite off Penelope's hit, to tide her over when Pul wasn't looking, but she's going to need a full load soon. Seeing Penelope getting off for the first time burst a dam of memories. She's always chasing those memories herself. She hates it but chases them anyway. The day she was transformed from pain to relief, from dejection to blissful flight, she became like a bird. She's not flown all the way home since.

"Yeah," she says.

He doesn't intend to torture her today. He puts the mousetrap away and picks out a baggie. "Catch," he says.

She does.

"Knock yourself out."

She will.

"Joris?" she asks before he's gone. "Does this do it for me? We done?"

He fabricates a smile. "Sweetie, baby steps. The day will come when you're the trap, not the mouse. Promise. This is not that day. A way to go yet. Aren't you pleased?"

"Yeah. I'm so thrilled."

Fair enough, her lack of sincerity.

"You know you're my favourite, don't you?"

Like she cares.

"Did she kill him? Zamarlo?" Pul jerks his chin to indicate Penelope.

"How should I know?" Libby reacts. "Did you?"

"Maybe it was you," Pul states. He squints while staring at her, to imply a threat.

Libby shrugs. She moves the heroin from one palm to the other. "Who knows? Maybe I did." She knows something he doesn't. She just found that out. She wonders what this means. How dangerous she is, now, to others.

"Don't mess with me, kid."

"Yeah, because if I did, then you'd need to watch your step, right?"

"You yours."

"There you go. Nail on the head." Then she asks, "Why, Joris?"

He knows what she's asking. Why addict Penelope? What's the big deal?

"Figure it out for yourself."

Joris Pul closes the door quietly behind himself as he takes his leave, his briefcase in one hand, a fresh bag of pretzels in the other. Libby St. Croix lies back against the sofa. She checks on Penelope, who's off in another world. She'll live. For now, she's long gone. Then Libby retrieves the ice cream spoon to use to warm her heroin, to join Penelope in her exquisite haze.

TWENTY-NINE

Two lists. The living. The dead. Troopers pick up the living for a discussion with Émile Cinq-Mars; for the others, he'll rap his knuckles on their gravestones. For now, he keeps pounding on a door when no one responds, not wanting to wake a ghost particularly but trying to get the attention of a young man enveloped by headphones. Perhaps the incessant pounding is detected between musical tracks – suddenly the lad looks right at him through the bay window.

Though modest, the home is too grand for a student working as a summer waiter. Cinq-Mars assumes he's living with his parents, which is obvious once he's admitted.

"I have an apartment in the basement. I'm like a reverse vampire. I rise from my tomb in daylight while my folks go to work."

"You prefer sun to basement gloom."

"Mainly I prefer my folks' audio system."

He likes this kid. He showed initiative at the restaurant when Émile and Sandra were dining with Hodges Marsh.

"Leo, I know you said I could come by the restaurant before your shift, but I tracked you down here instead." The state troopers saved him that task, providing the address. "I'm on a tight schedule and some things don't fit a narrow window. I hope you don't mind my showing up." He could explain that during his years on the force he always preferred to catch people unawares, but why bother to elucidate that?

"No problem. I wanted to tell you about my granddad."

"He died from heroin use."

"No, sir. He died of cancer."

"I see. I'm sorry."

"He was *using* heroin. For the pain. He didn't get what he needed through medical channels."

"Right. Can we sit?"

"Sorry, sir. I'm a lousy host. Not used to entertaining. I don't even invite my friends over."

"Why not?"

The young man whose name is Leo Ross is guiding him from the foyer into a living room that's crowded with furniture and tropical plants.

"They spill beer. They drop their ashes. They tear leaves off the stems. Worse than that in the basement. There they just wreck the place. Look, would you like some tea, or…"

Cinq-Mars waits for him to finish his sentence, but the lad says nothing more. Still, he encourages him as he sits. The arms on the chair are so high that he thinks he must look like that statue of Abraham Lincoln seated across from the Washington Monument. "Or?" he asks his flustered host.

"Or maybe a beer or…"

Once again, there's an unspoken further option. "Or?" Cinq-Mars repeats.

"Or, I don't know, don't detectives drink whisky, or bourbon? My dad has some Knob Creek."

This is how life should be. He demurs out of courtesy. "Kind of early, don't you think?" He doesn't let the boy dwell on that thought for long before correcting himself. "Sure, Leo. Why not? A little Knob Creek is just the ticket." If only every interviewee was this solicitous.

The bourbon *is* the ticket. As the liquor slides into his bloodstream, he grasps that he's been under a subliminal stress lately which he hasn't fully acknowledged. The strain of moving, looking for a home? The marriage again? The case? A second sip suggests an answer. He's accepted that he's ailing, but he hasn't tallied how the case has affected him. The same question: *Why?* Why kill old people, old drug addicts, for no known reason, not even for sport? By the third sip he begins to trace why that unanswered question has infiltrated his defenses and put him off his feed: it's because he knows the answer. *I know the answer!* He's amazing himself. An effect of the Knob Creek, perhaps.

"Sir?"

He's drifting off. Bourbon's kick.

"When in Rome," Émile says.

The boy's expression shows confusion.

"Back home I drink Scotch. In the States, American bourbon does me nicely. Thanks again. Tell me about your granddad, Leo." Émile nestles into the upholstery. "What did he do as a young man?"

Leo Ross warms to the subject. His granddad "sold things." Near the end of his working life it was cars, until the dealership bellied up, then shoes. "Really, he was an artist."

In the gentle fog of the bourbon, Cinq-Mars misses the inflection. "You mean, to him, selling shoes was an art form?"

"No, no. He was a landscape artist. He could never make a living at it. He painted slowly and sold quite a few, but most artists can't support themselves. He sold cars and shoes or whatever to earn his living, but all he ever wanted was to get back to painting."

Cinq-Mars looks at the walls that surround them. The paintings on display are of high quality, and vaguely familiar. A thought dashes through him, as if ping-ponging off his mental receptors. Muriel Cuthbert's furniture could easily have been cast off to a retailer somewhere, or the pieces could have wound up in thrift shops. What of her paintings? If the ones removed from the walls of her home downstairs were as poorly executed as those upstairs, they'd be worth a negligible amount. Why take them if they had no value? The paintings upstairs weren't touched, perhaps for that reason. They were trash. If the stolen ones matched the quality of these in Leo Ross' house, they'd also not be easily sold – as the boy said, earning a living as an artist is not easy – yet they might be of value. What happened to those paintings?

He returns to the matter of their familiarity. "I was in a lawyer's office in Hanover—"

Leo interrupts. "Hodges Marsh. The blind man at your table. He has at least four of granddad's paintings. I wanted to say something when you were having dinner. But didn't think it was appropriate."

When you don't believe in coincidence, connections are intriguing.

"So he became ill, your granddad. Sorry about that."

"Thanks. It was terrible."

"He started taking heroin," is Émile's assumption. "How did that happen, do you know?"

"He met a group of people. They were taking it for the same reason."

"If he was bedridden as you said, how did he procure his supply?"

Hesitation.

"There's nothing to worry about," Cinq-Mars says. "Just tell me."

"I got it for him. I mean, I didn't have to do anything. I'd go out to this guy's van and bring it in. He gave me the heroin. He'd give me a week's supply to dole out slowly. I then delivered his supply every day."

"You paid the guy in the van."

"I didn't, actually."

"How did he get paid then?"

"The man said it was free."

"Free heroin."

"That's what he said. When my granddad died, he was broke. He'd already sold his house years before, it was too much for him to take care of. After he died, I found out he used the house money to work off bad debts. He had debt because he never made much and took risks on the markets. That worked when he was younger. Later on, not so much. I don't know how he physically handed the money over or why the guy thought it was free."

"How did the man in the van explain it?"

"A way of looking after people is what he said."

"Then you did talk to him about it."

"He always asked about granddad. Kept tabs on how he was doing, how much pain he was in, stuff like that. He said he had an aunt who lost her jaw."

He's certain who they're talking about now. "A white van?"

"White, yeah."

"Did he have a name, this man in the white van."

"I didn't know it until the other day."

"Now you do?"

Leo shrugs. "His picture was on TV. His name was Reece Zamarlo."

Visiting the dead is more profitable than predicted.

"What was his name, your granddad?"

"William Ross. Often Will, never Bill. But I think he preferred William."

"Leo, thank you. Now, you already told me that he died of natural causes – cancer – and he was lying down."

"He couldn't sit up for days."

"Still, you brought him heroin."

"Oh yeah. I wasn't going to let him be in so much pain."

"I suppose he was cremated."

The boy scratches above his left breast pocket. "I don't think so."

The deceased was not sitting up and may not have been cremated. "Was an autopsy done?" He's not expecting the boy to know; not likely that he'd be included in the final paperwork.

"I'm pretty sure there was."

Another difference. "Why do you think that?"

"He was an organ donor. As soon as he died, they harvested what they could from an old guy. Obviously, the cancer affected that, and maybe the heroin if they knew, but he could still give some things. That's the kind of man he was."

Cinq-Mars takes it all in. "You have a right to be proud. I'm proud of you, by the way. You went through tough times with him."

"Even though some of it was illegal?"

"Even though. Did he have any special friends after starting on heroin?"

"Yeah. I used to drive him to meetings."

"Did you go in yourself to these meetings?"

"No. I'd return in two hours and take him home."

"These meetings were at people's houses?"

"Yeah. Across the river in New Hampshire. Mostly one place along the river."

Cinq-Mars described Muriel's house, and he agreed that that was probably the main place he'd go. There, and another place right across the highway.

"Near the end, he couldn't go out anymore," Leo explains. "His friends came to him. They cheered him up. They helped see him through it."

"Were any of these visitors a teenaged girl, with braces on her knees?"

Leo shakes his head. Of course, she'd have joined the group later.

"I know who you mean, though. She fell off a cliff, that girl. I know her."

A small, intimate world. The kids know one another. Cinq-Mars doesn't tell him that he suspects that the girl who fell off a cliff is still falling.

THIRTY

The sun's not yet up as Émile Cinq-Mars pulls into Muriel Cuthbert's drive. He procured a key from Hammond, who questioned the need. "Geoff, I'm borrowing a fishing rod. See if I like to fish before splurging on tackle and hip waders."

"Bullshit. What are you up to, Émile?"

He denied the inference. He wanted to borrow a fishing rod from Muriel's collection, nothing more. The trooper kept after him until finally, for the sake of expediency, the retired detective declared, "Fine! I'm up to something. Now may I have the key?"

All he wants is to borrow a rod.

He arrives at Muriel's hungover.

Émile slept soundly overnight. He woke up aware that his brain had been working overtime. After leaving Leo Ross's place, he was filtering a truckload of information when he caught sight of a real estate sign and followed a road into a contemporary development. He's railed against planned communities, he's unwilling to opt for one, yet a particular bungalow appealed. Merging back onto the highway, he spotted the sign again. The selling agent was Patricia Shaftesbury. That rang an alarm bell. Why was she showing houses to Sandra and him that they would never love when a home they might admire – on the river, and she's the selling agent – goes unmentioned?

Perhaps his animosity over housing developments warned her off, and yet he was feeling uneasy and wondering about doing business in America. Do people want to sell him their junk first, before moving on to better offerings? If so, he's got to figure this culture out.

Hammond buzzed him, and he pulled over to talk on his mobile. The trooper mentioned his absence from Muriel Cuthbert's funeral, and sitting in his car Cinq-Mars gave the side of his noggin a thump. He had wanted to go. In the old days, he never would have neglected something like that. You want to see who shows up to the funeral of a murder victim and, in this situation, he had wanted to pay his respects. After learning that he'd missed the funeral, he asked to borrow a key to Muriel's cottage.

"What are you up to, Émile?" Hammond pressed him.

Émile would have to concede that he was up to something when he wasn't, that his word was bogus, that he couldn't be trusted.

Hammond promised he'd get the key, then mentioned two reports. One from the Medical Examiner. Marcus Easton didn't think much of the notion that Reece Zamarlo did not die from a knife wound but he had agreed to investigate.

"Heroin?" Cinq-Mars expected to have confirmed.

"Nope. Still, Easton doesn't get to mock us. Pentobarbital. Know it?"

"I keep it at home."

"At home? Here in New Hampshire?"

"Geoff, in Quebec. Emergency use only and anyway it's not your jurisdiction. I'm sorry, but you can't arrest me."

"What kind of emergencies?" The trooper's tone suggests he might try.

"To euthanize suffering animals. Get off it."

"A few states are using pentobarbital for executions. Texas, the latest. Louisiana."

He was going off-topic. Cinq-Mars steered him back to the second report mentioned. This one was from the crew combing through Zamarlo's home. They found Muriel's necklace in a pair of jeans, and one of the televisions on his worktable was hers, already gutted for parts. They located the bill of sale in her home that confirmed the serial number.

Cinq-Mars found it curious that some of Muriel's belongings had stayed with Zamarlo, and most didn't.

"What does that tell you?" Hammond asked.

"First indication, he's not a lone wolf. He may have divvied up the spoils. Maybe a partner killed him."

"Why think that?"

"Most criminals who die violently are killed either by cops or by accomplices, and I don't think you did it. Statistically, not many exceptions."

Following their talk, Cinq-Mars drove to the cemetery. He had developed an inexplicable affection for an old woman he had never met and wanted to pay his respects. The gravesite had not been backfilled by the time he arrived. Workers were slouching in that direction. Muriel awaited her turn. The coffin was barely covered with loose dirt that friends had tossed into the grave. Cinq-Mars added a few clumps of his own, letting the earth run through his fingers. He suffered, right then, the impression that the deceased woman still guided him along. He called Hammond.

"Why," he wanted to know, "is Muriel in a coffin?"

"As opposed to what, a sack?"

"Easton warned us she was going to be cremated, it was in her will. So who needs a coffin for ashes? Why not an urn?"

Hammond didn't have an answer. "Does it mean something?"

"Something that does not make sense usually means something."

Another thought occurred before he left the gravesite, and once again he phoned Hammond.

"One of the names on our lists, a guy who lost a relative, Grant Labryk, do a background on him, will you? I want to make sure we can kick him out of the picture. Also, Patricia Shaftesbury."

"Excuse me? Why her?"

"Humour me, Geoff."

Cinq-Mars no sooner signed off on the call than his mobile buzzed. Sandra this time. She suggested they meet at the Farmers' Market on the Green in Hanover and shop for dinner.

A weekly affair, the market is a social potpourri. Amid the tables and shade tents, the gallimaufry of humans and their dogs, a cornucopia of foods from the fields and the harmonies of fiddle music and laughter, Émile Cinq-Mars failed to spot his wife but noticed Bitz Kincaid. Lacking a focus or diversion, he shadowed her rather aimless movements. He sheltered no suspicion: He was merely curious about what a heroin addict might be doing amid the stalls. Apparently, what other people do. Her daughter, whom Cinq-Mars had threatened with arrest if she misbehaved, pointed him out to her mom. He figured his tailing technique needed improvement if a seven-year-old could pick him out of a crowd.

Sandra tapped him on the shoulder right then. They wandered off on their own and agreed to fresh corn and hamburgers for dinner. Abruptly, the Kincaid woman came straight at him. She asked to have a word in private.

"What's up?" Cinq-Mars asked Bitz once they were alone.

"I talked to Libby."

"Where is she?"

"I don't know."

"Is that an honest answer?"

"You're right. I'm a junkie. What am I thinking? I'm incapable of an honest answer."

"Thought I'd ask. What's up with Libby?" he inquired.

"She has a plan. Whatever it is, it's a cockamamie idea. Some people want her to do something. She doesn't know what. She doesn't know when. They probably don't know what or when. She's on hold, in case something comes along, and they need a sacrificial lamb at their disposal. That's my thought."

Bitz had called Libby an angelic wolf, something like that, now she's a sacrificial lamb. He can guess which of the two might be closer to the truth. "What's Libby's big plan?"

Bitz kept an eye on her kids while they talked. Miraculously, they were behaving. They weren't even tussling.

"Don't know. Don't know if she knows. Except, she says when they really count on her to do something, she's not going to do it. She figures that whatever it is, not doing it will really mess them up. She says they won't expect it because she's going to let them believe they've got her."

"Sounds dangerous. And brave. And stupid."

"You don't understand."

"Then explain it."

"It's fucking suicide. Libby knows it, too. She expects it to go that way."

He understands now why she's talking to him again. She fears for her friend's life. When she says that she doesn't know where Libby is or what she's planning to do, or not do, she's not lying.

"Who, Bitz? Tell me. Who's manipulating her? Who's controlling her?"

Who, he wants to ask, is upstream in all of this?

"His name is Joris Pul." For the first time in his investigation, he has a name. A suspect. "Don't mention my name or I'll be the one who dies next."

"I'll find him."

"You might not. Nobody knows where he lives in his real life."

"What do you mean by his real life?"

"He only comes out at night. I don't know what coffin he lives in during the day. He drives a Mustang, top down usually. Black. There's an older lady, one of us, a junkie. Mrs. Birman is her name. First name Gladys, I think. Strangely, those two get along. Total opposites. Maybe she can help."

She goes on to describe him. His hairstyle especially will make him easy to spot on the streets of Hanover, whereas a man with his appearance would blend in on the streets of Manhattan.

"A black Mustang," Cinq-Mars murmurs.

"New Jersey plates."

Better yet.

"Sometimes he drives a van. Black or dark blue."

By the time Émile locates Sandra again, she has already bumped into Trooper Hammond and Hodges Marsh and invited them and their wives to a barbecue dinner out at the farm.

"You what?"

"We should entertain for a change."

"Are they coming?"

"With bells on, apparently."

"When?"

"Tonight!"

They'll be entertaining for a change.

That being the case, he's in the mood to drink.

The key's an ill-fit. Jiggling's required before Cinq-Mars enters Muriel's old home. Inside, the silence feels profound. Windows are open a crack, yet the air is motionless. The close atmosphere pulls him up straight.

He stands in the foyer. Waits. He does not know for what.

Something to transpire.

Light has become visible above the mountaintops, although the sun has yet to scale the higher peaks. He reaches out. Blindly finds a light switch with his fingers and flicks it on. He steps into the front den and switches on a standing lamp. Opens the closet where Muriel kept her fishing gear. Not knowing the difference between one rod and another, he selects the one nearest him. She used to keep a tackle box down by the river, the police probably have it but another rests on the floor. He's set.

Thanks, Muriel. Hey, let's go fish.

Turning back to the hall he can see into the living room and stops short. How can this be? He enters the room and turns on a bureau lamp.

On the mantelpiece, above the empty space where Muriel's TV once stood, the figurine of an elephant wearing the ceremonial garb particular to India has resumed its former position. When last seen it was in Reece Zamarlo's workshop, an area cordoned off under police jurisdiction. Cinq-Mars goes over and confirms what he expects to find: a tusk on the animal has been nicked. This is the same one. The cordon around Zamarlo's place has been breached. As has this house.

He wonders if he's not alone there.

The stillness. The silence. As though someone is holding his or her breath with such intensity that heartbeats are stifled and the air can't move. As though the house itself strains to hold its breath.

Cinq-Mars goes through to the kitchen. Flicks on a light. Remembers how things were left when last he was here, but he notes changes. Dishes have been cleaned up. Cops didn't do that. He checks: under the sink the trash has been emptied, a fresh bag placed in the bin.

He looks out the window. Poking out from the side of the house, the rear fender and tire of a bicycle are visible. He knows who's here.

Upstairs? Sleeping in Muriel's bed? Holding her breath as he moves about down below? He wants to talk to her. Now is as good a time as any. And this is as good a place.

He thinks first. She's found an excellent spot to hide. A better place than the police might locate for her. He's had enough experience to know that the ability of the police to keep an individual safe is readily compromised. If she is upstairs, frightened about who's downstairs, now might not be the moment to announce himself. Take up the fishing rod instead, depart. Let her see that he means no evil. She may deduce that he'll be back to return the fishing gear, or not, and continue to feel safe. That's needed here more than anything else, perhaps: Libby St. Croix's safety.

Hell, he's not really a cop anymore. He no longer has to do anything by the book.

Cinq-Mars gazes up at the ceiling. Not so much to address the girl upstairs, but to speak in silence to Muriel, who may yet be resident here. Is this your doing? Are you guiding me along, and her, too? Kind of feels that way.

He will go fish. Then return. See what the lay of the land brings to bear. Gear in hand, he goes out the front door, locks up again, sets off down the road. He inscribes a memo to himself: Get another key made. When he returns this one to Hammond, he may still want to access the cottage. He may choose to borrow Muriel's fishing tackle often after today, while assuring the trooper that, of course, he's up to something, he's just not sure what.

The man won't buy it, but will that matter?

THIRTY-ONE

She breathes. Barely.

Libby St. Croix sits up in bed, arms wrapped around herself to prevent the slightest quiver. Any infinitesimal movement will betray her as the bed is creaky. She holds her breath until her skull might burst, then breathes again. She tries not to gasp; she must not gasp. After the front screen door bangs shut, she remains still, praying the intruder has left. Then rises, which requires lifting her encumbered legs in their braces off the bed and setting her feet down on the floor. Libby retrieves her crutches and hobbles to the window to see who has come and gone.

That policeman. The French one. Him.

He's almost out of sight, a fishing rod in one hand, a tackle box in the other. Who does he think he is? Taking Muriel's stuff! He's left his car behind, so he must be coming back.

Libby needs to get out.

She's been sleeping in the house and keeping it immaculate in case cops come by. She leaves no trace; no one will detect her overnight presence. She expects to pass her days at Penelope's, helping her out, the two of them getting by. She won't sleep at Pen's. Not with how Penelope snores. You'd think a runaway 18-wheeler was careening off the highway and crashing through the walls. She sleeps at Muriel's and apart from it being a whole lot quieter, being in the cottage has helped her grieve. Her folks don't want her home anymore, they can't handle the heroin use. They don't want her arrested but don't want her in the house, either. Anyway, the authorities could find her there, and she has no desire to talk to them. Old friends could find her at her parents and Joris Pul wants her to run with those old friends and get them hooked. She won't do that. Penelope is bad enough, but she won't do that to former classmates. Better to escape that scene, let no one know where she hides out these days.

People talk. Apply pressure to them, they talk. The cops are looking for everyone in the group. They took poor Penelope in and she's not even a full-fledged member. Libby doesn't want to face the police. She knows too much. If cops question her, they'll figure it out. When Pul calls she can say, meet me here, meet me there, meet me at Penelope's, but she doesn't tell him for a fact where she sleeps. If he comes for her in the middle of the night, he won't find her. Even Penelope doesn't know she goes across the road at night. She's been fooling her with evasive tactics. This way, Penelope can't tell anybody what she doesn't know.

Libby's on the run.

This is her life now.

She doesn't mind.

With that detective roaming around, fishing, then coming back for his car, she decides to hang out at Penelope's. If someone snoops over there, she can hide in the basement.

Upstairs at Muriel's, Libby makes the bed. Fluffs the pillows as Muriel used to do. Makes everything look just so. She leaves no trace of her presence.

She holds her pee. She doesn't want a flushing toilet to give her away.

She hobbles downstairs on her crutches and checks the premises. Is there anything anyone might notice that could give her away? Dusty footprints? She came in on sock feet and carried her small boots upstairs, so no. There's the elephant, which she returned to the mantel. A gift she gave Muriel – she couldn't believe she found it at Zamarlo's. Why did he steal the keepsake? She couldn't retrieve it right then. He was still alive. He might have noticed. Going back after he was dead, she strategically placed it to interest investigators. Showed them where he kept his killer dope. She didn't know what came of that. Nothing in the papers about it. She'd been back since, to see if he left any clean smack the cops hadn't found out about – he hadn't – and this time took possession of the figurine again.

The day Muriel was buried, and she couldn't go, Libby held a ceremony of her own. At the end of it, she restored the figurine to its rightful place.

Hopefully, the cop didn't notice the elephant. Should she leave it? If he sees it he'll think it's a message he won't understand. If he already noticed it, moving it now means she's close by. Libby sneaks out the back door, replacing Muriel's key under a rock where the old lady used to hide it, and mounts her bicycle.

Her crutches she tucks away in the sheath her dad made for the purpose and pedals off. Next time, she'll leave her bike in the woods, well hidden. Only luck kept that detective from noticing it. Luck, or he's just not as good as people say.

She never expected anyone to show up at sunrise.

Libby glides down the hill from Muriel's place, her hands on the brakes to not go fast, to make less noise on the gravel in the quiet of early dawn. Birds are greeting the pale light of the misty morning. She carries her momentum ahead of a honking car and clears the highway onto Penelope's property and rides up to her door. She has a hard time dismounting without letting the bike fall to the ground and this time she works at it to be quiet. Once she's disentangled and is about to stash it away, Émile Cinq-Mars speaks up.

"Good morning, Miss St. Croix. How are you?"

She spins around. Faces him. She says nothing. She keeps her bike between them.

"I've been meaning to have a chat. Oh, yes, I see what you're thinking. Don't bother. You cannot get back on your bike and dash away sooner than I can stop you. I might be old, but I'm not a fossil. No offence, but you're not that quick."

With her legs, escape is futile. "What do you want?"

"Staying at Muriel's is fine. I don't mind. I'd like to talk, though."

She shrugs. "I have nothing to tell you."

"Sure you do, Libby." Rather than move toward her, Cinq-Mars steps away, going over to a hefty round boulder where he puts the tackle box on the ground. He's already leaned Muriel's fishing rod up against a sapling. He sits and folds his arms. "Only lies can trick you into thinking otherwise. Have you heard the old adage?"

He wants to see if she will answer, engage in conversation. "What old adage?" Her tone, how she looks and answers, suggests to him that she's intelligent.

"The truth will set you free. I'm sure you'll have a lot to say if you choose to be truthful. If you're planning to lie, then I agree with you, better to not say a word."

She's thinking about it. She moves her crutches in order to lean forward. She lifts one foot from the ground to take her weight off it. Cinq-Mars can tell that she's in pain.

"What you offered Bitz," she says.

"I'll offer you the same. I'm not a cop anymore. I don't have to do anything by the book. I told you that I'm fine with you staying at Muriel's. What cop would say that? So, yeah, I told Bitz that it goes in one ear and out the other as far as me and the law are concerned – as long as you didn't kill anyone. Let me start there. Have you killed anybody lately?"

At first, he's alerted by her silence. Then sees that she's genuinely uncertain. "Maybe," she says finally, and Cinq-Mars knows then that they are overdue for a serious conversation.

THIRTY-TWO

He has more to think about down by the riverside.

Cinq-Mars was heading there with fishing rod and tackle box in hand, eager for the adventure, when he stopped to see if Libby St. Croix would emerge from hiding. She did. They talked. The sky pale now, the sun baffled by cloud, the temperature escalating into the day. Through the trees, wisps of mist rise off the river, vanishing into the clear air.

So much to put together. The only way out of the maze is to map a route through the impediments. Cinq-Mars believes that regions of the mind operate without language yet prosper with full cognitive function. Images stitched to impressions. Outlier notions percolate. Crazy guesses float upward. Wild ideas intersect conscious data to dovetail with darker ruminations to produce, when a case is truly complex, a theory of evidence.

All bubbling away this morning after a fitful night.

Émile feels the mental computations in his bones travel through his bloodstream. That his skin feels clammy is probably the difference between body and air temperature, yet he suspects that he's in a slow-cook mode, his synapses reducing a sauce of possibilities down to a workable consistency. Deduction and reduction, he calls it. He needs more time for everything to bind together, and nothing more is necessary now than a sprinkle of salt – a seasoning of information, or an additional ingredient.

He won't be handed the sort of evidence that can be taken into a court of law. He'll cop to that. To support his gastronomic metaphor, he assumes that what he needs next is to catch a fish, any fish, that rises to the bait. Fry it in a pan. He needs to plot and plan, and he needs someone – who? – to blunder. To bite on a lure.

Libby admitted to dropping off heroin on the instruction of another. She brought up the dead guy but declined to mention the name, Joris Pul, and Cinq-Mars did not suggest it to her as that would betray Bitz's confidence. He hasn't figured out how these interconnections and relationships have worked. Many in the heroin support group might call one another friends, and that might be true in the everyday fabric of their lives; still, he does not know how deeply the alliances are cemented, or how stress might bend them out of whack. The principals probably didn't know that, either. Who trusts whom? Who will crack under assertive pressure? Or lie for another until the bitter end?

Libby made drop-offs while riding her bike to earn extra cash to support her own habit. One typical stop was at the Upper Valley Health Club. When Cara Drost failed to re-emerge from a closet upstairs where she was shooting up, Libby checked on her. For the sake of her deliveries, she had a key. She told him that she, not the janitor, had been the first to find Cara dead.

"I didn't leave her enough to OD on. Did she take bad shit?"

"Seems likely."

"I delivered it."

"Nothing but a drop-off?"

"What do you mean?"

"You weren't her supplier?"

"I don't sell drugs."

She made it sound like a crime.

"Who gave you the dope for Cara?" Cinq-Mars asked.

He found her shrug to be a bit elaborate, rife with unspoken words. Then she said, "Reece."

"Okay," Cinq-Mars mused aloud then, "so Reece Zamarlo gives you the dope that kills Cara, then Reece dies. That could be convenient for someone."

"Convenient?" Libby asks. "For who?"

"Well, for you. Shows you though, doesn't it?" he leads her.

She thinks about it, then says, "Shows me what?"

"How a person, me, for instance, doesn't need to take extreme action."

When he doesn't continue, she prods him. "Extreme action?"

"No undue risk."

"What risk?" Now she's confused. Which is how he wants her to be.

"Have you noticed? You have a tendency to repeat what I say back to me. I just want to get to the bottom of these relationships."

She waits, hobbles on her crutches, and rearranges how she carries her weight on them. She pushes a thick strand of hair back behind an ear.

He points out, "This is where you could ask me, *relationships?*"

Libby cracks the semblance of a smile. "I'm trying not to," she admits.

Cinq-Mars smiles also. "I understand. Nobody likes to be repetitive. You'd rather tell me something I haven't heard before, or something I haven't said myself. We both have to be careful here. Careful to buy ourselves time to figure this out. For me, I'm going fishing. Fishing might help me figure this out. Know why?"

She wants to jump in. Chooses to weigh her options first. Finally, Libby concedes and asks, "Why?"

"Because that old gal," Cinq-Mars says, and with a jerk of his chin he indicates Muriel's place, "is coming along with me. I can feel it. Not in a real way. She's not a ghost. In her way, she's coming along. I've felt it from the beginning, she's helping me with this case."

"Who," Libby needs to verify, "Muriel?"

"Muriel. You bet. Now I'm doing it. Repeating what *you* say. I just feel that in a real way, Muriel wants me – us – to succeed. Figure this out. Get it resolved the right way. Give the lady some justice."

Libby ponders this. "You mean so she can move on. That type of thing?"

Cinq-Mars gives it a moment's thought. "Actually, no. Muriel has already moved on. I've felt that, too. She is not looking back. She's free to go and we should let her. When Muriel was alive, she made her mark. I think for those who knew her – even for those, like me, who didn't, but who now investigate her murder – our job is to find our way through this, for her sake. For justice. And so," he finishes up.

"And so?" Libby repeats.

"I'm going fishing with her gear. To see what that tells me. We'll find out, hey?"

Libby had more that she could tell him. Cinq-Mars believed that she'd say less than what she knew. He was willing to give her a break for now, to earn her trust later. He had a source. He could develop her. The more she might trust him, the more she might reveal. Her information could be a tipping point.

Earlier in the talk, Libby had confirmed what Cinq-Mars was beginning to fear, that addicts in the north country were nervous about supply. Penelope was not merely everyone's NTB friend.

"NTB?" he inquired.

"Not too bright."

"I see. What else was she?"

"Her house, that's where our supply was kept." She seemed to think he'd understand.

"I don't get it."

"You don't want to deliver to every person every day, right?"

"That's how most of the world operates," Cinq-Mars pointed out. "A week's supply would kill most addicts. That's what street corners are for. Why we have dark alleys."

He succeeded at working a full smile out of her. "You seen any dark alleys around here?" she asked him.

"You have trees. Dark forests."

"Yeah, and we have Penelope's house."

"Penelope's not a pusher," he stated. If she wanted to convince him otherwise he'd have Hammond take her away as uncooperative. He and Libby had already made that deal. She could limit what she told him to what she was willing to tell him but only if she was truthful with what she put out there. She had to be generally cooperative. Otherwise, she was going to Twin Mountain for a talk that might last longer than she could sustain.

"Of course Pen's not a pusher," Libby scoffed. Cinq-Mars felt better then. "She had her purpose in our group. Keep everybody's heroin and dole it out as required. Under lock and key in a safe in her basement. Nobody else could be trusted, because we're all users. Only Pen was clean. She got to keep our stuff, dole it out, and if anybody wanted to take it from her, hey, she's big. She could even lick the men, one on one. Nobody tried."

These days, they were anxious. Some supply was going around, but Pen didn't have any and Zamarlo was dead and who knows how important he was to the whole operation. They were waiting, they were hanging on, they were scavenging for the *H* they knew was out there. But they didn't know how to find it.

She wouldn't bring up Joris Pul.

Instead, she said, "We can't let our fingers do the walking."

"Excuse me?"

"Through the Yellow Pages."

Desperation was setting in.

"You're high right now. You're not desperate."

"I get what I beg for. That's not pleasant."

She still had spirit, but he could detect despair behind her eyes. She had not succumbed. Yet. She was beginning to yield to its persuasion.

"Do you know where Muriel kept her stash?" Cinq-Mars asked.

Libby hesitated a little too long.

"So you do know."

"We were friends. I'd never take hers."

226

"While she was alive? Maybe that's true."

"I'd take it after, sure. I didn't. Never got the chance."

"Who else knew?"

"Knew what?"

"About her fishing boots."

She shoots him a glance. Sometimes she doesn't get this guy. Sometimes, she's impressed. "Just me, I guess."

"You and who else? Who else did you tell?"

That telltale hesitation again.

"I'd rather not say. I'll think about it."

"Was it Bitz? She's someone you talk to. Or Penelope?"

He didn't give her much reason to deny it.

"I told Bitz, yeah."

"She might have been down here looking for Muriel's stash. Just like you might've been down here. You know, the morning that Reece Zamarlo was killed."

"I didn't kill him. I'm sure Bitz didn't."

"You don't know that."

"Nobody knows anything. Not these days. Well, *I* didn't do it. That I know."

Walking on down to the riverbank, Émile mulls over what Libby St. Croix just told him, a reflection repeatedly interrupted by snapshot memories of the previous evening. The men had drunk heavily to the chagrin of their wives, Émile leading the way. He regrets now the physical toll and his mental lethargy, and wonders what else he might regret, should a broader review of the evening occur.

An outburst of his: "Why does anyone need a watch that costs fifty grand?"

Astounded, Hammond pitched in, asking Marsh, "Your watch is worth fifty grand?"

"Not even close," the lawyer scoffed. Only to add, "Twice that, easily."

Cinq-Mars threw his hands up then. Later, he bragged that he was going to solve the case in the morning. "I'm going fishing."

"Don't count on it," Sandra inserted, taking note of his inebriation level.

He resorted to dramatic intonation. "I'll stroll down to Muriel's old spot, use her tackle. Cast a line into the river and reel it back in. When I do, I'll either hook a fish or snag an answer to this case. One of the two."

The night ended with the women guests driving their men home as his own wife helped him crawl into bed.

Against the odds, he's up and set to fish. For the first time since his adolescence, Émile Cinq-Mars casts a line into a river and waits for an accommodating trout to bite. Like a fish wriggling upstream in search of a tasty morsel, he feels the case wriggle inside him, also ready to be hooked.

On the east bank of the Connecticut River, Émile Cinq-Mars proves an old adage true, that you never hear the shot that kills you. He crumbles. He hears the shot next, proving himself alive, not at all instantaneous as he slams into the water and strikes hard against the rocks. In this sudden lifting away, in this avid brightening, this rising amid the river mist, a quiet and diminutive voice unfamiliar to him that's way deep in his larynx contradicts his own opinion of himself and adamantly contends that he's still alive.

He lifts further away and knows nothing more.

IV

THIRTY-THREE

The shock of the gunshot pulls her skin tight to her scalp. Stunned a moment, then, as though she knows what happened, Libby swings on her crutches and lurches toward the sound.

Penelope reacts differently. She clamps her hands over her ears, less to block out the echo of the blast than guard against a second shot. "Libby!" She glimpses the girl outside. She was awakened when she heard Libby talking to that French detective, now it's a gunshot when hunting season hasn't started and Libby is hobbling toward the sound. She bursts onto her porch. "Libby! Somebody's shooting! Get back here!"

"Follow me! Come on!"

She does so. She doesn't want to. This happens when someone takes control of her life. She does whatever the heck they say.

"You're scaring the pants off me!" she yells. She complains all the way down the trail. Indecipherable jumbled laments. She can barely keep up to the girl on crutches. The excesses of her body jounce inside her tracksuit, nudge her off-balance. She screams again when she sees the detective lying face down in the river, the water around him red. Bloods Creek is up the road. This is real blood and there's a river of it. "*Libby!*"

"Come on, Pen! Drag him out!"

"Is he dead?"

"We don't have time to find out. Pen! Help me!"

"What if somebody shoots?"

She thinks the question's legitimate, but Libby exclaims, "Pen! Christ!"

Penelope helps. She does what she's told. They have a hard time of it but manage to drag him off larger rocks and get his smashed face turned up so he can breathe – if he can still breathe. Blood on his chest burbles up.

"I think he's alive," Libby insists. She's down on her knees. She lost her crutches in the fray. She's half-dragging him, down on her sore and cut knees.

Penelope falls. Smack on her hip. A big splash around her and a lot of that is blood. Libby is covered in dark red now.

"Pen, Pen," she's saying. "Pen! Get on your phone!"

"Who do I call? Bitz?"

"Pen! No! 9-1-1! Now! We need an ambulance!"

Her fingers dig out her wet phone. Her thumbs find the numbers, but she misdials. Libby snatches the phone away. She dials and hands the phone back. "Tell them your address. Tell them to send an ambulance right now. To rush! Tell them a cop's been shot."

"He's retired."

"Don't say that! Just say cop! They'll come faster."

Penelope shouts out her address as if the woman on the other end of the line can't hear. "A cop! He's been shot! Send an ambulance!"

The woman's asking a question that the older woman relays to the younger.

"Is he alive?"

"Tell them he is."

She tells the woman that and receives another set of questions, which she refers to Libby. The young woman is cradling Émile Cinq-Mars in her arms and talking to him. His eyelashes are flickering, but his eyes aren't focused. He's not moving except for the lashes. She's pressing down with the base of her right hand on his wound. She doesn't know if she should do that but that is what she's doing. "Pen. She's asking me. Is he bleeding?"

"Pen! For Christ's sake!" Libby cries out. Half-pleading-weeping.

Penelope says, "Oh yeah," and then she says to the woman she's talking to, "He sure is. There's blood all over everybody."

She sees that Libby is openly weeping now, her face cracking into pieces.

"Oh don't cry, Libby. Don't cry. The ambulance is coming, all right? She said. The woman. The ambulance is coming. On the way. This woman promised me that."

They wait, the three of them on the riverbank – the man bleeding, the teenager weeping, the older woman with her phone to ear and repeating that he's still alive as they wait for the sound of a siren, until she finally says, "I don't know. I think so, okay? Okay? I only think so. Libby says to say he's alive or you won't come fast enough." She feels so disoriented that she starts to cry herself and she really doesn't know why, or what's going on, or why men die on her property these days, or what might happen to her because of this mess.

Libby comforts her. "There it is. Do you hear it? Do you hear it, Pen?"

She does. She hears that distant wail.

"He looks so dead," Penelope says.

"No," Libby says. "I can feel him. I can feel him alive. I'm pushing on his heart. His heart is pushing back."

To Penelope, it doesn't sound as though he'll be alive for long. She doesn't argue. The siren screams onto her property and she says to the woman on the phone, "Tell them to go straight down to the river. Don't dilly-dally! Real fast, please."

The ambulance drives farther toward the river than the women expect, and when the medics get out and grab their stuff, they race toward them. Libby falls away as the paramedics take over and Penelope asks her if she's bleeding, too. Blood all over her.

"Are you? Bleeding yourself?" a medic asks as well, as he works swiftly with his partner on the limp body of Émile Cinq-Mars.

"No," Libby assures them both. "It's only his blood on me."

THIRTY-FOUR

Behind her mother's barn, Sandra Cinq-Mars is thwacking her goat with a tennis racket. Gentle taps, really, to help stimulate circulation through its stubborn stern. As a police car races onto the farm creating a storm of dust and gyrates wildly on the potholed drive, she turns as numb as the animal. Cops have charged onto her farm in Quebec with alacrity; never like this. Never did they exhibit this haste and inhibition.

The troopers don't spot her. When the car brakes, one officer races out of the ensuing dust cloud toward the house. Sandra discovers that she doesn't have the voice, or the will, to shout. Then an optimistic thought strikes: they would not arrive in a mad rush to deliver news of Émile's death. They'd do that with reluctance and sorrow. Émile's alive! Believing that, she sprints toward the troopers.

The cop behind the wheel alerts his partner, and the two hurry across to the paddock. All three arrive at the gate simultaneously.

"What's happened?" she demands to know. Her tone warns them to omit the preamble.

The officers are compelled by urgency. "A shooting, ma'am."

"He's alive."

"Yes, ma'am. We'll drive you." When she doesn't move, as though the news hits her with an effect that is both sudden and delayed, the officer adds, "To the hospital."

"I'll need my car." She's not certain where that thought comes from, as though two halves of her brain are working with different criteria. She fails to grasp what either side is figuring out.

"Ma'am, don't drive right now. We'll get you there quickly."

She understands what they don't want to say. She must go fast. Or risk being too late.

The notion that the Cadillac must come with her persists. She'll need the car to go back and forth to the hospital later. She needs to believe that there will be a *later*.

"There's two of you," she says.

"Ma'am?" the first trooper is confused.

The second gets it. "Trooper Treichel will drive you. I'll follow in your car if you give me the keys."

Almost mindlessly she passes her keys over the fence to him. House keys, car, barn, tractor, trailer, the shed: the works. Trooper Treichel swings open the gate. She again fails to move. "Ma'am?" he urges her. "We should go."

Sandra snaps out of it. She starts out at a fast step, then breaks into a run. The last ten yards are a dash. The car door is open. She leaps in and slams it shut. The trooper does the same. "Go!" she orders him. "Go!"

She hangs on for the rough ride off the property. Only when they reach the relative quiet of the highway will she pepper him with questions. He'll decline to answer, of course. He's not authorized. She's been through that crap before. Sandra assails him with questions anyway.

"I wasn't on the scene, ma'am. I was close to your farm when I got the call, told to fetch you on the double."

The highway's quiet terminates when he turns on the siren. The needle on the speedometer rises past any number she's seen before. Break the damn sound barrier, she's thinking. Go ahead. Break it.

He's in surgery. Beyond that, no news.

"Missed his heart by a tick," Hammond tells her. "Another fraction…"

Another fraction and they'd be having a different conversation.

They might have that conversation yet, as that "tick" may only provide a delay. They understand the circumstances, an awareness that envelopes them in the hospital corridor.

Sandra asks what happened. She's perplexed and horrified that it had been such a blatant assassination attempt. She thinks briefly that this would never happen in Canada, but not for any reason an American might think. Back home – and Canada feels both far away right now *and* like home – people commit murder, as in most places on earth; but the really bad people who knew Émile were aware of his reputation and connections, they feared him, his power, his scope. Rare for a bad guy to take liberties. Back home, a bad guy knew that killing Émile Cinq-Mars amounted to signing his own death warrant, and the authorities might not bother involving the courts, either.

"My husband fought the Hells Angels. Their preferred weapons were car bombs and chainsaws. He's been in gunfights. I armed myself at one point. I couldn't walk to the barn without my shotgun. But nobody, in all that, went out and shot him at long range. That damn fucking coward. If Émile survives—"

She stops, as though saying "if" comes across as a betrayal and can't be permitted into her lexicon. Not now. Not ever. He must survive.

"We can sit over here," Hammond suggests.

They go through to an anteroom. A fridge and a microwave are available. She doesn't know how long a wait she's in for. She doesn't know whether a lengthy time in surgery yields a better result than a shorter spell but thinks a short one might presage death. Illogical, but she's glad the fridge and microwave are there.

"Can we call someone for you, Sandra? I believe you have a sister in town."

He wants to get on with his job, and she wants him to do that. "I'll call Charlotte, my sister. Go, Trooper Hammond. Find him." She won't call him Geoff at the moment, even though he partied at her house last night. She needs him to be an officer of the law, a state trooper, not a mere friend. "Find—" She must stop herself again, for she almost says *his killer.*

"We'll do everything in our power. Your husband, yesterday, gave me a lot of names, people to look at, question. We'll be on it, Sandra, I can assure you of that."

Be on it now, she wants to say, but reconsiders. She doesn't have it in her to be critical in this moment.

A young woman, a teenager, struggles to get in through the door on crutches. Once in, she waits for Trooper Hammond to be free. Sandra sees her glancing over at them, as if she's expecting something. "That girl," Hammond whispers, "saved Émile. He might've drowned. She hauled him out of the river and called the ambulance."

Through tear-filled eyes, Sandra looks across at her. She can't make her out and fails to wipe her tears away. "Can I speak to her?"

"After I talk to her. I need to nail down a few things. First, can I dial your sister's number for you?"

"I will," Sandra says. "I've got her on speed dial."

She makes that call herself. It instigates more tears. Her sister will race over. After that, Sandra observes the trooper and the young woman. The two whisper in a corner of the room. Waiting, Sandra finds herself wishing she shared her husband's faith. Wishes that she had someone, some specter even, to talk to at a time like this. That would be welcome. Hypocritical to do so now, although Émile would probably understand. Rib her about it later, too. She'll be able to talk to her sister soon, a real live person, but she has to steel herself for that, for she expects to break down. She keeps wanting to talk to the young woman. She thinks that that might help because the girl looks distraught herself. With her, perhaps, Sandra can do the comforting rather than be a recipient of the kindnesses of others. She can handle being the caregiver. She's not sure she can handle being the one in need of support. Yet the chance to speak to the teenager is lost. Before Trooper Hammond is done, Sandra's sister arrives. By the time the two of them look up from their bout of hugs and tears, both the policeman and the girl have slipped out of the room.

THIRTY-FIVE

Four days later.

She's chock-full of secrets.

Libby St. Croix on her crutches has become integral to the hospital watch. Sandra appreciates her care. Whenever she leaves Émile with her, so that she can eat, or change clothes, or sleep herself, she's confident he'll be diligently supervised.

Yet she finds the girl unusual.

She is watchful, curious, generous; also, defensive and furtive. She's pleasant but can be awkwardly shy. Indeed, Sandra thinks of her as a young woman at one moment, the next as a child. She's intrigued by her disposition as an outcast. Through it all, she's come to trust Libby. She has already saved Émile's life, and while Libby is not a nurse, the girl knows firsthand what it means to lie in a hospital bed, having spent months in one herself. She knows what it is to be helpless. Libby's been through the wringer. Whatever the connection between her husband and this intense waif might be, Sandra is not going to come between them while Émile recovers from being gunned down.

She assumes that he will recover.

Permits no other thought.

Libby is positive that way, too. Consequently, indispensable.

Officially, Émile is doing as well as can be expected. The terminology used.

He's on track, they say.

On track. For what?

Remain positive. She must. Remain positive.

As positive as Libby, who's a fortress that way.

Trooper Hammond informed her that Libby St. Croix has nowhere to go. Relations with her family are strained. "To put it mildly." Apparently, her folks pay for her mobile phone in case she needs to keep in touch. The father implied to Hammond that that proves him a generous and forgiving man.

"A regular saint," Hammond said back to him, meaning to be sarcastic, but the man skipped the nuance and wholeheartedly agreed that he was a saint to be putting up with his own kid. One more reason why Sandra sees to it that Libby is welcome in the hospital corridor and at Émile's bedside, along with her sister, while everyone else is frisked by a trooper. If she has nowhere to go, she's welcome to stay.

The trooper at the door interrogates visitors. Sandra hates that part. His presence is a reminder that someone is out to harm her husband, and that no one knows who or why. Only the three women are exempted from a pre-emptive pat-down.

Sandra desperately wants her husband to wake up, to emerge from his torpor, to drift back to her from the realm of the drugs designed to keep him in a coma. She has an unfounded belief that once he's awake, he will solve this. She wants him safe, but to be safe he needs to *wake up*! She can't imagine that anyone can protect him better than he can protect himself.

The three – her sister, the strange girl, and Sandra herself – hold the fort. They adjust his pillows. Check his urine bottle and moisten his lips around the inserted oxygen tube. They make sure the nurses execute their routines on time. Each of the three takes a Kleenex to his impressive honker when he drips. Cool compresses comfort his brow. The women lift and lower his feet, spread his legs apart and back again. They don't want him stuck in the same position for hours on end. They wash him, although only the nurses venture below the waist. Troopers take turns guarding the door, doctors and nurses administer to him, but it's the three women who perform the most serious function: They remain present. As if they guard against death. They wait and, in Libby's case, pray. Sandra is comforted by that. The girl prays – at least someone around Émile thinks to do that – something her husband, the religious one in the family, will appreciate hearing one day.

If only he will wake up.

If only he will stay on track.

By the second day Libby took an interest in what nurses do. Sandra has a hunch she might discover her life's calling. She half-expected her to grow bored with the dreary vigil. Instead, Libby is stimulated by learning about nursing procedure. She's even learned to identify what the blips on the monitors indicate.

"That one?" Sandra quizzed, pointing to a stagger in her husband's heart line.

"A skip."

"A what?"

"His heart skipped a beat," Libby explains, then catches how the other woman's face just fell. "Perfectly natural, Mrs. Cinq-Mars. Everybody skips beats."

"Everybody skips beats?"

"Slight exaggeration. Most people. Anyway, a lot of people, really a lot of people skip beats. Mr. Cinq-Mars has probably always skipped beats. Perfectly normal."

She'd make a good nurse someday.

Or doctor. Maybe that's it. Her calling is up the ladder. She wouldn't put it past this one. If whatever strangeness in her life subsides.

Under supervision, Libby is given the opportunity to change Émile's glucose drip. Sandra agrees to let her learn to do that and to proceed with her husband. She told her sister, "I'm not saying she can experiment with a scalpel."

"Not yet," her sister noted.

Much of the girl's strangeness surrounds her comings and goings. She works both long and short shifts. She never asks for time off or to be spelled, and consents when Sandra or her sister request relief. Night shifts, day shifts, lunch time, dinner time, evening, it doesn't matter. Sandra calls and Libby accepts. Sometimes she sounds groggy, but she still agrees. That's a part of her strangeness in large measure: where she goes when she's not at the hospital is unknown and she won't say. Trooper Hammond advised Sandra not to bother about it, that he had the situation under control, or Libby did. Sandra doesn't worry too much about it, in part because she doesn't have sufficient worry left in her. Still, thoughts creeps in.

Such musings don't affect her level of trust. She's found herself trusting everyone around her. Nurses, doctors, strangers. Libby, her sister Charlotte, Trooper Hammond, Patricia Shaftesbury when she comes by – she giggles and makes flirty suggestions while being patted down, loving it – and Hodges Marsh, often with his wife, is a frequent visitor. Trust implies hope. The others constantly bolster her spirits, and she must abide with them for she won't relinquish an ounce of her massive hope. Sometimes her friends even astonish her, such as Regina Marsh dropping by with a food basket for the women, sneaking in a few drinks on the side.

They lined up shots of Jägermeister. The naughtiness of doing shots in a hospital room, with her husband in grave condition, provided Sandra with oodles of fresh hope.

Being a touch tipsy didn't hurt, either.

They make the best of it, even as a single day feels interminable, and she is forced to fight back against a premonition of despair.

Libby used the transport bus for the disabled whenever its schedule jived with her own. The driver felt sorry for her, so the ride was free. Bitz often picked her up as well, driving over to Muriel's old place where she was hiding out, a secret she confided, or across to Penelope's. She and Pen might open a can of beans for lunch or dinner, sometimes for breakfast. Or they drove to Bitz's place. Libby would babysit while Bitz pulled a short shift at her clinic. Sometimes Libby just came over. She'd shoot up while the kids were acting up, then sleep over, or mind the kids while Bitz fell into her own heroin daze. From time to time, she simply sat down wherever she happened to find herself, such as at the hospital, had a quick bite or a snack bar, which she considered a meal, and waited for Sandra to call her back to Émile's bedside.

She had to get high herself. Take time for that.

Tricky. Not easy. The group was working an old supply line. She had Joris Pul, but an alternative source was welcome. Word was, that source could be drying up soon. Then what? Then Joris Pul was it.

Libby kept an eye out. That's mainly what she did all day.

On guard constantly.

She had no clue what was going to happen. Something might. She had fished Detective Cinq-Mars out of the river, and figured that, for some people, her action was not a good idea, not the recommended response.

She tried to tell herself that she didn't care if they killed her. Sometimes at night, alone in Muriel's house, she woke up shivering, and really, she did not want to die. She didn't want the mousetrap, either, but she also did not want the people she hated to win. She wants to defeat them. Flatten them out. At whatever game they're playing or intending to play, she wants them beaten down without getting her friends hurt or killed. That's the hard part. What she did and what she knows has put her life in jeopardy. Hard for her to imagine how she can survive.

Who knows, she thought, where it all begins and ends. Pul could have a boss who has a boss who has a boss. This could go back to New York City. The mob, maybe. Where the drugs come from. Or the whole damn works was local.

All she knew was that she knew too much. And that was almost nothing.

"I'm a junkie," she wrote on a scrap of pink paper when she woke up shaking one night. She thought the line suited the beginning to a journal. "I'm a junkie. I don't care. Kill me. I don't care. Hit me. I don't care. I'm not sticking my tongue in your goddamn mousetrap again." She folded the paper to the size of a dime and stuffed it in the coin pocket of her jeans. Perhaps the start of a journal someday. For now, it was a solemn vow to herself.

If they wanted her to spring a trap so badly, she wanted to spring it on them. Kill me, she thought, and patted the pocket where her vow was written out, knowing that that could be the outcome. I don't care. She tried to tell herself that, that she didn't care.

Sometimes, high on smack or desperate to get high again, she believed it.

Bitz, late that morning, drops her off at Penelope's where she'll have lunch. Bitz isn't coming in herself, so Libby unloads her bicycle from the trunk and wheels it around back. She likes to keep her presence anywhere a secret. Bitz drives away, up the gravel slope to the highway, and Libby swings on her crutches toward the front steps.

Penelope bangs open the door. "We're on the news!" She's thrilled.

"What? Pen, what are you—. Hang on."

On account of her knees, Libby has to take the stairs one-by-one. It takes a while, then she goes inside.

"What are you on about?" Libby asks.

"Us! We're on the news! I tweeted it!"

"Penelope—. What—. Pen, what are you talking about?"

"We're on TV!"

"*We* are? Pen. Please explain what you're saying." Penelope can be exasperating. Libby realizes how much she enjoys talking with Mrs. Cinq-Mars lately, because those conversations happen on a whole other level. She won't find that degree of discourse here.

"We. Okay, *we* means people from here. New Hampshire. Vermont."

"This is not about us specifically."

"Well. Sort of. Yes and no."

"What was on the news?" Libby figures that Penelope has misunderstood, that soon she'll have to explain it to her, shed some light. She sits at the kitchen table and stands her crutches upright in a gap next to the fridge.

"There's an epidemic, they're saying that on the news. Heroin users in Vermont and New Hampshire. An epidemic! You know, among ordinary people. That's us, right?"

Libby gets what she's on about now. "Ordinary. Sure. Why not? That's us. What do you mean you tweeted this? What did you tweet?"

Penelope could misconstrue things, no big deal; what she tweets might be dangerous.

"We're a pack of junkies! Hashtag, junkieville!"

Libby tries to steady her with an intense stare, to get her to settle down and pay attention. She regrets that she started her on the path to getting hooked. She'd been given no choice.

The stare-down works. Penelope squirms, and asks, "What?"

"You told the world we're junkies? Us? Think, Pen, did you?"

The older woman understands that she's supposed to concentrate on the question. She's accustomed to getting this sort of guidance from others. "Not *us* us," she says.

"Then who?"

"Ordinary people in general. Oh Libby! I didn't name you! Or me! Is that what you think? I'm not that stupid-o!"

Close, Libby is thinking, but not *that* stupid-o.

"Good. How about lunch? I'm hungry. I don't know why."

"You high?"

"Halfway down. You?"

"Halfway up."

"What's the difference?"

"I feel good!"

"Good," Libby says. Pen can be a trial sometimes. "Food?"

"Beans."

Yes. Beans. As always. "Beans'll be great, Pen. God, I'm starving."

"I have bread and butter, too."

A veritable feast.

Penelope starts into preparing their meal, and after a minute or two, Libby's eyes close and her chin falls, then she arranges her head on the table under her wrists, and catnaps. A long dull night. She had slept in a chair by Émile Cinq-Mars's bed, fitfully. She's tired now. After lunch, she plans to walk across to Muriel's and sleep there. She doesn't know how long her head is down but hears the gentle pop of beans boiling in their sauce, then hears a car pull into the driveway. Penelope is already going to the door to have a look. Libby waits on her report even while she keeps her head down.

"Pul," Pen says.

"Shit," Libby replies, and sits up.

The older woman returns to stirring beans. Libby waits for Pul's entrance, feeling for all the world like a bean boiling in a pot. Her heart rate, her adrenaline, ramp up a notch.

"Ladies," Joris Pul says.

He comes deeper into the room and plunks his briefcase down on a chair and digs into it, pulling out the mousetrap. He places the trap on the tabletop and sets it. "So we understand what's what," he says.

The women stay silent.

"Good," Pul says, as though he's already accomplished something. He drops his briefcase onto the floor and sits in the large chair. With his legs spread apart, he slumps into a deep slouch. His head is barely above the seat back. He sticks his left thumb inside his belt, and with his free hand rubs his whiskers. Usually he shaves. Today he has a day's growth. He's staring at Libby as though he's amused about something and she does her best not to look back at him.

Finally, she says, "Something bothering you, Joris?"

"Nope. Something bothering you, Libby?"

"Nope."

"I bet," he says.

"What do you mean?"

"What do you think is bothering me?" he asks her.

She shrugs, indicating that she's not interested in the subject. "You said nothing. So I believe you."

"I don't," Pul says.

"You don't what?" Libby asks.

"Believe me."

"You don't believe yourself?"

"I lied," Pul says.

"What are you two talking about?" Penelope asks. She's stirring beans.

"Tell her to stay out of this," Pul tells Libby.

"Pen," Libby says.

"I heard him," Penelope says.

"This is just between me, you, and the mousetrap," Pul warns Libby.

She looks at it. She's not going to stick her tongue in there again. She doesn't know how she ever did it once. Trouble is, she doesn't know what she's going to do if he makes her.

Libby has stopped stirring the beans and turns the heat off under them. She doesn't serve them yet. Knows not to.

"You know what they say?" Pul asks.

"What do they say?"

"They say that fucker is still alive."

This is about that.

"Who?" Libby asks. She thinks she must.

"Don't play dumb – Detective Frenchie Motherfuck! He's got a big nose. Why—" He waves a hand in the air, the one that was scratching his whiskers. "Why did you and Sister Stupid pull him out of the river? Why not let him sink in the mud, die happy? That question will bother me until the day the sun comes up at night."

Libby asks him, "How come you think it was me?"

"You mean, how'd I know it was the two of you? Because you're on the fucking news, kiddo."

She looked at him for about as long as she could stand, and then she said, "No, I'm not."

She glances at him for a second, as though to apologize for being defiant. That amused look returns to his face.

"No? Then I guess I know because I was there."

Libby doesn't like this. She doesn't want to know what she doesn't want to know. Knowledge is dangerous in this world. She takes a quick look at Penelope to see if she comprehends what she just heard, and she has. She's standing by the stove with her mouth open. Libby's glad that she's staying silent. She doesn't want to hear anything really stupid-o right now. She thinks that maybe Penelope recognizes that.

"Happy now, kiddo? I was there. All right? I saw you there, too, dancing around, pulling Detective Frenchie out of the river. You and Miss Flabbyguts here. Playing the heroes. *Heroines*, that's the right word for stupid girls. What the sweet fuck were you doing?"

Libby shrugs again, not to convey disinterest this time. She wants to help forge a path, somehow, toward forgiveness. "We just, I don't know, we just reacted."

In a single motion Pul sits upright and simultaneously pounds both fists down on the tabletop, making Libby jump an inch and Penelope half-a-foot. His shout is loud and furious and causes not only fright but an uncontrollable despair to flood her veins.

"You don't know the trouble you caused me!" At the top of his lungs. The echo ricochets off the walls. Anything but this, Libby's thinking. Anything but the mousetrap.

Pul, strangely, works to regain control of himself. He tugs down the sleeves of his shirt, somewhat ceremoniously, and tries to settle back into his chair. He adjusts his shoulder blades; his anger settling.

"You don't know the trouble you caused me," he repeats, his voice calm. "Gotta be consequences for that. What else you expect?"

The three remain silent in their places. Even Pul is looking down, vaguely toward his knees. When finally he looks up again, Libby, showing no resistance, meets his gaze.

"You can be the mouse or set the trap. Your choice, Libs. We'll be done after this. The one shot you got. So. In or out? Whatever you do, don't fucking hesitate. Don't waste my time with shit like that. Don't fucking say you don't know what I'm talking about. Say something real stupid like that, you know where you'll be wiggling your toes. Where you'll wiggle your tongue. Not to mention, this time – think about this now if you say no – where we'll plant your little girl nips."

"What's he saying?" Penelope asks. She doesn't understand but she knows enough to be terrified.

Simultaneously, as one voice, Libby and Pul tell her, "Be quiet."

Pul waits, staring at Libby then, permitting this momentary delay.

"All right," Libby whispers.

She thinks she knows what it means to say that.

Pul thinks she does, too.

THIRTY-SIX

Libby St. Croix is sitting in the hospital room when the situation transforms. Two nurses and a physician enter. They let her stay.

She's curious as they fuss over the patient. She wants to call Sandra, but first needs to know what's going on. The nurses begin to alter the fluids that enter his body.

"What's happening?" she whispers quietly, her voice made almost inaudible by dread.

The nurse who has been helping her to learn about procedures, teaching her what the dials and instruments mean, explains, "We're waking him."

"I should call Mrs. Cinq-Mars."

"Yes. Do it."

She can hardly contain herself. Sandra was taken out to dinner by her sister, Charlotte, who believed that Sandra needed to break her routine before her routine broke her. Libby blurts out that she's sorry to interrupt her meal.

"No worries, Libs. I'm only into my second cocktail."

"They're waking him up! Right now!"

"Oh my God! Libby!"

"It's exciting!"

She's hoping the procedure takes time, so Sandra can be there, but it happens fast. Émile blinks. She remembers him blinking near death by the river. This time the doctor speaks to him, "Mr. Cinq-Mars? Can you hear me? How do you pronounce his name?"

"Not that way," Libby says.

The doctor smiles. He's not put out. He's fractured the French language before. He says to Libby, "You speak to him then."

The nurse nods, to affirm that the doctor is serious, and Libby approaches the bed. The nurse, who's been holding Émile's hand, places it in Libby's.

"Mr. Cinq-Mars?" Her accent is excellent, passed on, perhaps, by her own French relations. Then she remembers her instruction from school, and says, "Monsieur Cinq-Mars?" At least to her ear, that sounds about right.

The nurse, who has taken a shine to the faithful girl with the crutches and the interest in nursing, whispers close to her ear, "We've been keeping him under. He's still receiving medication for the pain, but he may be disoriented. We're hoping to discern his level of pain. Libby, he may not know where he is or even who he is. Be prepared for that." She instructs, "Keep repeating his name."

She does so. She sees him wakening.

Then his eyes fully open.

The doctor takes over, easing Libby out of his way, examining Émile's eyes with a probe light and addressing him. Émile does not speak yet, not even after they pull the tube from between his lips. He nods though. He responds yes and no with movements of his head. In a question about his pain threshold, the patient seems to think about it, then gasps, indicative of his discomfort. "On a scale of ten – ten being the worst pain you've ever experienced – how do you rate your level? Squeeze my hand when we've found the right number."

The doctor has to count backward down to three before Cinq-Mars squeezes. The physician, though, is sceptical. "Something tells me he's a tough nut. Isn't that right, detective?"

While it appears that Cinq-Mars wants to speak, either to answer the question or say whatever else is on his mind, his attempt fails and is never expressed. The doctor meets his gaze and reassures him, explains his whereabouts and condition, asks if he understands. Not a hand-squeeze this time, Émile Cinq-Mars replies with an affirmative nod.

Everyone in the room is smiling.

The nurse confirms with Libby that Mrs. Cinq-Mars is on her way, and the doctor agrees to permit the young woman, along with the second nurse, to watch over him in the interim. The doctor and the principal nurse depart the room, to be back in a few minutes.

They are close in the quiet of the room when Émile squeezes her hand and utters a word for the first time. The sound is not clear; Libby gathers that he means to say, "Water."

She gives him a drink. Then another.

"Does it hurt?" she whispers. She means his wound, where he'd been shot and sliced open by the surgeons. He looks down at his chest, as if trying to assess the damage.

He nods that it hurts.

Then says her name, "Lib."

His voice is quite clear. She's stunned for a moment. "Yes?"

She takes the movement of his chin to indicate that he wants more water. She provides it, dabbing the spillage off his chin.

"Libby," he says.

His voice has a lower volume than normal, perhaps meant to be a whisper, out of earshot of the nurse.

"Yes, sir?"

"Help me."

"Of course. What do you need?" She's anxious, not knowing what to do. Somehow, the look in his eyes settles her down. As Émile whispers to her, only to her, she listens.

"You did good," Joris Pul tells her. "We're okay with you."

"We?" Bitz asks him.

"Don't be smart. Just when I'm making this big effort to be like a friend to you."

What's wrong with this picture? she wishes she could say to him, wishes that she possessed the nerve. *Be friendly why don't you while I reach into my purse for my gun.* Bitz pulls out her car keys instead, as if she has somewhere to go.

"Sorry," she says. She never wants to irk him. "Me being me."

"I get that. You are your own breed, Bitz."

He has her on edge. Her kids are out in the backyard, quiet for a change, which means that at least one of them is up to no good. She longs to do more for her kids; being a good mom is not compatible with being a wayward junkie. She has to quit one or the other, and she knows which life she longs to leave behind. Except that this man won't let her.

"What's up, Joris? I'm fixed. You must want something."

"Don't be that way. Like I said. This is friendly-like."

"Who knew? Sorry. Me being me again. Be a pal, Joris, since we're being so friendly. Tell me what's up?"

"You can help us out, Bitz."

Of course. He wants something from her. Another pound of flesh. She never expects otherwise. She can take the other way out, too, she's thinking. Reach into her purse and pull out her pistol and shoot him between the eyeballs. Except that she can't do that. The consequences. Her kids. Her life. Her hands would shake. She'd miss. No. She doesn't have the nerve and she knows it.

"We need a heavy barbiturate-type-thing," Pul explains. "Your choice. Whatever you can acquire. Has to be liquid. Easy to use. Clear. To put in a needle. Morphine will do nice if it's an option."

"What dosage? Anyway, I don't know why you're—"

"Didn't I say heavy?" he interrupts. "I believe I did. Enough to stop a bull in its tracks. Don't deny me now. Get into supply rooms. At the hospital or your clinic. Places like that. You know you can. A nurse like you. Figure that one out for yourself."

"What you're asking—"

"It's simple, Bitz. Not saying easy, but simple. Used to be when Zamarlo was around … well, what's past has gone past us, right? Fucking whirlwind. Water under the bridge." He shoves his hands into his pockets to jiggle his keys in one, his spare coins in the other. He knows the fear he creates merely by being casual about desperate measures. Bitz doesn't want to show fear – but Joris Pul is easy to fear. He shakes his right hand free to pat down his ridiculous hair where it flops over the crown of his scalp. "Heavy duty," he reminds her. "Then guess what happens, Bitz? Whatever bugs you flies away. Did I mention? This here's your lucky day. Your troubles? Wave bye-bye. They'll fly away like little birdies. Hey, if you want to do the steps, you got my permission. All you do, bring us a vial to stop a bull."

"Pul—"

"Oh, come on! First names, Bitz. You know that."

"Joris."

"That's it. That's better. That's friendly."

"I'm not going to kill nobody for you."

"What? Why'd you say something like that? Are you kidding me? You're not killing nobody," he scoffs. "Give me a break. What a laugh. Look, if somebody needs to be whacked – I'm not saying it's the case – do you think I'd send an amateur to do a professional job? No way, José. All we're asking is – think of it like this – be a good nurse. Get us what we need. Doesn't have to be morphine. Something clear and heavy-duty. Enough in a vial to drop a stallion to its knees. The rest we figured out. Think livestock, Bitz. Nothing else."

She wishes she could do it, just reach into her purse and take out her new pistol with the gunmetal shine on it and spot the look in his eyes when she aims straight at him. She'd love to see the realization on his face before she squeezes the trigger. Then let him drop, like a dead horse. See if he's still thinking about livestock then.

She wishes she could do it that way. Instead, she'll find him a vial of something clear and strong. It won't be easy. Like he said, she can find a way. Call it survival.

"For just a few moments," Sandra says, a wry look crossing her face, one which Émile is glad to see as her visage is usually marked by her recent distress, "imagine what it's like if you don't have your particular tolerance for pain."

The request is both leading and confusing.

"Tell us how much pain you're in if you were a normal human being," she says. "If you were an NFL linebacker, for instance, would you be bawling your eyes out at this moment, or asking to get back in the game?"

"I'm not an NFL linebacker," Émile counters. "They don't know pain."

"So you're hurting."

"Leave the room, I'll scream into my pillow."

"Émile."

There's love in the evocation of his name, and a spouse's sense of frustration, too.

He helps her out. "Remember the time that horse kicked me in the chest? Nearly tore my heart out. Cracked a few ribs?"

"Like it was yesterday." He was hurting then, and she knew it, too.

"Along those lines. Or it would be if the drugs didn't buffer it. I understand why people get addicted. The drugs are sublime."

"Émile," she says with a different tone, as if she's about to scold.

"Sandra, I don't press the plunger too often. I want to feel some pain. How else will I know if I'm getting better?" He doesn't add: How else will I know if I'm still alive?

She doesn't favour his logic. Arguments can be raised, such as the benefit of blocking pain channels between the mind and injury. Once they set up, they can remain. She won't argue, though, not while he's lying there, cranked upright, the semblance of a smile on his face. Alive. That's the main thing. Her man is alive.

"They're going to put me under again."

"They don't want you to move much. Not even in your sleep."

"When they bring me back out again, that's the strange part. I feel I should've been, might've been, dreaming, except my head's a blank. I feel I've been somewhere interesting. But with no recall."

A light tapping on the door. With the fall of evening the ward is rife with visitors. Émile's under orders to stay as quiet as possible. Libby St. Croix pokes her head in. She's been dealing with folks outside, as the news has gone over the airwaves during the last several hours that Émile Cinq-Mars has been awakened from an induced coma.

"Hi," Libby says, and adds, "Sorry."

"Come in," Sandra invites her. "Is there a problem?"

She shuffles in on her crutches. The weight of the door makes her entry awkward. Then she stands still, not wanting to intrude on an intimacy between husband and wife.

"I sent the press away. I sent a bunch of people away. I collected a stack of flowers I'll bring in later."

"Thank you, Libby," Sandra says.

"Two people won't take no for an answer. Not from me, anyhow. They insist I check with you."

"Who?" Cinq-Mars wants to know.

"Mr. Marsh, the lawyer. He's been here before. The other one's also been in. Miss – or is it Mrs.? – Shaftesbury."

As if on cue, three loud knocks are heard at the door behind the young woman. "That'll be them," Libby says. "They're persistent."

"I'll shoo them off," Sandra says, rising.

Émile interrupts. "Let them in. Put a stopwatch on them. Two minutes, max. Then I'll kiss you goodnight, San, before the nurse sends me back to la-la land."

Libby looks disappointed, as though she'd rather see the two annoying people dispatched. She swivels on a crutch and is nearly knocked over as the first of the visitors, Patricia Shaftesbury, barges in.

"Oh my God, but that was a lovely, *lovely*, pat-down!" Entry remains restricted to those willing to be searched.

More tentatively, being blind, Hodges Marsh follows, and Libby has to hop out of his way, too. He's headed in the wrong direction before Émile's greeting has him alter course.

Libby, half-hopping and half-swinging, leaves the room.

"You're on the clock," Sandra tells them. "Two minutes." She's adamant: the visitors may have overridden the young woman's objections in the corridor, but her edict is final.

Patricia Shaftesbury has arrived with flowers.

"You should smell the bouquet outside!" the real estate agent exclaims. "You could open a floral shop. Three shops are kept in business, just by you."

"Pass them along to brides or the bereaved."

"He's back to being rude," Sandra explains. "He thinks people only send flowers in case they're not around when he kicks the bucket."

"Sandra!"

"I'm only the messenger. Tell *him* you're shocked."

"I'm shocked!" Patricia Shaftesbury announces, with a broad grin.

"Great to see you up," Hodges Marsh remarks, and everyone looks at him to determine if that's meant as a joke. "Seriously," he adds.

"Great to see you, too, Hodges. How've you been?"

"Anxious about you. How do you feel?"

"Apparently," Cinq-Mars explains, "the question has lost all relevance. I'm supposed to feel as though I fell off a motorcycle doing a hundred and ten. But whenever I feel pain, I give myself a squirt and I'm ... sublime."

"Kilometres or miles?" Marsh asks, and the question gets a delayed laugh out of the detective who reaches for his chest to quell the hurt laughter causes. "Sorry," Marsh tacks on. "We just needed to see for ourselves that you're awake, and to see Sandra's sunshiny face now that you're back among the living."

Hodges Marsh startles everyone in the room, especially himself, by bumping into a mobile tray. He reaches out to settle the moveable platform but makes the matter worse. In the ensuing kafuffle, Libby shoves open the door to announce, "Nurse on her way! Time's up!" Sandra detects an underlying joy to her report, as it will get the two interlopers out. The girl has taken a proprietary interest in the patient and is defending her turf. Sandra wonders if she'll be shooed out herself.

Taking his leave, the lawyer apologies for his clumsiness. He'd rather not attribute the crash to his lack of sight. He then paws the blankets in an apparent search for Émile's hand. "Careful, Hodges," Sandra warns him. Should he press down upon the centre of her husband's chest, the day's progress will be maddening. Fortunately, he comprehends her caution, the risk involved, and permits the patient to guide his hand so that he and Émile can shake.

"My God, the strength in that grip! I have seen what I came to see," he states, deliberately using the language of the sighted. "This man will recover his full health. His grip confirms it. Good on you, Émile. Sandra, take care. Be of good cheer. He'll be well again."

As promised, the nurse arrives, the doctor in tow, with the intention of putting Émile under. Not a clinically induced coma this time but an imposed blissful sleep. Only Sandra and Libby remain in the room, his wife holding his hand as he nods off. Libby waits by the door to walk Sandra out. She holds her crutches like an armed sentry and awaits her instructions for the night – who will sit, who will sleep. All is different from previous days: Hope has been ignited with the overwhelming velocity of a shooting star.

THIRTY-SEVEN

"That won't work," Libby says.

"Actually," Bitz counters, "it might."

"How do you figure?" They're crossing the Connecticut River into Vermont. Libby's slumped down in the front passenger seat, crutches behind her. Seated so low she barely sees over the hood. Her friend is high but driving with care.

"I have a plan," Bitz attests.

"A plan," Libby scoffs. "The junkie has a plan."

"It'll work, too," Bitz says. "Has to."

They know the consequences if it doesn't.

"I'm doing this for you, Libs."

"Sure you are. You know what they say," Libby says.

"I don't know what anybody says." She steps on it to pass a slow-poke.

"Never trust a junkie."

"Ah, that. Libs. Trust me. All right? Trust me."

She has little choice.

Bitz turns off onto the ramp for White River Junction, bursts into town, then stops outside a modest cottage. Libby checks the address. Bitz got it right.

"So what about this?" the older one inquires. "Safe?"

Libby shrugs as she opens the door. "Dunno. I guess."

"Why does he want you to talk to this guy?"

"He's got questions. He's investigating everything. Like, who shot him."

"Like who shot him? How is that safe? And what the hell do you mean, investigating? He's in a freaking coma. He's in a hospital bed."

"He's investigating anyway. Can you help me out here?"

Hanging onto the front door, she can't get around easily to fetch her crutches from the back seat. Bitz climbs out of the car and does that for her. She looks up at the cottage situated on a gentle rise. "Maybe I should come in with you," she says. Thinking of the gun in her purse.

"Should be all right," Libby states. Then she says, "It's a free country. Come in if you want to."

Bitz stretches back across the front seat and retrieves her purse, then settles the strap over a shoulder. She walks slowly beside Libby who's swinging on the crutches. The door opens before they're up the stairs as Libby takes them one at a time.

Leo Ross is expecting them.

"I know who you are now," the young man says. Her crutches have identified her to him. "He talked about you."

"Detective Cinq-Mars?"

"Him, yeah."

"I'm Bitz," Bitz says, and sticks out her hand. Leo Ross shakes it. Libby doesn't bother with the formality when finally she's on the stoop.

Leo Ross invites them in. They're impressed with his digs and compliment him. He explains that he lives in the basement. This is his folks' house.

"Neat to have a basement," Libby says. She's wistful. Her folks might have tolerated their daughter had she lived in their basement.

"How's he doing?" the young man asks after they're seated.

He means Émile. Libby replies, "Slowly. Surely."

"Good. Good. Holy fuck! I'm such a lousy host. Can I get you something?"

They beg off, and Libby says that Detective Cinq-Mars has a few questions.

"Sure. Shoot."

"About your granddad."

"Really? What does he want to know?"

Neither the questions nor the answers mean anything to the three of them. Libby promises to faithfully report back to Émile Cinq-Mars all the same.

"I have some Knob Creek. Bourbon," Leo Ross says as they're about to depart.

The visitors glance at each other. "A smidgen," Bitz says.

"Just a taste," Libby says. "I've never tried bourbon."

Leo plies them with ample amounts, and they toast their health. On the subject of health, they toast Émile Cinq-Mars. That reminds Libby that she has another question, one she almost forgot. She can't recall if it was on her mind or on Émile's.

"What's that?" Leo asks.

"How did you get along with Reece Zamarlo?"

The young man seems mystified. She remembers now. The question is on her mind.

"How was working with him?" she presses on. "Back when you were pushing?"

His eyes switch between the two of them.

"Hey, we're all junkies here," Libby assures him. "Don't need to get your back up."

He doesn't reply immediately and resorts to the bourbon, instead.

As Libby St. Croix and Bitz Kincaid were crossing the I-89 Bridge over the Connecticut River, Grant Labryk was travelling in the opposite direction, from Vermont into New Hampshire. He continued to the home of Penelope Gagnon.

Her mouth fell open when she answered the knock on her door.

"Mercy me. It's been a while," she said.

He agreed.

"Were you at Muriel's first? She's dead, did you know?"

"I was at her funeral. I saw you. I guess you didn't notice me, Pen."

"People all dressed up. Hard to know who's who. I put on a dress myself. Found one in my closet under some stuff. Had to let it out some."

"How are you?"

"I'm all right. You?"

"May I come in?"

She opens the screen door wider for him, and Labryk steps inside.

"To what do I owe the honour?" she asks as they sit around her small circular kitchen table. She brushes a few toast crumbs onto the floor and pulls her bathrobe more tightly around herself, making sure she's covered. She tries to sit up straight.

"You're still in the group, Pen. Only now, I heard, you have reason to be."

Penelope keeps staring at him, as though she's still waiting for him to speak when really the onus is on her to reply.

"Pen?" he prompts her.

"What?"

"I know, it's probably none of my business."

They sit together quietly a few moments. Each waits for the other to speak, although their body language makes it seem that they're waiting for the other to leave. Then Grant Labryk gets to his feet, which suggests he'll do just that.

He looks down at her while she dolefully looks up. "Pen, do you still hold the drugs for everyone else? I'm betting you don't."

"You're here to rob me?"

"I'm asking the question."

"So am I. If you think you're gonna rob me, you're plain out of luck."

"Did I ever rob anyone?" Labryk asks her.

"You tell me. Did you?"

"I don't know why you'd think that way."

"Because I don't know why you're asking me if I keep those bad drugs in my house. The ones not from the pharmacy. Who asks me that if they don't want to steal them off of me?"

"Pen, I'm checking up on you. Making sure you're safe. We don't live in a safe world. People have been dying around you. Like my brother did."

"He had cancer."

"He died sitting up, Pen. Just like Muriel."

"That's funny," she says. "I didn't know that."

"Just like you might, too. Die. Sitting up. What's funny about that?"

"What do you mean? Are you threatening me, Grant? Why? I never done nothing to you I can think of. Did I? I never done nothing wrong to nobody."

"I'm checking up on you, Penelope, like I said. Not threatening. I don't know who wanted you to be a junkie when up to now that was never necessary. The contrary. The opposite was necessary. You should stay clean, that's the way it was, so you could hold the drugs without being tempted to use them yourself. You can never ask a junkie to hold your drugs for you, that's ill-advised. Now, suddenly, you don't have to be clean anymore, and somebody even *wants* you to be a junkie. Forces it on you, I heard. There can only be one logical reason for why that is, Pen, when you think about it."

"To make money off me."

"Junk is cheap. You can't make much. It's something else."

"Like what?" she asks.

"Think hard about it," he instructs her.

"I can't," she says. "Just tell me if you're so damned smart."

He looks around at her kitchen. Then offers her the comfort of his smile.

"Pen, this is how it goes. These life-lessons can be tough to learn. Pen, a junkie is easy to kill. Once somebody's a junkie, all anybody has to do is see that he or she takes an overdose. Or takes a dose that's too pure. Game over. Bingo bango, death arrives, and the thing is, the beauty is, nobody gives a hoot. That's a beauty you only find in the eye of the beholder, if you take my meaning."

"I don't."

"Pen," Grant Labryk explains to her, "nobody asks questions when a junkie passes on."

"That French detective asked his questions," she points out to him, rather proudly as though she's tripped him up.

"Look what's happened to him. Where is he now?"

She puts her head down after that.

"Penelope, answer me. This is important. Do you hold onto the drugs for the group? Are you still the holder? I'm not here to rob you, Pen."

She shakes her head no.

"You see? I can't rob you because you have nothing to steal. Right?"

She nods, agreeing that that's true.

"Since you are no longer necessary, since you no longer have a job to do, you've become dispensable. Do you see that? You're somebody who can be discarded. Nobody needs you anymore, Pen, and because of what you know, for the knowledge you have, maybe, just maybe, you might be better off dead. Just like Muriel, who knew way too much. It would be good – are you catching on? – the safest way to do this, is to make you a junkie first."

"Why? To do what?"

"To kill you, Pen. Make you a junkie first, then kill you, second. You have to pay attention here. You have to listen to me. You're on your way to being a junkie now because junkies are easy to kill. Be afraid, Pen. You need to be very, very afraid."

"I am," she said. And looked up at him. "You made me."

"Good. Now I need you to think, Pen. I need you to think of every person you know, then tell me, who among them scares you the most? Who really scares you? The most. Besides me, of course."

"Why do you care about me, Grant? I don't know you much."

"Whoever may want you dead, Pen, for what you know, that person or persons unknown, is killing people. I think I know why. I thought I knew who, but I was wrong. The man I now think it is must have shot that detective, too. The man I used to think would have been the one, if it came to that, he didn't do it. He couldn't've. He's already dead. See? Put it this way, Pen. I'm not pretending that I care about you, but I find myself on your side. I know that Muriel was your friend, right? My twin was my friend. Both were killed. That puts us on the same side. Mostly, Pen, I want my revenge. For my brother. You should want it, too, for Muriel. Now, tell me. Who scares the hell out of you, Pen?"

She's reluctant to say. When she looks up, she tells him, "Maybe you do. Ever think about that? Sure, it could be you I'm scared of the most. You know why, too."

"Pen, don't think that way. I used to blame all of you, that's true. You took my brother's money. I used to think that. I think differently now. That's the truth."

"Is it?" Penelope asks.

THIRTY-EIGHT

Overnight, Libby sits with Émile Cinq-Mars in his hospital room. He'll flinch, a spasm, or lift his forearm an inch as if he wants his IV removed. She aimlessly reads a pocketbook filched from Muriel's collection. When she feels a vibration in the hip pocket of her jeans, she pulls out her smartphone and reads the text.

She puts her book down and exits the room on her crutches.

To the policeman on duty she explains that she's off to the washroom down the hall. He murmurs something that's sleepy and unintelligible. She was planning to explain that she doesn't want to disturb the patient by flushing the toilet in his room, but given the trooper's disinterest, doesn't bother.

Libby swings down the hall to the women's washroom, where she waits for Bitz to arrive. Bitz is in her nursing scrubs.

"Got it?" Libby asks.

"Your turn," Bitz says.

"Sure?" She takes the vial from her and the needle even as she poses her question. Libby puts the vial up to the light and studies it.

"Trust me. Don't give me that never-trust-a-junkie crap. Trust *me*."

From one side of her, maneuvering around a crutch, Bitz abruptly takes her in her arms and plants an emphatic kiss on her left temple. She breaks it off quickly, whispers, "Bye," and Libby smiles as her friend leaves. She stuffs the vial in a front pocket, then returns to Émile's room.

Her pockets are full. She tells herself that everything's in there except a needle and thread. Then corrects herself, because she does have a needle, but not the kind that requires thread. She has the vial, her smartphone, a notepad, a pen, a carpenter's tape measure taken from Muriel's cottage. In Émile's room, she waits for the pneumatic arm to slowly shut the heavy door, then takes out the tape measure and places an end against the base of the door. She measures straight back to an imaginary line formed by continuing the first side of the bed outward. That gives her a distance and she writes it down in the small pad she slips out of her hip pocket, using the ballpoint plucked off the hem of her shirt. Next, she determines the distance from that imaginary spot to the edge of the bed. Then the width of the bed, and she writes down those figures. She calculates the distance to the visitor's chair. Then the distance to the nurses' serving tray beyond the patient's food tray. Then the length between the outside edge of the serving tray and the wall, and the depth of the bedside table. She inscribes those figures. She retrieves Scotch Tape from a front pocket and takes out the vial. She tears off a piece of tape. She sticks the vial inside the Kleenex box, to the underneath side of the top of the box on the bedside table next to Émile Cinq-Mars. The needle is trickier. She finds a bar under his bed to tape it to, out of sight but right below his shoulder, and she measures the distance from there to the head of the bed. She writes down that distance. She returns next to the kitty-corner edge of the bed where she started and measures down that length to the stand for his IV, painkiller, and sedative drips. She writes down the correct numbers, then readjusts the speed of his sedative drip.

She hopes she's got it right.

Émile Cinq-Mars is prepped to die. No gunshot this time. No women pulling him out of a river before he drowns. He's on his own. She watches his body fidget as pain throbs through him again. Amazing, really, that he doesn't automatically scream. His pain threshold is beyond hers. In the loneliness of a hospital bed like this one, that's what she so often did: scream.

THIRTY-NINE

Bitz shows up at Penelope's in her rusty Chevrolet Malibu. The right front fender has started to wobble. It sets up an unseemly shuddering, then goes on for a bit after she's shut the engine and pulled the keys. Or maybe that was her nerves. She drops the keys into her purse and zips it, then leaves it on the seat.

She knocks on Pen's door.

She hangs onto the door handle as a bad moment shimmies through her, nudging her off-kilter. She's feeling rancid.

Penelope doesn't answer. Bitz opens the door and calls in. "Pen? It's me, hon. You up?"

The only response is an eerie silence throughout the house, augmented by the buzz of the refrigerator cycling on.

"Pen? It's me. Bitz. Come on, answer. I'm in trouble." Nothing.

She enters, and as she moves through the house, she looks out each window to see if her friend is somewhere outside. She checks the bedroom, an unholy mess, piles of clothes on the floor. No one's in bed. The bathroom door is wide open, the room unoccupied. Bitz hollers into the basement, then takes a few steps down to give herself a visual confirmation. Nobody's there. The tempo of her heart is suddenly frantic. She feels nauseous again. Her pulse erratic. She puts a hand on the nearest wall to prevent a topple.

This is a disaster. Penelope isn't here and that's a rare circumstance. The timing for Bitz couldn't be worse.

"Christ, Pen! I need a fix!" She summons a higher power: "*God!*"

Which way to turn?

Bitz works through the clutter on the coffee table, where she finds Pen's gear but no *H*, then the kitchen table, where she's staggered by a

rush of pain in her gut. She churns her way across the countertops and
rummages inside cupboards. She leaps to the bathroom on a whim and
juggles everything in the cabinet but finds ño heroin. There's none in
the goddamn fridge. She can't find any in the fucking pantry. "Pen!" she
hollers, uselessly. "God!"

A car pulls into the drive. Joris Pul. She almost runs to the door,
desperate. Then retreats. She needs to massage a carotid artery that's
suddenly in flames. Pul! Pul! He might have what she needs. He better
have what she needs. He'll know where to get it if he doesn't. She'll do
what he asks of her. Anything at all. He owns her now. She's at his mercy
but no longer cares.

She knows why Libby says to never trust a junkie.

She can't trust herself. *Especially* not herself.

"Say, hey," Pul says as he opens the door.

"I did your damn job!" Not sure why she yelled.

"I heard. Easy, girl. Who's eating you this morning?"

"Come on, Pul."

"What?"

"I need fixing. Don't make me beg. I did what you said."

"True. You did what I said. We're pleased."

"I'm glad."

"Just one more thing," Pul stipulates. "That's it. That's all."

"What? Pul! Come on."

"Your fault. You put the idea in my head. I need a solid from you."

"I'm not going to kill nobody! I told you." She will though, probably,
if he asks her to.

"Shape you're in, I wouldn't ask you to buy me a six-pack."

She slumps down at the table, puts her head down on top of everything there. "Pul. I can't talk. I'm hurting."

"First names, Bitzy. Start with that."

"Sorry. Joris."

"What you said. Go ahead. I'm listening."

"What?"

"Beg me, Bitz. Daddy will provide if you beg."

Her body cramps up at that moment, and she contorts.

"You can start on your knees. I like that."

"Joris."

"You want to please me now, Bitz? On your knees. I love to see a sick junkie begging. Can't explain it. A thrill, you know?"

Her body is on strings and he's the marionette master. She slumps to the floor. Pul spreads himself out on the sofa, his big hands on his thighs.

"I got what you need, Bitz. Tell me how much you want it."

She's so sick now.

From her knees, "Oh God, Pul – Joris! Joris! I'm sorry. Joris. I want it bad. You know I do. Please. I'm hurting real bad, Joris. I'm saying please."

"Hey. Hold on," Pul says, and he holds a hand up and cocks an ear. They both listen to the crackly buzz of the old fridge.

"What?" Bitz asks.

"Where the hell's the other one?"

"I couldn't find her. She's not here."

"What?" He shoots upright. "Where is she?"

"I just got here. She's not around. Joris. Please. I'm begging you, see? My fix. I'm hurting."

He seems totally disinterested in that now. "Where the fuck is she? She's supposed to be here when I drop by."

"Why?"

"What do you mean 'why?' When is she any place else? Is she across the street? Is she down by the river?"

"Want me to go look?"

"You? You're a wreck, Bitz. Don't fucking move. I want to find you where I leave you."

"Please, Joris! Fix me!"

Joris Pul goes outside again and Bitz slumps right down onto the floor. Her chest spasms. She cries out as if in the throes of dry heaves. When that passes her mouth remains wide open, gulping air, and she holds her forearms tight to her chest, her fists tucked up under her chin. Pul seems gone forever and when he comes back, she's doing a cycling motion with her legs while lying on her side, trying to get somewhere but only turning in circles on the dusty floor.

"Christ," Pul says. "I got to cook it for you, too."

She hopes he means what he says. He does go over to the stove, a very hopeful sign even though she wants to die now. Her chest is spastic again and she convulses, and this time she vomits slightly into her mouth. She spits the foul fluid onto the floor.

"Junkies are disgusting," Pul says.

He's heating a spoon. Her body aches, from her shins up through her hips, her bones feeling compacted and crunched while the blood in her neck pounds and her eyes threaten to burst from her face. She senses also, at a distance, a subliminal peace here. A possibility. A wild hopefulness that soon she'll be whole again. She'll be invaded again. Be high.

Where she is right now is too low to bear.

Pul has located Penelope's gear and uses that. He binds Bitz's arm to pop a vein and she's only half-conscious of that, only half-aware of him. She's rocking herself on her side, her mouth wide, her eyes bulging. He pokes her with the needle she requires. He slips off the band. Her head falls back then, her body relaxing. "You got it bad, Bitzy," he says in a voice that is soothing now. "Hope you don't mind. Extra big dose in the syringe today. Ha-ha. Yeah, you don't mind. Extra, because that's the guy I am. Extra low gets you extra high. See if you can take it. Shove your problems right out the door, Bitz. Moon them. Remember this when you wake up. *If* you wake up. And yeah, right now that's doubtful."

The dose is stronger than usual, although Bitz cannot realize that as she's swept away upon a mere thread of consciousness. The world vanishes. She hears no words.

In motion to the sway and bump of the van on the gravel path that takes them up the mountainside, Bitz's torso lolls forward and back in her seat. Perhaps the jostling helps her to return to consciousness, although she feels sick differently than before. Rather than jagged with pain and convulsions, her body feels like putty, loose and disjointed. She can barely contain her bowels and is not sure she has, her energy returning at the same moment she feels it dissipating. She's distant from herself.

When she first opened her eyes, she sighted a waterfall – high and narrow and shining in the sun, a sliver of reflected light tumbling over stone with ease. All sparkly. Then trees blocked any semblance of a view, and they drove on under the canopy of foliage. She closed her eyes again, trying to sleep legitimately. A sharp rut gives her a jolt, and Bitz straightens up. She takes a deeper breath. Looks over at Pul, who's driving. Where to, she does not know.

He's wearing a light summer jacket, blue, with a thick purple stripe down either sleeve. A team's colours, she imagines.

"What's this about?" she wants to know.

"Look who's back among the living."

He hasn't answered the question. She guesses he won't. She drifts off.

She listens to grasses and weeds brush the undercarriage. A sound she enjoys.

Later on, she asks, "Where're we going?"

"Pick up my stash," he says. "Everybody's low. We need fresh supply."

"Seriously?"

He looks across at her, then concentrates again as the ruts in the road try to command his steering wheel. She keeps staring at him, which has the effect of provoking an answer.

"Don't you get squirrelly. I'm not ignorant. You been half-dead. You don't know your way in. I'll blindfold you going out. You can't come back here to rob me."

"Blindfolded. I'm so thrilled."

He gears down. The slope grows steeper and from time to time the rear wheels lose their grip. Bitz hangs on as Pul guns it.

They arrive at an outcropping of rock with sparse vegetation and patches of moss.

"This it?"

"We hike."

"Shit," she says.

"Now what?"

"My purse. Left it behind."

"It's at your feet. You don't fucking need it here anyway."

Considerate of him to bring it along. She digs it off the floor, tests the weight, and fishes out her lipstick. He shoots her a scornful glance. Bitz dips the rear-view mirror to suit her. That's when she sees the shovel in the back.

And the pickaxe.

A shiver slinks across her bones.

She knows why he brought her purse. He considered every detail.

Thank God I'm high, she thinks.

Bitz straps the purse over her shoulder and follows Joris Pul into the trees. The trail wends uphill, Pul puffing more than she is, although she's feeling done-in herself.

"What the hell did you give me?" she complains. Mushy, and her joints feel scarcely connected, as if laced up with thread.

Pul chuckles under his breath. "A treat."

They travel across contours of rock. Pul knows where to go, he doesn't hesitate despite the lack of indicators. Bitz notices that they leave no trace.

She's never felt so alone.

Eventually they emerge onto a small clearing. Underfoot, the earth feels spongy.

He needs to catch his breath a moment and Bitz pulls back a zipper on her purse. "There's no stash, right?" she says.

"I'll get you what you need. Nothing more."

He undoes the top button on his jacket. Turning to face her he discovers that she's pointing a pistol back at him.

"Hey," he says.

"Hey, yourself."

His scoffs. Then gets curious. "Where'd you get that?"

"That's your business, how?"

"Think about it, Bitz. You're a nurse. You help people, right? You don't have the guts. You're a loser junkie and you know it."

"Seriously? You want to insult me?"

"Hey, Bitz. Come on. This is a misunderstanding we got here. Ask yourself, what'll you do when you need a new fix?"

Her eyes dart once to her right. She doesn't have an answer.

He sees that.

"Didn't Daddy take care of you today?"

"I begged."

"Fun and games, Bitzy. You know that." He moves closer to her.

"Stay there."

He does, only for two seconds, then takes another step.

"The thing is, Bitzy—"

"Shut up. Stop talking. Stop walking."

"Aw, Bitzy, don't be that way. It takes nerve to shoot somebody. You don't got that. You're not like me."

"That's what people say in the movies. Stay where you are, please."

"Sure, Bitzy. All right. I'll stay put. We'll talk this out. What movies you talking about?"

"Any movie. The hero says to the guy holding the gun, 'You don't have the nerve, you don't have the guts,' and a bit after that the hero or whoever takes the gun away."

"That's usually how it goes, Bitz. Yeah. I agree with you."

"In the movies, yeah. In real life, things are different. I read this."

"You *read it*? This is not something you read in a book."

"I read it. When somebody says that, you know, challenges the person with the gun, man or woman doesn't matter, in real life the opposite happens. Most times."

"What opposite? What real life? I'm not following you, Bitzy."

"The person with the gun fires. Even if he or she *did not have the nerve,* as soon as somebody points that out to him, or her, a funny thing happens. The shooter rises to the challenge. The shooter finds the nerve. I read that."

"Yeah, you think so? I can see how much your hand is shaking. This is reality, Bitz. You're no killer-woman."

"This wasn't your first mistake, coming out here to kill me. Just your last."

"Take the van, Bitz. Find your own way out. I'll walk." He takes another step forward, close to a distance from where he can lunge forward, seize her weapon that way.

"No," she says.

"No?"

She's read this, too, that nobody shoots straight. Cops don't aim for somebody's kneecap, because they miss. They don't aim for somebody's head, too small a target. They aim for the centre of the chest, the biggest mass. They don't usually hit the centre of the chest, even at close range, too many factors, like nerves, sudden movements, fear.

She aims for the centre of his chest and fires.

Like she's read she should do. Like the guy at the gun shop said. Like in boot camp only it's a pistol now.

The gun goes off in her hands. He falls.

She's shot him.

Bitz puts a hand over her mouth, gasping now, in danger of hyperventilating. She knows she's supposed to shoot him twice, three times. Empty the chamber. That's what you're supposed to do. That's what the man in the gun shop said, but she can't, she just can't. He doesn't seem to be moving, and definitely he's not coming toward her anymore.

Birds. She hears them scream in the sky, taking to flight above the trees.

Blood is streaming, running downhill away from him toward her.

She can still hear the echo of her gunshot off the hills a distance away. But that can't be possible. It must be only in her own head that the blast reverberates, again and again, through her and through her flesh and bones.

She's shot him. That's true. That's real.

She must take command of her breathing, and she does so, slowly.

She approaches Pul. She uses her boot to turn him a bit, and when she jumps away, he falls back again. What they say is true. You're likely to miss. She aimed for his chest, and the bullet hit him right between the eyes, deviating slightly to the left of his nose. This isn't like in the movies where the victim suddenly reaches out a hand and grabs the other person's ankle and the audience screams. Like Pul said, this is reality.

He's dead. And she killed him.

A further reality: she must go back to the van, fetch the tools as Pul planned to do, bury him as Pul expected to bury her. Way up here, once the snow falls and the spring grasses grow, he won't be discovered, not ever, even if someone happens to trespass into this clearing. Although even that is unlikely.

He's dead. He's gone.

She must do her best to make certain that he's also forgotten.

She intends to bury the gun with him. She might not need it anymore. To make sure of that, she gets down on her knees and turns him over. She opens his jacket to see what he went for. Yep. A pistol. If ever she needs to put a salve on her conscience, she can remind herself that this was self-defence. One of them was not coming back from this ride.

She helped them in their plan to kill a man. She brought them a vial. Consequently, she had to be eliminated. Their plan all along. Use her, then kill her. She'll return down the mountain, alive but still in danger, not knowing her enemy. Who was in it with Joris Pul? He'd said *we*. Who else?

Worse: she doesn't know how to get fixed again.

Another problem. Where did Penelope go? What's happened to her? Bitz Kincaid goes back to the car and returns with the tools Joris Pul brought with him to dig her grave. Now she'll dig his. She wonders if Penelope lies in one now.

She scrapes the earth with a spade, then puts her back into it.

FORTY

After lunch, Hodges Marsh pays Émile Cinq-Mars a visit. The trooper on duty is loath to pat him down yet again, but the lawyer is a stickler for procedure.

"If you're not thorough, my pal is vulnerable." He spreads his arms straight out from his shoulders. The guard does his thing. "Tickles," Marsh says.

The guard pulls out a miniature bottle of liquid bandage and questions him by raising his eyebrows. That doesn't work, so he reads the label aloud.

"Paper cuts," the lawyer explains. "My line of work."

The bottle is returned, and Hodges Marsh enters the room.

Émile is being minded by his sister-in-law, Charlotte. Sandra had a rough night, her morning no better, and for the first time, their young helper didn't answer her phone. Maybe she's finally done-in, too.

"I've had lunch. Have you?" Marsh asks.

Charlotte demurs, as though it will be impolite to answer honestly.

"Go. I'll watch him until you're back. At least, I'll keep an ear open. I have Sandra's number if he makes a peep."

Charlotte consents to being relieved, and off she goes.

Hodges Marsh sits in the visitor's chair near the bed and listens to hospital sounds. The infernal blips on a computer monitor. Corridor voices. The thrum of internal machinery through air ducts and the muted attestations of traffic outside. The distant wail of an ambulance, constantly drawing closer before falling inert.

"How're you keeping?" the man who sees figures only in shadowy relief asks the man who can't hear him at the moment. He doesn't know how the women do it, sit in the room hour after hour. Or why.

The hospital is not bereft of staff. Still. Loyalty. Perseverance. The will to be helpful. Good qualities all. "You have a good bunch around you, Émile."

He stands, and does a full body stretch, suitable for a man in his sixties who spends too much time in a chair. With his pernickety back, Cinq-Mars would approve. Hodges Marsh reaches the end of the bed, on Émile's right.

"I have to say. So do I."

He moves down one side of the bed. Stops. Stretches his right arm forward until he locates the outer edge of the headboard. That provokes him to slip forward two more inches, level to the patient's shoulders. Marsh reaches below the bed and pulls away the tape there and in the process a needle clatters to the floor. He has to get down on his knees and feel around to retrieve it. He tests the integrity of the needle in his fingers and examines it dangerously close to his right eye. The instrument appears to have survived intact.

Next, his fingers locate the edge of the bedside table and the Kleenex box there. He reaches inside and identifies an object taped to the inside top cover. He removes his secret prize: a vial. By touch alone he inserts the needle into the head of the vial and extracts fluid into the needle's stem.

Tape and empty vial are slipped into a suit pocket.

He walks around the bed. His movements silent. His small steps are fleet, as though he glides. On Émile's left side now, he locates the bag with a glucose drip. Hodges Marsh inserts the needle into the bag above the level of the remaining fluid. He presses down on the needle's plunger. Then draws the needle back out.

He removes the empty vial from his jacket, reinserts the needle into it to protect himself from any accidental poke, and deposits the conjoined needle and vial back into his pocket. Next, he pulls out his compact bottle of liquid bandage. Uncapping it reveals a tiny brush and Marsh locates the pinprick on the glucose bag by feel, then seals it with several swift, invisible swipes. He twists on the cap again and pockets the tiny bottle.

Finally, Marsh runs his fingers down the upper length of the tube that leads to Émile's arm until he intercepts the valve. He rotates the knob a quarter turn, counterclockwise, to marginally reduce the flow. "I don't want to be here," he explains to the man in his bed in a confidential whisper, "when the deal goes down. We'll go slow. If someone resets the flow after I leave, that's fine. Still works. Either way, you receive your dose and when you do, guess who won't be in the neighbourhood? No one will ever know."

Hodges Marsh returns to the opposite side of the bed, adjusts the position of the chair, and sits. He'll wait there for the man's sister-in-law to return from lunch.

"How're you doing, Émile?" he asks after a few moments pass. He gives the unconscious man time to respond and acts as though he has. "By the way, the watch I'm wearing? In your honour, my beautiful Calatrava by Patek Philippe. My absolute favourite. It tells the time with exceptional accuracy. Not that I can tell. Some things in life I just don't get to see for myself. Your dying face, for example. I guess we can't have it all."

He's quiet then. And waits.

FORTY-ONE

Bitz Kincaid negotiates the nervy ride down the mountainside. Complexity when climbing: forks, junctions, tangential roads. Mere pathways leftover from logging days. Going down, she takes whatever route water would travel, descending to the base, then onto a highway.

She makes it out. Now what?

She does not have a plan. She needs one.

She's driving the van of a man she shot and buried.

On TV, cops get lucky, finding criminals accidentally. With that in mind, she sticks to the speed limit, and she will avoid anywhere a camera might observe her. The clown didn't leave himself a whole lot of gas, but she won't refill, that would be insane. Nor will she park where she can be spotted walking away. Things to think about! And more: She tries not to touch anything other than the steering wheel and the shifter. She'll wipe those clean and the door handles when she abandons the vehicle.

In a moment of inspiration, Bitz adopts a destination.

She expects a cop to be hidden behind every road sign, a judge and jury around the next bend. Over the next hill, a hangman's noose. Even so, she feels a weight lifting. She might yet be saved, get away with this, go straight, beat the habit, be a proper mom again. Thank God Libby's got the kids. She's long overdue at home but Libby won't abandon the kids, although, she thinks again, she might. Libby will need a hit, too. She starts checking the back of the van in the rear-view mirror. Did Pul leave any *H* behind? If she can bring that to Libby, or set herself up for later? The wheels slip onto a gravel shoulder. She yanks the wheel over and swerves erratically a moment, then waits for cops to pop their sirens, pulling her over for drunk driving.

"No, officer, I don't need a Breathalyzer, I'm only high on smack."
Right. That'll work.

She enjoys a laugh.

Thank God, though, that Pul loaded her up pretty good.

A plan. She needs a plan. Get rid of the van first. Figure out Libby later. If Libby's desperate herself – who knows? She might have her own stash. She said she didn't, but she could've lied. She would've lied. She'll deliver the kids next door or across the street or something. Libby'll do something like that. That's Libby. It'll work out. *So get rid of the van.*

She drives on. Her spine seizes in a vice-like grip when a cop passes her racing in the opposite direction. Concentrating on the cruiser, to see if it does a quick spin, she nearly runs off the road again. She's cross with herself for being foolish. Resolved, she drives on.

Bitz Kincaid arrives at Reece Zamarlo's house. She can ditch the van here, pulling it in behind Zamarlo's. She doubts anyone will notice or be bothered enough to care. That buys her time. The move also gives her an exit strategy. Zamarlo lives down by the river. She's been here before. Out behind his workshop in the tall grasses lies a canoe. He used to paddle up to Muriel's and Pen's.

Exiting the van, she looks around. She doesn't want to leave her prints all over it, but she does want to search through it first. By the foot of the stairs to his cottage she finds a cloth that's useful. A bit oily, but it'll do. She returns to the van and opens the back end and gives everything a look-through. No dope. Bastard brought enough for her to practically OD on but nothing more. Gave her the bare minimum to nearly kill her so he could take her up the mountain and kill her properly, saving himself the trouble of dragging her body through the woods.

She knows why he wanted her dead, too. Knows what he was afraid of.

She uses the cloth to wipe and smear her prints on the shovel and pickaxe – the oiliness helps – then does the steering wheel and the shifter. She slams the door shut holding the cloth and takes it with her in search of the canoe.

She doesn't want her prints on the canoe, either. She'll take the cloth with her.

The canoe is red and scratched up. It's sound. It'll float. Bitz turns it over and is disappointed that Zamarlo didn't leave a paddle inside. She searches the perimeter of the workshop and house. No luck. He kept his paddles indoors. She'll make do.

Bitz drags the canoe down to the river and launches it over the rocky shore. The current carries her downstream. She paddles with both hands and steers with one. Then the canoe lies in the stream a while, spinning on its axis, the stream carrying her toward a new life. She's filled with hope in equal measure to the dread that squirms through her bloodstream.

At least, on the river, there are no cop cars.

In the current, her weight in the stern of the canoe turns it, and she sails on, facing backwards.

Her progress is incremental, a mile an hour, a mile-and-a-half. In a mile, the Connecticut receives the outflow from the Sugar River. She'll go ashore there and walk a distance into the village of Claremont. From there she'll catch a cab close to Penelope's house. Nobody will connect her to whatever might be discovered later if she sets out from that direction and from that far away. She'll make up a story for the cab driver about her car breaking down, then from Pen's she'll drive home in her own vehicle.

Check in on the kids.

She has another choice to make.

A decision. Her mind, the whole of her soul, feels wracked.

When she arrives at Penelope's, on foot after a short tramp from where the cabbie dropped her, she discovers that her friend is still absent. Missing.

She gets in her own car and drives.

Bitz is pretty sure she knows what she'll do now, what decision she'll make when the time comes, as long as her courage holds up. She shot a man today. Killed him. After that, she's ready to do just about anything.

FORTY-TWO

The hospital room feels inexplicably quiet after the physician and nurses depart. Émile lies flat and still, wrists crossed over his chest. The solemnity of the moment will be fleeting, Sandra knows.

For now, seated, she rests.

Four o'clock. The others will arrive shortly.

The first rap on the door brings in her sister; Sandra rises to greet her. The two women wrap together in a fulsome hug. Charlotte, an arm in full circle around Sandra's neck, seems determined to not let go. Hugs have been plentiful recently; this one acknowledges that that phase is terminating.

Charlotte releases her, looks her in the eye, and states, "Brave girl."

"Hardly."

"The bravest. Look, I've brought muffins."

"Muffins," comes the gravelly voice from the bed. "Outside food?"

"You hate muffins," Sandra reminds her husband.

"Not today I don't."

"You're awake," Charlotte says. His eyes remain shut.

"A matter of degree."

"This time for good?"

"Except when I'm sleeping," Cinq-Mars stipulates. Eyelids flutter.

He will no longer be heavily sedated or in an induced coma. Painkillers, yes, but sleep is optional, and he's no longer dependent on intravenous drugs. A relief to everyone. Not only is Émile Cinq-Mars out of the woods, but he's also recovering.

Sandra now accepts that *on track* is a legitimate prognosis.

Charlotte breaks off a bite of muffin for Émile. Cranberry, which, if there must be muffins, is his favourite.

The next knock on the door admits Patricia Shaftesbury. She received the text to drop by without knowing what to expect; she doesn't enter full of chortles and felicity, her usual aplomb. Instead, she peers into the room, a tentative survey, probably expecting a sad result. Seeing Cinq-Mars with his eyes open consoles her, and before she's halfway across the room her usual go-lucky demeanor ignites. "Then it's good news!"

"The best," Sandra assures her. "A wicked celebration. We want to thank everyone who's been helping us. If my tone made the invitation sound urgent, it's because we really wanted everyone to show up."

"A party? In late afternoon? In a hospital room?" She looks around with her mouth open, her hands spread wide, as if flabbergasted, then says, "What's not to like? I dig it!"

"With muffins," Charlotte says.

"I'd have baked a cake if I'd known," the real estate agent declares, "and brought wine."

"Oh, we have wine. We have party hats. But that's my point," Sandra says. "You guys have done too much already."

The three women enjoy a gabfest, much lighter than their subdued chatter of late. They break out the plastic glasses as a Chardonnay is uncorked and poured. Paper party hats emerge; everyone puts one on, the patient included. Not drinking, thereby left out of that ceremony, Émile closes his eyes again, at rest without a heavy drug cloud around him, pacing himself for the day's festivity.

Another knock, and Libby St. Croix arrives, all shy and retiring among such a large group of older adults. A secret smile passes between her and the patient, and they share a laugh when Patricia offers wine. She declines. "Underage," Sandra explains, then can't comprehend why her husband finds that so funny.

"Inside joke," he says to deflect her curiosity.

With Émile, the girl discussed a methadone plan. For now, she has a new heroin supplier, a college kid across the river in Vermont. She dutifully puts on a paper hat. Purple. Cut to resemble a crown.

Libby no sooner settles into a corner than Hodges Marsh enters the room, not sure that he's found his way through the right door given the racket of conversation.

"Hodges! Hodges!" Sandra Cinq-Mars exclaims, noticing his momentary consternation. "Émile's no longer sedated. He's awake on his own. Isn't that great news?"

"Goodness. That's fantastic. Is he awake now?"

Émile speaks up. "You don't have to ask her, Hodges, you can ask me. Either I'm talking in my sleep or I'm awake. Put a party hat on. Are we tearing you away from your work? If so, we can celebrate that, too."

"My day's done," he admits.

"Perfect. You enjoy conversation – understandable, given that talk does not require 20/20 vision. I thought you might enjoy my report."

"Sounds good. What report?" the lawyer asks.

Sandra takes hold of the lawyer's right hand. Given the humble nature of the plastic glass, filled close to the brim, she warns him to be careful, then asks her husband, "Yes, what report?" Others were unlikely to detect a nuance familiar to her. She's wary that he might be scheming. Today of all days she doesn't want him overtaxing himself.

"A few things I've mulled over. I haven't only been lying here, conscious and unconscious, twiddling my metaphorical thumbs. With a little help from my friends – thank you, everyone! – I managed to knock a few items off a checklist. I'll explain when we're all accounted for."

"Who else is coming?" Sandra inquires. Then she remembers, and her suspicions regarding her husband's motivations increase. She glares at him.

Patricia pulls out a chair from a corner, plops it down on one side of the bed, and insists that Hodges Marsh be seated. He's willing to do so, given the bustle of the women while he's balancing a plastic wine glass. He's fitted with an orange hat, which he readjusts but leaves on. He looks off to one side. What vision available to him discerns a shape, a movement, that of a figure vaguely present in the glow of light next to the far window. "Who else is here?" he inquires.

"It's Libby!" Sandra tells him; then whispers, "She prefers to be in the corner. Her way."

The attention does not induce the girl to forsake her private spot and join the older crowd.

"Of course," the lawyer Marsh says. "Hello, Libby. Good to see you again."

In a rare note of discourtesy, Libby does not reply.

Within the minute, Trooper Hammond arrives and is informed that a party is underway. "What are we celebrating?"

"Émile is out of the woods!" Patricia Shaftesbury exclaims.

"That's nice. What are we celebrating?"

He gets his laugh. "All guests," Sandra lets him know as she plies him with a glass, "are welcome. Even bloody cops."

"You had us going for a while, bud," Hammond remarks.

"Sorry to worry you. I know, you worried about paying overtime for another homicide investigation. I'm glad to spare your budget that expense."

"Only reason I care," is Hammond's retort.

"We have so many of you to thank," Sandra repeats, wanting to clip the wings of police bravado before they get off the ground.

"Getting to that," Cinq-Mars gently interrupts. With an effort, he pushes himself a notch higher on his pillows, a difference that helps him assume command of the room. "A few notions have nagged me as I lie in bed all day. My body has been goofing off, but my thinking cap went into overdrive. For that, I thank my wonderful drugs." That draws down skittish laughter in the room. "Permit me to share my observations before I lose the thread. I get foggy. I hope I won't go on, although Hodges appreciates a man who talks at length."

"Only if you're illuminating, Émile," Marsh responds, "even in a fog." A challenge Cinq-Mars brushes aside with a wave of his hand.

Trooper Hammond has chosen to remain by the door, taking his ease by supporting his back against it. Not interested in the wine, he has put his glass down, scrunched his yellow paper hat and stuffed it in a pocket. He won't be offered another. Libby remains seated in the opposite corner on the broad windowsill, while the two sisters are parked on Émile's right-hand side. Patricia Shaftesbury is down from them by the foot of the bed, with Hodges Marsh across from her, also off the end of the bed. To the patient's left is an array of gadgets and trays and equipment. Fewer tubes probe him than has been the case, and he's no longer breathing oxygen piped directly to his nostrils.

"Ladies and gents," Cinq-Mars announces, "I've busted the case wide open."

Sandra's sceptical. "Émile, you've been lying in bed."

"Who knows? I may solve all my future cases in bed. Safer, more relaxing. Beats getting shot while fishing."

Sandra declines to share in the soft ripple of laughter that scurries across the room. Secretly, though, she's also amused.

"Tell us *everything*!" Patricia Shaftesbury exhorts.

"I will. To start, poor Muriel Cuthbert was killed by Reece Zamarlo. Trooper Hammond, tell us why we think this way."

While he does that, Libby gets down from her perch at the back of the room and comes around behind Hodges Marsh to gain access to Émile's left side. She's noticed that he's a bit dry and passes his water glass to him. He takes it, sips, nods his thanks, and keeps the glass in his right hand while Libby returns to her nook. He listens as Hammond mentions finding Zamarlo's fingerprints on the shells of the eggs he cooked at Muriel's house, and on the frying pan handle. The trooper speculates that Zamarlo didn't want to burn his latex gloves on the hot pan, and probably planned to wash his prints. He never got around to doing the dishes. He either forgot or something shooed him on his way. As well, Émile spotted Muriel's elephant figurine in his workshop. A tire print in the parking area by her cottage matched his vehicle, Muriel's necklace was stuffed in a pocket, and the troopers have been accumulating evidence that he was involved in a series of deaths of shut-ins who happened to be hooked on heroin.

"Our theory," Émile Cinq-Mars attests, "is that whenever someone hooked on heroin and diminished by disease came to the end of his or her rope, Zamarlo was available to step in."

"An angel-of-death-type thing?" Marsh asks.

"That type of thing," Émile confirms. "Except we have reason to believe that Zamarlo himself was manipulated into believing who wanted to go. We don't believe, for instance, that Muriel Cuthbert wanted to die when she did. She loved to fish. Casting her line, her life was worry-free. She had friends who kept her spirits up. She kept other people's spirits up. Right, Libby?" The young woman accepts that evaluation with a nod. "Zamarlo was informed otherwise, so agreed to kill her."

The sadness inherent in his conclusion sinks in around the bed.

"What Reece Zamarlo did," Émile goes on, "was legally and morally wrong, obviously. That's not in dispute. He had no right to terminate people's lives."

"My God," Patricia Shaftesbury intones, "terminating?"

"In his mind, he was providing folks with the ultimate service. He thought he was on the side of the angels, of what was right."

"Fallen angels, more like." Patricia thinks she's being humorous and attempts to laugh. That no one joins in puts the kibosh to that.

"For Zamarlo, the matter begins with an aunt who raised him from childhood as if she was his mother. He loved her dearly. He was torn apart when she was dying by the duration of her suffering. Quite literally, in his mind, he put her out of her misery. She wanted to die, and he made that happen. He did not, subsequently, become some kind of crusader for assisted suicide. I'm not saying that. Nevertheless, he was induced to do it again, for another in need, then for another, and then he did it for someone when neither the need nor the desire was present. A different party, upstream in all of this, with a personal and rapacious agenda, manipulated him into doing it again."

"But why?" Sandra's sister, her voice softened by trepidation, inquires.

"Charlotte, that's the seminal question in this investigation," Cinq-Mars remarks. "Why? If dealers and pushers have customers who buy their product, why would they want their clients dead? Bad for business, no? Does anyone have a suggestion?"

"They didn't pay," Charlotte puts forward.

"They paid, as far as we know."

"They were talking to cops!" the real estate agent pipes up. "They were squealers! They were finks! They were ratting out their friends!"

"Not that the police are aware," Émile responds, calm in contrast to her gush. "Good suggestions, all. Yet, there's no evidence to support either theory. Actually, Patricia, you helped me gain insight into this investigation."

"Me?" She's taken aback. "Hardly. I never said boo. How could I?"

"Ah." Cinq-Mars takes a sip of water before continuing. "You created a curiosity for me. A curiosity is always of interest to an investigator's mind."

She looked around the room for help, then asked, "What curiosity?"

"You were showing houses to Sandra and me that we'd never buy in this lifetime."

She checked around the room again, hoping others might spring to her defence. "Excuse me? I did the best I could for you."

"Émile." Sandra reproaches his tone. "Rude?"

He attempts to mollify Patricia Shaftesbury. "I don't suppose it matters to you whether Sandra and I move here or not, apart from your commission. You must admit, though, you did your best to make sure that we did not buy a house. The antithesis of what a real estate agent is meant to do."

Reddening, she drops the pretense of her usual enthusiasms. "I'm sorry, is my leg being pulled? This is not amusing."

"Émile," Sandra implores him, her voice low and biting.

"Sandra," he explains, "I came upon, in my travels, the most perfect house for us, which I have since learned is perfectly priced. Absolutely a gem—"

"Perhaps I haven't discovered this *gem* as yet," the agent storms. She stands up. "I can't be expected to have perfect knowledge of every house available. If I missed one or two, I apologize. Maybe it *just* came on the market, did you think of that?"

"Guess," Cinq-Mars asks his wife, ignoring the agent, "who the selling agent is for the house that's perfect for us?"

This time, Sandra shifts her gaze to Patricia Shaftesbury.

"I'm not going to just sit here," the woman says, as though that's a threat.

"Don't," Cinq-Mars advises.

She jumps up in a huff, turns to address Sandra, decides against it and stalks out of the room. Trooper Hammond holds open the door for her.

"Whoosh," Hodges Marsh remarks. "Now that was an exit."

"Not showing us decent houses is not a crime. Although perhaps it should be. She's free to go."

"This makes no sense, Émile," Sandra complains. "Why would she not offer us a home that we might want to buy?"

"Agreed. It makes no sense. Learning from you that she's a long-time friend of Hodges Marsh here, that helped my deliberations."

"How so?" Marsh strikes a stony attitude, even under the aura of an orange party hat.

"You're the one, Hodges, who doesn't want Sandra and me to live here. You influenced Patricia to keep us away."

Although he cannot see anyone clearly, Marsh looks around at the others in the room, then returns his attention to the man lying in bed.

"Émile, we're starting to question, not your sanity exactly, but your perspective, perhaps? Your clarity of mind? Why on earth would I not want you to live here? Even if I had something against you, which is not the case, why would I care? Please, Émile. This might not be the ideal time for your so-called report."

"Everyone is being helpful with excellent questions!" Émile attests. No one's sure if he intends to be sarcastic. An exception is Sandra, who is sure. "Such as, why would you not want me to live here, Hodges?"

"Émile," Sandra says, and this time means for him to moderate his tone.

"Fine," Émile consents. "I'll behave. The point is, Hodges, your question is one that I had to ask myself. Would you care to be briefed on my conclusions?"

"By design, Émile, I'm all ears."

"By the way, Hodges, pardon my curiosity, but which of your fine watches are you wearing today?"

Hodges Marsh can only identify it from memory. "If I'm not mistaken, my Micro-Rotor, by Laurent Ferrier."

"Ah. Not the Patek Philippe you wore the other day."

The women in the room, and Trooper Hammond who is behind the man, notice him stiffen. "What," he asks, "other day?"

"Yesterday," Cinq-Mars reveals. "When you visited."

"I relieved Charlotte. How do you know, Émile? You were unconscious at the time."

Émile adjusts his pillow behind his shoulders and performs a cranking motion with his right hand. Sandra reaches onto his bed and presses the button that raises him farther upright, until he nods that he's high enough. His party hat falls askew; rather than remove it, he tugs it on tighter.

"Don't be perturbed, Hodges. I don't see things in my sleep. The guard at the door – the various guards – have enjoyed a sport with me. Also, it was a way to make sure they did their job religiously. In your case the guards had to identify the brand name of your watch every time you arrived. Record it in their logs. I warned them that it would be some time before you wore the same watch twice, that I'm aware of the marques. I lied, said I had other ways of checking that they weren't inscribing a name for my benefit. Honestly, I hoped to make the guards' days less boring. Each time you were frisked, my watchdog – that's a pun, by the way – recorded the brand. Yesterday, the Patek."

"I was happy to give Charlotte time for a bite."

"Very kind. Much appreciated. Now, to my report. I concluded that my real estate agent was secretly discouraging us from moving here, and discovered, through my good wife, that you and the agent are long-time associates. Could it be that you were the one who didn't want me here, and if so, how come? I then asked Trooper Hammond if he told anyone that I might be involved in his investigation on the murders of addicts. He said no. Isn't that right, Trooper Hammond?"

"Actually," Hammond corrects him, drily, as if disinterested, "I qualified that remark."

"Right. You said no, then qualified that remark. You remembered informing the Governor. You required his approval for additional funds and a change in protocol. And you, Hodges, the first day we met, mentioned having dinner with the Governor where my name came up. You see how my mind works. Hammond talks to the Guv, the Guv talks to you, I'm included in the chit-chat, and suddenly you plot with Patricia Shaftesbury to get me out of the state. You can at least begin to *see* how a suspicion might arise."

A further stiffening of his posture, then Marsh says, "I'm making allowances for your health, Émile, for your lengthy term of sedation. You're not making sense. The destruction to our friendship is regrettable, although I'm willing to make allowances. Please, though, bear in mind that I am a lawyer by profession. In any court of law, I'd rip your testimony – this report of yours – to shreds."

"Why was Muriel robbed?" Cinq-Mars asks him.

"Excuse me?" Marsh says. "How the hell would I know?"

"None of the others were robbed. This was something new. I could see where it might have been pitched to Reece Zamarlo as a way to shake things up, to make the various deaths look different. You'd say that you wanted to keep him safe on his missions of mercy, to foil any police investigation. The cops would be looking for a robber, you'd tell Zamarlo, never a good citizen like him. In my mind that explanation sufficed for a time. Until something else jumped out."

Everyone can tell by a quick read of his body language that Hodges Marsh wants to leave and is on the verge of doing so. Cinq-Mars has tweaked his curiosity just enough that he's willing to hang on for another moment or two. "What was that?" he asks.

"A corollary question. Why was the downstairs robbed and not the upstairs? The answer? Her paintings upstairs were of no interest to anyone. They were amateurish, and that's as kind as I will be on the subject. I assumed the stolen paintings were equally poor, until I learned of a gentleman from Vermont who'd been in her support group. Also an addict toward the end of his life, when he died a sorry death to cancer. That gentleman was a fine painter. Out of appreciation for Muriel he bequeathed four of his canvases to her. Please, correct me if I'm wrong. I believe the thief was beguiled into stealing a whole slew of useless items from Muriel to cover up for the fact that four desirable works of art were included. I think the crappy artwork upstairs was left behind because it had no value, but also because the works bolstered the assumption that the missing paintings were equally worthless. I now believe that somebody wanted those four works."

Cinq-Mars lets his response be absorbed before continuing, and he is about to forge ahead when Charlotte interrupts him.

"The four paintings are worth a fortune, I suppose."

"As fortunes go, no," Cinq-Mars attests. "The works of that artist tend to run between four and seven thousand. Not a fortune, at least not to someone of considerable means. They're not easily resold. Wouldn't you agree, Hodges?"

The lawyer half-snorts. "How would I know? I haven't bought them. Or sold them. Or whatever it is you think."

"True. I didn't mean to imply anything of the sort. You've neither bought nor sold those paintings. You do have another four, rendered by the same artist, hanging in the waiting room to your office, which you purchased. As well, when Trooper Hammond visited your home this afternoon—"

"Excuse me?" Marsh barks out, indignant now.

"Yes, he came straight here from there. Called me right after he left. What did you find, Trooper Hammond?"

"Sir," the trooper says, addressing the blind man, "your wife showed us three more of the artist's paintings in your living and dining rooms."

"So it appears, Hodges, that you're a collector, not only of fine watches, but of the work of a certain local artist. This is when artwork takes on greater significance, don't you think? When it is desired merely for the sake of extending a collection. Especially true in your case, as you can't properly view the paintings, or really, see them at all. Do you agree?"

"Why were you at my house?" Marsh asks instead. Then he stands, as though he's not going to wait for an answer but leave now.

"Of course," Cinq-Mars tells him, "I'm not suggesting for a moment that you conspired to have Muriel Cuthbert killed, or anybody else, merely to acquire four paintings. Such people exist in the world. You're not one of them. We both know you could have bought the paintings with pocket change."

"That's the most sensible thing I've heard you say today." He sits.

"Not really," Émile contemplates quietly to himself. "You had a far more complex interest in these poor people, did you not?"

A thought skips through Sandra's head, that Marsh, having stood to leave, then reseated himself, is now trapped. He'll look absurd if he suddenly bolts onto his feet again.

"Continue with your report, Émile," Marsh advises him. "Bear in mind that I am a lawyer. I reserve the right to poke holes through your rather flimsy thesis. I admit, I find it as fascinating as it is absurd."

"Fair enough. One issue I had a devil of a time resolving is why addicts across the border in Vermont did not also die sitting up. There they entered a decrepit state before their demise, that is, before Reece Zamarlo came along and ended their lives. Another issue: why so many people on this side of the state boundary were cremated. Does everybody put that in their wills these days? Yet every addict dying here in New Hampshire did exactly that. Take Muriel, she had a coffin on order, picked out and paid for, yet abruptly her will stated a desire to be promptly cremated. No open coffin. Some people choose cremation, I know I will, but *everyone*? That's cause for suspicion."

"Seems perfectly natural to me," Marsh says.

"Not to me," Émile counters. "Let's consider the wills. They all said cremate. What else was similar? Wills divvy up the assets, right? Oh, look, there were never any assets left – not from any of the deceased. Heroin was given as the explanation for why that was so. They all died broke. Yet they didn't, did they, Hodges?"

"How would I know?"

"Please. There's no point insulting each other's intelligence. In every instance you were the lawyer who processed the estates. You depleted assets, moved sheltered funds into your own numbered accounts, told surviving family members that heroin was to blame, and made sure the bodies were cremated so that your little scheme, your murders, would have that additional firewall if investigated. The other thing is, regarding the people in the support group who lived in Vermont – you could not handle *their* wills. Outside your jurisdiction. Your licence is only for New Hampshire. When they passed away, they went either in God's own good time, or thanks to Reece Zamarlo's sympathy for their agony. Since you could not materially benefit from a dying junkie in Vermont, you had no part in those deaths."

A sighted individual would notice the judgement on the faces around the room. Blind, Hodges Marsh feels their condemnation as acutely. He remains still; yet expresses a rising fulmination through the interplay of his fingers. His digits unravel rapidly, then knot together. He's working to locate an equilibrium, to project both innocence and outrage through a relaxed, superior, disposition.

"Mere conjecture, Émile. Obviously, we will discuss this down the line. I've already tallied one major failing to your position. My God, this is incredible! Lucky for you I'm keeping my composure here. I look forward to my day in court. You might not."

"Your day in court. About that. Care to guess what the charges might be?"

"I'm referring to the day I sue your ass, Émile. You plan to concoct something against me. That should be a hoot. Very publicly, the reputation of the great detective will be annihilated. In the meantime, I shall do what I should have done sooner and follow Patricia's lead. I'll stomp out now."

"No, you won't, sir," Trooper Hammond, by the door, tells him. "Stay where you are."

"Excuse me? I know my rights."

"You and your rights can stay put. You are being questioned as part of an official investigation."

"I don't need to answer."

"We can do this the hard way."

"Is that a threat? I'll have your badge."

"I know the Governor as well as you do, sir."

Cinq-Mars gives him advice. "Hodges, you're not going to hear this again, not this succinctly. Listen now and give yourself a heads-up. Otherwise, you might be charged without knowing the extent of what we have against you."

Hammond adds, "I'll arrest you right now if you decide to leave."

Marsh does not officially yield yet stays put.

"Cara Drost," Émile says, as if the interruption never occurred. "She was a puzzle. Until I realized – while I was fishing, actually, I had an eureka moment as I cast my line, before some fool shot me."

"Wasn't me. Unless you think the blind are sharpshooters."

"Not you, Hodges. But Cara Drost, why her? Zamarlo didn't know her. If he did, he'd know she wasn't ready to die. Her supply was compromised by pure *H* because you told Zamarlo that she was worse off than she was. Really, you just didn't want her to sell her house and move away, which was her plan, because you'd already depleted her assets. You didn't want to get caught with your hands on her accounts. If she died *later* rather than *sooner*, possibly in a different jurisdiction with a new lawyer, you'd be in a pickle. If she went promptly, you could tell her relatives the sad news that she had mountainous debts, due to her habit, and therefore nothing much was left for them to split. Not wanting her addiction to be known they'd walk away. Everything your clients owned, came to you. Tax-free, under the table. So you could buy another of your ludicrously expensive watches, I suppose."

"Trooper Hammond," Hodges Marsh says over his shoulder, "I'm enjoying this too much to leave now. All of it will be debunked when the time comes. Go ahead, Émile. What else you got?"

The others in the room seem to hope there's more.

Cinq-Mars sips his water again, then continues. "Let me tell you about a big break in the case, which came about when I went to the cemetery after Muriel's funeral, to pay my respects. I noticed a plethora of small metal American flags in honour of veterans on various graves."

"You're back to flags and flowers again, Émile? Still drunk from our party night?"

"Did I mention at the party meeting Grant Labryk? An older gentleman from Vermont. He did the same thing with flags in his garden. I wanted another visit with him, but somebody shot me before I was able. Fortunately, Libby went on my behalf."

Sandra asks, "Libby?"

Cinq-Mars nods. "She and I have been catching time together whenever I was brought back to the light of day or sometimes the dimmer lights of night. Good talks. Also, at night, she manipulated these infernal machines to delay how quickly I went back under. Libby's a clever girl."

"Hold it," Sandra says. "Wait. Libby did what? Libby? You did that?"

"Take it easy, San," Cinq-Mars advises her.

"I'm not going to take it easy! Are you kidding me?"

"A lot worse than that is coming down the pike. You may want to save your rage for later."

She crosses her arms and hoists one knee over the other in an attitude of determination. "What's worse? Émile? Right now. Out with it. What's worse?"

"Sandra, I'd like to ease you into that knowledge, if I may?"

"You may not! Out with it now. Please and thank you. You're saying that you confided in her and not in me?"

Émile takes a gander around the room, at Libby, hanging on his every word; at Charlotte, looking as though she's entered a twilight zone, she never expected a day like this; Trooper Hammond, relaxed and waiting, secretly expectant; and finally at Sandra's stern countenance. He doesn't bother to glance at Hodges Marsh. He doesn't particularly care what he's feeling. As well, he's never been able to read a blind man when they can't have eye contact. Although he gains an insight by noticing his fingers.

Cinq-Mars could hum and haw, try some tangential pathway, but Sandra won't be budged. He sees that. Knows she's right. Her beef with him is entirely legitimate. He confided in Libby because he could persuade her, whereas his wife would have insisted that his health be paramount, the case be damned. So he kept her out of it. A confession for another hour. He comes to the point.

"This man – our friend, Hodges Marsh – conspired with a woman by the name of Bitz Kincaid, working in concert with our friend Libby, to augment my glucose drip with an abundance of opiates that, in combination with my regular regime of drugs, would ease me beyond this vale of tears. After his last visit here – wearing his Patek Philippe – I was not supposed to reawaken."

"Wait," Sandra interrupts. "What? They tried to kill you. Libby, too?"

"Not Libby. She's saved my life more than once. Not Bitz Kincaid, either."

He cannot explain further, as Hodges Marsh barks out questions of his own. "Where's the needle? Show me the thread. I mean these opiates you speak of. Show us physical evidence or for God's sake shut up. I'm torn between this savaging of our budding friendship, Émile – these outrageous charges – and my lawyer's gut instinct. You could have broached your suspicions in private, that might have spared you the discord I shall now bring into your life. You won't know what smacks you in the snout. Here, with a public audience, *this* is slander. Welcome to your funeral."

Marsh finds the bedside table where he puts down his glass of wine. He's already spilled half of it. Cinq-Mars fixes him with his most penetrating glare, which in the past has caused felons to capitulate. He must remind himself again that the technique is useless in this circumstance.

"No needle," he admits, "no thread. No missing vial. Obviously, you took the incriminating evidence away with you. Although we do have the paintings."

"I collect paintings. Big—" About to release a vulgarity, he decides against it, perhaps in deference to his audience, or perhaps to simply maintain his cool.

"Trooper Hammond," Cinq-Mars says.

"I didn't mention it earlier," the trooper remarks casually, "but in addition to the three paintings in your home, we found four more in your garage. We've identified them through one of Muriel's friends as being the four stolen from her house."

"One of Muriel's friends," Émile repeats. "That would be Penelope Gagnon, presently being cared for by none other than Grant Labryk. Remember him? His twin brother *did* want to die early, helped along by Zamarlo. He may have legitimately lost his fortune to heroin, as he was paying for the habit of the entire support group at the time. The narcotic was more expensive then, too. I'm holding a suspicion in abeyance that you aided his slide into penury. Perhaps his death gave you the idea. Arrange for addicts to die broke, and no one will question either their deaths or their lost fortunes."

Hodges Marsh offers up mild disagreement with a slight shake of his head.

"No needle," Cinq-Mars points out, speaking slowly now. "Something of a thread. Four paintings stolen from the murdered woman. Your garage. Explain."

"In due course, I will. I'm sorry, but stolen artwork, purchased legitimately, I thought, does not involve me in murder or attempted murder. Others were involved? I suppose you coerced your drug addict friends to testify against me. In court, I'll break them down in minutes."

"Libby's not an addict," Sandra pipes up.

Libby says, "Ah—"

Sandra looks at her, then back at her husband, who shrugs, then back at Libby. Sandra takes in the girl's infirmity, the pain her accident must have caused, and puts together peculiarities in her activities and bearing. She then locks eyes with Charlotte in mutual sibling commiseration.

"I think they're viable witnesses myself," Cinq-Mars confirms.

"Yeah? Where's the other one? I'd like to see what she's made of."

"Not here at the moment," Cinq-Mars admits.

"Probably sticking a needle in her arm somewhere."

"Possibly. In case you're interested, she's not dead."

Marsh hesitates, a speck of time that feels telling. "I didn't say she was."

"She's been talking to Trooper Hammond. Strangely, she's not talking to me. I find that compelling because she and I had an agreement. She could tell me anything without recrimination, as long as she didn't kill anybody. Now, she's not talking to me. Makes me wonder. You? Does it make you wonder?"

"What are you on about? I doubt that you're in your right mind. You've been through a trauma, but Émile, that excuse is wearing thin."

"Bitz Kincaid moves among the living. Did you think otherwise? Trooper Hammond tells me she's feeling brave. Unafraid. As though a weight has been lifted from her life. Libby, has a weight been lifted from your life, too?"

The girl looks up. With her right hand in the air, she makes a springing motion with her forefinger and thumb, emulating the action of a mousetrap being sprung repeatedly. She looks quite crazy doing that. She replies, "Pretty much."

"As you are blind, I'll report that Libby is executing a strange motion with her fingers. Suggestive of a trap being opened. You see? I'm not the only one who's in recovery these days. I'm not the only one who's been on drugs who's feeling much better and thinks the future holds promise. You, Hodges, despite what you say, might dread what's coming."

"Wishful thinking, Émile. No one minds if I leave now?"

Cinq-Mars stalls his exit. "If I may, be mindful of this. Libby feels that a weight has been lifted from her shoulders. Reece Zamarlo was killed by a needle to the neck loaded with pentobarbital. Easily done by a blind man, don't you think? One friend and associate to another? I can imagine you walking down to the river with your confederate to collect Muriel's secret stash. Also, you wanted a private chat. He trusted you, of course. You'd accomplished so much together. You were his lawyer when his aunt died, and if you happened to discern that he killed her, then, well, out of compassion you helped him slip that noose. Probably after you placed it around his neck. Reece would assume that if someone was sent to kill him, surely it would be Joris Pul. You were a friend. You kept a hand on his shoulder as he guided you down the path. At a certain distance, you punctured his neck with the needle. Not hard to do when you have a hand on his shoulder, walking a step behind. Then you dragged him off. You made it look like a savage killing, a knifing. On the face of it, a murder a blind man would be incapable of pulling off."

"Nice theory. Now, tell me, how did I get there? Drive?"

"Zamarlo drove you there, Hodges."

"I see. Now that he's dead, who drove the van away again? The blind man or the dead man?"

"You're forgetting, aren't you, that Libby is in the room?"

The man has no immediate response.

"Confirm for Mr. Marsh, Libby, that you're still in the room."

Everyone turns toward her, as if they need this confirmation themselves. Sandra, for one, must admit that she doesn't really know who the young girl is. As she continues to make the springy motions with her finger and thumb, a smile emerges on her face.

"I'm still in the room," Libby answers, her voice quite assured.

Cinq-Mars explains, "Libby biked to Penelope's house that morning at Zamarlo's request. While you walked with him – she didn't know what happened there – she deposited her bike, as instructed, in the back of his van. Interesting that you mentioned Pul's van, rather than his car. You came out of the woods alone. She didn't know why you were alone. She then drove you downtown, dropped you off at a coffee shop, then at your command returned the vehicle to Zamarlo's place. She then biked away, as you instructed her to do, and eventually showed up at the crime scene again, all curious. She kept her mouth shut, at your command. Right, Libby?"

She affirms his hypothesis with a nod. Still springing the mousetrap.

"Hodges can't see you, Libby. Would you mind answering out loud?"

"Yes!" she says. Very loudly. Startling everyone.

"Which implicates her in a murder, obviously," Marsh points out. An attitude of triumph.

"Good point. Now tell me, how will you testify to that effect while keeping your own involvement out of it? Or do you intend to confess?"

Marsh is quiet a moment, digesting that dilemma.

"All she's guilty of is giving a blind man a lift. How was she to know a crime had been committed? And once she found out about Zamarlo's murder, she chose sides. Not yours."

He interlaces his fingers together and remains mute.

"Consorting with you and Zamarlo put her life in danger, no doubt," Cinq-Mars goes on, "except that you had plans for her. You and an associate – one Joris Pul – who may have been the trigger man with respect to me – the two of you have done well with the heroin trade among the elderly and invalids. Expansion is in the works, however, and that means enticing the young. New York dealers like to have sex with their local distributors. They prefer young women to be part of their clientele. Having available sex gives them an extra kick when they arrive north, and it also confirms that the young women aren't undercover cops. Heaven forbid that a drug dealer would have sex with a cop. Especially vice versa. Libby would make a good local distributor for you. Young. Under your control. A junkie. Then you found another job for her to do first. Kill me. No, not shoot me, she didn't do that. But she could come into this room and hide the drugs onsite for you to put me under. Smart. Of you. No one would ever know. The hospital administered too much opiate? Come on, they'd probably never notice, cover it up if they did. Touch and go with me anyway. How could a blind man pull it off? You'd be home free."

Cinq-Mars sips his water before continuing.

"Hodges, Libby will testify when you have your day in court. She wants to. She finally gets to do what she wants to do. How about them apples?"

Hodges Marsh remains seated. Impassive. Not serene, but detached, and decidedly still. As though he is the one who has been made immobile from a wound.

"Recall, Hodges, my homily on black holes. Before I was shot, even as I was being shot, certainly as I was lined up in a scope, I cast a line. That's when I had my revelation that connected you to all this. The pure simplicity of that action, the beauty of it, even though it wasn't much of a cast, combined rather succinctly with the complexity of it all. My life was literally falling over an event horizon into a black hole – I was being shot, falling face-down in the river, little hope of survival and in the same cosmic moment, as it were, I'm figuring out the case! Time compressed, space distorted and expanded. Bizarre that way."

"What drug are you on this morning, Émile? You remain distorted. I think someone should ring for a doctor."

Cinq-Mars returns a smile his opponent can't see. "Bear with me. You are the one, after all, who entreated me to demonstrate my mental processes. The DNA of fish, the course of a river, an evocation induced by morning mist: Within the simplicity of my action and the complexity of life as a gun was being fired, I thought of you, Hodges. And your watches! How, without seeing them, you adore their intricacy. That's why you are the criminal you are, so that you can govern with complexity and simplicity, yet be unseen. Let the world be blind, not you. Pull the wool over the eyes of us all. There you have it. Your watches your undoing."

"You're full of shit," Marsh states.

"Charming. Admittedly, you have nothing more to look forward to now. Other than monthly visits from your wife and kids. Unless they abandon you. They might. That happens when you disappoint people sometimes. Just think. We might have been friends if you weren't so shamelessly corrupt."

"Walk a mile in my shoes," Marsh retaliates under his breath, his voice both irritable and muted.

"I'd probably trip. Please, don't play the blindman's card. You accomplished much in your life; you tossed it away. When things grew complicated you resorted to murder. Or murder was always your game. A killer is in you, that's for sure. By the way, only three people knew I planned to fish that morning. Sandra, Trooper Hammond, and you. I ruled out the first two. But do you want to know what really did you in on my event horizon?"

"I'm all ears. Babble on."

"The river. There's a myth about a mathematical formula. Should someone want to calculate the actual distance for a canoe trip down the entire length of a river, to account for the zigs and zags, measure the straight-line distance on a map, then multiply by *pi*. Three-point-one-four. You'll be surprisingly close. That's more or less what I did here. Every distance had to be predetermined. Look upstream and down but not beyond that set distance. To know the scope, I straightened out the zigs and zags. Then spun that line into a circle. To see what comes back on itself. *Pi*. A circle's circumference to diameter, that ratio. Bear with me on this one, as you did with my talk on black holes, but it's what you asked for. I can't even say for sure if I was still about to be shot, or being shot, or lying in the water, but space and time were distorted when I understood that the reason the experiences of drug addicts on either side of the Vermont-New Hampshire border were different had to do with the law. With jurisdiction. That's what came back in a circle to me. Because that's what changes across a border. Criminals don't care, they circumvent the law. Drug addicts freely cross state lines. Cops cooperate if they have to. What group is left among those involved with the law, and yet, unlike a criminal or the police, is limited by jurisdiction on one side of a state line and not the other? Why, lawyers, Hodges, and that completed the circle – do you see the symmetry in this? Think of it as the symmetry of a fine watch. Full circle like the face of a watch. *Pi*. In thinking of lawyers, I considered the only one courting my favour. You."

"My interest in listening to your erratic slants of mind has concluded."

"Really? Just when I'm about to reveal how the criminal side in your
nature goes around the law? Your lawyer side, drawing up people's wills
where their fortunes vanish and they request cremation, *that* side is
inhibited by rules. You've not been called to the bar in Vermont. The
only addicts dying prematurely were on your side of the border in New
Hampshire. They were also your clients. Their savings ran dry, Hodges.
Everything they managed to dam up in their beaver ponds, so to speak,
flowed downstream into your hands. Into your accounts. You blamed
addiction for their losses, although heroin is cheap now, but you,
Hodges, you were the addicted one.

"Amazing," Cinq-Mars ruminates. "*Pi* times the straight measure of
a river equals its actual length. Way more than 90 per cent of the time
that's true with the slimmest of margins for error. That mythical, magi-
cal, mathematical formula gave me a thought, a way into this, and will
now land you in jail. There! You've heard some of my so-called high-
minded talk. I've sung for my dinner. I hope you enjoyed it."

"Scintillating," Marsh murmurs, his snide tone a switch for him.
"You err, Cinq-Mars. This may embarrass you, I'm afraid. May I point
that out?"

"Only fair, Hodges."

"I was called to the bar in Vermont long before I was called in New
Hampshire. I can practise there, still. Oh, look, I maintain a second
office in Woodstock! Around the corner from where we dined. A mere
room, but, nevertheless, it shoots down your premise. One wants to be
in close proximity to the truly wealthy, after all. Poof! There goes your
precious thesis."

Cinq-Mars slides his glance across to his wife, as though to seek
comfort there. He has misfired on this one issue, she can tell. He takes
a breath, as though reconfiguring his summation, before resuming that
advance.

"Hodges, you're a capable lawyer. You've tripped me up. I should have done my homework. That that's difficult from a hospital bed is no excuse. I assumed that you brokered death on one side of the border because you were limited by your legal practise. Now you've proven me both wrong and infallible. I'll have to search the laws in both states to discover why one suited your crimes and not the other. Or is it simply that your Vermont business requires the appearance of serving only the supremely wealthy? You didn't want to sully your practise with middle-class addicts on your stoop?"

"You will discover, Émile, that you're screwed."

"Will I? My error helped guide me to the truth. The luck of the draw, Hodges. In the interim, you leave now. Not quite Scot-free."

"As mentioned, Émile, there will be damages. I will see you in court."

"Don't bet on it, Hodges. I enjoyed your monologue yesterday. Remember, when you added glucose to my glucose drip and spoke to me? You didn't know it was more glucose. I was awake. You mentioned in your speech good people being on your side. Sorry, those good people were on mine. You may have tripped me up, but I've knocked you onto your keister."

Marsh falters in an attempt to stand, catches himself, and tries again. He grafts his legs on under his hips and locates the way out. As Hammond opens the door for him, the trooper remarks, "Sure, why not? We'll do this in the hall." And follows him out.

The hospital room remains quiet. Nobody speaks or moves.

Until Sandra says, "Émile."

"Mmm?"

"I'm going to brain you."

FORTY-THREE

The next day.

Émile Cinq-Mars is attempting to walk when Trooper Geoff Hammond enters the room.

"Progress," the policeman says.

"Gets rid of the bedpan," Cinq-Mars agrees. "We won't discuss the catheter. My God, that's an evil device."

While the patient repeats his short steps, the officer who sits on the edge of the bed takes a load off. They share a laugh and tidy up a few details of their recent investigation. Cinq-Mars detects that the trooper has something on his mind beyond the niceties.

Hammond finally gets around to it. "You might be freelancing these days, Émile, but I'm still an officer of the law."

He knows what he's referring to.

"Don't let it bother you. If a certain Mr. Joris Pul is missing, wait for him to show up. Hear what he has to say for himself."

"Don't kid me. You don't expect him to drop by anytime soon."

"Libby and Penelope say he admitted taking a pot-shot at me, right?"

"More than a pot-shot. A tick off your heart."

"If anyone wants him dragged before the courts, that would be me. If he's gone missing, what's anyone to do?"

"You alluded to a theory yesterday, talking to Marsh, that was a little different. Don't play coy. I know what you think. The same as me."

"Theories come and go. Hear what Joris Pul has to say if ever he pops in."

"We found his van," Hammond reveals. "Parked on Zamarlo's property."

"He's still alive, then?"

"Didn't say that."

"Wait for him to show. In the meantime, life goes on."

The trooper reflects on their talk, having gotten nowhere, sighs, and appears to succumb to the same conclusion. If Joris Pul is indeed a sleeping dog, he'll let him lie. If Bitz Kincaid put him down, where's the evidence?

Any further discussion ends with the arrival of Sandra Cinq-Mars, who's delighted to see her man up on his two feet. Then she asks if that's permitted, and by his response she can tell it's not. She hustles him back into bed, and Trooper Hammond, with a big grin, wishes them both a good day.

Later on, they're sitting side by side, Sandra on the bed also, the top end cranked upright. Holding hands.

"Glad you're still with me, Émile," she says.

"Glad to be here with you."

"I thought I'd lost you. Sorry. At times, it looked grim."

"Death will be patient with me yet, San. I may have some time left."

She covers the top of the hand she's already holding with her other hand. Then rubs her palm across the back of his wrist. "I'll be patient with you, too."

They enjoy several minutes of silence. Sandra won't let him nod off.

"Émile, I was talking to people back home."

"People?"

"Our medical travel insurance people."

"Sounds ominous. Don't tell me they won't pay for gunshots."

"They'll pay. The thing is, as soon as you can be moved back to a Quebec hospital, you're obliged to return. They insist."

He hadn't given a thought to this aspect. The financial and insurance arrangements have rested on Sandra's capable shoulders. "Of course. Private insurance pays while I'm here. Government when I get home. The private firm wants me out of here."

"ASAP. Government insurance also contributes here, and they don't want to. We have to go home, Émile."

He gazes at her, their faces inches apart. They rub noses.

"Do you think a hospital will take me?"

She smiles. "We'll find a dog pound and a vet, if necessary." Then she turns solemn. "Funny, how some people didn't want us to be here."

"True, but I'm having them thrown in jail. Or they're dead."

They chuckle together, and she meets his eyes.

"Émile," Sandra says. "Let's go home. You know what I mean by home. To where we live. Everything else, we'll work out later. I'm worn out. All I want to do is sleep in my own bed, not my mother's old bed, and to feed my own horses, not Mom's. I'll arrange things here. We'll pack up. Head for the hills. And home. At the very least, for now. Get better, then we'll decide what comes next."

He releases a long gush of air. "San, can you believe this? I'm retired, supposed to be anyway, yet I get shot. I've never been shot before. Shot *at*, but I never took a bullet before. I retire, then get gunned down. How does that happen? When you think about it, maybe I should go back to work. Safer, no?"

She snuggles in closer to him, also into the pillows, and takes his near arm which she slings around her shoulders. "You could do that, Émile," she says. "You could ask for your badge back. I happen to know for a fact that the department will *not* reinstate you. Of course, if you finagled it, pulled your famous strings, I'd take out your department issue—"

"Sandra, really, no—"

"—and shoot you myself. Unlike that dreadful man, the curiously absent Mr. Joris Pul, I won't miss."

That said, they kiss. They enjoy their moment, and both shut their eyes. Sandra's fingers find the control that operates the bed, and slowly the top end glides back down to bring them to a comfortable, nearly prone, position. They rest up.

The end.